A sound close to her had her tense, and she found herself hauled to her feet as her back slammed against the tree. A large hand slapped over her mouth driving her skull back against the bark. Pain radiated down her neck from the impact.

Blinking, she tried to focus on the dark blur in front of her. The light was at his back, masking his face in shadow. He stood motionless for what felt like an eternity. When he slowly lowered his hand from her mouth, as if testing to see if she was going to scream, it dawned on her what was happening.

"I guess you didn't do your research," she whispered roughly, "because if you had, you'd know that none of that supernatural gobbly-guck works on me." The hand that had been over her mouth wrapped around her throat in a tight hold. "Vampires can't compel me, spells don't work on me," she gasped trying to get the words out, "I am completely resistant to *your* kind." His hand squeezed her throat, tighter. "Now get your hands *off* me," her voice was barely a whisper now.

Remi pushed at the chest in front of her, not even moving her attacker. Before she could think of her next move, the hand that had held her pinned to the tree swung out and cuffed her on the side of her face. He shattered her cheek bone, the pain making her eyes water. She tried to knee any part of his body she could reach, only to be rewarded her with another slam against the unforgiving bark behind her.

The next thing she knew she was sliding down, suddenly free.

By Jacqueline Paige

ANIMAL SENSES
1 *Heart*
2 *Scent*
3 *Passion*

MAGIC SEASONS ROMANCE
1 *Beltane Magic*
2 *Solstice Heat*
3 *Harvest Dreams*
4 *Autumn Dance*
5 *Winter Mist*

Dreams
Three steamy stories that started with a dream

Curses
Two tales of curses.

After the Silence
Volume 1 Bree

SINGLE TITLES
Solitary Witchling
Salvation

Writing As: J. Risk

THE ALTEREALM SERIES
1 *The Huntress*
2 *The Seer*
3 *The Empath*
4 *The Witch*
5 *The Chronos*
6 *The Warrior*
7 *The Telepath*
8 *The Healer*
9 *The Kinetic*

CAFÉ SERENITY

By Jacqueline Paige

Published by FRP
Copyright © 2020 Roxane Kerr
Edited by Gaele L. Hince
Cover art by: Off the Wall Creations

Previous edition released in 2015

Excerpts from *Heart* by Jacqueline Paige and *The Huntress* by J. Risk
copyright ©2014, 2017 Roxane Kerr

ISBN: 978-1-7774682-1-7

DEDICATION

To my CC crew (you know who you are)
—every day was an adventure working with you. You kept me laughing,
scowling and always wondering if I was insane to show up each day or you were....
I think we achieved a whole new level of sarcasm together and I'll never forget it or you.

1

"Remi. This *guy* wants to know what's on the bacon, egg, and cheese bagel…"

Remi winced and dropped the paperwork she'd been struggling with. She looked out the kitchen window to see Iris, one of her waitresses, standing in the middle of the café surrounded by customers. Every single one of them now looking at her.

"Guess we don't need to ask how her hot date went this weekend," Darien mumbled behind her.

Betany came running through the door and slid to a stop, her eyes wide. "She didn't."

Remi glanced above the door Betany stood in to see the yellow light glowing. The light that let the staff and patrons know that there were *normals* in the café. Normals was the term they used to describe completely vulnerable, none-the-wiser humans.

Betany waved her hands in Remi's direction. "Stay. I've got this." Taking a deep breath, a sweet smile appeared on her face as she stepped out into the customer area.

"Well," Berk cleared his throat and glanced from Darien to her. "Happy Monday morning." With that, he turned back to the grill and flipped the French toast.

"She's been doing so well," Remi whispered as she watched Betany smile and charm the customers.

Leaning his huge body on the counter beside her, Darien nodded. "Yeah, she hasn't stunned anyone in months."

It was only seven in the morning, too early for anything but coffee as far as Remi was concerned, never mind a faerie with an attitude. "I don't think she's cut out for mornings."

"No one in our world does mornings." Darien lifted her chin and forced her to look into his chocolate-brown eyes. "You, for example, look like you haven't slept."

Sighing, she pulled away from his touch. "I didn't, really. I'm trying to get all the paperwork caught up before that stupid audit." Glancing into the dining area, she almost groaned in relief to see the customers Iris had embarrassed smiling and joking with Betany. Thankfully Iris was looking after another table, a stubborn set to her chin. "How can they be so different?"

Darien chuckled. "Just because they're the same race doesn't mean they have the same personality."

Picking up her cup, she sipped her now cold coffee while thinking about everything she had to do in the next few days.

"Hey," Darien leaned closer, "why don't you get Iris to give you a hand in the office?" He shrugged. "She's got one hell of a brain in her head, and with Nadine's little one teething and keeping her up all night, I'm sure she won't mind covering the dining room and not having to worry about the extra responsibilities for a while."

Remi turned to see Iris heading to the counter. Her small frame was rigid. Her expression clearly said she wasn't in the mood for human *or* para interaction right now. "It would solve a few issues."

Darien hissed out a sigh of relief. "Whew. I was half afraid you were going to put her back on nights." He wiped his hand down the front of his black t-shirt over muscles she tried not to stare at. "Then I'd have to deal with Pascal and Attis PMS-ing non-stop because they had to work with her again." He shrugged. "Everyone loves Iris. She's great to work with if she's in a good mood, otherwise, we're all terrified."

Remi doubted that Darien was afraid of anything. Rolling her eyes in his direction, she smirked. "I didn't know vampires got PMS."

He grinned. "They don't, but they bitch like they do."

Glancing at the time, she picked up the papers. "Order has to be put away." She glanced at the stack of boxes in the backroom. "Are you sticking around for the meeting?"

Moving around her, he reached across the counter and picked up the coffee pot, and then grabbed her cup. Filling it, he handed it to her and smiled. "I've got the order, and I'll do this morning's meeting, but I'll be late for this evenings." He winked at her. "If I don't grab a nap, I'll be grumpy tonight. We can't have a grumpy werewolf running Serenity After Dark." Giving her a heart-stopping grin, he sauntered out the door, grabbing a stack of boxes on his way past.

Remi watched the muscles flex in his arms and back as he lifted them with ease. Averting her eyes, she blew out a soft breath. Watching him made her flush all over her *whole* body. Turning, she noticed Berk was also watching Darien. He gave her a cheeky grin and then turned to serve up an order.

"It's not a crime to look," he wiggled his eyebrows up and down. "And I know better than to touch. I like all my appendages, attached and undamaged." He sighed dramatically. "It makes me sad though, so much man-meat, and it's untouchable."

Shaking her head, Remi hugged the stack of papers into her chest and went over to lean at the end of the counter to wait for Iris to reach her.

Clipping her orders to the rack, Iris heaved a sigh and came to stand in front of her. "Sorry," she said in a somber voice. "They were so annoying, asking about *every* single item on the menu. I mean if it says with cheese, they asked if it came with cheese…"

Remi could sympathize with her. Out-of-towners were so picky that way. "You could have passed them off to Betany. You know she doesn't mind."

Iris nodded, her short red hair bouncing with the motion. "I know. I just…" she sighed again.

"Listen," she gave her a hopeful smile. "I'd like you to help me get caught up in the office. With the auditors coming in two days, I need everything picture-perfect."

"Really?" Her eyes lit up.

"Yes."

She began untying her apron. "I'm all over that."

Remi looked over to where Betany was leaning, waiting for Berk to hand an order through the window. "Can you handle it for a few? Soren and the twins will be here shortly."

Betany nodded. "No problem, it's just coffee and a few orders right now."

Darien came back through the door and stopped to grin at the girls. "Disaster averted once again?"

Iris rolled her eyes and glared at him. "I wasn't going to harm them."

He chuckled. "Sure thing, Tink."

The ding of the door chime had all of them turning to see who came in. Back-up had arrived. Soren was moving quickly through the café in smooth, graceful steps, like a cat, which made sense as she was a lynx shifter. Her smile was warm and friendly as she greeted the regular customers on her way past.

"Get Soren to help you if you get backed up before the girls get here." Remi told Betany as she motioned Iris to go down the hallway."

"I'll give them a hand," Darien added, rubbing a reassuring hand down her back.

Remi smiled, even though she really wanted to step into his space and hug him. She'd be lost without him most days. "Thanks, Dare."

By nine-thirty the breakfast customers were gone, and a few regulars lingered watching the news channel while drinking their coffee. Most of them were retired or self-employed and didn't have to answer to the clock.

The elf twins, Ranae and Deanne were clearing tables and prepping for the next rush. Soren and Berk were in the kitchen preparing lunch items while singing show tunes. She didn't know how they did happy all the time, but it was better than working with grouches. Iris was content in the office, entering data into the computer while Darien put the order away. Betany was helping him by restocking supplies. This left Remi time for some peace and quiet before more of the staff arrived for the meeting.,

Taking a stack of papers with her, she went outside to sit under the tree at the picnic table behind the café. It was silent out here for the moment; only a slight breeze was blowing; the sun was warm. The only sound was the gurgle of the water in the river as it moved downstream.

Flipping through the papers, she began to put them in order by date. Having to back-track into files that were five years old was an enormous task, and she was looking forward to it being done. Some of the papers in this pile went back as far as two years ago when Doyle was still alive. She really needed to sort out the entire system he used to file and fix it.

Pausing, she looked up and stared toward the river. She still missed him. He'd been more of a father to her than any of the foster parents she'd had. Although, when she'd first met him, she thought he was insane, or she might be having some sort of psychological breakdown.

She'd been eighteen the first time she'd looked at the *Café Serenity* sign hanging out front, and the next seven years became a blur of edification that changed her life. Not just her life but her mindset and beliefs.

After leaving the foster system the second she turned eighteen, or as close as possible considering no one was one hundred percent sure of when she was born, she'd hopped on a bus with her starting-out allowance and ended up in Riverside.

On the bus, she'd met a girl close to her age, Astrid. They'd hit it off right away. Astrid had invited her to stay with her and even helped her get a job at the diner she worked at. Remi hadn't known a thing about waitressing, but with the customers demanding attention, she'd soon learned.

Things had gone well for about six months until her life began spiraling downward again.

Astrid's boyfriend, Carl, had tried to force himself on Remi. Thinking she was friends with her roommate had been Remi's first mistake. The second was telling Astrid about Carl; she freaked and kicked her out. Remi realized now that she probably shouldn't have told her that he'd been screwing around on her for months with other girls.

The next thing Remi knew, she had no job or place to live. After sleeping in the post office for three nights, she'd gotten on the bus and headed to the other end of Riverside, setting out to find a place to live. Then she'd noticed the help wanted sign in the window of a unique-looking Café. Intrigued, she walked through the door. A café by day and a bar by night sounded interesting.

"Daydreaming?"

Remi jumped and turned to see Darien standing behind her, holding two plates.

"I brought you something to eat."

"Thanks." Setting her cup on the pages so the breeze wouldn't take them, she accepted the offered plate. "I was just thinking about Doyle," he handed her a fork, "about when I met him."

"You looked like a street rat when you came in." He took a bite of the hash browns.

"That's right; I forgot you were there that day." It was a lie; she could still remember seeing the large, muscular man unloading the delivery truck. She'd never seen someone with *that* much muscle up close before. Darien was one of those people that everyone looked at, it didn't matter whether you were a man or woman, you noticed him. He had soft understanding eyes, but his features were chiseled and hard, his body was too. All too often, she'd overhear female customers calling him sexy and dangerous in the same sentence.

He nodded slowly. "Yeah. I couldn't help wondering what Doyle was up to when he started showing you around without even knowing your name." He grinned. "Sneaky bugger that he was, placing a sign in the window only someone like *you* could see."

Remi took a few bites as she recalled. Doyle was a demon, what type she couldn't remember. There were far too many to know them all. A few days later, when he sat her down and explained how he'd placed a sign in the window looking for her and all about the para world, she'd thought he was crazy. He'd been seeking out an *almost human* to take in and train to run Serenity someday. Remi had never felt like everyone else, never quite fit in, but to be considered 'almost human', well even that was more than her off-center imagination could grasp. "You know, I thought he was crazy when he told me I was almost human, but not quite."

Darien grinned. "You and me both. I thought he'd lost all sense bringing in a kid to mentor."

Pushing the plate away, she avoided the look he gave her, the one saying he wasn't happy she hadn't eaten all of it. "I was just grateful to have a place to live. I figured going along with his delusions wouldn't hurt anyone."

"Until your gifts started making an appearance…"

Stacking her half-eaten plate of food on top of his empty one, he leaned forward, his dark brown eyes moving over her face slowly.

"The first time you walked into Serenity After Dark and Pascal and Attis stopped and stared at you, I knew something was going on. I'd never seen them not be able to get inside someone's head."

Remi smiled. "Pascal is *still* trying to get inside my head."

He chuckled. "You'd think after seven years he'd give up."

Glancing down at the papers, she frowned.

"You're really worried about this audit."

"I am. They're looking for something. The questions they asked were specific, not ones that you'd ask for in a random audit."

"You think someone pointed them in our direction?"

Nodding, she bit her lip. "How else would he know to examine the purchase orders?"

Darien reached across the table and squeezed her hand. "They're not going to find anything. Doyle's system keeps the unusual items in plain sight."

Closing her eyes, she exhaled slowly before looking back at him. "I hope so. Explaining bottled blood is not something even I could do."

"Remi."

Both turned to see Caitlyn leaning out the upstairs window. Caitlyn lived in the apartment at the back that Remi used to live in. She was nineteen and had been in Remi's care since she was thirteen when her family had been killed.

Most days, she was Remi's sunshine, that brightness in an otherwise dark world. Cait was a troll which, to Remi's mind before she met her, had meant big, ugly, fairy tale creature. The reality? Caitlyn was a petite, curvy beauty with snowy blonde hair, golden eyes, and a smile that could thaw a glacier.

"I think you'd better come see this." She nodded to Darien. "Both of you." Her tone held a note of panic.

Remi glanced at Darien, his dark brows were drawn together in concern. Grabbing her cup and the papers, she got up and moved to the back door. She met them at the stairs, talking quickly and animatedly. Remi was only able to catch the main points, at least, she hoped she did.

"So, Mel texted me telling me to check it out..."

Mel was one of Caitlyn's many admirers. He was a techie geek, a young werewolf that hung around whenever Cait was at work.

Cait practically danced on the spot as she turned her laptop around for them to see. Remi's stomach lurched as she looked at the gory pictures on the screen.

"Did Mel take these?" Darien asked, his disapproval clear in his tone.

Cait gave him an annoyed look. "No. Mel would pass out if he'd seen this in person."

Reading the banner didn't help Remi understand. "Is this online for everyone to see?"

Cait tapped a polished nail on the screen. "No. It's only for our community, and you have to have a membership and password."

A glance at Darien's face told her this was news to him as well. Still confused, Remi looked away from the grizzly images of a shredded body to her charge. "So why are you showing us?"

Rolling her eyes, Cait leaned over the table and clicked on the screen. "Look." She enlarged photo.

Bending down, Remi focused on where she pointed. It was a picture of what was left of one blood-covered arm, with a barely visible tattoo. Recognition had her straighten suddenly, her back bumping against Darien where he'd been looking over her shoulder.

"It's that inspector that was harassing us a few weeks ago." She tapped the screen. "He had this tattoo on his left arm. It's him."

Darien's hand rested on her hip as he stood close to Remi's back. The warmth from his higher body temperature didn't stop a shiver from going through her.

"Does it say what happened?" She swallowed and looked away from the screen to Cait.

Nodding, she brought up another page. "Word is he was ripped up like some crazed animal shredded him, but there are no bite marks to prove it."

"It's gruesome, honey, but what does that have to do with us?" Darien's breath brushed against the side of Remi's face, drawing her attention to the fact that he still stood close.

Moving further away from him, she clutched the papers in her hand and shrugged at Cait.

Caitlyn gave a dramatic sigh. "He got all nasty and in your face when you told him to take a hike."

Shaking her head, Remi glanced at Darien. "I didn't tell him to take a hike. I told him I had a business to run and couldn't have his minions getting in the way while they played with every wire and plug-in appliance."

"Still, he was pissed and left saying he'd be back with a court order giving him the ability to do what he felt was necessary."

Darien rubbed the back of his neck. "We've scheduled the electrical updates. They'll be done in a few weeks."

Cait groaned. "They're going to look at *anyone* that had a problem with him."

"He was a pompous ass, Cait," Remi said quietly. "I'm sure a lot of others had a problem with him."

Sighing, she closed the laptop. "Okay, but don't say I didn't warn you." With that, she flounced from the room, muttering under her breath.

Remi looked at the laptop.

"Hey, don't worry; it has nothing to do with us." Darien's voice was soft and reassuring.

Remi glanced over her shoulder at him. "I hope you're right. With this audit, I have more than I can handle."

Grinning, his eyes sparkling at her, he shrugged. "You don't give yourself enough credit, *Álainn*. You're stronger than anyone I know."

She hoped he was right.

2

Remi leaned against the wall outside the break room and glanced at the clock. A few people were still missing, so hopefully, the supplier came back to the phone soon. She hated being put on hold, and any other time would have hung up and emailed, but their blood supplier had short-shipped them, so it was a top priority. Customers relied on them for their blood source. Without it, humans would become menu items. And she couldn't forget the four vampires that lived in the well-hidden rooms beneath Serenity counted on having a meal, or two, every day.

Darien came around the corner carrying two steaming cups. He stopped and gave her an inquiring look; she shook her head. With a sigh, he moved by her and took their cups into the break room. He sat beside Nadine as she went through the order book while waiting for the meeting to begin. Leaning close to her, he must have said something funny because she laughed quietly, shaking her head at him. To look at Naddy, you'd never guess she was a scary, powerful witch with her pale blonde hair and soft blue eyes, but inside, that petite beauty was enough magic to alter history if she deemed it so. A good thing that she had the sweetest disposition and a truly loving heart. As Remi's assistant manager, she was her savior. Without her, she would never sleep, rarely eat, and probably lose her mind.

Sitting and chatting while they waited were Berk and Caitlyn. At least Berk was one of the males in Cait's life Remi didn't have to worry about trying any moves on her, not that Remi doubted she could take care of herself. He was one of the wolf-shifter quadruplets, and he was gay. Her heart went out to him; it couldn't be easy being so different in a race that was all alpha personalities. Thankfully his three identical-looking brothers seemed to support his choice. Berk liked to tell everyone that the three Lewis brothers set loose on the female populous was unfair enough, so he was balancing the scales and spreading some of their hotness to the other side. Remi wasn't sure about all that, but they were good-looking boys; with short brown hair, hazel eyes, and dimples.

Sighing, she glanced at the clock again. She'd been on hold now for twenty minutes, and her patience was almost at an end.

Ranae's laugh distracted her, it was one of those bubbly, infectious laughs, and everyone in the room had no choice but to smile. Whatever she and her twin, Deanne, were talking about was entertaining Ranae. If you didn't look at Deanne's dyed black hair, they were exactly alike. They didn't fit the elf image most people thought of. They were short and curvy with big beautiful dark eyes and soft voices that could lull anyone that listened long enough. As far as waitresses went, there was no competition. They were the best at what they did, making every single person they served feel like they were the most important in the world. Remi often wondered if it was due to their personalities or their race. She didn't know any other elves to compare it with.

Iris and Betany sat with their heads close together. Whatever had been bothering Iris wasn't now, and for that, Remi could only sigh in relief. What Darien had said was true. Everyone loved Iris, except those few times she lost her cool. Those ramifications were messy to clean up and get past.

She met Darien's dark eyes and shook her head. She was still on hold. Sighing, he got up and picked up his cup. With his large body and long legs, he was in front of her before she could blink—one of these days, she would get used to everyone except her having supernatural speed. With a smile that said he knew what she was thinking, he gently pulled the phone out of her hand.

"I've got this. You remind everyone to keep things clean during the audit."

"Use your growly voice when they take you off hold."

Chuckling softly, he turned and headed for the supply room. Sighing, Remi turned back to the staff that all sat watching her. "Relax, this isn't one of those *bad* meetings."

By the time she got through answering all the questions about the audit, the early lunch rush had started. Pulling her long hair into a loose braid, she went out behind the counter to cover the regular customers that Iris usually dealt with. The same customers sat at the counter almost every day.

Nadine followed her and started fresh coffee.

"Hey Joe," Remi greeted the old troll beside the door. "How are ya' today?"

He gave her a toothless grin. "Good, Remi."

Pouring his coffee, she set in on the counter in front of him and gave him a genuine smile, not one of her customer service smiles.

"I think I'll try some of Soren's soup today with toast."

"Sounds good, Joe." Writing on the order pad, she turned and clipped it to the holder. All it said was *Joe's lunch*, but Soren and Berk would know the order. The old guy ordered the same thing every single day.

Nadine came around behind her to fill a drink order. "Don't worry, Rem. No one is going to start anything with the auditor here."

Reaching around her, Remi grabbed the next two customers' drinks. "I'm more concerned with the privacy of our in-house residents."

Picking up the tray, she gave her a big smile. "No worries. You know Pascal monitors everyone's thoughts to make sure the dungeon stays a secret." With that, she walked away.

Deanne went by giggling, having heard the nickname the staff used for the downstairs. Grabbing Joe's soup, she took it over to him just as Ranae walked around behind her with an order.

"Les wants to know if we have red on tap, Remi."

Eyebrows raised, Remi sent Les, a wolf shifter, a shake of her head. "Les is just trying to rattle my chain, Ranae. Tell him to behave."

"Will do." She left again with a large glass of milk in her hand.

Remi turned to get the next order ready and caught Soren's frown through the window. Looking in the same direction, she spotted a couple sitting in the corner. One she'd never seen before. A familiar chill went through her veins. Moving down to the end of the window, she looked back through it, "Yellow light, Berk."

With a nod, he flipped the switch and continued with the order he was working on. Glancing over at Les, she watched him stare at the light for a moment and then turn to her and raise his glass of milk. "Swear he only comes here to drive me nuts."

Nadine moved by her with the coffee pot in her hand. "He comes here because it feels like home," she said softly and kept going.

"Remi."

She turned to see Darien standing at the door to the kitchen.

"I'm going to grab a nap." He rubbed a hand over his face, the only sign that he was tired as far as she could tell. "The supplier is sending the rest of our order this afternoon."

"Thanks, Dare."

"Anytime." With a mock salute, the muscles dancing in his arm along with it, he went back through the door.

"Why can't you look like that, Stanley?"

Remi grinned, keeping her back to Mr. and Mrs. Reece, and quickly moved to the other end of the counter before the couple started bickering, another thing that happened daily at Serenity.

3

Tossing the pillow across the room, Darien muttered every curse word he could remember until he ran out of breath. If he didn't start sleeping more, he was going to end up with grey hair fifty or sixty years before he should.

Flipping onto his back, he glared at the ceiling in the dark. How long had he been surviving on a few hours of sleep each night? He'd lost track.

For the first few years after Remi's arrival, he'd gone straight to bed when Serenity After Dark closed each night and stayed there until late afternoon. Doyle thought it was best if he let Remi learn the ropes and adjust to her new life without Darien doing everything for her. He'd agreed with the old demon even though it pained him, mentally more than physically, if she was stressed or upset.

That hadn't changed. Right now, she was freaked out over the audit, and here he was, lying awake after only two hours of sleep. Even after working out until his muscles screamed just to fall asleep in the first place.

When he'd started having trouble the first year keeping his distance, he tried drowning his natural instincts with various forms of alcohol. His werewolf metabolism made getting drunk hard work, not to mention expensive. Having to drink himself sober two or three times a night just to get some rest hadn't been one of his wisest plans. But, he'd felt so lethargic the next day that he'd been able to curb any desires.

Doyle had finally found a potion that would help with this, and for the most part, it worked. Darien still had to fight the need to be with Remi, but with proper rest, he'd been successful.

It was when Doyle passed away, and Darien had lost his main outlet for rants, control, and someone to talk some logic into animalistic instincts that made no sense at all, that he'd had to turn to others for help. Pascal and Attis had jumped on board and were all for being on team Remi as a defense to keep Darien under control. It was lucky for him that they were two very old vampires and had the strength to rein him in when his emotions got out of hand.

Darien had actually been naïve enough to think it was going to work, and mostly it did until Remi hooked up with that arrogant pig Randell. Even the vampires had trouble keeping Darien from ripping his throat out with his teeth. This was when the rest of the staff, and especially Nadine, were brought into the loop. None of them liked the cop, but everyone agreed that if Remi was happy, they weren't going to do anything to ruin it for her.

Rubbing a hand over his chest, Darien could still feel the pressure of how much it pained him to watch her with that man. Sure, she'd had a quick fling here and there, and he'd managed to keep it together because he wanted her to grow and experience life. That and they were always brief. As long as he didn't think about what happened when they were out of sight, he managed to keep things under control with minimal damage to walls, doors, and various other inanimate objects.

When Randell broke her heart, Darien could feel it to the bottom of his soul. He ached for her; his wolf mourned for the pain she was in. Nadine had to increase the dose of her herbal concoction at that point, leaving him so doped up that the sky could fall, and he'd have just let it happen with a stupid grin on his face.

As the months went by, the mixture became less effective, and he'd had to resort to working out, vigorously each night before trying to sleep. Were metabolism was a bitch to maintain, but if he burned enough energy, his wolf was too weak to drive him mad for being denied what fate had deemed was his. The end result was that his body had never been in better shape. Unfortunately, his mental state wasn't fairing nearly as well.

Six months ago, the concoction began failing completely. He had to double, even triple up during the week leading to the full moon, and even then, it was touch and go if it worked at all. Of course, kissing her the first time had been by far *the* stupidest thing he could have ever done. Now his wolf had her taste and tore at him relentlessly to claim her.

If she'd pushed him away and ripped into him when it had happened, he may have been able to control his actions, but she hadn't. To make it worse, she responded in a way that made his animal content but then would spout off about her rule of not mixing business with pleasure. That was complete bollocks as far as he was concerned. Couples and spouses ran businesses together all the time. She had this fear of things going bad, them breaking up, and Serenity suffering because of it.

Did she care if the rest of the staff messed around with one another every once and a while? No. They did too, always around the full moon, and, of course, where was he when this was affecting the others? Locked in a damned cage going through his version of hell. It was worse for him when he was in the moon's thrall now because the beast part of him knew damn well that his mate was on the other side of the bars and steel, and it still couldn't get to her.

For the past five months, he'd had to contend with all of that, plus have the staff riding him non-stop to clue her in. They swore that if she knew that she was his mate, she wouldn't be worried about them breaking up because that didn't happen in the para world. His argument was a sound one: she'd never accept that once mated, he was going to turn into a dominating, possessive man that impinged on her freedom. He knew he would. He also knew that she wouldn't just accept that and smile prettily.

Groaning, he closed his eyes. His emotions were all over the place again. Still taking deep breaths, he focused on trying to settle down. Snorting, he opened his eyes and studied the empty space above him. It didn't matter what he was feeling, all it took was one touch from Remi, and he was a mellow puppy, at least until his hormones kicked in.

Turning, he squinted at the clock. He should get up; the night staff would be upstairs getting ready. If he could just get through tonight without seeing her, it would be an accomplishment. He'd meant to be in bed before she came down to open for breakfast, but his feet refused to leave, and then he'd stayed to put the order away, argue with the blood supplier, go to the staff meeting, and of course spend some quiet time with her. *He was his own worst enemy.*

His phone buzzed across the table. Sighing, he picked it up and checked to see who it was. Baker had texted him. Sitting up, he opened the message, and his blood pressure rose before he had his feet on the floor. Detective Randell Peterson was upstairs, and Baker didn't know why, but Remi was getting upset.

"Fuck." Getting up, he tossed the phone on the bed and went over to his dresser to get some jeans. "Why can't that asshole take a fucking hint and just leave her the hell alone?" He growled and jerked the material up his legs. "Should have ripped out his throat a few years ago." Snarling at the shirt as he turned it around to find the front, he quickly pulled it over his head.

Grabbing the phone, he stomped over and put on his shoes, and then gripped the doorknob. Before he turned it, he straightened and took a deep breath. "Think of Remi." He whispered, trying to lock down his temper. "Just keep it together for her." Exhaling loudly, he opened the door.

4

With an hour to go before the evening staff meeting, Remi reclined on her couch and put her feet up on the coffee table. The Café was closed, and they didn't serve dinner. The downtime allowed the evening staff to come in, open the liquor cabinets, draw the shades, and set up for Serenity After Dark.

"Pretty good rush today." Caitlyn came in and leaned against the door frame.

"It was a good day." Remi turned to study her. She had her makeup bag and a towel in her hand. "Are you going out tonight?"

Caitlyn gave her a half-shrug. "Not sure yet. I'm supposed to meet Mel and Alcina downstairs. We'll decide from there, I guess."

Remi quickly calculated the moon's cycle. "Just be careful. It's getting close to *that* time again."

Chuckling, Cait waved her hand around. "I have Allie to watch my back."

Knowing that did nothing to comfort Remi. Alcina was a witch, but a young and unpredictable one. "I know, but that didn't help when I had to come and get the three of you at the station a few months ago."

Gasping, her jaw-dropping in the dramatic way she loved, Caitlyn flung the towel onto her shoulder. "*That* was all because *Randell* was being a dick, and you know it. *We* didn't do anything wrong."

Realizing she'd just axed her own downtime by bringing it up, Remi dropped her feet and sat up. "I know. Just be careful, something's going on, and it's gnawing away at me."

Completely disarmed, Cait came over and sat beside her. "Something like what?"

"I don't know," she gave her an exaggerated roll of her eyes. "I just… this audit, and the atmosphere is off right now."

Blowing out a breath, Cait nodded slowly. "Okay. We'll stay close to home tonight."

"Thanks, kid." She glanced at the clock. "You better go get all beautified, or you'll be late."

Looking at her phone to check the time, Caitlyn jumped up. "Crap. If I don't hurry, pretty boy will nab the shower." She turned and went quickly down the hall.

Pretty boy was Emery, Remi's other adopted para. Emery was a nineteen-year-old vampire and stayed downstairs in his own room for the most part, but the highlight of his day seemed to include coming upstairs to harass Caitlyn. If she didn't know better, Remi would swear they actually were siblings. According to Pascal and Attis, the fact that Emery could get up this early in the day was unusual, highly out of the ordinary for a vampire so young. Remi told them he was driven to annoy his adopted sister. They didn't buy it, and to be honest, she didn't either, but she hid her worries and was thankful he had, for the most part, adjusted to the fate that had been shoved on him.

Just after Remi had taken in Caitlyn, she'd been attacked by a vampire. The vampire was Emery. He'd been turned and left to fend for himself to figure out what being a vampire was all about. It had been Attis and Pascal that had saved her and would have killed Emery if Remi hadn't stopped them.

There was something in Emery's pale blue eyes that had called to her, even though he'd just taken a bite out of her neck, coming close to killing her.

Darien hadn't been happy about her taking in another stray and had ridden Emery hard for months after. Even Doyle had reservations. That had been almost four years ago, which meant Emery was actually twenty-three, and two years younger. Still, she saw him as that nineteen-year-old boy with fluffy blond hair and pale haunted eyes.

"Evening, *Mom*."

Grinning, Remi turned and glared at the tall vampire leaning against the doorframe, a cheeky smile on his ashen face. "Em, don't call me that. I am not old enough to *ever* be your mother."

Shrugging, he strode across the room, his long legs making it a short walk. Dropping down beside her, he slumped down and leaned back. "I know, but I love the look of death you give me when I do." His eyes flashed at her. "How was your *day*?"

She couldn't help her smile. His sarcasm always did that to her. "Busy. How was your *night*?"

With a roll of his shoulders that reminded her that he was forever frozen in a teen's body, he sighed. "Same old boring."

She studied him for a moment. He looked tired and possibly even paler than normal. "Have you eaten?"

Grinning wide, he wiggled his eyebrows at her. "You offering?"

He teased her all the time, but they both knew that wasn't a possibility. "There's blood in the fridge."

Sighing, he sat up. "Thanks." Giving in so quickly wasn't something Emery usually did.

"Are you all right?"

Nodding, he moved toward the door. "Just peachy."

She could hear him moving around in the kitchen.

"You still planning on a meeting tonight?" he called back to her.

"It's not really a meeting, just a reminder. The auditor will be here, and I don't need any hassles while he's here."

Emery came back and leaned in the door with a cup in his hand. "We all know." His pale eyes moved over her slowly. "You're pretty worked up about it."

Trying to shrug it off, she shook her head. "It's just a pain."

"Cait texted me the link for that inspector guy. Guess he won't be bugging us again."

A chill went down her spine. "Yeah, but it's a pretty gory way to go."

With another shrug, he turned. "Maybe he deserved it."

She opened her mouth to reply, but he'd already moved down the hall to the bathroom, where he began calling out to Caitlyn to get a move on so he could get ready for work. She debated on sitting and doing absolutely nothing or go scrounge up some sort of meal in the kitchen when her phone started to vibrate across the table. She didn't look to see if it was important, the only people that ever texted her were staff, and whatever the reason, it was important.

Sighing, she grabbed the phone and slid the screensaver off. The text was from Vienna, the evening head waitress. *Need you down here. Randell just walked in.* If Vienna messaged, she knew it was important. Vie didn't do dramatics. She jammed the phone in her back pocket and ran her fingers through her hair.

"Where are you off to?" Emery asked from where he leaned against the wall.

"Randell's downstairs."

Emery's eyes flared red so briefly she wasn't sure they had. "Why doesn't that asshole leave you alone?"

Patting his arm as she passed, she offered him a smile that she hoped said he didn't bother her, even though he did. "Probably because he's a cop in the supernatural division, and I run the biggest hangout for the supernatural community."

"He should still piss off."

Not bothering to comment, she moved down the stairs to take the back way into Serenity. She didn't want to see

Randell any more than she wanted to have a double root canal. It still hurt every time she had to look at him. They'd been a couple. A real couple for almost a year, and she thought she had found her happily ever after. He was as normal as she was, yes, he had some sort of para ability, but she'd never been able to figure it out and hadn't wanted to know in case it took away what normalcy she found with him. When he'd asked her to marry him, she'd floated around on a cloud for weeks, thinking she'd finally been rewarded for all the misery of her short life. He'd taken all that away when he told her she'd have to give up Caitlyn, Emery, and Serenity if she was going to be *his* wife, leaving nothing but a huge, gaping hole where her heart had once been.

They may not be her own, but Cait and Em *were* hers. They lived in a part of her that she doubted could have been stronger if she had given birth to them, and to ask a mother, real or not, to give up her children was the lowest of lows. As for walking away from Serenity, that would never happen. Ever.

Things had gotten ugly between Randell and her. For months he'd tried to take his anger out on every member of her staff after she gave him the boot. Her staff had held strong and persevered against him, and it humbled her to know they all had her back. Now, a year later, she could tolerate seeing him, it was never easy, but she wasn't going to give him the satisfaction of knowing he still got to her.

Vienna met her in the backroom when she got downstairs. Remi had never been able to tell what specie Vie was, only knew that she could do things with her mind that any army would love to do. They had an easy relationship. Neither asked questions they didn't want to face the answers to. "Any idea why he's here?" Remi glanced down at her jeans, hoping she didn't have any food spills or anything on her.

Shaking her head, Vie flipped her black hair back over her shoulder. "Nope. Pascal's not upstairs yet, so we don't even have a preview." She grinned, her dark eyes sparkling. "He brought some guy with him, and I have to tell you he's not hard to look at…at all."

"Really?" Knowing that her taste in males was all about cute and sexy, Remi smiled. "Then at least I'll have something to look at, so I don't have to look at Dell. I hate the way he looks at me like he owns me."

Laughing, Vie nodded and turned to head back into the bar. "Just say the word, and I can have him drowning in his own drool."

The part that scared Remi? She knew Vienna could do that to a person.

One of the Lewis boys met Remi at the door. Baker gave her a somber look. "I could bite him."

Patting him on the shoulder, she moved past him. "I'll keep that in mind, Baker. Is Darien up yet?"

"Nope." He turned and went into the kitchen.

Taking a deep breath, Remi stepped out behind the bar. She knew it was hiding by keeping the counter between them, but it helped to keep busy. Attis nodded to her from his perch at the other end. It only took a glance to know he was less than happy that Randell was here just before they opened, putting a damper on the mood before the night even got started.

Attis she'd never been able to figure out completely. He was a vampire of unknown age and origin. If she had to guess by his sheer size and slightly darker complexion, for a vampire, she would lean towards Greek, and his name seemed Greek to her. He told her he'd never changed his name, as many vampires did from time to time. To her, he looked like a Greek warrior from movies of gladiators and philosophers, which would make him *really* old. Despite his hulking size, he was very peaceful. Then again, if you could climb inside someone's head and make them think and do whatever you wanted, there wouldn't be much reason to project anything but calm. It was Attis' calm that finally had gotten through to Emery when he'd first come here, and for that, she would always be grateful.

Unable to stall any longer, she moved to lean on the bar

across from Randell. He hadn't gotten ugly and unappealing in the last few months, she thought with dismay. He was still easy on the eyes with his dark hair, and brown eyes that made you think of sleepy Sunday mornings, even with his bad-boy aura. "Dell." She didn't pause long enough for him to give her that look, the one that, when they had been together, made her feel cherished but now came across as more proprietary which made her skin crawl. Sitting beside him was a real cutie with blue eyes that gleamed with humor and mischief. He had dirty blond hair that was short enough to be appropriate for appearance's sake, but it was rough cut and on the messy side, giving him a boyish look.

"Remi. This is Kyran Nelsen. He's new to my division."

Remi gave Dell a sideways glance and then held her hand out to the new guy. "Remi Foster." She ignored the odd look Dell was giving her. He knew it was unusual for her to touch someone voluntarily. If she couldn't sense what race a being was, sometimes she had to touch. Right now, the Kyran cutie appeared nothing but normal, but she liked to make sure.

"Nice place you have," Kyran said, squeezing her hand gently.

Releasing his hand, she inclined her head. "Thanks. We like it." As far as she could tell, he was just a normal human with dimples and pretty blue eyes. Turning away from his playful smile, she met dark disapproving eyes. "So, what brings you here?"

Dell leaned closer, and she had to fight the urge to step back.

"You may have already heard, but one of the city's inspectors was killed yesterday." His eyes held hers, waiting for her to panic.

"I heard. What does that have to do with Serenity?" She just wanted him on the other side of the door.

"He wasn't killed by a normal."

Remi fought to hold his look without reacting. One thing Dell had never been able to do was read her, and she wasn't about to let him start now. "How was he killed?"

"Brutally," he said, glancing around at her staff as if they were suspects.

"I'm afraid you'll have to be a little more specific." She tucked her shaking hands into her back pockets, hoping to appear less interested than she was.

"We won't have the exact details for another hour, but we have a few ideas."

Glancing at his partner's face, she thought he seemed uncomfortable when he lowered his eyes to study the counter in front of him. "Is that your way of saying you don't plan on sharing that information with me?"

"Yes." He leaned on the bar and looked around the space again, pausing on Bates and Boden Lewis as they moved a few tables back to make room for the small dance floor. "I will tell you it was a para that did it, so," he turned and pinned her in place with a hard look, "Kyran is going to be helping out around here for the duration of this investigation.

"What do you mean?" She frowned and looked at Kyran. He had an apologetic expression on his face letting her know this was not his idea.

"It means find something for him to do so he has a reason to be around here."

His demanding tone set every part of her off. She wanted to reach across the counter and smack him. Opening her mouth, she closed it and looked at Kyran again before giving Dell a look. "You want him to pretend he works here every night?"

"Daytime too."

Sighing, she studied him. How could she seriously have thought she was happy with this man? "I…"

"Remi." Darien's voice growled from the kitchen door.

Hiding her relief, she turned back to Dell. "Excuse me." Quickly she walked into the kitchen. One look at Darien told her he'd barely gotten out of bed, and he wasn't at all happy.

Letting the door swing closed behind her, he leaned closer. "Why is he here?"

Glancing behind her, she made sure they were alone. "It's about that inspector's murder."

Darien's brows furrowed. "What does that have to do with you?"

"It was done by a para."

"Yeah, I gathered that from the pictures." Resting his hand on her waist, he looked down at her questioningly. "*What* does that have to do with you?"

"He wants his partner to hang out here day and night. He wants me to give him a *job* so he has a reason to be here."

Darien's jaw clenched a few times. "That the guy sitting beside him?"

Remi nodded.

"What is he?" His tone was quiet, but she could tell he wasn't pleased.

"Human, completely normal."

His dark eyes searched hers. "You're sure?"

She nodded again. "Yes." Closing her eyes, she let out a soft sigh and then looked back at him. "Can he do that? Just make me give this stranger a job?"

Vienna came out of the back room. "He can. Well, usually, the department makes a formal request for cooperation, but to decline will make it appear you have something to hide."

Without thinking, Remi might have thought Vie said that only because she thought Kyran was cute, but this is Vie. Her mind gifts are lethal and intelligent. "What do I do with him?"

Darien growled softly, his annoyance clear. "He can help me at night. I want to keep him close. I don't trust him." He squeezed her hip lightly. "And I don't like how he was looking at you."

Surprised, Remi gave him a puzzled look. "I didn't notice."

With a smirk, he shook his head. "You never do." Hooking his hand in her belt, he moved to the other end of the kitchen, dragging her along with him. Pulling out the cup rack, he grabbed two cups and set them on the counter.

Remi glanced out at the two men sitting at her bar. Would it be too much to have one week of her life run smoothly?

"Hey."

Turning back to Darien, she gave him a look.

"I can crush him into rubble and make it impossible for him to be top cop and macho."

Rolling her eyes, she shook her head. "Knowing him, he'd find a way."

Lifting her chin gently with his fingertips, he looked at her gently. "It's been a year. Either break or move on."

"I already broke. I just allow my own pity party from time to time."

He released her chin and shrugged. "I prefer tormenting myself." Without warning, he pulled her into his solid chest and picked her up until her feet were off the floor. His mouth crushed down on hers in one of his bone-melting kisses, making her glad she didn't have to stand. When she was as breathless as he was, he lifted his head and set her back down.

Grabbing the front of his t-shirt, she held on until her legs were steady again. "Did that have a purpose?"

He grinned. "A dual one, actually." With his chin, he motioned in the direction of Randell, looking through the window. "A reminder of what he lost and," he tucked the hair behind her ear, "because I would cut off my left arm to kiss you."

Shaking her head, she grinned. "It would probably grow back." She chanced a glance at the man on the other side of the counter; he had a dark look on his face. "I don't think he needs a reminder."

Darien shrugged and reached for the coffeepot. "Then I did it because I can't resist you." With a lust-filled look, he studied her for a moment. "Someday, I could ask for more."

"I'd have to fire you then. You know I don't believe in mixing work and play." It was only half truthful; under no circumstance could she ever ask him to leave Serenity. She needed him too much.

Shrugging again, he held out a cup to her. "There are other jobs, *Álainn*, there's only one you." Nodding, he picked up his cup. "I'll go deal with the jackass. You enjoy your coffee."

Turning, she watched him walk out of the kitchen.

"Damn, Remi, how do you keep telling that sexy beast no?"

Glancing at the door, she saw Vienna standing there with their other evening waitress, Elise.

"Well, Elise, to be honest," she shook her head. "I really don't know." Darien had always been touchy around her, light hugs, and his arm around her from time to time, but in the last six months, he'd really stepped it up. He seemed to kiss her whenever she least expected it. She wasn't going to complain, not with the way the guy kissed, but she didn't know what to do with it either.

Vienna grinned. "I don't usually go for the dark, brooding alpha types, but," she sighed dramatically, "he walks with this sexy predator aura that makes *my* knees go weak."

Elise nodded enthusiastically. "I would be all over *that* in a heartbeat if he'd so much as glance in my direction."

"He'd have to drag his eyes off Remi long enough to notice you, El." Vie said in a dry tone.

"I take it we're discussing our favorite wolfman." Pascal glided up behind the girls.

Remi grinned at him. "They don't give up."

Leaning down, he kissed Elise's cheek. "He's the only man present that doesn't notice you, my pretty Elise."

Elise blushed, which was hard to do to a water nymph, and turned to bat her big blue eyes up at the pale vampire that towered over her. "You're a complete flirt, Pascal, but thank you."

He inclined his head to her and then looked at Vienna.

She lifted her hand in his face. "Don't even think about putting those cold lips on my face. You know I don't do undead." Turning, she walked into the bar.

Elise grinned and flipped her long red hair back from her face. "I might consider it someday." She gave Pascal a lingering look and then pushed through the door.

Pascal turned his pale green eyes back to Remi. "What have I missed? The tension is this place makes it hard to breathe," he smirked, "if I still needed to breathe."

"Randell's here."

He straightened his large frame and suddenly looked like a man going to battle. With his heavy muscular build, he made her think of a Highlander. The red hair and bone structure backed it up, but he wasn't one to ever talk about his past, so she had no idea. "Why?"

That one word was spoken with enough venom to send a cold chill down her spine. "The inspector that was here from the city was killed, Randell believes it was done by a para, so he's planting a spy to work here."

Surprise flickered in his eyes briefly. "Never a dull a moment, is there?" Tucking a hand into his front pocket, he motioned to the door with a tilt of his head. "I think I'll go play in some thoughts and see what I can find out."

"Let me know."

"Of course."

She watched him glide through the door. He was a large man, as tall as Darien and Attis, and had a heavy build, yet he always moved with a smooth grace that left Remi feeling awkward and unrefined around him.

5

After Darien sent her back upstairs, Remi scrubbed the entire kitchen from floor to ceiling, trying to burn off her anxiety and frustration. It didn't work. Now she was looking out Cait's window at the river. A few couples lingered along the bank, leaning close to each other, believing themselves concealed in the darkness, although the three-quarters moon highlighted their every move. The tranquility should have brought her peace, but it just reminded her of what was lacking in her life.

Her phone chirped in her pocket. Pulling it out, she unlocked the screen to see Darien's name.

Turn off your brain and get some sleep.

How did he always seem to know when she was at odds with some part of her life? *Maybe I was sleeping; she* sent back.

If you were, that last reply would have been uglier.

He knew her too well. *How's Kyran doing?*

No one has killed him yet.

Shaking her head, she replied. *Finally, good news! Seriously...* She could almost see him sighing.

He's fine. I have him helping Baker in the kitchen.

Closing her eyes, she pictured the detective having to put up with Baker's odd sense of…well, everything. *Now I feel sorry for him. Get any more information out of him?*

No. Go get some sleep.

If there weren't several soundproof layers between them, she would never get away with chirping back at him for this long. *I'm not tired.* She responded before turning to watch one of the couples by the river get up and start walking toward the parking lot.

Stop thinking.

I THINK I'll go sit by the river for a bit. It's peaceful. She knew that would ruffle his fur, but it was also true.

It's after midnight, Remi.

Checking the time on her phone, she hadn't realized it was that late. She should really try to sleep. *I'll be fine. There's a couple hanging around, I won't be alone.*

Take your phone and be careful.

You'd think she was going to go swimming in the dark. Yes DAD!

She smirked at the phone, knowing he'd be clenching and unclenching his jaw because of her now.

GRRR! Was all he sent back.

Tucking her phone into her pocket, she headed to the stairs. It was a picture-perfect night. There was a gentle breeze, just enough to stir the muggy air but not be too cool. The crickets chirping and lapping water broke the silence.

Leaning against the big tree that sheltered her favorite picnic table, she picked up a large twig and twirled it on her fingers. An owl hooted, the sound echoing through the night. Vaguely she could hear a cat yowl, most likely a tomcat out prowling for companionship. The moonlight reflecting off the water was mesmerizing, and she finally found her sense of calm, something desperately missing in her life for the last several months.

Movement downstream caught her attention. She turned her head to see the couple getting up and walking away, holding each other close.

Poking at the ground with the twig, she sighed, hating the melancholy ache in her chest.

A branch snapping caused her to pause until someone moved into her sight. They stood by the bank staring at the river. Maybe its the tranquility would help them, she thought for a moment.

A sound close to her had her tense, and she found herself hauled to her feet as her back slammed against the tree. A large hand slapped over her mouth, driving her skull back against the bark. Pain radiated down her neck from the impact.

Blinking, she tried to focus on the dark blur in front of her. The light was at his back, masking his face in shadow. He stood motionless for what felt like an eternity. When he slowly lowered his hand from her mouth as if testing to see if she was going to scream, it dawned on her what was happening.

"I guess you didn't do your research," she whispered roughly, "because if you had, you'd know that none of that supernatural gobbly-guck works on me." The hand that had been over her mouth wrapped around her throat in a tight hold. "Vampires can't compel me. Spells don't work on me," she gasped, trying to get the words out, "I am completely resistant to *your* kind." His hand squeezed her throat tighter. "Now get your hands *off* me," her voice was barely a whisper now.

Remi pushed at the chest in front of her, not even moving her attacker. Before she could think of her next move, the hand that had held her pinned to the tree swung out and cuffed her on the side of her face. He shattered her cheekbone, the pain making her eyes water. She tried to knee any part of his body she could reach, only to be rewarded her with another slam against the unforgiving bark behind her.

The next thing she knew, she was sliding down, suddenly free.

"Remi?"

Darien's voice. Hands grabbed her shoulders. She swung out in their direction only to connect to a body that went with the voice next to her ear. *Why does he sound like he's in a tunnel?*

"Remi, talk to me." She felt herself being lifted into strong arms. "Come on, *Álainn* talk to me."

She could feel herself moving, but she couldn't even feel her legs. Her head was bobbing along like she was floating. *Did I go for that swim after all?*

"Attis. Get out back and see if you can find out who did this." Darien was growling.

Attis was here? Should he really be swimming when he was supposed to be manning the bar with Pascal?

"Remi?"

Emery? Why the hell wasn't he working? She was going to have to sit her night staff down and give them all a good talking to.

"Hang on, *A ghrá.*"

She could hear boots on the stairs now. *What is going on?*

"Cait, go get Pascal. Now."

Darien was really crabby tonight. Maybe she should have given him a night off, she'd tried but he always said no.

"I'm going out to help Attis."

Emery was so loud; gads, why was he yelling?

"You are going to stay right here. When she comes around, I don't need her freaking out because you're off playing avenger." Darien's voice bounced around in her head.

That's it, Dare, keep him in line. She loved Emery, but sometimes she needed to hammer it into him that he wasn't invincible. Nothing could happen to him.

"Was she conscious when you found her?"

Pascal? This was turning into some kind of party.

"Has she said anything?"

Why was Caitlyn crying? Darien? What's happening?

"Her eyes were open when I got there."

Darien's voice was softer now. Good, she hated it when he was upset.

"No, she hasn't Cait. I'm sure she's just a little dizzy."

Dizzy? She wasn't dizzy. *Oh, wait, yeah, I am.*

"Can you do anything? Cait, get some ice for her face."

Her face? *What's wrong with my face?*

"I don't know how my blood would affect her, Darien. We have no idea what could happen." Pascal sounded concerned. Pascal didn't do emotion.

"What happened?"

Oh great, now Randell's spy was here too. Seriously she needed to get a handle on these people, creatures, beings…whatever. She felt cold fingers at her throat. Oddly enough, they felt comforting.

"Her pulse is strong." Pascal sounded like he was right beside her, but she couldn't see him. "See if you can get her to respond. I think she's probably concussed, but if at any point she doesn't respond, you're going to have to take her to the hospital."

Hospital? *Oh, no. No! I am not doing doctors.*

"Remi? Come on, sweetheart. I need you to open your eyes for me." Darien's voice was so soft and rumbling. She loved it when he sounded like that.

"Here's an ice pack." Cait's voice echoed beside her.

"Come on, Remi," Darien's sexy voice again.

The side of her face was suddenly burning. It was so cold. Focusing, she tried to open her eyes, but they didn't want to.

"That's it, look at me."

Following his voice, she turned into his warm chest and rested her head against him; she felt his arms tighten and had never felt so safe.

"She moved on her own. That's a start." Pascal's voice sounded like it was moving away from her. "You, cop. Come with me. We have to find Attis."

Alarms went off in her head. "D-don't…" her stomach revolted, "hurt him."

"Not what I wanted to hear you say, but it's something." Darien's voice whispered against her ear.

Breathing slowly, she snuggled closer to his warmth. *Maybe if I just have a short nap, all of this will make sense.*

6

"Darien, move out of the way so Vienna can check her."

Darien looked away from the woman curled into his chest to snarl at Caitlyn.

"Please," she added softly.

"Vienna has medical training?" Kyran inquired from where he stood at the end of the bed.

Emery got up from the other side of Remi and sent Darien a knowing look. "Vie has *all* training." He looked back at Remi's swollen face. "And she can see inside heads so she can check how Remi really is."

Dairen exhaled slowly and then held his breath as he lifted her head and gently pulled his arm from beneath it. His wolf was riding him hard. Anxious and angry feelings were swarming inside him. She had to be all right. Any other outcome was not acceptable.

Lowering her head to the pillow, he slowly brushed the hair back from her face. Her cheek was red, and down into her jaw, a deep purple. Her mouth was swollen. "Her jaw could be fractured," he said more to himself than anyone in the room.

"Let me take a look, Darien. Nadine will be here shortly."

He looked over his shoulder at Vienna. "You called Nadine?"

Vie flipped her hair behind her shoulder and nodded. "She might be able to do something. I can only look inside. Healing is *not* my thing."

Clenching his jaw, he sighed. Even his wolf understood that they needed to get near her to help her. "Okay." He moved back hesitantly, afraid he might jar her. Emery still stood on the other side of the bed. Hating how he felt, he sent the young vampire a quick look. "Just," he sighed again, "just please... no males... I'm..." He closed his eyes and clamped down on his emotions. "I'm struggling."

"It's okay, Dare," Cait spoke from behind him. "We get it. Just move back so we can look after her."

Afraid to say anything else, he sat up. Before he could change his mind, Darien got up off the bed and stepped three feet away from it.

Pascal pushed off from the wall where he'd been leaning and stood in front of him. Darien recognized the stance of a warrior coiled and ready. It made him feel more at ease, knowing that the large vampire would stop him from doing anything stupid.

"We'll find out who did this to her," Pascal told him in a quiet, his tone lethal.

Darien clenched his jaw and nodded.

Emery and Kyran were both standing as far from the bed as they possibly could without leaving the room. Flexing his hands to relax his fists, he focused hard. It took every ounce of willpower he could find to stay where he was as Vienna ran her hands over Remi's body and face.

Cait sat on the bed watching. He could see she was shaking and close to tears, but if he moved to comfort her, he'd just end up pulling Remi back into his arms.

Attis came into the room unannounced, and Darien turned and growled a low warning.

He stopped and raised his hands. "I won't go near her."

Taking a deep breath, Darien forced his wolf to calm again.

"Anything?" His voice was deep, the tone hinting at the wolf near the surface. He knew he had a mouthful of fangs, but there was no one present that hadn't seen them before. He glanced at Kyran, who stood where he was, hands in his pockets, a serious expression on his face. He didn't seem to care if his fangs were showing.

"I couldn't find a thing," Attis finally said, his voice filled with doubt. "I followed the scent of the normals that were making out along the bank but couldn't find a trace of anyone near the tree but Remi." He looked at Pascal for a moment. "I don't understand why I can't pick up the scent. Any scent at all."

Darien swore softly under his breath. He'd never known a trail Attis couldn't pick up. Judging by the look passing between the two old vampires, they hadn't either. Rubbing the back of his neck, he closed his eyes and hung his head. His wolf was not happy to not see Remi. Opened them to look at her lying on the bed. She looked so pale and fragile. He looked back over Kyran. "You need to find out who did this."

Kyran studied him for a moment. "I know." He looked to Attis. "If Attis can't find a trail though, I'm not sure what I can do." Motioning toward Remi, he held Darien's stare again. "Hopefully, Remi can tell us more when she comes to."

"I got here as fast as I could." Nadine came rushing into the bedroom. "What happened?"

Cait jumped up. "Someone attacked Remi by the river. They were smacking her head off the tree when Darien got to them."

With wide eyes, Nadine looked at him. "Are they alive?"

A low growl came from deep in his chest. "They got away."

"And I can't find a trace of them," Attis added, stepping in front of her. "It's got to be some kind of magic."

Nadine nodded. "If they're cloaked from you, then yes, it is." She turned and looked at Remi on the bed. "Oh my god."

Moving over to stand behind Vienna, she looked down at Remi. "Look at her face. Is anything broken?"

Vie dropped her hands into her lap. "Not that I can sense. Her head's fairly clear, so I don't think it's too serious."

"I don't want to give her any blood without her being awake. I honestly don't know how it's going to work in her system." Pascal's voice was quiet and strained.

Nadine bit her bottom lip and nodded. "I agree. She needs to be awake the first time she tries that." Finally, looking up from Remi, she gave Darien a soft look. "I can't do much. Maybe try a little spell to make her more comfortable."

"Can't you just make her face better?" Kyran crossed his arms and looked from her to Remi.

Darien raised both eyebrows and looked over at him.

Nadine snorted. "You've been watching too many cartoon movies, Detective. *Real* magic doesn't work like that."

Lifting a hand in Kyran's direction so he wouldn't reply, Darien moved closer to Remi. He didn't know how much longer he could be this far from her. "Do what you can, Naddy."

Nadine nodded. "Who is working if you're all up here?"

Pascal blew out a breath. "I suppose Attis, Vie and I had better go back down. Who knows what mayhem is possible with two wolfs, a nymph and Finn running the show."

Emery straightened like he was going to go with them.

"You stay." Darien said giving him a narrow-eyed look. "I want you where I can keep an eye on you."

"I was just…"

"Going to slip out the back the first chance you got." Pascal said sounding bored.

Darien glanced at Pascal out of the corner of his eye, thankful he'd confirmed his suspicions. Looking back at Emery, he titled his head. "Remi would skin me alive if anything happens to you." He pointed to the other side of the bed. "So, you stay until she's awake again."

Emery watched the other three leave the room and then shrugged. "Fine by me." He moved over and sat on the edge of the bed looking down at the woman he considered his mother.

Rubbing a hand over his face, Darien exhaled loudly and watched Nadine holding her hands over Remi's face and talking softly. "I don't know how much longer I can keep my distance." He said it quietly, hoping all in the room would take it as a warning.

Cait came up to him and rested her head on his shoulder, her warm hand on his arm. "You can hold her again in a few minutes, Dare. No one is going to stop you."

Nodding, he wrapped his arm around her and squeezed her into his side.

"I sometimes forget that she's not a para or invincible," she whispered, sounding small. The truth of her words made his heart ache.

Emery snorted and looked over at his sister. "Well, she's not a regular normal. How do we know she's not immortal or unstoppable?"

Darien looked at him for a moment. It was true. They all knew it was. Deep down, he knew that Remi knew she wasn't just a plain, garden-variety human. She liked to believe Doyle was the reason she could read people and know if they were paras or normals. He suspected that wasn't the case at all. There was a part of Remi that was awakened after Doyle passed away. For whatever reason he didn't know, he'd never looked beyond who Remi was. He liked everything about her, even when they were butting heads.

"Should we try to wake her every few minutes?"

Emery's voice brought him back to the present.

"Isn't that what you're supposed to do?"

Darien glanced at him and then looked to Vienna. She nodded.

"As long as you can get some sort of response from her, I think she'll be okay." She shrugged. "Right now, her body is in what-the-fuck stage and just doing some regrouping."

Nadine sighed loudly and stood up. "I've tried to boost her own natural healing mechanisms."

"But nothing else can be done until she's awake?" Cait asked quietly.

"I'm afraid not." Nadine sighed and looked down at Remi. "Why would someone attack her?"

Darien's heart started pounding again as he looked at her. Her face was so swollen. Her neck had red welts on it in the shape of a hand. He clenched his jaw and fought his wolf's desire to kill at the thought of someone touching her.

"Shouldn't you take her to the hospital?" Kyran moved over to stand beside him.

A warning growl emitted from Darien's throat was the only warning anyone had. Before he could clamp down on the beast, he had Kyran by the throat and pressed against the wall. "Why don't you find out who did this?" His voice was deep and rasping as he spoke around a mouth full of sharp teeth.

"Whoa." Emery grabbed his wrist and tried to pull the hand on Kyran's throat off.

Darien could feel the strength he was using, trying to get his arm to move.

"What the…" Finn appeared on the other side of him and got in his face. "Dare, let go of the *human* cop." He said it slowly as he pushed his body between them, forcing Darien to back up.

He knew his clawed hand was around the man's throat and fought to get his beast under control.

"Come on, big guy," Finn's voice was soft and steady. In the back of his mind, Darien knew he was trying to use his thrall on him, but his wolf was immune. "Remi will be seriously pissed with you if you crush a human's throat in her bedroom."

Blinking, Darien looked at him. The only sound that could be heard was the rapid breathing of his wolf side.

"Dare…"

The rasp of Remi's voice had him opening his hand. Kyran slid down the wall as he spun to Remi. She'd said his name. He moved over to the bed and sat, leaning over her. "I'm here, sweetheart." Sliding onto the bed, he pulled her into his arms and looked down at her swollen face. Her eyes were still closed, but he could tell by the tension in her face that she was in pain. "We need another ice pack," he said, his voice cracking. He didn't look away to see if anyone heard him.

"I'll go," Cait said and rushed out.

Darien gently brushed the hair back from Remi's face and then looked up. Kyran was standing against the wall, and Nadine was checking his throat. "Sorry." Darien sighed. "I'm walking a thin line right now."

Kyran nodded abruptly but didn't reply.

Emery looked from Remi to Darien and then turned to Kyran. "Rem's his *mate*." He said it slowly, enunciating mate with flare. "Only she doesn't know."

Kyran's eyes changed, an understanding entering them. "Sorry," he croaked and then swallowed with a wince.

Exhaling slowly, Darien forced his body to relax and then really noticed Finn. The lanky vampire was staring at Remi, a look of pain almost on his face. "Why are you up here, Finn?"

Finn's eyes snapped to him, "We're shutting things down early." He glanced at everyone in the room. "Attis and Pascal want to go see if they can track the guy."

Remi moved into Darien's hold with a moan of discomfort. He looked down at her and nodded without looking up again. "Make sure Nadine and everyone gets home safely."

Cait came back in with the ice pack and handed it to him. Her eyes were filled with worry.

Placing the pack lightly against the swelling on his love's face, Darien cleared his throat and glanced up at her. "Can you make Kyran some herbal tea?"

Hugging her waist, she nodded. "Yeah." Turning, she motioned to Kyran. "Come out to the kitchen.

With an apologetic look on his face, Kyran straightened from the wall and started for the door. He paused and looked back at Remi. "I'm going to stay until she comes to." Not waiting for a reply, he walked out.

Vienna cleared her throat. "I'm going back down to help with clean up."

"Thanks," Darien mumbled but didn't look away from the woman in his arms.

"I'll see you in the morning." Nadine's voice was soft and fading as she walked out of the room.

He moved the ice pack down to her jaw, his eyes roaming over every inch of her face. "Come on, *Álainn,* open those pretty eyes and look at me," he whispered, lowering his head to kiss her gently on the temple.

7

Opening her eyes, she quickly closed them again. The pain in her head intensified, making her groan out loud. *What the hell?* Taking a few deep breaths, she explored her aches. It felt like her heart had moved up into her skull, pounding with a steady throb. She didn't feel nauseous now that she closed her eyes again. It hurt to swallow, and it was that realization that brought back the whole incident. Someone had tried to choke her, literally choke her, and then smacked her brain off a tree.

"Remi?"

She opened her eyes to see Caitlyn sitting on the bed beside her. She had red-rimmed eyes and looked worried. "Hey," Remi said, her voice was so hoarse she wasn't sure if the words were understandable.

"Oh my god, you're awake. I've been losing my mind sitting here." She leaned so close Remi could make out the size of her pupils. "Don't ever do that to me again," Cait whispered, her voice cracking with emotion.

"I'll try," she tried to swallow and winced. "Drink?"

Caitlyn moved out of her line of sight, and Remi didn't dare try to move her head.

"Next time you wanna be a ninja, let me know. I'll back you up." Emery's face appeared in front of hers.

"What time is it?" She really needed that drink.

"Sunrise in a half hour." He brushed the hair off her forehead, his eyes moving over her face. "I was ready to camp out in your closet if you didn't come around."

"I was hoping there was room for two in there." Attis leaned over Emery's shoulder.

"You guys should be in the basement," she whispered, forcing each word out through the pain.

Attis knelt beside Emery. "I didn't find him, Remi. Any idea what he, I'm assuming it was a he by the size of those fingerprints on your neck, was?"

Closing her eyes, she took a few slow breaths and tried to remember all the little details. "Wore gloves. Was trying something with eyes or mind…" She coughed, moaning when it burned her throat.

"That doesn't narrow it down much." He gave her an uneasy look. "I'll see what I can find out." He stood up and put his hand on Emery's shoulder. "Come on, kid, you're going to drop like a stone in a few more minutes, and I'd prefer not to carry you down as the sun rises. Bad enough that Pascal is going to come racing in as the horizon lights up."

Emery leaned down a few inches from her face. "I'll be back up as soon as I can move."

"Okay."

He knelt there for a few more moments, his eyes burning into hers like he was imprinting her image into his memory. "Go, Emery," she croaked. Reluctantly he stood up and turned away. As soon as he moved, Caitlyn was standing there holding a cup. Remi didn't care what the contents were, only that it was wet.

"Let's get you more upright." Darien appeared behind Caitlyn. He knelt on the bed and leaned over her. "Just roll slowly onto your back, and I'll take it from there."

Wincing the whole time, and it felt like a *very* long time, she rolled onto her back. Just that slight movement brought tears to her eyes.

"Pascal was afraid to give you his blood when you were out, not knowing what it would do."

Pain was shooting up through her shoulder into the side of her head. "Okay," she blew out a slow breath and waited for the pains to settle.

"I'll go get him if you want to try now," he whispered, watching her eyes.

"Later."

Nodding, he leaned closer and wrapped his arms around her, lifting her gently into his chest. "Grab the pillows, Cait."

With the arm that didn't hate her, she gripped the front of his shirt as he lifted and slid her body up onto the pillows. When he released her, she realized that what had felt like she was sitting meant she reclined on the pillows, only raised a few inches. Just enough that she'd be able to take a drink with help.

Cradling her head in one of his big hands, he held the cup to her lips. "Take it slow. Swallowing is going to hurt."

It took a lot of energy to manage to take two small sips of the drink. Feeling like she'd just run a mile, she relaxed into his hold so he would lower her back to the soft pillows. "How long was I out?" Now her voice just sounded hoarse instead of squeaking.

"A few hours." He sat down and looked down at her, Cait standing right behind him.

"You should go get some sleep," she tried to smile and then realized the side of her face was swollen. Lifting her hand, she touched it. She probably looked like someone beat the hell out of her. Oh wait, they had.

Cait leaned down and kissed the side that didn't hurt. "I'm going. I called Nadine so she could cover my shift if I'm not up in time."

"Okay. I'll be fine." Remi assured her. "Get some rest."

Darien sat there looking at her after Cait left. After a few minutes, he sighed. "Kyran is here. He wants details."

Clearing his throat, he glanced across the room. "He hasn't called it in because Randell would show up."

Swallowing, she winced. "Buy him breakfast for that."

Darien gave her a half smile. "I'll be sure to do that." He turned and nodded to someone.

Kyran came into her view. "Hell of a thing to get yourself attacked on my first night here."

Coughing, she closed her eyes for a second before trying to speak. "That was rude of me, sorry."

Crossing his arms over his chest, he leaned against the wall. "Any other details besides what you told Attis?"

"No, not really." She huffed out a breath. "I couldn't see his face."

"Did they say anything to you?"

"No." taking a deep breath, she released it carefully, testing to see if it hurt. "They weren't happy when I told them their supernatural gobbly-guck didn't work on me." Darien gave her a hard look. "I was hoping they'd run after that." She took another breath. "Not beat me against the tree."

Kyran's eyes moved over her face. "Do you know of anyone that has it in for you?" He studied her face some more. "How many times did they hit you?"

Closing her eyes, she inhaled through her nose. It hurt to breathe through her mouth. Opening them, she looked back up at him. "Once."

Darien's jaw clenched a few times. "No one has a problem with Remi."

Kyran nodded a few times. "Definitely a para to do that with one strike."

That? How bad did she look? Her eyes sought Darien's, asking him the question.

He turned to Kyran. "Hand me my phone."

Kyran moved out of her line of sight again, but there was no way she was moving her head to see where he was going. Before she could think about it, he was back with the phone. Darien turned and looked at her as he held it against his ear.

"You still able to come up here for a few?" He nodded.

"Barely," more nodding. "It's worth a try." Hanging up, he dropped the phone and looked back down at her. "Pascal will be here in a sec; he wants to try a little blood and see if it helps."

She couldn't possibly feel worse, she decided. "Okay."

"Try a little?" Kyran asked.

Darien didn't take his eyes off her as he answered. "His blood. It usually heals normals, but we're not quite sure what else Remi has in there, so we don't know how it will work."

Kyran glanced at her and then back to him. "That's a bit risky, isn't it?"

Darien turned, and she wasn't sure what his look conveyed, but Kyran nodded abruptly. "I'll go so I don't have to put that on my report." He glanced at his watch. "I'll be back by mid-morning."

"See you then." Darien's voice was harsh.

Remi searched his face. "Be nice."

He snorted. "That *was* my nice." Rubbing a hand over his face, he glared, even though his expression was softer than he wanted to convey. "You just took ten years off my life, sweetheart. I'm allowed to be pissy."

"Is this a bad time?" Pascal came into view. His eyes moved over her face briefly. "Your quite colorful, Rem."

"Bad?" She asked, moving her eyes enough to look from him back to Darien a few times.

"Bad enough." He moved around to the end of the bed and sat down on the other side of her. "Let's give this a try, I can withstand the dawn, but it was a hell of a night, and I need some solitude."

She'd never tasted blood before and wasn't sure if starting with an ageless vampire was something she really wanted to do. "Worst case scenario?"

Pascal paused with his wrist in front of his mouth. "You become a winged thing and start flapping around the room."

She gave him a steady stare.

He sighed. "In my estimation, nothing will happen." He shrugged, "which will be hell on my ego if that's the case."

Remi wasn't sure if it was because she was fuzzy-headed or if he was that tired, but she could have sworn he had a slight brogue now. "Just enough to kick-start your healing, okay?"

He gave her a fanged grin, his eyes flashing for a second before he inclined his head slightly. She winced when he bit into his wrist, but he didn't even hesitate, just ripped into his flesh and held the opened wound toward her lips.

Darien moved closer and lifted her head again.

"Just a bit, lass."

She swallowed, making a yuck face with his wrist still against her mouth. The taste wasn't as bad as she'd thought it would be. It was the idea that she *was* drinking blood. *Blech.*

"Take another before it closes," Pascal coaxed softly.

She did as he said and then swallowed and released his wrist. Licking her lips, she looked up at him. "Lass?'

He looked at his wrist for a moment and then lifted his long lashes to look at her. Slowly he raised his finger to his lips. "Shh." He grinned at her.

Someday she was going to ask, and she knew he realized it too, but for now, she just blew out a breath and assessed how she felt. Overall, she didn't feel any different. Everything still hurt.

"Get some rest, and hopefully, you'll be on the mend by the time you wake up." He stood up and nodded briefly at Darien before leaving.

"I knew he was Scottish," she whispered to Darien.

He grinned. "I don't care if he's the pope right now, just as long as that helps you." He touched her chin lightly and turned her head so he could look at the swollen side. "You should try to rest some more."

"Can I have more to drink first?" She wanted the taste of blood gone.

Darien helped her take a few more sips and then move back to her side. Pascal's blood hadn't made her feel any worse, which she was thankful for, but it also didn't feel like she was any better. Her shoulder and neck were still throbbing; her head wasn't feeling great either.

"Get some rest. I'll be right here." Darien stood up.

"Who is going to run the café if we're both here?"

He chuckled. "The staff will just have to step up for one day."

"I hurt, Dare. My shoulder is on fire, and my head is pounding. I doubt I'll sleep at all." She exhaled slowly, closed her eyes, and shifted as much as she could without moving her shoulder.

When she felt the bed move behind her, she opened them. The heat from Darien's large body was comforting, and she relaxed against him as he moved close.

"Do you mind talking to me for a few minutes until I fall asleep?"

He brushed the hair back from her neck then she felt her pillow move as he lowered his head. "What would you like me to talk about?" His hand moved up and down her side in a lazy caress that she found soothing.

"How old are you, Dare? I don't think you've aged since I got here."

She could feel his breath against her neck as he while silent for a few minutes.

"Weres age a lot slower than humans." He moved his hand in a slow circle at her lower back. "We grow at a normal rate until our late teens and then slow down…"

"Weres are born? I thought they only turned because they were bitten." She closed her eyes. Between the motion of his hand and his warmth, she felt more and more relaxed.

"Both, actually. A simple nip won't turn anyone, not like the movies portray. A turning from a bite is no accident. Only an elder can turn someone."

She loved how soft his voice was. The rumbling in his chest was against her shoulder blades. "Were you born this way then?"

"Yes." He moved his hand to her lower arm and began more gentle caresses.

"So, I guess you're a pureblood." She smiled, picturing the pride on his face.

"I am."

Typical Darien, she thought, have to drag every word out of him. "So, how old are you?"

"You're what, twenty-five now?" His fingertips moved up her arm to her shoulder, somehow soothing the ache away. "I'm roughly three times your age, *Álainn*."

She opened her eyes, or eye mostly. "Wow. You're one sexy geriatric, Dare."

He chuckled, his hot breath running across her neck. "I can assure you that none of me is geriatric. For my kind, I'm in my prime."

She attempted a grin, but it hurt too much. "If you say so."

"I say so." His tone was deeper but still playful.

"You should take more time off, go out more." It was too much work to keep one eye open, so she closed it again. She could feel his heartbeat against her back.

"I like working."

"Don't you get lonely? I've never seen any of your kind around here."

He was silent for a long time, his hand continuing its mesmerizing patterns up and back down again. "I walked away from my own." He said it, almost whispering. "For the most part, my own kind believes it's okay to mindlessly kill, especially during the full moons." She felt his lips brush against the back of her neck. "I don't."

"You're such a good man, Dare." Letting out a long breath, she felt the throbbing in her head ease a little. Her throat still hurt, and talking probably wasn't the smartest thing, but Darien rarely answered questions. "You're lucky you know what you are, that you know how long you'll live. I don't even know that." She licked her dry lips. "I mean, am I human and will live to somewhere between forty and ninety, or am I more?" His lips brushed against the side of her neck. "So, do you have one of those destined mates out there? I think all paras do."

"I do."

His hand brushed the back of her neck, the movement easing any tension. "You're lucky there too. I guess all paras are. Humans, not so much. I wish we did, have a mate. It would stop all the mistakes, heartbreak, and depression." She exhaled as his fingers stroked again. "What happens if your mate isn't a werewolf? I mean, that happens, right? What if yours is a specie that doesn't live as long as you?" She hissed out a breath when his teeth brushed against the tender skin at the back of her neck. Strangely enough, that felt good to her. "I guess that's the flaw with the whole destined mate thing."

"If I," his breath brushed over her neck, "any of my race find a mate from another specie, when they mate, their lifelines link together."

She felt the muscles in her shoulder relax. "That's awesome, Dare."

His lips brushed against her neck again. "Which part? What I'm doing or the mate link?"

Sighing, she relaxed back against him more. "Both. Between the blood and your warmth, I think my headache is easing."

His mouth brushed over the back of her neck again. "Just try to get some sleep. I'll stay right here."

"Thank you, Darien." She leaned back into him, "for finding me outside."

"I was heading out there to sit with you." He lightly wrapped his arm around her waist and held her.

"You're always there for me," a heavy feeling set into her eyelids and muscles.

"Always, sweetheart."

$$8$$

"Remi?"

Her eyes opened. Disoriented, she had no idea what time it was. "Come in."

A groan sounded behind her, and right at the same moment, she felt a warm hand against her stomach.

"Sorry to wake you guys." Cait stood at the end of the bed, a hesitant look on her face. "Nadine just called me. Randell is downstairs."

"What time is it?" Darien said in a sleep-filled voice.

"Three." She said softly.

Remi pushed up onto her elbow. "I slept all day?"

"You needed it," Darien's tone was flat.

Cait moved over to her side. "Oh, Remi, your face looks a lot better." She tucked her hands in her pocket. "I heard Pascal here this morning. I guess it works on you."

Darien shoved up until he was sitting and gently turned her head so he could see. "Slight bruising," his eyes moved to her arm. "How are you feeling?"

Remi dropped back onto her pillow. "Stiff from lounging in bed all day." Touching the side of her face lightly, it barely hurt now. "Call Nadine and tell her we'll be down in half an hour."

"Is there any coffee up here?" Darien swung his legs off the bed and stood up.

"I made some when Naddy called."

"You're an angel, Cait."

"No," she giggled, "I'm a troll." Turning, she walked out.

Darien came around to her side of the bed and held out a hand. "Get up slowly. You're going to be wobbly with no food all day."

Remi nodded and took his hand. "Do you think I have time for a shower?"

"Make time. He can wait."

He hadn't been kidding when he said she'd be wobbly, although mushy was a closer description. Her legs were shaking as she gripped his forearms to steady herself. "Do you think Dell found out who attacked me?"

Darien gave her an annoyed look. "Just focus on standing without shaking." Leaning forward, he gripped her waist lightly, giving her no choice but to put her hands on his shoulders to steady herself. "If Attis couldn't track them, I doubt *Dell* found anything."

She tilted her head up to look at him. Light-headedness had her squeezing her eyes shut and leaning her forehead onto his chest. "I think I need food."

He wrapped his arm around her, supporting more of her weight than she was. "Just get your balance and then we'll get you cleaned up and fed."

Remi nodded, not sure if speaking was going to make her feel sick or not. She took a few slow breaths.

"When was the last time you ate?"

She could hear the concern in his voice. "Dinner?"

"You mean the salad you barely ate while doing paperwork?"

She frowned at him.

He shrugged. "I asked."

Remi nodded.

"That was over twenty-four hours ago. Remi, you have to

start taking better care of yourself."

Exhaling slowly, she looked up at him, trying her best to give him an exasperated look. Straightening, she took a deep breath to assess how she felt.

"Are you going to be okay to stand in the shower?" His grip on her loosened to give her space to try moving.

"I'll let you know when we get there." She took an unsteady step, keeping her hand on his arm as she did. "This can't be from lack of food."

"You did get your head cracked on a tree, not to mention a smack to the face." His voice had dropped. "If it wasn't for Pascal's blood, I doubt you'd be able to stand right now."

"I'm glad I didn't get to see what my face looked like before his help. The expression on everyone's face was enough." She took a few more steps with his hand on her back, happy he wasn't moving too far away from her.

"It wasn't good. Did I mention you scared the hell out of me?" His voice cracked.

Remi concentrated on getting to the hallway before she said anything. "I think so." Nodding, she moved a little further from him.

"I don't think standing in the shower is a good idea right now."

She wasn't used to hearing Darien sound this worried and really didn't have the energy to argue her case. "Just get me in there, and Cait can help me clean up a bit."

He hesitated, his eyes searching her face. "I can go down and stall super cop."

Remi eyed him for a moment. His expression gave nothing away. "I don't think so. You haven't eaten either, and I know how easily you snap when you're hungry."

He smirked. "Afraid I'll take a bite out of super cop?"

She started to move slowly toward the bathroom, keeping one hand out in case she lost her balance. "Yes."

Darien followed her, his hand resting against her back. "I'll stay up here until you're ready to go down."

By the time she got downstairs, she felt a little steadier but not as solid as she would have liked. When they stepped into the cafe, Nadine was placing two plates at the counter and she realized Darien must have called down while she was getting changed. Sitting on the stool, she gave Naddy a grateful look and took a bite of her eggs. Only a few customers lingered; the café would be closed in a half hour for clean-up and to get the bar set up ready.

Kyran came through the door. He spotted Randell talking on his phone. With no more than a glance in his direction, he turned and started walking toward her. "You look better." His eyes scanned her face.

She'd seen what her face looked like now, and if the bruising was better, she was really glad she hadn't seen it before. "I'm a little shaky, but I'm sure this food will help."

"Speaking of food," Darien glanced at Kyran, "How do you take your eggs?"

Kyran leaned on the counter. "Sunnyside up."

Darien looked over at Nadine, who nodded and went back into the kitchen.

A few minutes later, Pascal came out carrying a plate, Remi glanced at the clock. "You're up early."

Setting the plate in front of Kyran, Pascal moved down the bar and reached into the fridge under the counter to get a bottle of blood. Without even warming it, he took a long guzzle and then paused, studying her. "I got up to check on you," he tipped the bottle in her direction. "Then I realized I'd missed this before going to ground."

Remi knew he slept on a bed, she'd seen it, but he still referred to sleeping as going to ground. Just one more tidbit that told her he was a lot older than anyone realized. "Sorry.' She said before taking another bite.

Finishing the bottle, he set it on the counter and came back to stand across from her. "It's hardly your fault." Reaching over, he tipped her chin up with two cool fingers and looked at the side of her face. "I guess the mystery of my effectiveness is solved."

She grinned. "I wouldn't want to wound your ego by not responding."

He released her chin and gave her a wink before his expression became serious. "You could use more from the looks of it."

Remi sipped her coffee while she considered the offer, now that she wasn't in agony. "Maybe later."

Pascal inclined his head in that regal way he had and then turned to look at Randell. "How long has he been here?"

Darien glanced over his shoulder and then turned back to the food in front of him. "Not long."

Pascal turned his attention to Kyran. "Any news?"

Kyran paused in eating and shook his head. "Not that I'm aware of."

"Ah, well," Pascal gave him a forced smile, "here comes our exemplary detective now, so I suppose we'll all find out together."

All heads turned to watch Randell walk across the bar. He was the type of man that didn't saunter or strut. His steps were always purposeful. He came to Remi and grasped her chin, turning her head to look at her face. She was momentarily shocked. Recovering, she leaned back out of his hold.

"Any other injuries?" he jerked his head toward Kyran. "He said it was too soon to tell this morning.

She looked passed Dell to Kyran, who sat there his expression giving nothing away. Turning back to her food, she played with it, stalling and considering what to say. "The pain in my head has eased, but my neck and shoulder are still quite sore." She kept her head down to avoid Darien and Pascal, knowing the looks of disapproval that she hadn't mentioned those injuries sooner.

Randell moved to lean on the bar, a little closer than she would have liked. "You're lucky, that's all." He lifted a hand, motioning in an agitated way. "What the hell were you doing out back alone after dark?"

Setting her fork down, she turned the stool to see his expression. It was hard and snide. "I go outside all the time." Randell glanced at his partner; a look passed between them that made her spine stiffen. "What aren't you telling us?"

Kyran glared at him, and at the same time, Pascal cursed softly.

Darien leaned forward, his posture suddenly tense.

We both knew Pascal had read one of their thoughts and we weren't going to like it.

Sitting down, his jaw clenched, Randell sighed. "The inspector isn't the first victim."

Darien's fork clattered on the plate as he dropped it and turned to face her ex. "What do you mean?"

Dell looked at Kyran, who nodded. "He was the third. All three are linked to here in one way or another."

Remi's heart started to pound. "How?" She swallowed the lump in her throat. "Who were the others?"

Tapping his fingers on the counter for a moment as if he was trying to decide what to tell her, Dell finally looked back at her. "That old woman you used to have clean here."

Remi gasped, "Mrs. Chaise? She retired last month and hasn't even been in here since…" her voice cracked. Wrapping her arms around her waist, she fought to keep the food down.

Darien stood up and put his hand against her back, moving it slowly up and down, trying to comfort her.

"Who else?" She asked, even though she was afraid to hear the answer.

Pascal leaned on the counter and hung his head down. "Mark." He said before Randell could say a word.

"He went back home," Remi said, sure there had to be a mistake. "He was only here for a few weeks and then decided to work it out with his family and go home."

Randell just sat there, not saying anything.

A gasp came from the kitchen door and then Nadine stepped up beside Pascal. She placed a hand on his arm. "Is it true? Was it him?"

Pascal looked down at her and then nodded. "I don't know how I didn't see it yesterday." He looked from one cop to the other. "You must have worked hard to keep it out of your thoughts."

Her ex didn't even acknowledge that he'd spoken, but Kyran's look became an apologetic one.

Randell leaned closer to Nadine. "I'd like to talk to you about magic."

Her eyebrows rose as she held his look. "Like what?"

"Could the attacker have tried to cast on Remi last night?"

Nadine looked at her for a moment. "Not from what I've been told." She gave Remi a questioning look. "Did they say anything?" Remi shook her head. "They wore gloves?" She nodded. Glancing back to Randell, she shrugged. "It wasn't magic, none that I know of anyways."

Dell nodded and then looked around Serenity. "How many males work here, Remi? Where were they last night?"

Remi jolted like he'd hit her. "What does that have to do with what happened to me?"

"There are nine males that work here," Darien replied with a cold tone. "All were here, inside, at the time Remi was attacked except two of the Lewis boys."

Nodding his head slowly, she watched him process that.

"It wasn't any of the Lewis boys, Dell. They're not tall enough." She added quickly before he could think about it much longer.

"How tall was your attacker?" He finally looked at her again.

"At least my height. Maybe taller." Darien's hand now rested on her shoulder as if sensing she was ready to freak out. First, she finds out people she knew were dead, and now he was trying to accuse her own staff of attacking her.

Randell finally sighed. "Okay." He looked back at Nadine. "Can you and your coven extend a no-harm spell to cover most of the property?

Nadine looked at her briefly before nodding. "We can try. It's a bit harder without walls."

"And you," Dell turned on her, his face a harsh mask; he pointed a finger at her, "go nowhere alone."

The hand on Remi's shoulder tensed.

"I always knew something like this was going to happen," Randell continued, "I…"

"We'll look after Remi," Darien said in a quiet tone, "You just do your job."

Dell stood up and moved into Darien's space. "Like you looked after her last night?"

Darien released her shoulder and stepped into Randell's chest, forcing her ex to look up at him. "Maybe if you'd told us *everything,* I would have known to keep a closer watch over her." A low rumble emphasized his displeasure.

Kyran and Pascal moved at the same time; they both pushed in between the seething males. "Enough," Pascal said in a firm voice. "Tearing into each other isn't going to solve anything."

Kyran pushed Randell to step back a few more feet. "I was here too last night, Peterson, and it *still* happened."

Dell spun away from him and retreated a few feet. "Just keep me posted." He stomped to the door and left without another word.

"He just makes me want to bite someone," Pascal muttered in a quiet tone.

Kyran turned to look at him, his eyes filled with surprise. "I thought you only drank from a bottle."

Pascal flashed him a fanged grin. "I do. Now." With that, he hopped back over the bar and went back to the small fridge for another bottle, this one he warmed in the microwave.

Remi sat, dazed. She couldn't focus on any one thought. "I can't believe they're gone, and no one told us."

Darien was behind her, resting his hands on her shoulders.

"We were told not to tell you right off." Kyran sat down again. "At least until I had a chance to see what the atmosphere was like internally."

"And what's the atmosphere like *internally?*" Remi shot

back, unable to keep the sarcasm out of her voice.

Kyran glanced around at the others standing near before making eye contact with her. "All of you are a family unit. You'd go to bat for each other in a heartbeat." Getting up, he rubbed a hand down the back of his neck. "I'm going to get some air." Turning on his heel, he left through the side door.

"I'm going to go get the kids from mom, and then I'll put in some calls and see if the others have any thoughts on how to extend the casting to the property," Nadine said quickly.

Remi nodded.

"I don't want any of the staff arriving or leaving alone, Nadine," Darien said in a somber tone. "Until we find out what the hell is going on, that's the way it's got to be."

Pascal set his bottle of blood on the counter. "I'll go call the rest of the staff and give them a heads up."

"Thank you." Remi finally said as the emotional haze started to lift.

Pascal paused at the door, holding it open. "Kyran is on our team if you're worried about that." He gave Darien a look she didn't understand and then looked at her again. "He'd go to bat for you too, Rem."

After he left, she looked at Darien, who had a snarl on his lips. "What does that mean?"

"I don't know." He moved away from her, grabbing their plates. "You better go up and talk to Cait."

Confused, she watched him go into the kitchen. "Just one normal day," she whispered, picking up her cup and drinking what was left. "Is that too much to ask?"

9

After sleeping the whole day, Remi knew she wouldn't be able to go back to bed any time soon, so she busied herself, making sure everything was ready for the auditor before seeing how things were going out front.

Kyran was sitting next to the kitchen door, so she went over and stood beside him. It wasn't overly loud yet, but it was close to being at full capacity. Darien was by the doors carefully checking IDs as another group filed in.

Kyran leaned closer to her. "It's not as rowdy in here as I thought it would be. Last night seemed a lot louder." He shrugged, "Although they nearly contained me in the kitchen, so I didn't get to see much."

Remi glanced at the clock behind the counter and smiled. "Pascal and Attis just haven't gotten it going yet."

"Got what going?"

Grinning, she motioned to the two vampires behind the counter serving the drinks. "Just watch."

Crossing his arms over his chest, he leaned back against the counter, looking at the line of customers waiting for drinks.

Remi tucked her hands in her pockets and rested her shoulder against the wall keeping a watch at the line of customers gathered at the bar. She wondered how long it would take Kyran to notice they were all female. Glancing at the yellow light, she noted it was off. The boys would get it going any time now. The tension had been high the last few hours; everyone needed to blow off some steam.

When Attis turned and looked at Pascal with a cheeky grin on his face, and Pascal smiled in return, she nudged Kyran with her shoulder.

Attis gave a quick nod to Vienna as she passed. With a smile on her face, she turned and went into the small sound booth. Kyran started to say something and then stopped with his mouth hanging open as the louder drums and guitars started.

Pascal was suddenly animated behind the bar, mouthing the words to *House Rules* as the girls lined up at his end. Remi wasn't much for country music, but this was more rock than twang, as far as she could tell. Even if you didn't like it, the beat just pounded its way into your body, and you'd be stomping your boots on the floor whether you wanted to or not.

Everyone in Serenity came to life. If they'd been here before, they knew the night had officially begun with Pascal's song of rules blaring through the speakers. If they hadn't, the commotion was so infectious it carried you away. Vienna, Elise, and Finn were busy moving through the crowd bringing the drinks that the two vampires had made with vampire speed without missing a beat.

She even found herself mouthing the words to the song. Remi glanced at Kyran to see a huge grin on his face. She bit her lip as the song ended, and another one began right away. She nudged him again and motioned toward the bar. Whereas Pascal liked the rocky country, Attis had his own theme song, as the staff called it.

The opening had everyone cheering just as the guitars cut in. Attis knew every beat and instrument in the song, and his movements followed as if he'd written it. When he started to mouth the words, Kyran's eyebrows shot up, and he gave her a questioning glance.

The girls were leaning over, ogling Attis now, their bodies swaying with the music. Attis smiled and mouthed each word of *Give me a Reason*. Pascal was smirking through the entire thing. Remi was sure their interpretation of the song had an entirely different meaning, but she could never bring herself to ask why they lit up when they sang some of the lines. Some things she just didn't need to know.

As the song faded, the heavy drum beat of *The Animal I have Become* started, and the night had officially begun, with movement everywhere.

Emery came out of the kitchen and leaned over to place a cool-lipped kiss on her cheek. She looked at him and smiled. He touched her bruised cheek lightly and then pushed away from the wall and, strutting in time to the music, went out through the crowd, greeting most of the female patrons with a smile, wink, or slight nod.

"What's the story there?" Kyran asked, his head close to hers so she could hear without him shouting.

She didn't look at him, just continued to watch Emery as he worked the crowd almost as well as the older vampires. "He was turned and left to figure it out on his own." She thought about all the details Kyran didn't need to know, being a law official. "I found him and pretty much adopted him." She finally glanced at him to see his mouth hanging open. Shrugging, she smirked. "I know, he's a vampire."

He blinked. "I thought you adopted Caitlyn?"

She laughed and then nodded. "I did. I have a troll daughter and a vampire son." Pushing away from the wall, she shrugged. "Not many can say that." Feeling like she needed to show her staff that all was well, even though she still felt like her body had been used as a punching bag, she moved to the bar and gave Attis a knowing look.

He paused to look her up and down and then smiled. With a look in Vie's direction, he inclined his head to her and then motioned to the small dance space. Darien watched her as she walked out onto it. A few hoots from some regular female customers sounded over the music as they quickly joined her. Elise and Vienna set their trays down, and they followed the line of females.

The male staff all stood back. Even Baker appeared out of the kitchen as the opening bars of *Ladies Come First* began to pound through the place. Digging deep, Remi found the energy to give the song justice and began to move in time. It didn't take long for the adrenalin to kick in, and she was soon bumping and grinding to the beat along with almost every female in the place. The males, Emery, Finn, and Darien surrounded the dance floor playing their part in the theatrics. Out of the crowd, Cait appeared as if the music had found her and brought among those that loved her. Taking her place between Remi and Vienna, she moved along with everyone else.

Serenity After Dark wasn't just a place to hang out and drink. It was a place that always felt like home. It may be filled with paras, but as far as Remi was concerned, they were just like normal people and deserved more than a dingy hole to hang out in.

By the end of the song, the males had moved onto the floor to move in time with a female or two. Darien was in front of Remi, a smile on his face, mouthing the words as he rested a hand on her hip and swayed in perfect movement to hers. The set of his mouth told her he was watching her closely and knew she wasn't at full strength, but the look in his eyes said something else as they held her gaze and sang to her.

When the song ended and another began, most of the customers continued to dance. Remi turned and worked her way off the floor, Darien's hand tucked into her back pocket, following her without skipping a beat.

As she headed toward the bar, his hand dropped away, but he still followed her until she found a home on the closest stool. Attis set a drink down in front of her and leaned on the bar. His eyes held her for a moment, seeing that she was all right before he grinned and moved back down the bar.

Darien's warm body leaned against her back; his lips pressed up against her ear.

"You okay?"

She took a sip of the cool water and nodded.

He squeezed her hip. "I have to get back to the door."

Taking another drink, she nodded again. As he moved away, Kyran came up and sat beside her. He leaned on the bar and smiled at her. "You guys know how to rev the place up."

Remi laughed and then nodded. She was still too winded to say much. Dancing wasn't the smartest thing, but she knew everyone needed it. She needed to feel some measure of normalcy right now too.

"I may have to get a job here for real." He said as he motioned to Pascal for a drink.

Feeling like things might be okay for now, she turned her stool and tapped her foot on the floor to the music as she looked around at her world of the last few years. Just when she felt like she may have had enough for the night, the door opened, and in stepped someone she hadn't seen in a while. Someone she could have done without seeing.

Through the door, Margo, an ex-employee demon, walked in like she owned the place. Beside her was her sidekick, Gemma, a troll. Margo smiled at Darien, as his expression echoed Remi's thoughts exactly.

With an abrupt nod, he motioned them in, his eyes glancing to Remi over top of the heads of those between them. The set of his jaw told her that if Margo started anything tonight, it would be ended very quickly. More often than she'd like, Margo would show up and create discontent among the staff of Serenity. Remi sat still, breathing slowly as Margo and her friend made their way through the crowd, zeroing in on Finn. From where she sat, she could see Finn stiffen as Margo's hand landed on his arm, and she gave him a charming smile.

With a frozen smile on his face, he inclined his head as he took her order, glancing briefly in Remi's direction as he did.

Margo turned and looked across the bar at her, a look of disdain replacing her smile before she turned back to Finn.

"Do I want to know what that was about?"

Remi looked away from Margo and shook her head. "She used to work here." She watched the way Finn's smile faded as he pried his arm free to head back to the bar.

"When did you fire her? Recently?"

Turning in the stool, she looked at him for a moment. "No, it was over a year ago now."

"Maybe we should look into her."

Shrugging, she glanced around for Darien. He was across the bar watching Margo also. "Randell was around when all that happened. Ask him."

Kyran leaned closer and studied her for a moment. Remi hated feeling like she was under a microscope. "I will if it bothers you to talk about it."

Glancing over at Pascal, she raised her empty glass and made a motion like she was holding a cup. With a nod, he swung around and picked up the coffee pot and a cup. "It doesn't bother me, really, I just feel dumb anytime I think about it." She jerked her chin in Margo's direction. "She was stealing and lying," she paused while Pascal poured her coffee, "she had me believing some of the lies about my staff. I still feel like an idiot."

"Ah, chronic liars are good at the stories they tell." He leaned both arms on the bar and stared at his glass. "How long ago did you and Randell break up?"

Narrowing her eyes, she looked at him.

Kyran grinned and looked down at her briefly, then at the glass in his hands. "*That* kind of tension can only come from a relationship gone bad." He tilted his head and looked over at her. "You want nothing to do with him, and he still cares."

Remi snorted and shook her head. "That's him caring?" Exhaling, she turned the stool and stared across the patrons enjoying themselves. "That's him being possessive," she glanced at him out of the corner of her eye, "he didn't want to be with me. He wanted to *own* me."

Kyran was silent for a long time before he looked back to his drink. "Well, everyone has their flaws."

Turning, Remi looked at him. He had a smirk on his face, letting her know he was going to leave that discussion alone. "What about you, Detective Nelsen? What are *your* flaws?"

Shaking his head, he tilted it and looked her in the eye. "I'm sure the list is long."

"At least honesty isn't one of them." She said, looking back at the crowd. "So, why a cop?"

He gave her a puzzled look.

"Why are you a cop? You seem like a nice guy."

"Ouch, Dell really did a number on you, didn't he?" He shrugged. "I like justice."

Quirking an eyebrow at him, she held his look. "That's it?"

Taking a drink, he watched her over the rim of his glass. "That's it."

"Hmm." Sipping her coffee, she turned her attention back to the dancers enjoying themselves to another song.

Darien left the door to Baker as the kitchen would be slow until later when everyone decided they should mix some food with their drinks. He motioned to Pascal, and both of them moved in her direction.

Kyran leaned closer and gave her a slight nod. "I think your nurses are about to end your night out."

"Ya think?" She said, narrowing her eyes and giving Darien a defiant look. She knew what they had in mind for her. She wasn't sure she could do it without feeling ill.

Darien stopped and turned her stool, so he could block her in with an arm on either side. He leaned down next to her ear. "You need a bit more blood, sweetheart. You're as pale as a ghost right now."

Leaning her forehead against his shoulder, she sighed. "I don't know if I can, Dare. This morning was one thing…"

He straightened up, his chocolate eyes searching hers. "You need it. You've got the auditor coming in the morning. The staff is all wired with the news…"

She waved a hand so he wouldn't continue. "I know. I

just…"

Pascal leaned across the bar, his head close to hers. "I can't compel you because we all know *that* doesn't work on you."

"I think I'll go mingle," Kyran said loudly and got up, giving her a look that said he agreed with the were and vampire but had to deny knowing because it was illegal. He moved past Darien and disappeared into the crowd.

Finn and Emery were suddenly standing beside Darien, looking down at her. It was like seeing in black and white with Emery's pale hair and eyes, and Finn's the exact opposite. She quickly felt defeated with three vampires and a werewolf ganging up on her. "You guys do know that I'm supposed to be the boss."

"Uh huh," Emery held out his hand, "and that's why we need you in full fighting form."

Groaning, she put her hand in his and gave Darien what she hoped was the look of death, almost meaning it.

Elise came up and leaned close to Darien. "Betany and Iris just came in." She smirked, "Dressed to kill." Emery and Finn both turned to look for them. "Iris seems to be zeroing in on Kyran."

"Oh shit." Darien looked from her to Elise. "I guess the flavor of the week is human." He tilted his chin to the two vampires flanking her. "Go run interference before she swamps him with faerie lust."

The two young vampires grinned. Finn moved away while Emery leaned down. "Go take your medicine and get some rest, *Mom*."

She glared at him as he chuckled and followed his friend through the crowd. Sighing, she looked up at Darien and at the big vampire now behind him. "You guys suck."

Pascal grinned wide at her words and then shrugged. "As often as I can, actually."

Rolling his eyes, Darien took her elbow and began to guide her in the direction of the break room.

"Is this *really* necessary?" She asked, hoping she was only imagining the whiney tone in her voice.

Closing the door behind them, Darien stopped and looked at her. "Would I really be asking you to suck on *his* wrist if it weren't?"

Pascal cleared his throat and then grinned. "Careful, you'll give me a complex." He glided closer to her. "Just relax, Rem. It's not going to hurt."

Rubbing her hands over her face, she groaned. "Just get it over with." It took all of her courage to stand there as Pascal bit into his wrist.

He grinned with red lips and fangs, "Sometimes it's a fight to get others to see things that are for their own good."

She glanced at Darien when the wrist was held to her mouth. He gave her a look and nodded. Taking the wrist with one hand, she touched her tongue against the blood welling on the cool skin.

Pascal continued talking as if this was a normal moment. It may have been for him, but not in her world.

"It's like those that find their mate and for whatever convoluted reasons do nothing about it." He looked from her to Darien.

She watched Darien's face turn to stone as he glared at the vampire.

"If *I*," Pascal said softly, "were to find the one to revive this dead heart of mine, heaven, hell, and all that lies between wouldn't stop me from ensuring she was mine for the rest of eternity." He shrugged, "But there are *some* that would rather be a fool and allow her the time to be more complete than they've ever been."

Swallowing again, she pressed her hand against her stomach and released his arm.

"Look at that face." Pascal chuckled. "You would think I taste like battery acid." His eyes flashing at her, he licked the healing punctures on his wrist and made smacking noises. "Mmm, thirteen twenty-nine. A perfect year." He gave her a fanged grin, and she forgot all about the taste of the blood on her tongue as the meaning behind his words registered in her head.

"She's going to get a bit of a buzz off that. Don't let her do anything she wouldn't normally do." Pascal said with a nod to Darien and then left, closing the door behind him.

"Did he…" she looked at Darien and then back to the door.

"Just tell us his age?" He gave her a wide-eyed look. "I think he did."

"That would make him," she struggled to focus on the math, "six hundred and eighty-something years old."

"And you thought *I* was geriatric." He said in a dry tone.

Remi giggled loudly and then slapped her hand over her mouth, giving him a horrified look. She was not a giggling kind of gal.

Chuckling, he grabbed her hand and pulled her toward the door. "Let's get you upstairs before you get too giddy on me."

"We could go dance again. Wanna dance with me, Dare?" She laughed after she said it, never having asked anyone to dance before.

"Sweetheart, if your eyes weren't glazed like an addict's, I would love to take you out there and bump and grind for hours." Darien tightened his hold on her hand and tugged her in the direction of the back stairs.

"I can take myself up, Dare." She felt so much lighter, and it wasn't an all bad feeling.

"Yes, you can, but I'm checking the apartment before I leave you there. I'll call Cait to stay with you when I leave."

She snorted. "I don't think Dell meant I *literally* couldn't be alone, not when I'm at home."

Darien stopped and gave her a once-over. "I don't care what *Dell* said. I won't feel right if I'm not sure you're safe."

Relaxing her arm, she let him lead her up the stairs. "Who's going to watch over me when I shower?"

His hand flexed around hers, and she stifled the urge to giggle again.

"Don't tempt me, *A ghrá*. You might get a surprise." He pushed open the door at the top and pulled her through it.

"What does that mean? You've called me it before." She tripped over the trim of the step and had to brace herself against his chest so she wouldn't fall.

He caught her with a strong arm around her waist and stood there looking down at her. She loved when he gave her those tender looks where his dark brown eyes softened. It made her feel cherished, something she'd never felt before.

Shrugging, he released her. "It's just a term I picked up." He turned away from her and went down the hall.

Remi stood there, watching after him. Sometimes that man was hard to read. He was her best friend in the whole world but could just shut down in a heartbeat. He went in and out of all the rooms before he came back toward her. Remi wasn't sure what Pascal had spiked his blood with, but she suddenly wanted to hug Darien. Just to get lost in the safety of his big arms against his warm body. When he paused a few feet away from her, she swayed in his direction and wrapped her arms tight around his waist.

Darien stiffened for a second before he hugged her back. "It's going to be all right, sweetheart. You know that, right?" He whispered into her hair.

Burying her face against his throat, she nodded. "It has to be," she squeezed him. "This is all I have."

His arms tightened, his warm hand stroking up and down her back. "Let's get you to your room. It's going to be a long day tomorrow." Turning, he walked with his arm hugging her into his side. Darien stopped just inside her bedroom door. "Get some rest, Remi." Kissing the top of her head, he turned to leave.

Remi grabbed his t-shirt to stop him from going. "Kiss me, Dare." She didn't know where it came from, only knew she'd like to kiss him once when she was expecting it. Maybe it was brought on by the effects of Pascal's blood, but she didn't care. She just wanted to feel a connection with someone, most specifically Darien.

He opened his mouth like he was going to say no and then closed it and grasped her chin lightly, searching her eyes for a long silent moment. Whatever he was looking for, he must have found because he released her chin and cupped her jaw gently. Tilting her head back enough that their lips were only a few inches apart, he stood there, his breath mixing with hers.

She felt everything stop before his warm lips caressed hers in a touch so light it was more like a whisper than a kiss. Stepping into his hard body, she pushed her hand into the back of his hair, encouraging him to stay close. "Again," she dragged her mouth over his.

He wrapped one arm around her waist and pulled her in, kissing her again with more passion this time. Her body responded to the movement of his mouth on hers, heating. It always happened whenever Darien kissed her. She loved the feeling, no matter how short-lived it was. It made her feel wanted, needed in a female way.

Darien's mouth suddenly ravished hers with a kiss hotter than any other she'd had before, and then he pulled back, leaving her shocked he had stopped so abruptly. "I have to go. You need to rest."

Taking a second, she caught her breath. "Just like that?"

His eyes bore into hers. "Just like that. I'm not a monk."

Dropping her hand to his shoulder, she looked up at him. There was something in the way he was looking at her, but her brain was too hazy from the blood and the kiss to grasp what it was. Regardless, she knew Darien well enough to know when he wouldn't bend, and she was certain this was one of those times. "Okay."

Leaning down, he brushed the hair back from her neck and placed a tender kiss on the side of her throat. "You can have whatever you want, Remi. You just have to ask." He straightened and gave her a sad look. "But not while you're stoned on vampire blood."

Sighing, she stepped back and rested her hip against the wall. "Got it."

He looked over his shoulder at her bed. "Are you good from here?"

Nodding, she hugged her arms around her waist. "I'm fine. Go."

It wasn't like Darien to linger, but he turned back to her and ran a hand through his hair. "Call if you need me, okay? Follow your gut feelings. If something doesn't feel right, I want to know about it."

"I will." She sidestepped past him. "Promise."

10

Darien set a drink in front of Berk and leaned on the bar.

Berk looked at the pink concoction and grinned before looking around at the others. "So," his eyes moved over each of the nine men present, "it's just males at this middle of the night *meeting*?" He smirked. "Not that I'm complaining.

Darien tipped his beer bottle in acknowledgment before taking a sip. "It wouldn't be a meeting if all the women were here."

"No, it would be a party," Baker added with a grin.

Kyran tasted the drink in front of him carefully, unsure if he should be drinking it. "Not bad. What is it again?"

Darien saw the look pass between Attis and Pascal. He knew the look and felt a twinge of pain for the unsuspecting detective.

Pascal grabbed several shot glasses and placed them on the bar. "It's a python," He picked up a bottle of tequila and started to pour it, "patent pending."

Shrugging, Kyran drank some more of it. "It's good."

Darien looked away when the human glanced at him. "Before we get sidetracked with libations, I'd like to brainstorm to see if we can come up with a list of suspects with something against Serenity or Remi."

Finn downed his tequila and washed it down with a mouthful of blood. "See, I don't believe that anyone could have a thing against Remi." He shrugged. "She's…"

"The most brilliant…" Boden paused and studied his empty shot glass.

Baker winced as he swallowed his drink. "Graceful," he croaked.

Darien watched as Pascal set another drink in front of Kyran. He looked at the glass the vampire pushed toward him and downed the rest of his previous drink in one gulp, placing it in the hand waiting for it. Raising an eyebrow at Pascal, Darien tried not to smirk at the nonchalant expression on the scheming vamp's face. He'd be pouring the detective into a cab later, Darien decided.

"Remi's the most fucking understanding person I know," Emery added in a strained voice.

Bates pointed at him. "And you'd know," he blinked a few times. "You tried to fucking kill her, you supreme *asshat,* and she forgave you, *then* adopted your sorry ass."

Choking on another shot, Kyran looked at Emery with his eyes wide. "You did what?"

Tipping his beer bottle toward the startled normal, Emery took a long drink and nodded. "When I was turned, I was left on my own to figure out what the fuck I was." He shook his head quickly. "I didn't even know about paras," he waved a hand motioning to the others sitting along the bar, "never mind that I'd need to drink blood to survive." He chortled softly and looked at the bottle in his hand. "I spent three nights dragging my ass from one abandoned dive to the next, puking my guts out every time I tried to eat." He glanced at Attis and Pascal, who, Darien noted, had a look of understanding on their faces. Leaning forward, he stared down the bar at Kyran. "And *then* this tall sexy chick walks by," he waved a hand around, "I think this was the fourth night of the new me." Shaking his head, he briefly made eye contact with Darien, then looked away quickly. "I remember thinking if I wasn't dying," he grinned, "because let's face it, I couldn't even find a fucking pulse in my own body and thought I was, well, dead." He snorted. "Who knew?" A serious look appeared on his face. "So, I see this woman and briefly thought if I weren't dying, I'd jump that." He sighed. "And then, like a possessed man, I did." Eyes wide, he looked at Darien. "I was just going to ask her for a buck or two, so I could try some juice or something, and the next thing I know, I can *smell* her blood." He cleared his throat and glanced at Attis. "She smells like fucking paradise and my favorite meal all in one…" He stopped talking and picked at the label on the bottle in his hand.

Darien knew he was reliving it. The curse of a vampire, as far as he was concerned, wasn't that they couldn't go in light and lived on blood. It was that they felt intense emotions repeatedly. Forever.

"You bit her?" Kyran asked, his voice slightly slurred.

Emery opened his hands and then clapped them together, and leaned on the bar. "Yeah, I lost it and bit her, and it was…" He waved his hand around, searching for the word.

"Tasty," Finn added with a nod.

Darien turned and glared at him.

"Sorry." A serious look covered his face.

"What happened?" Kyran accepted the next drink from Pascal without taking his eyes off Emery.

Watching him take a drink, Darien hid his smile behind the bottle against his lips and looked back at Remi's son.

Blowing out a breath, Emery leaned both elbows onto the bar. "I'm thinking I'm going to drain this poor woman, but I can't stop myself. Then the next thing I know, there's this enormous guy flashing fangs at me and pinning me against the wall." He motioned to Attis and continued. "I'm scared shitless staring into the face of this red-eyed seething man while another larger-than-life guy is holding Remi and licking her throat closed where I bit her."

Kyran accepted the shot of tequila from Pascal and downed it. "So, how did you get from *that* to being her precious son?"

Emery lifted a hand, a confused look on his face.

"I'm ready to rip his throat out," Attis said in a lethal tone, "when Remi comes to and tells me not to hurt him because he's *scared*." He glanced from Emery to Darien, "and to bring him home with us."

Darien shook his head, still remembering how conflicted he was when they did just that. Setting the empty bottle on the back counter, he moved to the fridge and grabbed several more. "I'll never forget you walking in carrying her," he glanced at Pascal, "it was a week before my heart rate settled down."

Pascal laughed. "At least you got to look after Remi," he jerked a thumb toward Emery, "we got left with Junior here."

"Hey, I didn't know," Emery added with a grin, accepting the bottle Darien handed him.

Kyran nodded his thanks to Pascal as he slid him another python. "I'm just gonna forget I heard *any* of that." He waved a hand around and then pointed at Darien. "Now you." He took a sip of his drink. "Remi's your mate?"

Darien leaned back and crossed his arms, knowing he was about to be harassed by all of them in a few moments' time.

"So why the fuck," Kyran paused in a dramatic way, "haven't you told her?"

Several sounds of agreement sounded. Taking a deep breath, he looked down at the floor. "It's complicated."

Finn leaned forward so Darien couldn't help but see him. "It *was* complicated. Now he's just procrastinating."

Darien stood there and kept his eyes on the floor, someday, they would all get tired of nagging him.

"Complicated, pffft," Kyran muttered. "Have you *seen* Remi?" Darien looked up at him. His eyes were wide and glazed over. "Seriously, aside from the fact that she's *smoking* hot, she has a brain *and* a personality." He finished his drink and pushed the glass toward Pascal with a nod for another. "Don't even tell me what the hell she was doing with a dickwad like Peterson. That's just *wrong*." He slumped against the bar and squinted at Darien. "What the fuck are you waiting for?"

Darien felt his wolf stir. He knew Remi was the type of woman every man looked at, but hearing it wasn't always a welcome thing. Or particularly safe for anyone.

"New topic," Berk said loudly. "Anything. Now." He stood up and tapped his hands on the bar top. "Why are we here?"

Finn moved around to behind the bar, putting three vampires between Darien and the detective, that shouldn't be talking about his mate.

"To make a list," Baker added quickly. "Which we really need to do before we drink much more."

"I'll drink to that." Boden chimed in, toasted Darien with his bottle before raising it to his mouth.

Taking a deep breath, Darien exhaled slowly. "Yeah, let's get this list going." Turning, he picked up his beer, trying to ignore the multiple sighs of relief behind him.

11

Cursing at the phone under her breath, she scowled and tried again. *Stupid game. I don't know why I keep playing it.*

"Maybe I'm wrong, but it looks like you're out here *alone*."

Lifting her eyes from the screen, Remi looked over to see Darien leaning at the door with a cup of coffee in his hand. "I'm five feet from the building, it's daytime, and the door is open." She looked him up and down slowly. Darien always looked rumpled when he first got up, but today he just looked ragged. "Long night?"

He sighed and blew on his black coffee. "We decided to have a man meeting last night," he shrugged, "try to get a handle on what's happening."

"Do those meetings always involve large quantities of alcohol?"

He winced against the light as he stepped outside. "Not always."

"Kyran looked like he was on his last legs when he crawled in an hour ago."

Darien chuckled. "He's slumped over in the supply room with his head on a box right now."

Tucking her phone into her pocket, she shook her head.

"If he didn't try to keep up with you supernatural boys, he wouldn't be wishing for death right now." He gave her a sheepish grin. "I was a little surprised you all included him in your *meeting*."

Darien cautiously sipped his coffee. "I almost like him."

Crossing her arms over her chest, she tried to read his face. "Almost?'

"Yeah, he's all right for a normal. I just don't like how he stalks you with his eyes."

She gave him a wide-eyed look. "No, he doesn't."

Shaking his head, he stared at her. "You never notice," he said quietly, more to himself. "One of these days, I'm going to record it so you can see how every male takes notice when you pass them."

Feeling uncomfortable, she kicked at the dirt with her boot. "It's because I'm not *petite*." She shrugged. "Why they look at me." As far as she was concerned, she was tall and skinny with no appealing curves like all those other types of females.

Darien chuckled. "Remi, you're petite." His eyes moved down over her. "Just not short." He opened his mouth like he was going to say more and then stopped and took another drink.

Shrugging again and wanting to change the subject, she looked around them. "So, other than several hundred dollars of alcohol poisoning, did you guys come up with anything?'

He rubbed a hand over his brow. "No. We went back as far as you first coming here, and there's no one that has cause to target Serenity."

"I thought the same."

"How's the audit going?" He smirked. "The accountant isn't at all what I pictured."

Remi nodded. "I know. I expected clean-cut and geeky."

"Well, he's none of that." Shaking his head, he took a small sip.

She thought about the accountant sitting in her break room. He was middle-aged, very much overweight, and sweaty.   Remi had only been able to sit in there for a few minutes as he made little grunting noises as he worked. It was worse when he spoke. He gasped randomly during sentences, pausing each one at least three times. When he first started, everything seemed fairly routine, she knew about audits, but then he started asking questions that didn't have much to do with checking the numbers.   "There's something not right about this audit, Dare."

His brows rose in question.

"He's asking some things that don't have a lot to do with the books."

With a subtle move, his whole posture changed to alert. "Like what?"

"He's verifying everything, even if they don't have anything to do with balance sheets. He's questioning the high electricity bills, asking about employee addresses and files, which have nothing to do with inventory and costs."

Darien's jaw clenched a few times. "Give Vienna a call and get her take. She knows more about this sort of thing than either one of us." He stepped closer. "Be careful. Don't answer anything you're not comfortable with." His voice was lower so no one could overhear them. "He's definitely sniffing around for something."

A large green box truck pulled up, ending the conversation. It was Jose with their produce delivery.

"Just in the nick of time, Berk ranted about lettuce for fifteen minutes this morning."

Darien grinned and took another drink. "Berk was hungover this morning." She turned and looked at him. "He joined our meeting last night."

Shaking her head, she grinned at Jose as he climbed out of the cab. "My staff is out of control."

Darien laughed and set his cup on the bumper of the truck as Jose opened the door. Remi took the offered clipboard and began to check off the cases as Jose handed them down to Darien.

"Sorry I'm a little late today," Jose added as he handed

over the last case. "We have a new packer, and he's slow."

Signing the invoice, she tore off her copy and handed him the clipboard when he climbed out. "It's no problem, Jose. Everyone has to learn."

With a smile, he nodded. "I'll see you at the end of the week."

"Thanks." She watched him pull away and glanced at Darien. "I didn't even realize he was late."

Handing her his cup, he leaned down and opened one of the cases. "Better get Berk his lettuce." He stopped and cursed under his breath. "Go revive the dying detective and tell him to get his ass out here. Now."

Frowning, she went over to him and looked down into the box. There was red all over the lettuce, and a single page sat on top. The words *next time* were written in red. "Is that blood?"

Darien leaned down and inhaled. He nodded and then gave her an ice-cold look. "Get inside and get Nelsen out here."

Nodding, she turned and stumbled into the backroom, rounding the corner to the supply room on numb legs. Shoving the door open, she flicked on the light. A low moan came from the corner. Kyran was slumped forward, resting his head on his arms on top of a stack of boxes. "Kyran." He raised his head slowly and looked at her with bloodshot eyes. She wanted to tell him to never mind, but the alternative would be to call Randell. *Damn.* "We need you out back. A note was left inside a case of our lettuce." She dragged in a deep breath. "It's written in blood."

Kyran stood up and then teetered for a moment. Using the boxes to steady himself, he took a deep breath and winced. "Did you touch it?" He closed his eyes, and she watched his Adam's apple bob as he swallowed.

"No. Darien opened the box and then sent me to get you."

"Good." Opening his eyes, he ran his fingers through his hair, brushing it back from his face. "Stay inside." He took slow steps in her direction as if he was trying to build up the momentum to keep going.

"Nadine makes a pretty effective hangover cure if you want to try it."

He stopped and looked down at her, and placed a shaky hand on her arm. "I would try anything at this point. Thank you." Exhaling slowly, he took a few more steps. "I don't know what the hell was in those python shooters, but I'm never touching them again." He kept walking, "or tequila."

Remi cringed. She knew a python was a concoction Attis and Pascal had come up with. The fact that Kyran was even out of his bed today would win him the respect of all the men on staff. Taking a deep breath, she went to find Nadine. They needed him to think coherently right now.

Carrying the herbal brew, she stepped out the back door. Darien was opening the other cases and checking them before carrying them inside. Kyran was pacing and talking on the phone.

"No, Peterson, I don't need to send it to the lab to know it's blood." He groaned. "I'm pretty sure Darien could smell blood at twenty paces." He glanced at the paper in his hand, and she recognized it as the invoice from Jose. "Yes, I'll have the lab guys come and pick it up." He nodded. "Let me know." Hanging up, he jammed it into his pocket and looked at her. "Is that my fix?"

Holding out the cup, she nodded. "It doesn't work on paras, so it should help you feel better."

Coming over, he took the cup and sniffed it. "I was afraid it was going to smell like this."

"It will help." She hugged her arms around her waist. "What did Dell say?" She looked at the case of lettuce sitting open.

"He's going to head over to the produce company and find out who packed the order."

"Jose said it was a new packer."

He took a sip and then made a face. "Unfortunately, I'm pretty sure that means whoever did it will be long gone."

Remi nodded.

"Didn't I tell you to stay inside?" Darien stepped between them and looked down at her, his brows furrowed.

Surprised, she touched his arm. "I'm standing here with Kyran. I think I'm safe."

Darien looked down at her hand, his expression softening. Turning slowly, he gave Kyran and blank look.

Kyran grimaced. "Yeah, I don't think I'd be much use to you right now, Remi."

Darien grinned. "You're standing. That says more than you know." He turned to grab the last box of food. "First time the boys fed me pythons, I didn't move for two days."

"Oh, well," Kyran took another small sip and shook his head as he swallowed, "then I feel much better knowing that." He smirked at her. "Go inside; leave me to my quiet death."

Remi turned. She'd have to send someone to buy more lettuce.

Remi was so distracted waiting to hear from Randell or the lab about the bloody note she forgot about the accountant until he came into her office.

"Miss Foster?"

She dropped the receipts on her desk and turned her chair. She couldn't for the life of her remember the man's name, so she just offered her most cordial smile. "Yes."

"I just wanted to let you," he made a quiet gasping noise, "know." Another gasp. "Everything I have checked seems to be," one more gasp, "in order. Your evening supervisor, Vienna, was most," and gasp, "helpful clearing up some questions." He made a wheezing sound and grinned. At least she was pretty sure it was a grin; either that or he had gas. He was sweating a lot more. "I have started my report and will be," quick gasp, "back tomorrow to finish up."

"Oh." Oh, she had to see what Vienna had done to him. "That's wonderful," she paused, hoping the name would come to her. It didn't. "I'm glad Vie was able to assist you."

He nodded and seemed like he was prancing on the spot.

"I'll be going now."

Standing up, she looked down at him and nodded. "Let me walk you out."

As they passed through the café, Remi turned to watch Vienna as she stood at the end of the counter sipping a drink through a straw. To her questioning glance, she shrugged, not telling Remi one way or the other if she had done something. Closing the door behind him, she turned, zeroing in on Vie as she walked quickly in her direction. "Did you do something to Mister…" she waved a hand, "whatever his name is?"

Vie gave her an exaggerated innocent smile. "I spoke to him."

"And?"

Vienna shrugged and walked into the kitchen. Remi followed her. "I didn't *do* anything to him, but I wanted to."

Remi stopped and studied her. Vienna cracked a smile and looked at the corner of the kitchen. Turning, she saw Attis sitting on the edge of the counter. She narrowed her eyes at him, and then he began to chuckle and raised his hand.

"I *may* have suggested a few things to him." He lifted his hands in a helpless gesture. "He was a dick to Vie. I technically saved his life."

Vienna snorted a laugh. "Oh, you saved his life," she growled.

Taking a deep breath, Remi looked from one to the other. "I don't approve," she looked at Attis, "but I thank you." She turned on Vienna. "And thank you for going to Attis instead of giving in to the urge." She shook her head. "Just don't tell Darien."

"Don't tell Darien what?"

Closing her eyes, she opened them and looked at Attis, who now had a big grin on his face. Turning around, she looked at Darien leaning against the door. He raised his eyebrows at her. "Vienna had a few problems with the accountant."

Darien immediately looked concerned.

Vie raised both her hands. "I didn't do anything."

Attis sighed and stood up. "I did." He went over to the fridge and pulled out a bottle of blood. "And you're welcome for dragging my cold ass out of bed *way* too early to come help." Opening it, it put it in the microwave.

"What did you do?" Darien asked, looking a little more at ease but still tense.

Attis shrugged and pulled the bottle out of the microwave. "I made the suggestion that he loved how Remi's books looked and that he was completely happy with things here."

"Won't he know you did that?" Remi asked, still not sure of the way Attis's skills worked.

Lowering the bottle away from his mouth, he smirked at her, "Do I look like a fledgling?" He took a small sip. "He doesn't even know he had the pleasure of meeting me." He raised an eyebrow and gave Remi a fanged grin.

She looked over at Darien. His expression mirrored her thoughts: she wasn't sure if this was a good thing. She gave him a hopeful look. "He said he was finishing up his report tomorrow and that everything was in order."

Darien looked from Attis to Vienna and then finally back to her. "As long as it doesn't come back to bite us on the ass," he sent Attis a hard look, "and you don't get into the habit of doing that again, I guess we're good."

Attis raised his hand. "I have been the paragon of virtuous intentions for more than a year now."

Shaking his head, Darien glanced back at Remi. "I think we're good." Patting Vienna on the shoulder, he smiled at her. "You did right, using Attis instead of handling things on your own."

She beamed a huge fake grin and flipped her hair over her shoulder. "Well, I can't be employee of the month if I fry someone's brain, now *can* I?"

"We have an employee of the month?" Attis asked.

Vienna shrugged and started laughing as she walked into the back room. Attis looked from Darien to Remi and then started to go after her; he stopped two feet later and glanced at Darien over his shoulder. "I got your text. I checked out that thing in the place, and I'll see what I can do." With that, he bolted after Vienna.

Rubbing his hands over his face, Darien dropped them and looked down at her. "Sometimes it's like we have a house full of kids instead of a business."

Remi grinned. "Yep. What thing in the place where, and what's he going to do?"

Darien rubbed his face again; he rested his hip on the wall. "Kyran let me take one of the leaves with the blood to see if one of our in-house trackers could pick up anything."

She nodded. "Let's hope so." Rubbing her hands up and down her arms, she tried to stave off the chill that went over her skin. "I just want things to go back to normal."

Darien leaned over and wrapped his arm around her waist, pulling her into the warmth of his body. "We'll figure it out, sweetheart."

She leaned into his chest. Just being close to him made her feel safe. His warmth, his touch, his scent, all of it was home and comfort to her. At least as long as he only held her. She'd been trying not to think about it all day, the way she'd acted when he'd taken her up to bed last night. What possessed her to break her own rule, she didn't know, but she had to try to keep it to business and friends between them. Serenity was too important for her to screw up the relationship with Darien. Darien was too important in her world, period, to take a chance.

"Are you all right?" He whispered into her hair, his warm hand moving up and down her back.

Leaning back, she looked up and him. "Yeah. It's just been a hell of a week so far."

He chuckled. "Well, if it makes you feel better, there's only four more days, and then we start again."

"Oh, goodie," she rolled her eyes. He stood there looking at her with those chocolate eyes; the intimacy in them made her knees weaken. She knew this was exactly what she had to avoid but couldn't have looked away from him if her life depended on it. His hand moved to the back of her head and lightly grasped her hair.

"Either kiss her or get out of the way. You're blocking the fridge."

They both jolted like teenagers caught doing something they shouldn't be. Remi stepped back and looked at Emery standing in the doorway. She hated that he could sneak up on her without warning, all the vampires could, and it irked her. Huffing out a breath, she studied him for a moment. He looked completely ragged. "Everything good?"

He moved past her and pulled out a bottle of blood, and opened it. "Just great, *Mom*. I woke up early, lucky me, and then I find out someone left you a lovely note in the lettuce." Shoving the bottle into the microwave, he slammed the door and stood there watching it count down.

Remi glanced at Darien over her shoulder; his brows were drawn. That made her feel better, Emery had his moods, but they usually leaned toward dry sarcasm. "Kyran sent it to the lab, and Randell is following up with the company."

Emery took a long gulp and looked at her, his lips coated with blood. "Well, that makes me feel *bunches* better. The *humans* will keep you safe." He tipped the bottle at her and then took another drink.

Glaring at the back of his head, she scowled. "Hey, I think you're forgetting I'm also human."

Lowering the bottle, he stood with his back to her, staring at the wall for several seconds. Slumping his shoulders, he turned slowly and looked down at her, his blue eyes filled with regret. "Sorry." Leaning down, he kissed her cheek softly. "I do forget sometimes." Straightening, he cupped her cheek. "You're like superwoman, not some weak human." Shifting past her, he started to back out of the room. "Just ignore me. I'm having a difficult time lately."

Blinking, she stared at the door he'd gone out. "Has he been like this a lot?" She glanced at Darien, who stood there rubbing the back of his neck.

"Not that I've noticed." Squeezing her shoulder, he turned toward the door. "I'll keep an eye on him." Shoving the swinging door, he went out front.

Turning, Remi looked around the kitchen. Sighing, she followed him in search of Nadine. With everything going on, she'd forgotten to ask what the word was on the no-harm spell. Right now, it looked like Serenity could use it.

<h1 style="text-align:center">12</h1>

Rounding the corner, Remi nodded as Baker and Boden walked by her toward the kitchen. Turning, she watched them go through the door, something wasn't right, but she couldn't say what. Shaking it off, she started to Nadine in the corner. A few steps later, she watched Darien take something out of her hand and stuff it in his pocket. Nadine was shaking her head, worry clear on her face. Darien rubbed the back of his neck and then looked at Nadine again. She didn't need to hear what he said. She could see clearly that he was upset. Nadine patted him on the shoulder and returned to what she had been doing.

Feeling like she shouldn't be staring, Remi spun around and went into the kitchen. The Lewis boys were standing at the counter, pulling dishes out of the dishwasher. She watched them for a moment before clearing her throat. They both stiffened and turned slowly. She looked at their name tags, slowly raising her gaze up to their reddened faces. "Why are you two wearing Baker and Boden's name tags? Where are your brothers?"

Bates cleared his throat and took off Baker's name tag. "They're going to be late, and with everything going on, we didn't want to stress you out more."

Raising an eyebrow, she looked at Berk. "So, you thought you'd pretend to be your brothers?"

Berk raised his hands. "Only you would notice."

"Our own mother can't tell us apart," Bates added with a sigh.

Shaking her head, Remi took the name tags and tossed them on the counter. "Why are your brothers going to be late?" She really hoped it was trivial.

Berk looked around the room, and Bates cleared his throat.

"Guys?" Remi looked from one to the other.

"Uh," Bates finally looked at her, "they're still at the station."

"Station? As in police station?" Berk nodded. "Why?"

Bates opened his mouth and then looked at his brother. Berk nodded. "For questioning. We have to meet Randell there when we leave here."

"Unbelievable!" She pointed at them. "You are not going there." Growling, she spun on her heel, digging her phone out of her pocket. Shoving the door open, she sidestepped a surprised Nadine and stomped toward the door. "I'm going to feed him his badge." She snarled, shaking her head. *The nerve! To go, behind my back and question my staff, my family. He had absolutely no reason.*

"Whoa," Finn slid in front of her. "Where are you going?" He shifted to stay in front of her, even as she went to step around him.

Remi glared at him. "I'm going to beat Dell over the head with a," she tried to go around him again, "desk." When he stopped her again, hands out like he would grab and hold her, but didn't. She put her hands on her hips and huffed out a breath. "Get out of my way, Finn."

"Ah," he stuttered and looked over her shoulder for a second, "I can't let you leave."

"What?" Pointing up at him, she growled. "*Move.*"

Emery appeared beside Finn. "What's going on?"

Finn looked relieved.

Looking from one to the other, she went to step around them both, but they out-maneuvered her each time.

"Remi," Emery was in front of her again, "come on. You shouldn't go out alone."

"Emery, get out of my way."

"I," he stuttered, looking to Finn for help. Finn just shook his head, "uh…"

A strong arm wrapped around her waist, and she was lifted off the floor. She didn't need to look to know who held her. "Darien, let go." She tried to pry his arm loose.

"You're not going to beat Dell with a desk," he said next to her ear, "as much as I'd like to see that."

Growling, she struggled in his hold. "He's questioning *my* staff…" she stopped struggling, "my family behind *my* back." Her feet were on the floor again, but his arm held her in place.

"He's what?" Darien loosened his hold enough to turn her and look at her expression.

"Berk and Bates were pretending to be Boden and Baker because Dell has them at the station questioning them." She grit her teeth. "Where's Kyran?"

"He's walking down the street, should be here in about twenty seconds," Finn told her with a smirk. Darien turned and glared at him. Finn shrugged. "It's a kick seeing Remi all revved up. I'd like to let her loose."

Pointing a finger, Darien scowled. "Go find something to do, or I'll let loose on you."

"Spoilsport," Finn mumbled as he quickly strode from the room.

Relaxing slowly until his hand was just resting on her waist, Darien looked down at her. "We'll find out what's going on. Just calm down."

Tapping her foot, she held out her phone. "Fine. You call him."

Taking the phone slowly, watching her for signs she would go crazy at any second, he nodded. Taking a deep breath, he looked at the screen, slid the saver off, and pressed call.

Remi heard the door open and spun to face Kyran walking in, pissing her off all over again. Before Darien could stop her, she was in his face. "What the hell is going on, Kyran?" She barked. Raising her hand, she intended to smack him on the chest for effect when she was lifted off her feet and found herself halfway across the room.

Seething, she glared at Pascal as he held her in his arms, a few inches off the floor. "What have I missed?" Lifting his head, he glanced over to Attis was looking amused, Finn right beside him. "Seriously, Finn, if there's to be a beating and blood spilled, I'd expect you to inform me first." He gave Remi a fanged grin. "What's this about you feeding people their badges and beating them with a desk?" He wiggled his eyebrows at her. "A woman after my own heart."

A low rumbling growl echoed across the room. Looking over, she saw Darien still standing where she'd been, and he wasn't at all happy.

"See now," Pascal set her on the floor, "you've made me step on toes by distracting me with violence."

Huffing out a breath, she stepped away from him and gave Darien a puzzled glare. "I just want to know what's going on."

"Me too," Kyran said, gobsmacked.

"I just saved your life, detective," Pascal told him.

Kyran raised both hands and looked back at Remi. "I just found out, and I expressed my opinion loudly, and the boys are right behind me."

Taking a deep breath, Remi tried to settle down. "No more of my staff will be questioned, Kyran."

Lowering his hands slowly, he nodded. "Agreed."

Remi closed her eyes and took a few deep breaths before opening them and looking around. Finn and Attis were far too amused. She rolled her eyes at them and turned to see Emery shaking his head.

"I will never cross you again." He grinned. "And *that,* ladies and gents is *my* Mom." He pumped his arm in the air a few times. "Mess with her and pay. Yes!"

Hissing out a breath, she threw her hands up and walked out of the room, all eyes following her. When she reached the kitchen, she brushed past Nadine and went straight to the break room, Nadine close on her heels.

"Are you okay, Rem?"

Remi leaned on the table and took a few deep breaths. "I feel like everything is going to hell lately."

Nadine sat down and a heartfelt sympathetic look on her face. "I know." She shook her head. "I'm afraid to leave the house now." She clasped her hands together. "I don't know how you're holding it together."

Remi snorted. "Clearly, I'm not." She grinned and looked at her. "I can't believe I just did that."

Nadine grinned. "Neither can I, but at least we know it takes all the guys to stop you."

Remi laughed. "I guess that's something, huh?" Taking a deep breath, she straightened, remembering what she'd seen before she apparently lost her mind. "What did you give Darien?"

Nadine took a deep breath and held it; shaking her head, she exhaled slowly. "That's not for me to tell. You'll have to ask him."

Knowing that when Naddy gave her word, she was true to it, like most witches, Remi nodded. "Okay, I will."

Nadine stood up. "I better go get the kids." She let out a loud breath. "My husband is picking me up."

"Good. No one is to be by themselves for now." Tucking her hands into the back pockets of her jeans, Remi offered her a smile. "I'm glad you have someone. The nights seem to be closing in on me in the last month with inspections and audits…"

"And everything else," Nadine finished for her.

"Yeah."

Nadine turned to leave and then looked back at her. "Honestly, Rem, you need to let loose and get yourself laid soon." She shrugged. "It works wonders during times of high stress." She smirked. "It's been what, six, seven months for you? That's a lot of stress built up."

Groaning, Remi rubbed her hands over her face. "Don't remind me." She waved a hand at the door and then froze to see Darien standing in it. She felt her cheeks heat. How long had he been standing there? How much had he heard?

"I'll see you tomorrow," Nadine said quickly and left before Remi could reply. She bailed on her, plain and simple.

Darien was looking at her cautiously. "You okay now?"

Shaking her head, she looked hopeless. "That's questionable."

"Do I need to lock you in my cage?" He smirked.

Huffing out a breath, she shook her head. "No. Not yet, at least." Pulling out a chair, she dropped down into it. "I just," she waved her hand in exasperation, "feel like everything is happening at once, Dare." Dropping her hands onto the table, she studied them for no reason. "The inspector driving me nuts, now he's dead, the audit being randomly called, being attacked," she glanced up at him, "and it's like I'm losing touch with everyone that works here."

He perched on the edge of the table, not interrupting her, just listening.

"Emery is acting weird now, and I just went…"

"On a rampage," he finished for her quietly. "You're allowed to blow off a little steam, you know." He leaned over closer to keep her attention. "You're twenty-five years old, Remi, and running a place that's open twenty-one hours every day." Holding her eyes captive with his for a few tense moments, he shook his head. "I do what I can. We all do. When Doyle left this place to you, he didn't mean for you to do it all on your own."

"You guys are great," she sighed. "I can't even imagine doing it all on my own. It's just…" she closed her eyes to gather her thoughts before looking back at him. "I don't want to screw it up, you know. I had nothing, *was* nothing until I walked through that door, and Doyle gave me a chance."

Squatting down beside the table, he grabbed the leg of the chair and pulled it until their faces were only a few inches apart. "You were never nothing, Remi, *ever*."

His dark brown eyes bore into hers. At times like this, when she could see his emotions as he looked at her, she wanted to cry, knowing that there was someone that did care about her.

"You were meant to be here. Doyle knew that the moment you stepped inside and no one," he lowered his voice until it was almost a whisper. "No one will ever say differently." Brushing the hair back from her face, he gave her a weak smile. "None of us would be here if it weren't for you, do you know that? You have the loyalty and love of each and every being that works here." Leaning back, he smiled. "You were right; we are your family. This is our home, even for those that don't live in the building."

Taking a shaky breath, she nodded. The lump in her throat stopped her from saying anything.

"Now," he stood up and held out his hand, "let's go get some dinner tossed together and have a little piece of serenity before the night begins." He pulled her to her feet. "You spend too much time working in the place and not enough time enjoying it."

On their way out, Darien warned Kyran to keep Randell away from her tonight. He told all the staff that she wasn't the boss for the next few hours; she was just Remi, and if they had any problems, they would wait until tomorrow.

13

Taking a night just to be Remi Foster and not the person that ran Serenity was such a nice feeling that she decided she was doing it more often. The bar was packed tonight. The full moon, just two days away, could be to blame, but she wasn't complaining, or the boss she'd be tomorrow wouldn't when she did the deposits.

Pascal slid down to where she was standing and leaned down. "I know you're not working, but can you go grab me a few bottles of Jack Daniels? Seems to be in high demand tonight." Remi set her drink down and nodded. "Sure thing." Weaving her way between Pascal's groupies at the end of the bar, she pushed through into the kitchen and nodded to Baker as he stood at the counter, bopping to the beat of the music. Jack Daniels was always a sure sign that the full moon was only a few days away. A weird fact, but still true.

Going into the storage room, she flicked on the light and froze at the sight of Emery and a girl. He had her pinned against the wall, and her first thought was, *oh no* and then she saw the girl wrapped around him as much as he was her.

"Oh." Was the only thing that came out of her mouth as Emery spun around and glared. His eyes flashed red momentarily. Remi could tell by the way his jaw was set that he had a mouth of fang going on.

The girl, half hidden behind him, peeked out. That was all Remi needed to sense she was a normal. *Now what?*

"Corey," Emery put his arm around her and pulled into full view, "this is Remi." His eyes pleaded with her. "My sister."

Trying not to look surprised, Remi smiled. "And boss." She raised an eyebrow at him, daring him to deny it.

"Yeah." He looked down at the small blonde at his side. Remi's heart jerked in her chest when she saw the look in his eyes.

Crap. He really had it bad for her, *and* she was a normal.

"You have two sisters?" She turned her pretty green eyes back to Remi. "You guys don't look alike."

Emery's eyes sought Remi's. "Remi looks like..." he smirked, "Mom." Clearing his throat, he held her stare. "I was just on break."

Remi nodded, not sure what to say, knowing she *really* couldn't say what she was thinking.

"I'll let you get back to work, Em." The girl stretched up to place a lingering kiss on his mouth as her hand rubbed a circle on his chest. Stepping away, she smiled at Remi. "Nice meeting you."

Remi smiled at her and watched until she was out of sight. Pointing at him, she shook her head. "Stay. I have to take some J.D. out front."

He crossed his arms and stared down at the floor with a slight nod.

Remi grabbed two bottles from the shelf and spun on her heel. She made it out front without seeing anything. What was she going to do? The safe sex talk was kind of irrelevant for a vampire. Added to that, she was pretty sure Emery was long past a virgin. The normal meets para sex talk was entirely different; forget allowances for blood lust. She was way out of her depth with this one.

Stepping into the flashing lights and loud music, she set the bottles on the back counter and turned to see if she could find Darien. He was halfway across the sea of bodies but still paused and looked her way. A wide-eyed look that she hoped said *mayday* was what she gave him. Brows furrowed, he started to head her way.

When he reached her, she pulled him into the kitchen.

"What's wrong?" His eyes immediately began scanning her body.

Shaking her head, she leaned closer to him. "I just caught Em in the supply room with a girl." He didn't even react. She filed that away for later; obviously, things happened at Serenity After Dark that she wasn't privy to. "She's a normal."

His eyes widened. "Is she all right?" He looked at the door.

"Yeah." Remi brushed the hair back out of her face. "Pretty sure she wasn't a snack."

"Oh." He glanced over his shoulder to where Baker was standing, and a knowing look passed between them. Baker cleared his throat and then began whistling.

"So, we should talk to him…" She said, meaning it, but it sounded more like a question.

"Ah," he looked uncomfortable for a second and then nodded. "Yeah." Placing a hand on her back, he guided her toward the door.

Emery was standing right where she had left him. The look on his face was one that Remi didn't need to question. His head was full of Corey. He straightened and looked embarrassed when he saw Darien come in behind her.

"I wasn't going to hurt her." He held his palms out.

Remi went over to him. "I know." She tucked her hands in her pockets and glanced at the floor. "Em, she's a normal."

He snorted. "Yeah, I noticed, heartbeat and all."

Darien stayed over by the door, almost like if he wanted to make a fast escape; he could. "Does she know what you are?"

Emery rubbed the back of his neck and looked hesitantly at Darien. "I think so." He shrugged. "I mean, she's said things that make me think she does."

Remi looked at Darien, who just seemed to be perplexed. Filing that information for later, she turned back to the tense vampire. "Em, sex with normals is…"

He held up a hand to stop her. "I don't need the sex talk, Remi. Trust me, I'm long past *that*."

Shaking her head, she rolled her eyes. "I realize that I'm just…"

"I don't know what to do." He suddenly sounded like a teen, angst filling his voice.

"About?" Darien finally spoke.

Emery looked at him and then at her. He looked embarrassed all over again. "I," he rubbed a hand over his face and took a deep breath, which was weird because he didn't really breathe. "When I'm with Corey, I, it's…" he closed his eyes and stood there for a moment.

Remi glanced at Darien. He shrugged, looking as confused as she felt.

Emery's eyes popped open. "I can't seem to differentiate between sex lust and blood lust." He said it quickly like he needed to get it over with before he changed his mind.

"Have…" Remi's heartbeat picked up.

"No." He stopped her. "I haven't bitten her."

Nodding, Remi closed her mouth and looked at Darien. He glanced from Emery and back to her before shaking his head. "Don't look at me. I don't suffer from blood lust." He tipped his head, "Well, except one day a month." Jamming his hands in his pockets, he shrugged. "I don't have the urge to bite while having sex," he looked over her at Emery and then avoided her eyes, "or I haven't yet."

Emery made an exasperated sound.

"Would you like to talk to Pascal or Attis about it?" Remi kept her voice steady even though she wasn't feeling calm.

He looked relieved. "Yeah."

Darien backed out of the room. "I'll go grab one of them."

When he was gone, Remi turned and looked at Emery for a few seconds. "She's cute."

He grinned, relief in his expression. "Yeah, and she's really smart too. I love talking to her."

Oh dear, was all her brain registered.

"Hey," he gave her a sheepish look, "thanks for not freaking out, even though I know you want to." He looked at her chest. "I can hear your heart having a conniption fit right now."

Remi laughed. "Well, as your *sister,* I'm trying to be cool."

He cleared his throat. "I couldn't say you were my mom, even though you are to me." He motioned with his hand. "I look older than you most days."

She grinned. As compliments went, she'd take it.

Attis glided into the room. "I hear my assistance is needed." He winked at Remi, "Darien gave me the low down."

If she couldn't feel blasé about this, relieved was as close as she was going to get. Crossing her arms, she leaned back against a stack of crates and looked at Emery. He was staring at her. Glancing at Attis, she saw he was also just standing and looking at her, a small smirk on his face. "Oh," she straightened up, "I'll go help Pascal until you're done."

Attis inclined his head and gave her a little smile. "I'll help your boy, no worries."

Help her boy have sex with a normal human without draining her blood; yeah, this day needed to end now.

Going back, she bypassed her drink of juice on the back counter and went to Darien. It wasn't often he was behind the bar when they were open; as she got closer, she was shocked to see a glass in his hand. He drank, then turned to pour more whiskey. When she reached him, he handed over the glass. Accepting it with a small nod, she gulped it down. It burned a path all the way to her stomach, but the warmth that followed helped to calm her. "Thanks." She gasped out, her eyes watering, and she handed the glass back. He took it with a smirk and set it in the wash bin.

Pascal handed the customer their drink before turning around to give her a big grin. "So, our little boy is growing up."

Huffing out a breath, she winced. "I guess it was bound to happen."

He laughed for a moment and checked the bar to see if he was needed. Looking out across the crowd, he motioned with his head. "Which one is it that has our boy's head a mess?"

Scanning the bar, Remi looked for Corey and found her in the corner talking to some other girls that were paras. Leaning closer to Pascal, she pointed. "Little blonde in the corner, her name is Corey."

He shrugged. "The boy has good taste." Glancing from Darien back to her, he placed his hands in his pockets. "Would you like me to take a quick look inside her head and see what she knows?"

Remi bit her lip and looked at Darien. They didn't encourage Pascal to mind-surf, frowned on it normally. Darien tilted his head, his expression saying what she was thinking. "Yes," she said to the tall vampire, that appeared frozen on the spot, not moving as he waited.

With a slight tilt of his head, he turned and made a drink. "Watch the bar. I'll be back."

Remi glanced up and down the bar to see that no one was waiting to be served. "Do we tell Emery he's doing that?"

Darien rubbed his jaw and looked down at her. "It might be better if Pascal tells him and keeps us out of it."

She nodded. "Depending on what he finds out."

"That too," Darien added quickly and moved down to the two girls waving for service at the other end.

Remi kept busy by giving the bar a vigorous wipe. Every few seconds, she looked over to Pascal, leaning against the backrest of the booth the girls were in. She didn't know what he was talking about, pretty sure she wanted it that way, but the girls were smiling and laughing.

Feeling like someone was watching her, she turned to see Attis and Emery standing at the kitchen door. They were both watching Pascal. Emery pointed and smiled at Attis, who nodded and patted him on the back.

Attis strode toward her and gave her a reassuring smile, reaching over to grasp her hand and give it a slight squeeze. "All is well, mama bear. Your cub has it all sorted out now."

Remi sighed. "Thanks, Attis." She squeezed his hand before releasing it.

He shrugged. "It's good to take all these years of living to help someone." With a grimace, he pulled the cloth from her hand. "I would have killed to have my kind of help," he laughed, "or killed less."

Eyes wide, she watched him go down to talk to Darien. Those were just the sort of tidbits she didn't need to know.

"Can I talk to you?" Emery was suddenly standing behind her. She glanced over to see Pascal weaving his way through the crowd.

"Sure." Motioning to the end of the bar, she followed him down to the kitchen door. Stopping, she tucked her hands in her pockets and looked at him, then held her breath.

"Thanks," Emery said with a bashful grin. "I've been a mess the last few days with all this."

Not even knowing what to say to that, she rubbed her hand against his cool arm.

Glancing over at Pascal as he came towards them, he gave her a questioning look. "Pascal looking to see if she knows what I am?"

Remi nodded, holding her breath again.

He nodded slowly. "Okay." Turning around, he raised an eyebrow at Pascal as he stopped in front of them. "Well?"

"Well," he smirked, "she thinks you're cute and sweet and hot," he said with enthusiasm. "She knows her friends are not all normals and has a really good idea what you are," Pascal gave him a serious look, "and she doesn't have a problem with it."

"Really?" Emery's expression turned from somber to relief.

He grinned and looked down at Remi. Dammit, she loved seeing him look that happy.

Smacking Pascal on the shoulder, he laughed. "Thanks." When he went to go around the old vampire, Pascal put his hand in front of his chest and stopped him.

"You have work to do, young one. Your break is over."

Shoulders slumping, Emery nodded. "Got it." Straightening, he turned and picked up his tray, and moved back out into the crowd.

Remi looked up at Pascal and made a motion for him to bend down closer to her. "That's the truth?" He nodded. Stretching up, she kissed his cold cheek. "Thank you."

With a shocked look on his face, he stood to his full height again. "Anytime." Clearing his throat, he turned and went down the bar to the girls that were gathering.

Darien came over and stood in front of her. "Now we just have to get through Caitlyn having sex, and then we'll have dealt with every crisis."

Remi laughed. "Dare, Cait has been having sex for over a year now."

His eyes grew huge. "No."

Remi nodded and laughed again. "Yes."

Groaning, he rubbed a hand over his face. "I'm getting old."

Snorting, Remi patted his arm. "And I'm getting tired. I think I'll call it a night."

He glanced over to where Kyran was at the door and then gave her an abrupt nod. "I'll walk you up."

14

Jolting, Remi sat up. Cait was standing over her. "What's wrong?"

Cait flipped the blankets off. "Come downstairs."

Untangling her legs, Remi stumbled from the bed. "Why? What's happened?" She rushed over to pull the jeans she had dropped on the floor up her legs. "What time is it?" Looking down at the T-shirt she wore to bed, she decided it was fine.

"It's two thirty. Darien just bellowed from downstairs, telling us to get down there." Cait struggled to get her arms into her sweatshirt.

Nodding, Remi slipped her feet into a pair of running shoes and quickly followed Caitlyn. Her heart was hammering as they ran down the stairs and through the back rooms. Hitting the door out from the kitchen, she gasped. Emery stood at the end of the bar with blood all over himself, including his face. "What happened?" She ran down the length of the bar and then almost tripped over her feet when she saw Darien leaning over Corey, where she sat on the floor, leaning against the front of the bar.

"She's okay, Remi." Attis steadied her by gripping her arm.

"It's not our blood," Emery added, prancing on the spot,

looking back to Corey.

"What happened?" Remi demanded, her voice shaking with emotion. Shaking off Attis' hand, she rushed over to Emery and pulled his face down toward hers. His pupils were huge, obviously from the adrenalin. Grabbing a napkin off the bar, she wiped the blood from his face.

"We were jumped." He said with venom in his voice. "I was walking Corey to her car, and they came out of nowhere."

Remi looked down at Corey, who was nodding to whatever Darien was saying. "Was she parked in our lot?"

Emery shook his head. "No, which is why I insisted on walking her."

Kyran and Pascal came through the door. Pascal locked it behind them and looked at Emery. "They're long gone."

"Shit." Emery paced away and clasped the side of his head. Dropping his hands, he shook his head. "I had to get her back here. I couldn't leave her there alone to go after them." He cursed again. "It's like they knew about the spell; we were only two feet past the boundary when they came at us."

Darien helped Corey stand up; she nodded and released his arm.

Remi watched Emery as he looked at her; his face was filled with pain. Corey stepped away from Darien and went to Emery, wrapping her arms around him. Remi had to look away when she saw him relax as he wrapped his arms around her, cradling her into his body.

Turning away from the couple whispering softly to each other, she looked at Kyran. "You have to figure out who is doing this." Glancing at Pascal, she gave him a desperate look. "You couldn't track them?"

Pascal shook his head. "No, couldn't even find a trace."

"Which is quite the puzzle considering Emery injured one of them, and the smell of blood should have led Pascal right to their doorstep," Attis added, his voice filled with disbelief.

"What are we going to do?" Remi glanced at Darien and then turned to Emery and Corey before he could say a word.

"Corey, I'd like you to stay here tonight. Is there someone you have to call to let them know?"

Corey turned her head, her arms still wrapped around Emery. "No. I have my own single unit across town."

Nodding, Remi glanced at Emery and then back to her. "You can stay upstairs." She ran a hand through her hair and then nodded to Emery. "Take her upstairs, Em." She watched them turn to go. "Are you sure you're both okay?"

Corey looked up at Emery, her eyes filled with wonder. "They didn't even get near me; Emery wouldn't let them."

Emery hugged her into his side. "Only thing hurt is my pride."

Sighing, Remi gave him a relieved smile. "Good." She wanted to hug him but was pretty sure that would embarrass him. "Why don't you take Corey up, make her some herbal tea?"

Moving over, Corey, still glued to his side, he kissed her cheek. "Thanks, Remi." His look said a lot more to her than words. He was more thankful that she was accepting Corey than he was anything else.

"Go." She offered Corey a reassuring smile as they went past her. Turning, she looked over at Cait. "Go up with them. Try to get some sleep."

Cait nodded, her eyes wide as she hurried to catch up to her brother.

Sighing, Remi glanced back at Darien. Attis and Kyran stood beside him, their expressions mirroring one another; they had to put a stop to these attacks. Pascal moved back around from behind the bar; he held a bottle of blood.

"Do I close up Serenity temporarily?" She asked, glancing from one to the other.

Kyran sat on a stool and crossed his arms over his chest. "I can't tell you not to, but they're going to be harder to catch if you do." He motioned around the empty room. "They're right here under our noses, and we're just missing it."

"You think it's someone on the inside?" Attis asked.

"No." Kyran shook his head. "Not necessarily, but it is

someone that walks in and out of that door," he pointed to the entrance, "every day or knows someone that does."

"You think someone is mind-surfing one of the staff?" Pascal took a sip and waited for an answer.

"It's the theory Randell and I are working right now," Kyran answered in a tired voice.

Darien nodded. "That would explain how they knew the boundary has been moved and about the inspector and the others."

"And how they knew when we get our deliveries." Remi mused out loud, more to herself than to anyone.

"Exactly." Kyran nodded and then looked from Attis to Pascal. "Is there any way either of you can do something with that?"

Pascal took another drink while looking at Attis. "I can check every mind that comes in: it's possible I'll get a whiff of who it is or a thought that might lead us in the right direction."

Attis moved over and leaned on the bar. "If he can give me a target, I could make a suggestion or two."

Kyran rubbed a hand over his face. "All of that breaks so many laws," he sighed, "but I just don't know how to put a stop to this without it." He lifted his head and looked around at them. "Peterson will flip if he finds out."

"People are dying and getting hurt, Kyran," Remi said in a quiet voice.

"I know." He waved his hand around, "That's why I'm asking for help."

Pascal raised his bottle to him. "Consider it done."

"Agreed," Attis added.

Remi looked over at Darien, who stood there without comment. "Darien?"

Blinking like he'd been elsewhere, he gave her a blank stare and then shook his head. "Yes. I agree." He blew out a breath and rolled his shoulders. "I'm just battling my own demons right now."

Remi winced. She'd forgotten how close to the full moon it

was and how it affected him.

"Demons?" Kyran inquired.

Remi dragged her eyes away from Darien to nod at Kyran. "Yeah, when it's close to the full moon, Darien has to work harder at being a nice guy."

Kyran's eyes widened. "And on the full moon?"

Darien grinned. "She locks me in a very strong cage."

Smirking, Kyran looked from her to Darien; he paled as the smile left his face. "For real?"

Pascal patted him on the back and nodded. "Welcome to Serenity. We have our very own live werewolf that turns into a vicious beast once a month."

Kyran looked Darien up and down while he stood perfectly still. Wiping his hands down his jeans, Kyran slapped his hands down on his thighs and then stood up. "On that note, I'm going down to the station to fill Randell in, decide if I'm writing everything in my report, and then I'm going to get some sleep."

"Are you sure you should go out there?" Remi asked hesitantly.

Kyran shook his head. "No, but it's my job, and as much as I like this place, I don't think sleeping on the bar would be very comfortable. I don't know how you guys do these long hours every day."

"I'll walk him out," Pascal set the bottle on the bar.

Kyran waved a hand to everyone as he walked to the door.

"I'll finish the cleanup, and then I'm going to bed," Attis said with an abrupt nod to her and Darien. He glided to the corner booth and started to collect glasses left at the end of the night.

Darien rubbed a hand over the back of his neck and then rolled his shoulders a few times. He had to be suffering from all the extra stress added to the moon's effects. "I didn't think you'd want me to wait until morning to tell you."

"You thought right." Tucking her hands into her back pockets, she gave him a tired look. "What did you say to Corey?"

Shaking his head, he leaned against the bar, "Just a bunch of nonsense to calm her down." His expression mirrored her thoughts; this was getting out of hand. "It was a lot for her to take in." He sighed, "At least she didn't freak out over Emery's faster-than-human movements as he fought them off."

Remi wanted to sigh in relief. "So, we can assume she pretty much knows about the para world."

He nodded. "I explained a bit of what's been happening." He smirked, "Now she's all worried about *poor* Emery being in danger."

"Poor Emery?" She rolled her eyes. "Yes, with his speed, fangs, and blood lust, he's bound to be a sacrificial lamb."

Attis came back over and stepped in between them. "May I just say you look *fabulous*, all rumpled fresh from the bed?" He looked her up and down and then grinned. "Absolutely fabulous." A growl came from behind him. Attis glanced at Darien. "I'm allowed to *look*. I'm not dead." He chortled. "Oh, wait, yes, I am." Winking at her, he turned to collect the glasses on the tables along the wall. "Anytime you want a snuggle buddy, call me, Remi."

Shaking her head, she didn't know what to do, so she turned back to Darien. He stood there. His arms crossed over his large chest, eyes hooded as he looked her up and down slowly. Feeling like she was exposed, she hugged her arms around her waist to hide the response of her body to his roaming eyes. "I guess I'll go upstairs and try to get some more sleep."

Darien's attention came back to her face. "I'll walk you up. I want to check on Emery." He stepped away from the bar. "He was freaked out when he got back here. Attis had to almost hold him down to stop him from going into a full bloodlust and going hunting."

Nodding, she headed toward the kitchen door. "You just want to make sure he's not using Corey as a *snuggle* buddy."

Darien made an exasperated sound from behind her. "Something like that. He shouldn't try to conquer any lusts when his emotions are this wild." He moved by her to hold open the door and looked down at her with a meaningful glare. "It never ends well."

Pausing, she looked up into his serious eyes, wanting an explanation but with everything else going on, she seriously didn't know if she could handle it right now. He held himself ridged, which for Darien wasn't normal. "Are you okay?"

Inhaling deeply, he let it out slowly. "I'm having a few issues, but I'm good." He motioned for her to go ahead of him.

Turning, she started up the stairs. "Issues? Because of the moon?" She glanced back at him.

He sighed loud enough that she paused.

"Let's just check on Emery and Corey, and then I'll explain."

Frowning, she nodded and continued up the stairs.

Remi sat on the couch and watched Darien fidget in the chair across from her. Darien didn't do fidgety. He was a straight-up kind of man, got right to the point. When he flopped back and looked at the ceiling, she sat forward and leaned on her knees. "Dare? *What* is it?"

Blowing out a loud breath, he tipped his head back down and looked at her. His eyes held her steady without so much as blinking. "I don't," he waved a hand around, "I'm not sure what to say."

Confused, she frowned. "I don't understand. Say about what?" Sitting back, she leaned on the arm of the couch and studied him for a few seconds. "What's bothering you?"

Rubbing his hands down over his knees, he gave her a pleading look, but she didn't know why. With a sigh, he stood up and went to the window, pushed the heavy drape aside, and stood looking out it for a few seconds before turning slowly and looking at her again.

"Darien?" This behavior wasn't the Darien she knew. In seven years, she'd never seen him act the way he was. Darien was a rock. He looked out for everyone that mattered in their world and was never hesitant or emotional. "You're starting to freak me out."

His shoulders lifted and fell, and then he came over and sat on the table in front of her. "I've been having a really hard time lately."

"With everything going on?"

He glanced at the floor and then back to her. "That's part of it. Emotions are all over the place around here right now." Shrugging, he wiped his hands down his legs again. "With good reason, but that's not what I'm talking about."

Leaning forward, she placed her hands on his knees and stared into his eyes. They were like looking into a storm. "I can't have you losing it right now, big guy." She offered him a wavering smile. "If you fall apart, I'm screwed." Letting a breath out slowly, she bit back emotions that were stuck in her throat. "You're my rock, Dare. I need you." Giving him a half grin, she flexed her fingers on his legs. "It's just you and me against all the insanity, remember."

Nodding, he reached out slowly, almost hesitantly, and cupped the side of her face. "I know." His eyes moved over her face, and she couldn't look away from him or the anxiety she saw. Sighing, he straightened, "Right now isn't the time." Stroking his thumb over her cheek a few times, he dropped his hand. "It's just my beast side misbehaving. I'm sure I'll be good after the moon is back in cycle."

"Is that why you were getting something from Nadine?" She watched him stiffen and then look over her shoulder instead of meeting her questioning look.

"Yeah, she makes a concoction that helps me keep my beast side under control." He nodded abruptly, and she had to wonder if he was speaking to her or his beast.

"Does it help?" Lowering her head, she leaned over so he would have to look at her again.

His dark eyes were a squall of emotion. "It usually does," he shrugged, "must be the added stress this time."

Patting his knee, she gave him a serious look. "Can I do

anything to help?"

Darien swallowed and stared at her for a second. His eyes flicked to her mouth twice before he looked away and closed his eyes. "I should be good." Looking at her again, he shrugged. "Tomorrow's cage night, so I think I'll be good after that."

Holding his look, she tried to read him but couldn't. She wasn't sure why she felt like he wasn't telling her something, but she decided to ignore it. "Let me know if it gets to be too much tomorrow." She slid forward on the couch so she was closer to him. "If it's too much, just take the day and watch a movie or something."

He shook his head. "I'm not going to hide in the damn basement with some psycho targeting Serenity." His jaw clenched. "It's bad enough I'm out of commission tomorrow night." He cupped her face in his hands, a serious look on his face. "Promise me no one goes outside tomorrow, out of the protected boundary, without Attis or Pascal with them."

"We'll be careful, Darien." She whispered; his intensity made her heart ache.

He gave a brief nod but didn't release her face. "*You* don't go outside at all. For *any* reason, and someone is to be with you at *all* times." His voice cracked as he said it.

Remi didn't know what was going on with him, but it frightened her that he was this emotional tonight. Maybe it was because of what had happened with Emery or the note, but she didn't like seeing him this way.

"Remi?" His tone was pleading. "Promise me."

"I promise." She wanted to reassure him, but how?

Darien leaned closer and brushed his lips over hers in a soft kiss. She could feel him shaking as he did it. He stayed there, so close his breath was brushing over her mouth. A shiver of awareness went through her. Normally when Darien kissed her, it was fast, hard, and unexpected, except the one time she'd asked him to.

"Ah," a groan came from the doorway, "shit. Sorry to interrupt."

Darien's hands dropped away as they both turned to see an exhausted, paler-than-normal Emery slumped against the doorframe.

A look of regret was on his face as he shrugged. "I just wanted to let you know I'm going down to my room." He looked over his shoulder down the hall and then back at her. "Corey is out like a light and," he looked from Darien back to her, "it's a little too much for me to stay with her tonight."

"You need blood," Darien said, standing up.

Nodding, Emery rubbed a hand over his chest. "Yeah, I'm long past due needing some, and with the way I'm feeling…" he jammed his hands in his pockets and gave Remi a sorrowful look. "I just can't lay there and listen to her heartbeat tonight."

Remi stood up and went over to him. "It's okay. I'm sure she'll understand." She glanced over her shoulder and gave Darien a soft look. "Emotions are playing havoc with everyone right now."

"I just," Emery gave her a hopeful look, "will you check in on her before you go back to bed?"

Placing a hand on his chest, she nodded. "Yes. Go get something to drink and try to rest. I will even feed her breakfast in the morning."

He looked down at her, a grateful smile on his face. "Thanks, Remi." Leaning down, he kissed her cheek and then backed up a step. "I really need to go. Even your blood smells like a snack right now." Stepping out into the hall, he glanced back to Darien. "Are you staying up here tonight?"

Remi turned so she could see Darien. He looked from Emery to her, a pained expression in his eyes.

"I'm just going to check the place from top to bottom, then try to get some rest." He lifted a hand in a helpless gesture. "The moon is riding my control hard right now."

Emery nodded quickly. "I hear ya." With a mock salute, he was gone from her sight in a blur.

Biting her lip, she turned to Darien. "You think he'll be okay?"

Darien grinned. "Yes, momma bear, he'll be fine." He shrugged. "This emotional stuff is just like growing pains."

Sighing, she ran her hands through her hair and flipped it back from her face and neck. "Attis once told me that when you're turned, everything you feel is intensified."

"It's that way for a lot of paras."

"You too?"

Clenching his jaw in thought, he looked her up and down once before answering. "In certain circumstances, yes, it is."

Huffing out a breath, she smirked. "I guess, when it's like that being a normal isn't so bad, then."

Darien came toward her, a look she didn't recognize on his face. "You are anything but a normal, Remi, and you know it." He stopped when he was right in front of her. "Normals can't just look at a being and know what specie they are."

Leaning against the door, she shrugged. "Blame that on Doyle." She shook her head. "I was perfectly normal until he passed whatever this is on to me."

"This," he tapped the center of her chest lightly with a finger, "is the way you were meant to be." Leaning down, he kissed her on the mouth and then straightened up before she had a chance to respond. "And I wouldn't change a thing." Taking a deep breath, he turned toward the door. "I'm going to check the windows and doors, then make sure everything is closed up downstairs."

"Thanks, Dare." She reached out and touched his shoulder to stop him. "If you need me, you know where I am."

He gave her a strange look and then an abrupt nod before he continued down the hall.

Blowing out a breath, Remi shook her head. This had been one seriously strange day, and she hoped tomorrow brought some normalcy back. With a grin at her own thought, she went to her bedroom. What she thought was normal would be so far from anyone else's idea of it.

15

Barreling through the kitchen door, Darien came to an abrupt stop when he saw Attis, Emery, and Pascal leaning against the bar—all three held bottles of blood.

Pascal set his down and moved over to grab a glass off the shelf. Pouring some J.D. into the glass, he slid it down the counter in a smooth motion toward Darien.

Picking up the glass, Darien tipped it in his direction. "Thanks." Swallowing the bitter liquid in one mouthful, he set the glass back on the counter and looked at Emery. "How are you doing?"

Emery stared at the bottle in his hand, his posture tense. "I'd like to go kill something right now." His tone was filled with venom.

Crossing his arms over his chest, Darien nodded. "I can understand that. Just don't give into that feeling."

Taking a sip, Emery lowered the bottle and sighed. "I won't."

"How are *you* doing?" Attis asked quietly, focusing on Darien.

Resting his hip against the bar, Darien lowered his head and stared at the floor for a moment. "I'm struggling."

"You've been struggling for years, wolfman," Pascal added blandly.

Rubbing the back of his neck, he let out a slow breath. "I know, but it's getting harder to control."

"*That* is because you aren't supposed to control it." Attis slid up to sit on the bar, watching Darien. "You're trying to fight against what nature intends." He tilted his head and gave looked serious. "We all know how well that always turns out."

"You need to tell her, Darien." Emery sounded tired. "The vibes coming off you when I walked into the living room almost suffocated me.

Pascal looked from Emery to slowly study Darien. "How hard is your wolf riding you when she's near?"

Darien snorted. "*Hard.* It takes all my focus to not change lately." He looked down and flexed his hand. The constant pressure in his fingertips where his claws would come out was ever-present.

"Lately, as in because the full moon is close, or before?" Attis inquired, leaning forward to study him more closely.

"All the time now," Darien whispered. He looked up, making eye contact with each of them briefly. "I want to tell her, but it's not the…"

"You can't *wait* for the right time." Pascal crossed his arms, exasperated. "You need to *make* it the right time."

Rubbing his hands over his face, Darien sighed and dropped them again. "I just… I know" He waved a hand around, "I don't want to force her to…"

Emery snorted. "There is no one on this planet that could ever force Remi to do something she didn't want to do." Chuckling quietly, he grinned at him. "Maybe you can't see how she looks at you, but the rest of us can."

"The air is electric when you two are close to each other," Pascal all but purred, "the pheromones have the rest of us walking around stiff."

Attis sent him a blank stare and then shook his head, giving Darien a look full of sympathy and understanding. "You're running out of time." He shrugged. "The fact that she's stayed single this long is mind-boggling."

"It's not from men not trying…" Emery closed his mouth when Darien sent him a look of death. Lifting his hands, he shrugged. "It's true, Darien. You can't pretend it's not."

His wolf was clawing at him again. Unable to stay still, he moved around the bar to check the doors. "She won't get involved with anyone that works here."

"Maybe if she knew what was going on and that you're not just a happy-for-now kind of guy, she'd rethink," Attis called across the room to him.

Checking the side door, Darien turned and jammed his hands in his pockets, and looked over at the three vampires watching him. He'd thought it for years but never said it out loud to anyone. "What if she says no?" Pulling his hands out, he moved slowly across the room. "I'd have to leave."

"What if she says yes?" Pascal countered in a nonchalant manner. "Then you'd live happily ever after."

"Are you just going to follow her around with your fuzzy tail tucked between your legs forever?" Attis asked, a smirk on his face.

Rolling his eyes at the vamp's poor attempt at humor, Dairen heaved another loud sigh. "I don't know…"

He stopped when Pascal moved away from the bar and started slowly and methodically walking toward him. Something in his expression made Darien's heart speed up. "What if she doesn't have forever?" He raised his eyebrows in question. "What then?" Lifting his hands slowly, he maintained eye contact with him. "We don't know exactly what she is. Her longevity could be that of a normal." Stopping a few feet from him, his eyes red and lethal. "She could die tomorrow of some normal affliction; then you would never have her."

A low growl emitted from deep in Darien's chest.

Pascal shrugged. "If you don't bind her to your life-line, that *could* happen, my friend." Shaking his head sadly, his eyes went back to green.

"Can we not talk about Remi dying? Please?" Emery was across the room in a blur. "I can't even…" he waved a hand around, "just don't." Glaring at Pascal briefly, his grief-stricken eyes turned to Darien. "I'm going to try to sleep."

"Yes." Attis moved by them over to the door and set the alarm. "We should try to rest now. It's going to be a long night tomorrow."

Emery nodded and turned toward the kitchen without another word.

Attis came over and stopped beside Pascal. "Depressing the fledgling when he's had an emotional night isn't the wisest."

Pascal shrugged. "The truth can hurt."

Holding his look for several silent moments, Attis inclined his head in concession, then gave Darien a weak smile. "I'll see you tomorrow."

Darien watched as he left, then moved over to the bar. Picking up the empty bottles, he tossed them into the bin under the counter. When he straightened up, Pascal was on the other side of the bar. "I know it's the truth, doesn't mean I want to hear it out loud."

"None of us want to think of the day we won't have Remi in our world." His tone was soft, almost understanding. "But she does deserve to know, Darien."

Closing his eyes to escape the steady stare of the man making him want to scream, he opened them again and nodded. "I know." Glancing around the empty space to see if everything was clean, he sighed. "Let me get through the full moon tomorrow, and then I'll tell her."

"That's all I ask. Give her the choice of making her own decisions and stop making them for her."

Motioning to the kitchen door, Darien waited until he moved. "I can't wait for the day you find the other half of your soul."

Pascal paused in the doorway. "I gave up my soul a millennia ago. I doubt any such fate waits for me."

With that, he moved out of Darien's sight so fast he

couldn't comment. Stopping to flick off the lights, he stood there in the dark. It felt like everything from this moment forward would change. He couldn't even fathom a day without Remi in it. Nothing could happen to her. Ever. His beast would wreak havoc in the world if her light were no longer in it.

Exhaling slowly, he pushed through the door. Trying to sleep was going to be the same old restless rerun from every other night, but he had to try.

16

The next day the atmosphere was thick with tension and suspicion. None of the staff lingered to talk to the customers. They kept close to one another. For the most part, the patrons didn't notice that they were the subject of distrust.

Corey came down with Caitlyn for breakfast, and Remi decided she should get to know her. Emery was obviously very serious about her, and Corey must have some deep feelings about him because she didn't run the other way after the attack the night before.

Corey watched the girls serve the customers as she ate. When Iris went by carrying an order, Corey looked at Remi. "So, *all* of the people that work here are supernatural's?"

"We call them paras," Remi smiled, "and yes, they are."

"Paras," Corey said quietly and sipped her coffee. "Except you."

Remi grimaced. "I'm mostly a normal."

"Mostly?" Corey set her cup down, giving her a wide-eyed look.

Not even sure how to explain, Remi shrugged. "I'm normal with a little extra, the ability to tell what others are."

Corey's expression changed to excitement. "So, you can

look at someone and just know if they're a regular human or not?"

Running her finger around the edge of her cup, Remi nodded. "Yeah."

"That's kind of cool." She took another small bite.

"It wasn't at first. I thought I was going insane." Remi remembered what it had been like at first. She'd known it was possible because Doyle used to rhyme off the natures of each body that came through the door. Then after he died and the Lewis quadruplets had come through the door, she'd turned to Nadine and said. "Wow, four identical wolves just walked in." It had been a heart-stopping moment in her life. She'd freaked out later when Darien got up for the night shift, and he'd just sat there grinning like it was a wonderful thing.

"I bet it was crazy finding out you weren't as normal as you thought."

Pushing her empty cup away, Remi looked at her for a moment. "How long have you known about the para community?" She grinned. "You're taking all of this a little too well to have just found out."

Corey wiped her mouth and placed the napkin neatly over her plate. "I grew up with a shifter for a best friend." She shrugged. "You can't be around a family like that and not know something's different." With a half-smile, she glanced around. "Since I've been on my own, I'm drawn to places like this." Leaning forward, she rested her arms on the table and clasped her hands. "I feel out of place with regular old humans." Her cheeks flushed slightly, "when I met Emery, I couldn't take my eyes off him." She smirked. "He's so…" she waved her hand around, "I'm not sure how to explain it."

Remi laughed, "I can see it on your face. You don't have to explain." As happy as she was that Corey seemed like a good fit, she still had to speak up to be sure. "You do know the risks of having a relationship with Emery."

A serious look appeared on Corey's face, and she nodded. "I know. I don't think he'd ever intentionally hurt me, but," a pained looked filled her eyes, "things happen, right?"

Remi sighed. "Yes, they do." Story of my life lately, she thought, things happening, one right after the other. "Just be careful. For your sake and Em's."

Corey studied her for a moment. "Emery told me you're not his sister."

Snorting, Remi grinned. "No. I'm not. I'm the mother in his world."

Corey laughed. "I figured that much out by the way he looks up to you." She shrugged. "Figuratively speaking." She offered her a small smile, "he loves you."

Remi didn't know what to say to that. Kyran came in, giving her a good excuse not to reply at all. He headed straight for her.

"I've come to the conclusion that you never sleep." He said with a grin as he sat down.

Remi yawned as if on cue. "It's not by choice most of the time."

Nodding, he looked at Corey. Remi couldn't help noticing that his eyes lingered on her neck more than once. "How are you feeling this morning?" He asked her.

Corey tilted her head, a look of anxiety on her face. "Fine. I'm just a little apprehensive about going outside today." She looked at the clock, "But I have to get home and change so I can get to work." Giving Remi a half smile, she stood up. "Thanks for everything, Remi. I'm sure I'll see you later."

Kyran stood back up again, "I'll walk you to your car." Looking down at Remi, he grinned. "I'll be right back. Hopefully, there will be a free cup of coffee waiting for me."

Stacking the dishes, Remi got up. "I'm sure I can find one around here somewhere."

She watched them walk away and then turned and almost walked right into Iris. She looked at the door. "So, that's Emery's girlfriend?"

Remi held out the dishes for her to take. "It looks that way."

Iris sighed. "Another one off the market."

Remi's eyebrows went up.

Iris shrugged. "What? I know faeries and vamps shouldn't hook up, but that doesn't mean I can't appreciate a sexy one when I see it, and your Emery," she made a dramatic moan, "he's sexy with a splash of boyish charm."

Remi shook her head and motioned for Iris to go to the kitchen and then followed her. "It seems to me that all the males around here are."

Iris leaned on the door so it would open. "Yes, they are. Lucky us."

Laughing, she held the door for Iris and then released it after she'd gone through it. Berk turned around and looked them both up and down.

"Only man talk would have you two looking so pretty and flushed." He waved the spatula at Iris. "Give. Who are we talking about?"

Iris put the dishes in the bin and grinned. "All the sexy, charming males that work here."

Berk fanned his face with the cooking utensil. "Boss lady does know how to pick them."

"Uh huh," Iris nodded and picked up a plate to finish the order for delivery.

"I don't pick them based on their looks or sex appeal, guys." Remi objected.

Iris looked out the server's window. "Speaking of sex appeal, here comes Kyran."

"No, we know you don't, Remi," Berk put the eggs on the plate, "but it doesn't hurt at all." Adding the toast, he nodded to Iris. "Now, if you could just hire one that leaned more to my way of thinking, I'd be one happy puppy."

"Oh, Berk," Iris grabbed a cutlery roll out of the tray, "I have a friend whose brother is just your type. I can hook you up."

Berk glanced up at the next order and then at her before she went out the door. "My type as he's sexy or gay?"

She laughed. "Both. But he's a normal."

Berk gave her a wide-eyed glare. "I'm in. I don't care if he's normal or not."

She winked and pushed the door. "Okay."

Kyran came through the door before it closed.

Berk made a soft rumbling sound in his chest. "Good morning, Detective."

Raising an eyebrow at Berk's purring, Kyran nodded. "Morning, Berk."

Remi moved down the counter and picked up the coffee pot to pour him a cup. "Any news we want to hear?"

Holding out his hand for the cup, Kyran shook his head slowly. "Not yet. We should know more later. Just waiting on some reports."

It wasn't good news, but it wasn't all bad either, so Remi decided she'd take it and go find something to distract herself.

"Need a hand?"

Remi glanced over her shoulder at Kyran. "Daytime a little slow for you?"

He smirked. "It's definitely quieter, with a lot less dancing."

Writing her countdown before she forgot it, she turned back to him. "Hey, dancing has been known to happen during the day shift too."

"Really? Who do I have to bribe to see this?"

"Remi, the accountant's office just called. Apparently, they can't reach him on his cell, so they asked if we could have him call in when he gets here." Nadine stood at the door, a case of coffee in her hands.

"I guess that means he should be here soon." Remi hugged the clipboard to her chest and gave Naddy a look. At the top of her list, right after Emery's attackers and her staff being safe, she hoped whatever Attis had done to the auditor yesterday held, and he'd be finished here today.

"I'll tell him when he comes in," Nadine said with a quiet nod before she left again.

"This really hasn't been your week." Kyran sighed with a quiet sound as he moved one of the cases so she could see behind it.

"And it's not even close to ending," she gave an exaggerated moan and shook her head. "At least the auditor will be done here today."

"Are you really locking Darien in a cage tonight?"

She nodded and wrote down her count. "Yes. It's heavily barred, surrounded by stone and concrete, sealed behind a solid steel door."

Kyran paused and looked at her. "That answers my next question."

"What question?"

Kyran leaned against the shelf, crossing his arms over his chest. "It's going to sound stupid to you," he shrugged, "you've been exposed to more of the para than I have, but I wondered how vicious Darien is when he shifts." He gave her a lopsided grin. "The cage you just described says it all."

Remi shifted a bottle to see how many were behind it. "He's only bad when the shift is from the full moon." Pausing, she looked at him. "Okay, he *can* be vicious if he shifts pissed off, but he still controls it." Remi got lost for a moment remembering the first time she had seen Darien shift. It had both scared the breath out of her and excited her. Of course, he had controlled it, and in seven years, she had never actually seen him during a moon shift, only heard him through the steel door. That was all she needed to know and never wanted to see.

"So, it's true. They have no control during the full moon."

"No, he doesn't. A few other paras have to work harder for control during the full moon, like wolf shifters, and some of the cats." She flashed him a big smile, "Most of the para communities are affected one way or another."

"I'm pretty sure a lot of normals are too," he added, straightening to move another case for her.

"They are." She flipped to the next page on her inventory list. "Serenity After Dark is insane on the full moon." Quickly counting, she continued. "The normals are all amped up, and the paras either want to bite them, spell them, or eat them." She gave him a forced grin. "It's never boring." Kyran pulled a case down so she could open it and see if it was full.

"So, what do you do?" He set it back on the shelf. "I mean, your main peacekeeper is locked in a cage. I imagine it drives Darien crazy knowing all of you are going through that when he's not there to help."

Moving over to the next shelf, she noticed an empty space and took a second to double-check what was supposed to be there by her list. "He…"

"Hates every second of it." Darien's groggy voice came from the doorway.

Remi turned to watch him come in, looking like he hadn't slept at all. "You're up early."

Darien shrugged and nodded a greeting to Kyran. "I wanted to get a few things done before tonight." He glanced at the clipboard she held. "Like finish the alcohol inventory."

Smirking, she held it out to him. "It's all yours. I was just killing time until Berk and Soren were done with lunch prep so I could figure out the order."

"Do they sing every day?" Kyran asked, stepping back from the shelf.

Remi glanced at Darien, whose eyes were laughing. "Yes, they do."

Raising his eyebrows, he looked from one to the other. "I don't think I've ever met two people that are always *that* happy."

Taking the cup out of Darien's hand, she took a sip. "I suppose it's better than having to work with crabby people." Handing the cup back to Darien, she smiled and headed toward the door. "I'll go get started on the order.

"Remi, hang on a sec." Darien handed a surprised Kyran the clipboard and followed her. "I need to talk to you."

She was afraid to ask what about because the way her week was going made her feel nervous when someone said that. She smiled at Kyran. "Just put the clipboard on the shelf and go grab some breakfast."

Kyran looked down at the list in his hands and set it on the shelf like it might bite him.

She waited until he went into the kitchen before really looking at Darien. He had that stormy look in his eyes again. "Let's go in the office."

He held out a hand for her to lead the way.

Remi stepped into the office and held her breath as he closed the door. "What's up?"

Darien looked at her for a moment, several emotions going through his eyes. "I'm not really comfortable about tonight."

Tilting her head, she gave him a bland look. "I don't think the moon cares much for your comfort."

Brown eyes glared at her. "Not about my change. About not being here with everything that's going on…"

The fact that he stopped talking made the hair on the back of her neck stand on end. "What are you thinking?" She held up her hand. "We can't be closed tonight. Not on short notice, they'd tear the building down."

Taking a deep breath, he lifted his hands in frustration. "I know. Too many rely on coming here during the full moon…"

Remi put her hands on her hips and looked at him. "So, what then? You look like you're going to combust spontaneously."

He snorted. "Close." He took a deep breath, his large chest noticeably rising and falling. "If I asked you to stay upstairs tonight…"

She shook her head. "Not a chance." Remi couldn't recall seeing Darien this anxious before. "Look, the harm none spell is good. Better than good. Baker and Boden tested it." She smirked, trying to lighten his mood. "Actually, it was quite entertaining to watch them try."

"Do I want to know?"

"Let's just say they can think violent thoughts toward each other, but as soon as they try to act on them, they're laid flat out staring at the ceiling."

Darien blew out a breath. "Still, it's magic, Remi. There always seems to be some kind of loophole. Some charm, talisman, or damn herb that negates a spell. Just…"

"Hey," she offered him a small smile, "calm down. I'll be

fine."

Darien paced on the spot. He looked like an animal trapped in a cage.

"Dare."

With a soft growling sound, he grabbed her by the waist and pulled her closer, leaning down so they were face to face. "Just stay inside the building. I don't care what's going on. You *do not* leave the building. Don't go upstairs alone. Take Emery with you." His eyes bore into hers with a look more serious than she'd ever seen. "Promise me, Remi."

Nodding, she tried to keep her pounding heart quiet. "Okay, I promise. Calm down…"

"I can't calm the fuck down. There's a sick killer out there," he released her and pointed to the door, "they've already attacked you and Emery, and I'm going to be locked in a damn cage." He took a deep breath; his fists were clenched at his sides. "Any staff that's here can stay here. There's enough room upstairs, and we have two empty rooms downstairs. I don't want anyone out there that doesn't have to be." He dropped his head down and looked at the floor. "Anyone that has to leave can park out back, within the spell boundary, so they can get to and from their cars…"

"I'll tell them," She moved over and stood in front of him, placing her hand on his chest over his heart. It was beating so strong she could feel it. "Everyone will be okay, Darien."

Heaving out a loud sigh, he placed his warm hand over hers. "I really hate this."

"I noticed." She could see the conflict in his eyes.

"If I had a choice…"

"You don't. You're a werewolf, and that won't change." She took a shaky breath, trying to appear calmer than she was; seeing him like this caused her to feel panicky. "Freaking out isn't going to help anyone."

"I'm just," he placed his other hand on her hip; she could feel his fingers flexing against her, "I can't even do what I'm supposed to do…"

"You take off *one* night a month, Darien, and not by

choice. I'm pretty sure that's allowed."

His eyes darkened as he looked down at her. "That's not what I meant." She watched him clench his jaw a few times as his eyes moved over her face. Releasing her hand, he cupped her jaw so she couldn't have looked away if she'd wanted to. "*Nothing* can happen to you, *A ghrá*." His voice was raw with emotion.

A shiver went down her spine, "Darien," wanting to ask what that word was he used, was stalled in her throat as she stood there and watched his brown eyes take on a yellow hue. That only happened when he was close to changing. He stood there, breathing deep, his breath brushing over her mouth, his eyes holding hers captive. The hand on her hip squeezed, and she gripped his arms, feeling the tension.

Remi didn't know how long they stood there like that, inhaling each other's breath, their eyes drawing the other in. His eyes didn't change, just stayed streaked with yellow. A knock on the door didn't move them.

"Remi?" Nadine called from the other side.

Darien took a deep breath and straightened away from her.

Blinking, she looked at the door. "Yeah?"

The door opened enough for Nadine to stick her head in. She looked at Darien, one eyebrow going up. "Is everything all right?"

Remi nodded, still feeling breathless. "Did you need me?"

Leaning in the small opening, Nadine shrugged. "The accountant's office called again; they're sure he should be here by now."

Darien rubbed the back of his neck. "Maybe he's just running late."

On any other day, Remi wouldn't have thought any more about it, but with all that had happened in the last few days, her stomach tightened. Placing a hand over it, she looked from Nadine to Darien. "I don't like it." She waved her other hand around. "Am I being paranoid?"

Opening the door further, Naddy stepped into the small space. "If your guts are telling you to worry, then you worry."

Growling softly, Darien closed his eyes. "Where's Kyran?"

"Sitting out front."

Darien looked over at her. "Go get him."

She nodded and then hesitated at the door and gave him a strange look. "Are you okay?"

Remi looked from one to the other. "What's going on?"

Giving Nadine a look before he turned to her, he shook his head. "Nothing."

Remi watched the silent appraisal Nadine gave Darien, then she turned and left to get Kyran. Darien went to step by her, but she stopped him with a hand on his arm. "Dare?" The last thing she needed right now was more secrets. "What was that? What aren't you guys telling me?"

Letting out a long breath, he reached over and brushed the hair back from her face. "It's nothing." He gave her a lopsided smile that was probably meant to put her at ease, but it didn't work. "Let's get through tonight, and then I'll explain." He rolled his shoulders. "With the moon right now, everything's more intense."

"You don't usually struggle this much."

Dropping a quick kiss on her forehead, he straightened. "The stress of bodies being found and people I care about being attacked isn't helping."

It made sense. Everyone was more on edge than normal. She hoped that was all that was going on. "Okay, but seriously if you need to take off for some quiet time or whatever, then do it."

Darien nodded but didn't look right at her. "Okay."

Remi glanced at the door, "Are you going to ask Kyran to track down the auditor?"

"Yep." He moved and put distance between them. "I'd like to know before I'm locked up that he's just a slow-moving man."

Flipping her hair back from her face, she gathered it behind her head to put it into a braid. "God, I hope he's just slow..."

"Rem, a customer wants a refund. He didn't like his food."

Nadine leaned around the door.

Remi shrugged, "you can do it."

She smirked, "he *ate* all the food he didn't like."

Remi just stared at her in disbelief. "So, there's no food to refund?" Nadine nodded. Sighing, Remi looked at Darien; even he had a grin on his face—the *joys of customer service*.

"Go help. I'll talk to Kyran." Darien stepped back so she could go out front.

17

Darien stomped on the box and flattened it. He'd rearranged and cleaned both supply rooms, did the inventory, helped with two rushes, and Kyran still hadn't come back. Tossing the cardboard into the pile, he paused and pulled his phone out. No messages.

How hard can it be to track down one very overweight, sweaty man?

Running a hand through his hair, he looked around the room. He hated that it was the full moon tonight. Absolutely, all the way down to his soul loathed it. Tonight, even more than normal. He wasn't comfortable leaving Remi and everyone else. On any full moon, he worried, afraid that some para would bite a normal, or worse, Remi would hook up with someone. The stakes were higher tonight.

Someone had it in for Serenity. At least, that was the conclusion he'd come up with. At first, he thought they had just had it in for Remi, but with the other bodies and then the attack on Emery, they had a gripe with all things Serenity.

He didn't get it. Everything this place stood for, all the people that worked here…what grudge could anyone have? Paras and normals were both equally welcome. It was a bridge that joined the two worlds. Many of the regulars were in mixed marriages, and this was a place where they could be themselves. Well, within reason. Over the years, anything from the weird to bizarre had happened, even that was accepted for the most part.

"Darien, we're going to open up."

Jolting, he turned to look at Emery.

The young vampire grinned at him. "Did I just get the drop on the wolfman?" He stood straighter. "It's a proud moment for me."

Darien gave him a void look. "You're lucky I have good control. Sneaking up on a werewolf on the night of the full moon could turn out badly."

His smile faded. "I didn't think of that." Crossing his arms over his chest, he leaned against the door jam. "Are you staying for a bit?"

Darien shook his head. "Not tonight." He rolled his shoulders. "I'm a little strung out, and my wolf is unpredictable when I'm like this."

Nodding, Emery dropped his hands. "I hear that."

"Corey coming tonight?"

His face lit up. "Yeah."

"Make sure you focus on work." Darien felt like a heel for pushing off his own bad mood to squash Emery's. "And maybe she should stay here tonight."

Emery smiled, a surprised look on his face.

"As many as we can fit should stay."

"Got it." Emery started to turn and then paused. "Are you coming?"

Rubbing a hand over his chest, Darien looked around. "Yeah, I'm just going to put the cardboard out."

He watched him leave before turning around and kicking the pile of cardboard. He could feel his wolf just under the surface, prowling, waiting. Taking a deep breath, he pushed back at it. Nadine's potion wasn't helping at all tonight. Up until last year, he could stay upstairs and function with a degree of normalcy. Now, he had to be locked up before by seven, like some toddler. It pissed him off and left the taste of self-disappointment in his mouth. He wasn't some young pup. He should be able to control this better.

With a growl, he leaned down and scooped up an armful of the cardboard. Shoving the door open, he went out to the bins. Nadine and her witch crew could spell the boundary around Serenity so no one could intentionally hurt another within, but they couldn't spell his were ass to have more control. It just didn't seem right.

Emptying his arms, he turned back to get the rest. He could feel the magic crawl over his skin when he was outside. Whether it was because the spell was stronger or his wolf was too aware, it had him rushing to finish and get back inside. Hopefully, if it did that to him, it would do the same to anyone that tried to come in tonight with ill intentions.

When he finished, he glanced up at the sky, his lip peeling back as he looked where the moon would soon sit. Shaking his head, he stepped back inside and closed the door. If he believed in any kind of deity, he'd be praying right now and asking that they not allow anything to happen to anyone he cared about.

On his way through the back, he checked his phone once more. Where the hell was Kyran? He wanted him present tonight as well. The more to watch over Remi and Serenity, the better.

18

Remi paced the length of the kitchen again. If she kept going at this rate, she'd soon wear a groove in the tile.

Emery came in a leaned against the door. "We're going to open the doors." She glanced at him and kept moving; he followed her with his eyes. "Are you warming up for a sprint or something?"

Stopping, she huffed out a breath and shook her head. "No. There's still no word on the auditor."

He smirked. "How is it that's a bad thing? According to Vie, he was a greasy jerk."

She rolled her eyes at him. "Being a jerk isn't a good reason to wish something bad on someone."

He held up his hands. "I didn't wish anything bad on him or anyone else." He looked away from her and then moved his eyes back slowly. "Okay, I'd be lying if I didn't want something to happen to whoever jumped us last night." He made a hissing noise. "Corey could have gotten hurt."

"Is she coming tonight?"

He smiled. "Yeah."

Brushing her hair back from her face, she studied him for a minute. "Darien doesn't want anyone of us leaving, so you

139

better find her a place to crash."

"You like her?" His voice was hesitant, an anxious look on his face.

It was the little things like that, she thought that reminded her how young he really was. "Yes, I like her." Going over, she stopped in front of him and looked up into his pale eyes. "Just be careful."

Doubt filled his eyes. "You trust me?"

"Yes." Remi watched the shock fill his eyes. "Why are you surprised?"

He opened his mouth, but the words came slowly. "You didn't seem so sure when you walked in on Corey and me in the supply room."

Remi smirked. "I wasn't exactly prepared to walk in on that." She gave him a serious look. "I know you'd never hurt her, Em."

He stiffened. "How can you be so sure?"

"Because," she held his eyes with her own, "I know you'd never hurt someone you care about. Just like I know that every time you see this," she pulled the collar of her shirt aside to reveal the jagged scar from a reckless bite. The one Emery had put there when he'd attacked her. "You feel regret and remorse." She rubbed a hand over his chest and smiled up at him as his eyes moved over the scar and then slowly back to her face. "That's how I know."

His eyes glazed over as a slow smile appeared on his face. "Have I mentioned lately how lucky I am to have you?" With a quick move, he wrapped his arms around her and hugged her into his chest. "Thanks, Remi."

Emery wasn't big on hugs normally, so she just smiled and enjoyed the closeness while it was on offer.

A low growl filled the quiet space. Slowly Emery dropped his arms away, allowing her to turn and glare at Darien where he stood behind her.

He clenched his jaw, "Sorry, Emery." Darien shook his head and looked at her. "We better go. The moon's pull is too strong right now."

Nodding at him, she turned back to the young vampire and smiled. "Go open up. I'll be back up in a few minutes."

Emery saluted her and started to turn.

"Emery." Darien reached out and took his arm to stop him.

With a wary look, Emery glanced at the hand on his arm.

"I'm sorry." Darien dropped his hand away. "I don't have a lot of control this close to…"

"Hey," Emery shrugged, "no biggie." He grinned. "Go get in touch with your wolf, and I'll see you tomorrow."

Darien nodded stiffly. He looked at her and then back to Emery. "Keep her safe."

Emery patted him on the shoulder. "Don't worry. I will." He gave him a somber look. "Everyone here will look after my dear *Mom*." He winked at her before turning back to Darien. "She's the most important part of Serenity. She's the glue that keeps all of us and this," he motioned around them, "together."

With a loud sigh, Darien gave an abrupt nod and then turned on his heel, heading toward the supply closet.

"I'll be right back." Remi followed Darien. Going to the closet, she stepped across the three-foot space and pulled the small panel on the wall open. Pressing the switch, she watched as the shelf slid out of the way and stairs appeared. Hurrying down the cement steps, she caught up to Darien as he reached the door to his room.

She closed the door and watched him pull his belt from his jeans.

"I'm sorry about that up there." He kept his head down, not looking at her and sat down on the bed.

Remi swallowed the lump in her throat; she could feel the anxiety rolling off him. "You've been growling a lot lately, Dare."

"Yeah." He still didn't look at her.

She sat and watched him take off his shoes. "I hate this time of month."

Darien gave a strained chuckle. "You say that when it's

your time of month too."

"Haha. The difference is I just bloat and get cranky. You eat people."

He stood up and pulled his shirt over his head. "I don't eat people." A somber look filled his eyes. "I kill anything."

Remi tried not to notice the perfect muscles in his chest. Turning his back to her, he slid the steel door open. The muscles in his arms flexed as the ones in his back danced with his movement. Unlocking the cage behind the door, he turned and set the key on the table.

Sighing, she stood up. Not everyone got to lock their friend in a cage of solid steel bars, surrounded by eight-inch-thick stone walls, once a month. "How much time do we have?" She already knew the answer by how tense he was.

"Not long."

When she moved over to the door, he reached out and wrapped his thick arm around her waist, pulling her into his firm body. His hold was tighter than it normally was, and, as odd as that was, she was used to it at this time of the month. For the last year, he'd changed the routine when she locked him up to include kissing her. She never asked why he did this, and he didn't offer any insight either. Remi wasn't about to complain. The way he kissed was more than worth the internal battle she always had about mixing work and play.

"You always look stressed when we do this." He brushed the hair back from her face. "It has to be done for everyone's safety."

Looking up into his changing eyes, she sighed softly. "I know, but that doesn't mean I have to like it."

His lips moved slowly into a smile. "Which is why I do this…" cupping the back of her head in his large hand, he lowered his mouth to hers and kissed her lightly.

Bracing her hands on his chest, she leaned into him until she could feel the outline of his body pressing into hers. She loved the feel of his solid chest beneath her hands.

With a soft growl of approval, he deepened the kiss, his tongue demanding entrance into her mouth. "I don't like leaving you unprotected," he breathed against her lips.

She could feel his muscles tensing and knew the rising moon was getting closer. Trying to step back, she stopped when she felt his arm tighten against her movement. "I have four strong vampires upstairs armed with fangs, speed, and tranq darts. I'll be fine."

With a quick move, he backed her up against the bars, caging her in with his arms. "Don't go upstairs alone. Have Emery check the apartment."

His lips were working their way down her throat; she tried to ignore the way it made her feel, knowing that in a few more minutes, he'd be locked up, and she'd be left cold. "I will."

He growled low against her skin, sending shivers through her. "Dare…" His mouth on hers again cut off any more words. His tongue stroked hers while his body rocked her into the cold steel.

She almost fell when he jerked away from her and stepped into the cage, moving quickly to the other side and bracing his hands on the stone through the bars. "Now," he growled in a guttural voice.

Moving fast, she grabbed the door and closed it. Her hands were shaking as she locked it; watching him, she lingered over, pulling the steel barrier back.

Breathing with ragged breaths, he turned his head. The yellow eyes of a werewolf looked at her.

"I'll see you in the morning," she whispered and then heaved the door closed. Securing it, she turned and flipped the switch for the air vents to open through the thick walls. She could hear animalistic grunts and growls as Darien took on his true form. It didn't matter how many times she did this, it still left her shaking. Turning away, she glanced around his tiny room. The cage took up almost half the space.

Pulling the curtain over the door, she grabbed the keys on her way out. Darien spent every day looking out for her and the rest of Serenity staff; one night a month, she watched out for him.

Moving through the tunnel, she went back up the stairs into the supply room. The sound of the music hit her as soon as she opened the door. Closing her eyes, she asked silently for an uneventful full moon and then went into the turmoil that was her life.

A wrestling match, impromptu strip tease, a table of drunk crying women, and an ice machine malfunction later, Remi slumped onto the stool at the end of the bar, dropping her head on her arms for a few seconds, maybe even a whole minute if she was lucky.

"You survive this every month?" Kyran leaned down beside her face and glanced at her in the low light.

A drink appeared in front of her; she looked up and gave Attis a grateful smile, then looked at Kyran. He looked as out of sorts as she felt. "Yes, we do." She took a drink of the ice water and motioned to the door where Finn and Boden stood. Neither one looked tired or stressed. "Those guys live for the pandemonium every month."

He sat down and leaned on the bar. "Yeah, I noticed the only ones dragging their asses were us normal humans." He gave her a serious look. "I just talked to Randell. Still no sign of your accountant."

Remi closed her eyes briefly before looking at him. "Let's hope he's just playing hooky."

"Think we'll be that lucky?" He asked, a hopeful look in his eyes.

She took another sip. "Nope."

"Me either."

"Uh, Remi?" Elise leaned down closer to her. "There's a couple in the bathroom," she looked over her shoulder toward the door, "in the same bathroom."

Remi exhaled loudly. "I'll go."

Finn walked by and shook his head. "Not alone, you don't."

Rolling her eyes, Remi turned to look at Elise, who just shook her head and motioned to the drinks on her tray.

Kyran groaned and stood up. "I'll go." He shrugged. "Two humans are better than one, right?"

Attis's laugh sounded from over her shoulder. "I couldn't agree more."

At least, she thought as they came back out, no one had all their clothes off.

"Your world is interesting, Ms. Foster," Kyran said in a low voice near her ear.

"Yes, it is." She picked up the glass as Attis slid it to her.

Loud cheering had them looking across the sea of bodies. "Looks like I'm up again." Kyran gave her a dramatic sigh and headed over to see if Emery needed a hand getting things under control.

Glancing at Elise as she moved out of the crowd, Remi was relieved to see her smiling. Whatever the commotion was this time couldn't be anything threatening. Swiveling around on the stool, she picked up her drink again and watched Attis and Pascal as they gracefully moved around behind the bar keeping up with the orders.

Pascal's movements seemed slower than they usually did. He came down and hefted a tray of dirty glasses up over his shoulder and took them into the kitchen.

When he came back out, she taped his arm as he went past. "Why do you look paler than usual?"

He finished making the drinks with his swift grace and put them on Vienna's tray before he leaned down close to her, his green eyes locked on hers. "I've been in more heads tonight than I can count."

Remi looked around. They were packed to capacity tonight, which was completely normal on the full moon. "Then take a break. I don't need you passing out."

He flashed a fanged grin. "I'm more likely to go feral and start snacking on throats than passing out."

Rolling her eyes, she stood up. "I'm serious, take five and have a drink," she moved behind the bar and gave him a bland look, "out of a bottle." She set her drink behind the counter and by him. "I'll cover you."

He hesitated for a few seconds. "You haven't asked if I've found anything."

Remi leaned over the bar so she could hear what Vienna needed and then looked at him. "You'd tell me if you found something." Moving down the bar, she grabbed a pitcher and started filling it. She was tired. All she had to do was keep busy until closing and then wait out the rest of the night or moon until Darien could be let out again. Setting the pitcher of beer on the counter, she flipped over two glasses and swung around to get the bottles she needed. Pascal was still standing where she'd left him. Giving him a questioning look, she finished the last two drinks and nodded to Vie so she would take them.

Pascal turned and went into the kitchen, but before the door closed, Baker came out and grinned at her. "You're needed in the kitchen. I've got this." He moved by her and leaned across the bar to three women on the other side.

Frowning, she grabbed her drink and went into the kitchen. Pascal stood there holding a bottle of blood. She looked around to see why she was needed.

"You look like you're going to drop," Pascal said in a low tone.

"You're one to talk." She leaned against the counter and took a sip of water.

He grinned and waved the bottle around. "The difference is, I can drink this and be ready for rounds two and three. Your water isn't going to revive you."

Sneering at him, she rolled her eyes. "Yeah, it sucks to be normal."

Pascal snorted and took another drink. "You've been vibrating around here all night." Setting the empty bottle down, he stood in front of her. "How are you really doing?" He rested his hands on his hips and stared down at her with haunting green eyes.

"Still drives you nuts that you can't just look inside my head and find out, doesn't it?" She wiggled her eyebrows at him, trying to lighten his somber mood.

Quirking one eyebrow at her, his eyes moved slowly over her face. "Yes, it does, but I've also discovered that watching you tells me almost as much."

"It does?"

"Almost." Crossing his arms over his chest, he stayed where he was standing and gave her a determined look. "I know you're stressed with the attacks and the deaths," his eyes locked on hers, "and we both know that the robust sweaty accountant isn't off somewhere with a mistress." He faked a shiver. "That's an image I'd like to erase."

Remi exhaled and let her shoulders drop. "Yeah, I guess we can assume he's the next body to be found."

Nodding slowly, Pascal squinted at her. "Have you noticed you're worse on the nights of the full moon?"

Shrugging, she looked down at the glass in her hand. "Our main bouncer is missing. Everyone has to do more without Darien on the floor."

He smirked. "Everyone has a blast on the night of the full moon, and you know it." He sighed. "Myself included, except that I'm on brain scan detail tonight."

She looked up at him again. "Have you found anyone?"

He shook his head. "No. Now don't change the subject."

Sighing, she closed her eyes and let out a slow breath. "I don't know what's happening with me. It's like everything is more intense lately." She opened her eyes and looked at him for a second. "It's probably just from the attack and threat of something else."

"Probably." He said softly, letting the end of the word linger for a second. Clearing his throat, he backed up but continued to watch her. "Have you noticed anything off with our favorite werewolf lately?"

His tone was nonchalant, but if Remi knew one thing about Pascal, he didn't bring things up without reason. "What isn't everyone telling me?"

He stared at her for a moment, almost like he was concentrating, and then he sighed. "Everyone who?"

Setting the glass down, she crossed her arms over her

chest. "Nadine, Darien," she gave him an accusing look, "you." As he stood there, she watched the expression in his eyes become masked. There was something going on. She was certain of that.

"I'm not sure what there could be."

Curbing the urge to smack him, she barred her teeth instead. Maybe she hung around with too many fang bearers, but it was how she felt. He glanced at her teeth, a look of amusement changing his expression. "Nadine tells me it's not her place to explain anything. Darien just says later or after…" Moving over, she craned her neck so she could glare at him. "What's going on? Is something wrong with Darien?"

Pascal rested a cold hand on her shoulder. "I'd love to say there are so many things wrong I can't list them," he sighed, "but I can hear your heart hammering away in that fragile chest of yours, so I won't tease you." He lifted one red eyebrow, "This time." Leaning down, he kissed the center of her forehead and then moved away in a blur of movement. He stopped and looked out the window into the bar. "I would love nothing more than to tell you all of Darien's deep dark secrets, but in truth, it's really not my place."

He gave her a sympathetic look that made her want to scream in frustration.

"What have you noticed with Darien lately?" Flicking his eyes from the window to her, he studied her briefly before looking back to the window to keep an eye on what was going on.

She felt like he was suddenly playing the role of her shrink. "Well, he's been anxious lately, but with the moon cycle so close and all the crap hitting us, I guess it's understandable."

"Is it?" He motioned out the window. "We're all catching the *crap* hitting us lately."

Remi shrugged and tucked her hands into her pockets. "Darien's more intense than everyone else…"

Pascal turned his head enough to give her a steady stare. "Darien is as mild-mannered as a week-old puppy ninety percent of the time, and you know it." He shook his head.

"Calmest damn werewolf I've ever met. Usually, they're all *grr* and growl."

She knew he was right and couldn't think of any other reason for the behavior lately. "I asked him why he was growling more lately."

"Oh?" He finally turned from the window to look at her. "What did he say?"

"He," she frowned, realizing that Darien hadn't given her an answer, "just agreed with me and didn't explain."

Pascal smirked. "So, he avoided answering."

Remi shrugged again. "I guess." Taking a deep breath, she let it out quickly. "Is there a point to all of this, Pascal? You won't tell me what's going on."

"Something's going on?" Emery came into the kitchen. He looked from Pascal to her and then back again. "We have a few food orders, so Baker needs to do *his* job now."

Pascal nodded and moved toward the door. "Go get some rest, Remi." He paused in the door. "Why don't you take Darien's bed? Then we can put Elise and Vienna in yours for the night."

"I was going to stay and help out…"

"We'll be fine. You have to work in the morning." He glanced at Emery, an odd look passing between them. "Darien will feel better if you're on the other side of his wall."

She frowned. "He'll know I'm there through all that steel?"

Emery grinned. "Yeah, he'll know."

"It will soothe him," Pascal said with a big smile. "I'm sure his beasty side is worse lately because he's worried about you with a killer running around." He winked at her. "With you secure in the basement, the rest of us won't have to watch over you."

For some reason, she felt like she was being set up, but she couldn't quite figure out for what. She did know that she hated being the weak human in the group, everyone feeling like they had to look after her. "Fine." She looked at Emery. "Do you need me to help out for a bit longer?"

Emery shook his head. "Nope. We're good. It's almost

one, so the crowd is starting to settle down." He smirked. "Somewhat."

She glared at Pascal. "We'll finish our conversation tomorrow."

Pascal inclined his head in that regal way he had and then left.

"What have I missed?" Emery was beside her, a concerned look on his face.

Remi rubbed a hand over her forehead. "Honestly, I don't know. Everyone is getting weirder and weirder around here."

He chuckled. "Or you're just beyond exhausted and think it is." Wrapping a cool arm around her shoulders, he turned them toward the back door. "Let's get you settled in downstairs so I can help to start clearing out the joint."

Sighing, she nodded and let him lead her to the supply closet.

19

Remi never really spent a lot of time in Darien's room. Other than to lock him up, she hadn't been inside the door. Most of their conversations or disagreements were always in her apartment. Looking around, she turned on the bathroom light to not be in complete darkness. There was no lamp; she supposed a werewolf's sight in the dark was better than hers.

Turning off the overhead light, she kicked off her boots and shoved them with her foot to rest beside the door. She checked the lock for the third time and then went to the bed. It wasn't a huge bed. How could a man the size of Darien be comfortable in such a small bed? With a grin, she pulled back the covers. Maybe she was a little spoiled having a king-size bed all to herself upstairs.

A growling noise from behind the wall had her jumping. What did he do in there all night? Unless he had a jackhammer, he couldn't get through the floor. If he managed to damage the stone wall, the bars would stop him. She knew this because of the new, improved cage design from a few years ago. The first few tries had held him but hadn't fared well against his beasts' onslaught.

Going over to the curtain, she pulled it back to place her

hand against the steel. There was a rumbling sound from the other side, loud enough that she could hear it through the thick barrier. Scratching against the hard metal sent a shiver down her spine, and it was quiet again. Backing away, she stared at the door. *Only four more hours, Dare, and then you'll be on this side again.*

She went back to the bed and stripped off her jeans. So tired, she took her bra off through the sleeves of her t-shirt, dropping it to the floor. Setting her phone and keys on the bedside table, she climbed under the covers and laid back. The pillow was soft and smelled of Darien. She smiled as the scent brought her the same peaceful feeling as he did.

She burrowed under the covers and closed her eyes. Things hadn't always been peaceful between them. The first few years, they did nothing but bicker and fight. She grinned, even though that hadn't been all bad. Mostly it was annoying. When she'd wanted to waitress at after dark, he said no. Anytime she tried to lay out back by the river and soak up some sun, he said no. She gave up trying to date because he always found a reason she was needed at the last minute. They could tear each other down six different ways, but if someone else were to try it, they'd face an attack. That's what Darien was; her verbal sparring partner, her sense of calm when she was freaking out, and that went both ways. The few times that Darien had lost control, she'd always been able to reel him in.

Where were they when he'd completely lost it and half changed? She was so tired. It had been a celebration or picnic of some sort. She must be tired when she couldn't remember one of the rare events away from Serenity. Thinking about everyone, it was only them that didn't have much of a life on the outside. Serenity was her life, and she really didn't mind all the time it required of her. Thinking of where she came from, what she'd had before walking through the door to owning every inch of a place that housed so many, and giving all, paras and normals, somewhere safe to be, was overwhelming and humbling all at once.

When Doyle had told her it was all hers, she'd thought he was crazy. She'd even argued for Serenity to go to Darien, she wasn't sure how long he'd been here before she'd arrived, but it felt right that his name be on the deed. Doyle told her that he'd asked Darien to be co-owner, and he'd declined. For the longest time, Remi was afraid that without Serenity to tie him here, he'd leave. There were still days when he seemed so preoccupied that she wondered if he was thinking of moving on.

Werewolves were supposed to be plagued by wanderlust; she hoped he was the exception. She couldn't do any of this without Darien, and hopefully, he knew that. Turning her face into the pillow, she inhaled his scent, that musky smell that calmed and excited at the same time. With a sigh, she wrapped her arms around the pillow and let her body relax.

A buzzing phone woke her. Lifting her head, she looked around and tried to figure out where she was—Darien's room. Picking up the phone, she squinted at the screen; it was the alarm letting her know it was time to open the cage.

Remi flipped the covers back and got up. Grabbing the keys, she went to unlock the steel door as quietly as possible. Darien was usually passed out on the floor after his shift.

Pushing the door open, she looked for him in the dark space. Sure enough, he was curled up on the floor. If he couldn't feel how cold it was, she wasn't going to wake him up to tell him.

As quietly as she could manage, she unlocked the door to the cage and then turned and jumped back into the bed. She didn't want to wake anyone upstairs, so the only option was to try to grab a few more minutes of rest. Grabbing the pillow, she curled her body into it and closed her eyes.

The next thing she knew, a warm body pressed into her back.

"Why are you in my bed?" Darien's voice rumbled quietly in her ear.

She smiled. "Was told to sleep here," she mumbled, "so

the girls could have my bed."

His arm wrapped around her waist and pulled her tight against him. "I'll get up in a minute." She could feel his breath on her cheek. He must have been looking down at her, but she didn't want to open her eyes to check.

"No," his mouth brushed over her jaw, "stay."

Remi felt him relax and put his head on the pillow behind hers. "I like seeing you here when I step out of the cage." His mouth moved over her neck.

She sighed. It felt good.

"I knew you were here." His lips brushed over her skin again. "Even under the thrall of the moon, I could sense you on the other side of the door."

Turning onto her back, she opened her eyes and looked at him. His hair was damp; he must have had a shower when he woke up. "I hope it didn't bother you."

He pulled her so she was against his body again. "No, I liked knowing you were close. Safe."

With each breath she inhaled, all she could smell was him. Even with a shower, that scent that was pure Darien was still strong. Turning into the warmth, she moved closer to his chest and relaxed in his arms.

"What fun did I miss last night?"

She could feel the rumbling in his chest against her cheek as he spoke softly. "Stripping, wrestling, crying faeries, almost sex in the bathroom…"

He chuckled. "Do I want to know who?"

Rubbing her face against the softness of his chest, she smiled. "I didn't know them. Thank the gods for that." His warm hand began moving in slow circles, caressing her back.

"Rem," he breathed into her hair as he shifted and moved her closer, "I want you to think about us." His bare leg moved between hers as he pulled her tighter into his body.

It felt so right, even though her brain told her no. They had to run Serenity together. "Dare, you're one of the most important people in my life." Knowing she should be moving away and getting up, she was clinging to the feeling of being close after too long being alone. Sliding her hand down his chest, she rested it against his waist. "Without you, Serenity…"

He cupped her chin and tipped her head back, holding his thumb over her lips so she couldn't finish what she was saying. "We could have more than just Serenity." Sliding his thumb off her mouth, he leaned down and brushed his lips over hers.

She took a shaky breath, trying to find the words as he did it again, lingering longer this time. When he kissed her, she always forgot why it was a bad idea to go beyond what they had. Her head told her to move away that the sleepy haze contributing to the slow, simmering heat building inside. Instead of slipping out of the bed, she moved closer and tilted her head back, giving him better access to her mouth.

Darien didn't waste time before his mouth covered hers, erasing all her thoughts as he did. With a quiet growl, he shifted her hips so she was completely against him. His kiss grew more demanding, making her head swim with lust. Tearing his mouth from hers, he looked into her eyes. Yellow eyes searched hers.

"Why do your eyes go yellow when you kiss me?" Her voice was breathless.

His eyes flicked to her mouth and then back to hers. "My wolf wants you." Leaning down, he nipped her jaw with sharp teeth; it sent shivers of need through her. "*I* want you, *A ghrá.*" Reaching to grasp her leg above the knee, he jerked her against him. There was no mistaking his arousal pushing against the dampness between her legs. A wave of heat went through her. She tried to find a reason to move away, even as her arms wrapped around his neck and her fingers burrowed into his hair, his mouth working its way up her jaw back to her lips.

He rolled to pin her beneath him, kissing her with such passion she was sure she'd ignite at any second. A rumbling growl sent a rush of heat to her groin, and she forgot all the reasons they shouldn't do this. It felt so hot, so out of control, and all they'd done was kiss.

Darien tore his mouth from hers, and she gasped, trying to drag air back into her lungs as his teeth traced along her throat. Wrapping her legs around his waist, she realized that there was only thin material between their heated flesh.

Rocking his hips into her, he groaned. "I can feel your need," he growled against her neck, "smell how wet you are." Reaching between them, he jerked her t-shirt up so their bare skin was touching.

The feel of his weight on her, his flesh burning hers, made her gasp. This was Darien… Her thoughts shattered as he reached underneath her and lifted her hips into his body. The friction of his hard erection against her swollen flesh made her moan. All she could think was that she'd never been this close, this ready in her life. She'd always thought she was a slow-building lover, needing the attention of foreplay to reach any completion, and Darien had her on the edge with a few kisses and grinding.

With each motion of his hips, breathless mewling noises came out of her mouth. She didn't want it to end. His lips crushed hers, his teeth scraping along her tongue, and need crashed through her. With a growl, he lifted his head, and she felt sharp claws trailing along her waist, causing the muscles of her womb to clench. She heard fabric tearing and realized he'd just cut her underwear off her body…and she didn't care.

With a whimper, she stretched up and bit the hard cords of muscle in his neck. He groaned and shifted on top of her with jerky movements. "Can't stop," he growled and crushed her mouth again as he pushed inside her with one powerful stroke. Remi moaned into his mouth as he filled her completely. It felt so good. She gripped his hips with her knees, biting his tongue as he rocked gently against her allowing her body to adjust to his size. She'd never been stretched like this before.

Tearing his mouth away, he lifted his head and looked down at her; his eyes were yellow, sending a jolt of excitement through her. Reaching down, he gripped her hips and slowly pulled out; her muscles tightened his length, not wanting him to leave her. With his jaw clenched, he thrust into her as her whole body quivered in response. She whined as he released her hips and took an arm, stretching it over her head. With a soft growl, he did the same with the other and held them in one of his strong hands. Pulling out of her gently, he reached under her and lifted her hips before plunging back into her with a force that shifted her up the bed.

She couldn't move as he began to pound into her, taking her breath away each time their bodies collided. Remi was spiraling out of control and was utterly helpless as he rode her. Lifting her hips further off the bed, he leaned down and gently bit one nipple. She cried out and crashed over the edge into a powerful orgasm that tightened every muscle in her body. Darien continued to thrust into her as she gasped and moaned, trying to catch her breath.

With the whole room spinning, she fought to catch her breath. He released her hands, letting her body drop back to the bed, but didn't stop thrusting into her. Before she could do anything, her body began to climb again, her muscles clenching tight, milking him. Grasping her hair, he covered her mouth and kissed her with desperation, shortening his thrusts and rocking into her tender flesh.

Another orgasm exploded through her, and she moaned into his mouth, her hands clinging to his shoulders. Darien released her mouth and slammed into her, his body tensing as he groaned through his own completion. She couldn't find enough air to speak. Her whole body was quivering; her head felt too light as he kept rocking into her, causing wave after wave of spasms to course through her.

The only sound in the room was their panting, trying to bring enough oxygen back into their lungs. Remi tried to gather her thoughts, but she couldn't focus. Darien shifted, taking some of his weight off her.

Her phone blared out, breaking the silence. She tensed and

looked over at it. Resting one hand on his chest, she reached over and picked it up. It was the café's number. Not knowing what time it was, she answered it with a breathless hello.

"Sorry to wake you," It was Berk. "Kyran just hammered on the door and scared the *hell* out of me." She could hear him talking in the background. "You need to come up here. Now."

Berk's tone cleared the fog from her brain immediately. "Give me five," she gasped into the phone and hung up. Darien looked down at her, his eyes still streaked with yellow. "Something's wrong." A look of sadness filled his eyes as he moved and pulled out of her body. Without a word, he moved off to sit on the edge of the bed.

Pulling her shirt down, she sat up and took a deep breath. She saw her torn underwear, and the air left her lungs all at once. Scrambling off the opposite side of the bed, she stood up with shaky legs and weak knees. Darien stood up on the other side, reaching down and picking her jeans up off the floor. He held them up, giving her no choice but to walk around the bed and face him.

With shaking hands, she took them and turned to pull them on. She'd have to go up to her room and change, but right now, she had to go see what was going on. Darien came up behind her, holding out her bra. With flushed cheeks, she put it on under her shirt and pulled the straps out of the sleeves to get her arms through them. Running her hands through her hair, she combed it back from her face and hoped she didn't look like she'd just had earth-shattering sex with Darien.

"Hey," he gripped her arm gently and made her turn to face him. His eyes were chocolate brown again, and searched hers. "Don't you *dare* regret what just happened."

She opened her mouth to deny it but couldn't say the words.

"I mean it, Remi." He pulled her into his arms and held her there. She realized he was dressed already and wondered how long she'd been standing there, lost in her own thoughts.

"I didn't plan it to happen like that, but it wasn't a mistake." He dropped a firm kiss on her lips and then released her. Going over to the door, he picked up her boots and brought them to her. "We'll talk about it later."

Taking her boots, she looked up at him. There was a vulnerability in his eyes she'd never seen before, and it made her heart jerk. She'd had sex with him *and* broke her number one rule, but it was still Darien. "Okay," she whispered and nodded briefly.

He watched her put her boots on and then pulled her back to her feet, grasping her chin lightly and forcing her to hold his gaze. When he winked and smiled as he released her, it was the last thing she'd expected. Sighing, she gave him a small smile. "Let's go see what's going on."

20

Stepping into the kitchen, Remi stopped and watched Berk mumbling under his breath as he peeled potatoes. Usually, he was humming and brighter than anyone should be at this time of day.

Darien brushed by her and went over to the coffee pot.

Berk lifted his head and gave her an exasperated look. "He's lucky I didn't *bite* him," he waved the paring knife in the air, "pounding on the door like some lunatic before the sun's up." He cut the potato with jerky movements, letting it drop into the bowl. "I don't know what he wants, but I had to step away before I hurt him," he stiffened before looking at her, his eyes moving up and down her slowly. Raising one eyebrow, he glanced at Darien getting coffee and then exhaled loudly. "If Kyran expects breakfast today, he'll be cooking it himself." He growled. "Especially now that I know he not only ruined my chi for the day but interrupted other things as well."

Remi felt her cheeks flush.

Darien handed her a cup of coffee while looking over at Berk; he smirked before lifting his own cup to take a sip. "We'll tell him, Berk."

Berk made a sound of annoyance and glanced at Darien out of the corner of his eye. "You do that."

Going out into the café, Remi sent Kyran a hesitant look.

He sighed loudly. "I think I pissed off your cook." He grimaced. "He threatened to give me a colonoscopy with a spatula."

Darien chuckled quietly from behind her. "That's an image I could have done without before breakfast."

Grabbing the coffee pot from behind the counter, Remi set it under the brewer and filled the basket with coffee before turning around. "What's going on?"

Kyran leaned on the counter and looked at her for a few seconds. "They found your accountant."

"Dead?" Darien asked quietly.

Nodding, Kyran rubbed a hand over his face. "Yeah. Same as the others."

Setting her cup down, Remi leaned back against the counter and wrapped her arms around her waist, staring at the floor.

"You didn't come here before dawn just to tell us that," Darien said, moving over to wrap his arm around her shoulder. She looked back at Kyran.

"No. I wanted…"

"Good morning." Pascal appeared in the kitchen door. He raised his eyebrows at Kyran and then moved aside so a tall, dark-haired woman could slip passed him. She looked up at him, her cheeks flushing slightly as she smiled.

No one said a word as he walked her to the door and unlocked it. Stepping aside to avoid the dim light of dawn as she opened it and went outside. Locking the door again, Pascal turned to look at Kyran. "You were saying?"

"Oh, joy, a pre-dawn meeting." Attis came out of the kitchen holding a bottle of blood. "I should stay up more often." He went over and sat beside Kyran. "Judging by the tension rolling off you, I'm guessing you're here for more than coffee."

Kyran nodded. "I came to tell Remi we found the

accountant.”

“Hmm,” Pascal came around behind the counter and went over to the fridge to get some blood, “and he’s dead.” It wasn’t a question. Leaning back while he waited for the microwave, he looked at Remi and then gave Darien an amused look. With a smile that told her he could smell sex on them, he took the bottle out of the microwave and drank without comment.

Attis slid a cup of coffee across the counter to Kyran. He nodded his thanks.

“I wanted to warn you, well, actually, Randell told me to come and warn you that he had to report the deaths to the para council.”

Darien dropped his arm from around her shoulders and went over to stand in front of Kyran. “Why?”

Kyran looked up from his cup. “The tests finally came back on the first few bodies found, and there were traces of magic.”

“Shit.” Darien stepped back and crossed his arms over his chest.

“I don’t understand.” Remi looked from Kyran to Darien.

Sighing, Darien looked up from the floor. “If magic was involved with a death, the para council has to be informed.” He waved a hand at Kyran. “Normal cops don’t stand a chance on their own.”

“So,” Remi stepped over and leaned on the counter, “the para council will be taking over?” She’d only heard of this council. All mentions of it had always been tinged with fear and apprehension.

Kyran nodded.

Attis groaned. “There goes the neighborhood.”

The sound of the bottle hitting the counter made her turn and look at Pascal.

Pascal looked like he blanched, as odd as that was for a vampire. “I respectfully request a leave of absence, Boss?” He looked at her, his eyes wide.

Remi frowned; Pascal never referred to her as boss. She

looked over at Attis, who was close to collapsing as he held in a laugh. Giving Pascal a wary look, she shook her head. "Denied."

His shoulders slumped as he placed his hands on his hips and looked at the floor, and sighed loudly.

"Am I missing something?" She looked at Darien, who raised his hands. He had no idea either.

Attis moved down the counter, attempting to keep his laughing under control. He cleared his throat a few times. "I do believe Pascal's ex is on the Para council."

"More like a stalker," Pascal muttered.

Attis sputtered again, laughing quietly.

Rolling his eyes, Pascal glared at him. "I'm glad you are amused by my suffering, old friend." He waved his hand around with a dramatic flair. "I can't believe I spent *six* decades outrunning her, and now she's coming *here*."

"No means no." Berk quipped on his way by, a grin covering his face.

Pascal snarled in his direction. "No, doesn't work on Elissia, or Elaine, or whatever she calls herself now."

Almost amused by seeing the always-composed Pascal out of sorts, Remi leaned on the bar and shrugged. "Why not?"

"She's *a lot* older than Pascal," Attis started laughing again and waved his hand in apology as he moved down the bar to calm down.

"Really?" Darien smirked and looked at Pascal.

Pascal sighed and gave Darien a pleading look. "You don't understand." He whined. "With her, I discovered *everything* I don't like about sex, and I thought I was open to anything up until that point."

Darien lowered his head, his shoulders shaking gently. Remi knew he was laughing now, and it took all she had to keep a straight face. "There's a killer out there, Pascal. If they can stop them, we don't have a choice." His eyes pleaded with her. "Not to sound like too much like one of the guys here," she paused until all eyes looked at her, "but I guess you'll have to take one for the team." Turning, she picked up her cup and focused on her coffee before she started laughing. Behind her, she could hear the snickers along with Pascal's cursing in several languages if she wasn't mistaken.

"When will they be here?" Clearing his throat after he said it, Darien reached around her for his coffee.

"Tomorrow," Kyran said quietly.

The sound of a door closing had Remi turn. All heads were looking in the direction of the kitchen door, and Pascal was nowhere to be seen.

"Well, he's going to be charming to work with," Attis mumbled as he moved by her. "I'll see you tonight." Whistling softly, he went into the kitchen.

Berk came back from pulling the blinds up. Kyran spun on the stool and looked at him. "I'm sorry for startling you, Berk."

Berk's hazel eyes moved over Kyran, studying him silently, and then he let out a loud sigh. "Don't do it again." He waved a hand toward the kitchen. "Come on, I'll make you breakfast."

Remi watched them leave and then turned to look at Darien. He stood there, his eyes moving over her as he sipped his coffee. Just the way he was looking at her sent a shiver of awareness through her as she remembered his yellow eyes looking down at her earlier. "I should go upstairs and see how many crashed here last night."

Setting the cup down, he closed the distance between them in a second and blocked her from moving from behind the counter. She backed up until the counter was against her back. He moved closer and caged her in, placing a hand on the counter on either side. "It wasn't a mistake," he said softly, "or a fluke." His dark eyes held hers so she couldn't look away from him.

"H-how do you know?" She swallowed, her eyes flicked to his lips and then back to his eyes.

Leaning forward, he spoke quietly beside her ear. "Because I still want you, I'm not even touching you, and you're shaking Remi. I can feel it."

A shiver went through her; she wasn't going to deny it because that would be a lie. "So."

Lifting his head, he grinned down at her. "No regrets, *Álainn*." He brushed his lips over hers once and then again before stepping back.

She stood there for a few seconds and then remembered to breathe. Watching him move back to pick up his coffee, she exhaled slowly. "We are going to have to talk about it."

Taking a sip, he lowered the cup and nodded. "I know." Setting the cup down, he came back over and cupped the back of her head, crushing her mouth with his before she had a chance to react. His lips moved over hers as if he tasted her over and over. With each stroke of his tongue against hers, more heat pooled between her thighs. Then as abruptly as it had begun, he stopped and straightened. "Just not now. I need a nap, and you have to get this place going for the day."

Gripping the front of his shirt to help keep her balance, she nodded and stood, looking up into his dark eyes. He did look tired; with everything that had gone on, she'd forgotten how much the forced change took out of him. "Go get some rest, Darien."

He looked at her mouth again and then inhaled, a lopsided grin appearing on his face. "If you don't want every para with a heightened sense of smell to know what we were doing, you might want to fit a quick shower into your morning." Chuckling, he stepped back and winked at her. "You reek of sex, *A ghrá*."

Her cheeks heated. "Go." She watched him leave and then fanned her face, huffing out a breath to calm down.

Berk leaned his head out the door and grinned at her. "It's about damn time," he whispered, "and I want details ASAP." He winked and then ducked back into the kitchen.

Covering her face, Remi closed her eyes. What had she done? As if things weren't complicated enough in her world right now, she'd just slept with her best friend. Worse than that, she didn't regret it, if her body's reaction was any indication, she'd do it again given the chance. Groaning, she dropped her hands and picked up her coffee.

Four hours later, Remi rested her head on her arms slumped at her desk.

"You want to tell us why you're one breath from a breakdown today?"

Turning her head, she looked at Nadine and Iris standing in the doorway. Nadine raised an eyebrow at her.

"Besides the dead bodies, the para council, and all of us being confined to secure locations around the clock," Iris said with a smirk on her face.

Nadine nodded. "Yeah, after all that." She studied her for a moment. "You look like you're off in space and about to un-tether at any second."

Iris gave Naddy a wide-eyed look.

"Sorry," she shrugged, "hubby has me watching this space program."

"How romantic," Iris purred, her voice heavy with sarcasm.

Sitting up, Remi turned the chair, so she was facing them. "I did something I probably shouldn't have," she frowned, "Okay, I shouldn't have."

"Really?" Iris said with a sarcastic flair in her tone. "Do tell."

"The last time you thought you did something you shouldn't have was when you slept with that hottie shifter who was stranded in town until his car was fixed." Nadine came in and sat on the filing cabinet. "That was almost a year ago now, right after asshat."

Iris nodded. "Who did you sleep with this time?"

Remi looked from Iris's animated expression to Nadine's expectant one and groaned. "Darien."

"Yes. Finally." Iris pumped her fist in the air. "I swear it was getting pretty sad watching him follow you around with his tail between his legs. If you…"

Nadine kicked her foot to stop her. "When? It was the full moon last night."

"This morning." Remi slumped down further in the chair. "I slept in his bed so the girls could have mine last night..."

"Does this mean we don't have to tippy-toe around now?" Iris asked.

Nadine glared at her.

"What are you talking about?" Remi shook her head and looked from one to the other.

"Ignore her," Nadine said firmly. "There's nothing wrong with what happened, Rem..."

Remi sat forward. "We *work* together. My number one rule is..."

"We know all about *your* rule, boss lady, and it's silly. I've seen the way he grabs you and kisses you." She snorted. "I don't know how you're not a puddle at his feet when he does that." Iris crossed her arms and leaned against the doorframe.

Nadine turned her soft blue eyes on Remi. "What did Darien say?"

Leaning back in the chair, she looked up at the ceiling. "That it wasn't a mistake, but Kyran showed up with the news about the accountant and the council, so we didn't get a chance to discuss it."

Deanne came around the corner behind Iris. "Can one of you give us a hand? A large group just came through the door."

Nadine and Remi both looked at Iris, and she sighed. "Fine, I'm coming." Shoving away from the frame, she waited for Deanne to leave. "If you ask me, I say ride *that* body as often as possible." She gave Remi a cheeky smile, "Because there is nothing *bad* about it."

Remi's mind went to places she had been struggling all morning to control. Places that involved Darien, his body, and hers.

"She does have a way with words," Nadine said with a smirk after she left.

"I'm worried, Naddy. I think Darien has really been struggling with his wolf lately, and I'm not sure what to do."

Remi watched Nadine sigh silently and then study the floor

for several seconds. "The only difficulty Darien has with his controlling his wolf has to do with you, Remi." She sighed loudly this time, "And you need to sit him down, tie him if you have to, and get him to talk." She stood up. "It's long overdue. Trust me."

That feeling of missing something hit Remi again. "I constantly feel like I missed a memo around here lately."

Nadine nodded and stood there looking at her for a moment. "Darien has the answers for that too."

"Wonderful." Remi turned and flipped on the computer so she could do the paperwork she'd come back to finish. "Then I guess Wolfman and I are going to have to have a long chat."

"Don't let him off easy, Rem. He's been a *very* bad wolf." Nadine smirked at her and left the office.

21

Sliding the curtain closed, Darien turned and went over to the bed. *Why the hell am I still awake?* After last night, and this morning he should be passed out, oblivious to the world around him. He should want to be unaware, just a short reprieve from reality.

Could things possibly get any more fucked up than they were? The staff were all paranoid and would be getting cranky if the restrictions to not traveling alone weren't ended soon. Once they got through the aftermath of the full moon, Darien wanted to talk to Remi about letting some of the staff take some time off. He didn't know if that would keep them safe, but he thought giving them an option would be good. All of it was for their safety, they all knew that, but not many in the para world liked confinement. With another body being found that involved someone from their world only made it worse. If it had been some normal human with a grudge that would almost be acceptable because the gods knew *that* happened more often.

Dropping down onto the bed, he let out a deep sigh. His whole room smelled of Remi. Of their scents mixed, of sex, Remi…

Inhaling deeply, he closed his eyes. His wolf was pacing inside him. He wasn't at all happy that Darien had mated Remi but hadn't marked her. It was the typical archaic were thought process, one Darien didn't agree with. It had been hard, the desire to not sink his fangs into her flesh and mark her as his had taken a lot of control, but he did it and would until she knowingly consented. Fifty years ago, that would have been unheard of. If a were found their mate, they claimed them, consent or not. He tried to imagine what Remi would have done back then. Grimacing, he knew the answer. He'd be gutted by her hand. One of the many reasons he was a lone wolf, not tied to the laws of the pack. Sure, some clans thought in more modern terms, but his hadn't been one of them. His own sister had been claimed without any consideration. She said she was happy with her mate, but there had always been something in her eyes that told him it was a lie.

Taking a deep breath, he tried to let some of the tension ease away. Remi's scent filled his system again. Opening his eyes, he glared up at the ceiling. Finally being with her after all the years had been…he didn't know how to describe it. He had been engulfed with need. After years of picturing how it would be when they were finally together, he'd been so consumed he couldn't have gone slowly if his life depended on it. The way her body responded to him broke his control and he thought he was going to go up in flames if he didn't have her right then. When he started, he thought she would stop him, but she didn't. By the time he realized it had actually happened, the damn phone rang and it ended before he could talk to her.

He had to tell her, there was no choice. Holding off his wolf was harder than ever now. With the council coming, things were going to get even more unpredictable. He knew who was on the council, and he was dreading that almost as much as Pascal was. His uncle had been selected to be on the para council forty years ago. It was a great honor to serve the community that way, or so he was told. Given the option,

Darien knew he'd pass on taking something like that. It wasn't that he wasn't for the community or justice, he just didn't agree with most of their methods. The only good side to them coming is the killer would be found and stopped from hurting anyone else. The bad meant he was going to be reminded of his clan and the way he *should* be living, according to his uncle. Maybe he and Pascal should make a pact to watch each other's back throughout this visit. In all the years he'd known Pascal he'd never seen fear in his eyes, until this morning. Whoever this woman was from his past, she had done what Darien always thought was impossible.

Flipping on his side, he stared at the door. He needed to get some sleep, yet all he wanted to do was go back to be near Remi. Snorting, he closed his eyes, all he wanted was not give her time to think about what had happened and regret it. If she did, he had no idea what he was going to do. The very thought of having to leave Remi left him with an ache inside his chest. He'd always known it was a possibility if she denied him, which is why he refused Doyle's offer to own half of Serenity but knowing and living with it were two totally different things.

22

When Darien finally returned from his nap, it was during the busy rush period of the afternoon. Remi was stuck in the kitchen helping Soren keep up with the orders. While the bar was usually pandemonium on the full moon, the café was chaos the next day. Remi often thought those people that swore the moon didn't affect anything were idiots that probably never left their house, lab, or wherever. She damn well knew the cycle of the moon messed with everything and everyone in one way or another.

Darien came through the door carrying another tray of dirty dishes. She glanced away from the salad she was making and watched him place it beside the dishwasher. He looked over and winked at her.

"I'll give you a hand getting the dishes done when it settles down out there."

She watched him walk back out again.

"Our wolfman seems pretty spunky today," Soren said softly in her purring voice. She took the salad from Remi's hands and set the plate in the window with the other two sitting there. Ringing the bell, she turned and grinned at her. "It's nice seeing him happy." She pulled the next ticket off and looked at it before putting it back up. "Two more house salads, one without tomato, both with ranch on the side." Humming, she turned around and went over to the grill.

Remi pulled two plates off the shelf and set them on the cutting table. She began to cut more lettuce.

Cait came out of the back room with a case of juice. "We're going to have to up the juice order. We're going through it really quickly lately." She swung through the door, letting it swing after she was out of the way.

Remi made a mental note to go over the order and adjust what wasn't selling if the juice was going faster.

"Can you add green onions to the produce order next week?" Soren asked her. "Berk and I were thinking of trying a new soup and it will be better with green onions."

"Sure." Remi put the lettuce on the plate and flipped the lid up on the salad bar to get the other ingredients. "I've been debating on cherry tomatoes for the salads too, just to give them a new look."

"Oh," Soren turned from the grill and nodded, "that would be nice." She gave her a smile and turned back to what she was doing.

Through the order window, a cup of coffee appeared. Remi smiled and watched Darien walk by with a grin on his face. Sighing, she pulled the cup down, took a sip, and then set it beside the salad table.

Caitlyn came back in and stood at the door. "So, with the council coming tomorrow, how is that going to affect things around here?"

Remi finished the salads and set them on the ledge. "I don't know. I've only heard about them, never had anything to do with them before."

She winced. "I've heard a lot of scary things about them."

Soren glanced at her. "They're only scary if you're the one they're looking for."

Cait gave Remi a look full of apprehension. "Let's hope so." She sighed. "I just want things to get back to normal around here."

"Cait, can you go get me some more oil out of the back?" Soren asked as she looked on the shelf beside the dish rack.

Remi wiped her hands on the kitchen towel and tossed it on the counter. "I'll go. I want to grab the order book."

Cait went to the sink. "I'll get started on some of these dishes."

Picking up her cup, Remi went into the back. As she rounded the corner, she stopped. Darien and Nadine were standing by the supply room door, faces close, talking quietly. Remi didn't need to hear what was being said to know that Nadine was upset, her face was flushed.

"What's going on?" She stood in the doorway and watched them jump.

Nadine huffed out a breath. "Just banging my head against the *same* wall as always." She glared at Darien and then spun on her heel and went into the office, closing the door completely.

Eyebrows raised; Remi turned from looking at the closed door to Darien. He stood there, hands on hips. the expression on his face showing he was almost as pissed off as Nadine seemed to be. "What was that about?"

Taking a deep breath, his chest rising, he exhaled loudly. Lifting his hands, he let them drop and slap on his hips again.

"Don't say *nothing*, Darien, because something has been going on around here for a while now and I'm sick of playing these guessing games."

He looked at her, several emotions going through his eyes before he closed them and shook his head.

"Just let me get the oil for Soren and I'll be right back." She went into the storeroom and grabbed a bottle of vegetable oil and headed back to the kitchen. Setting it on the counter, she looked at Caitlyn. "If you guys need a hand, Naddy is in the office. I'll be back shortly." Without waiting for a reply, she went to find Darien, but he hadn't moved from where she left him. She motioned for him to go up to her apartment.

With a sigh, he turned and went over to the door.

They went up the stairs in silence. He followed her into the living room and still didn't say a word when she walked to the middle, turning around to look at him. "What's going on, Darien? I feel like there's some big secret that everyone knows but me." She shrugged. "I know I'm only the measly normal around here, but I..."

He growled and closed the space between them. "You're no more normal than I am a goldfish."

She blinked up at him. "Interesting comparison."

"You know what I mean." He grasped her chin lightly. "You're not *just* a normal and you know it."

Squinting at him, she pulled her head back, freeing her chin. "Oh? Then what am I?"

"You're *my* mate, that's what you are." He flung a hand in the air. "*That's* the big secret that everyone has been nagging at me about."

Remi stepped back so quickly, she hit the coffee table and wobbled until she had her balance.

"Shit." Darien reached and took her arm to steady her. "That is not how I planned to tell you."

Opening her mouth, she closed it again with a snap, her teeth clacking together. Pulling away from his hand, she moved over and dropped down to sit on the couch before her legs gave out completely.

"Remi..." He came over and sat on the table in front of her.

"How," she cleared her throat, "how did you plan to tell me? How long have you known?" Her brain wouldn't focus on one complete thought.

"I planned to tell you soon," he leaned on his knees and looked at her, his eyes moving all over her face, "and then this morning..." he shook his head. "I didn't plan for that..."

Squeezing her eyes shut, she took a deep breath and then looked at him again. "You didn't mark me." She frowned. "I didn't think it was possible for mates to be together like that without..."

"It wasn't easy." He reached and brushed the hair back

from her face that had fallen out of her braid during the hectic day.

"How long have you known, Darien?"

He exhaled, leaning back. Shaking his head, he stood up and paced across the room. "Pretty close to that first day you walked in the door."

Remi knew she was sitting there with her mouth hanging open but couldn't move a muscle.

"For that first year, I was drawn to you, but it set off my wolf, which made me wary and uncomfortable. I knew something was up but didn't clue in right away." He turned and looked back at her, his whole body tense.

Remi finally forced her mouth to close and sat there frozen staring at him.

"Then I suspected," his voice was quiet, hesitant, "so I spent every moment I could with you, wanting to be sure." He shrugged. "And got attached to you even *more*." Coming back toward her, he slowly sat down on the table, his brown eyes moving over her face looking for something. "Doyle warned me off, saying you were too young, so I had to bide my time and fight my instincts to be close to you without," he smirked, "being *close* to you."

Leaning forward, he captured her hands and held them in his. "When Doyle died, you were devastated and mourning, and then your gifts appeared and there was that adjustment to deal with." His thumb stroked over her hand in a gentle caress. "Next thing I know, you're hooked up with Randell and you seemed happy." He looked down at their hands. "I couldn't take your happiness away even if I was in pain and miserable." Lifting his long lashes, he looked at her for a moment. "For the last year, I've thought about it above all else, to the point I think and breathe only you…" He took a deep breath and let it out slowly, "But every time I see you look at *him*, I see the grief from the loss of what you thought was your *normal* happiness." He dropped down off the table and kneeled in front of her. "I'm not normal, you'd never have normal with me, Remi." Releasing her hands, he reached out and brushed his fingers slowly down her cheek.

She sucked in a breath from the tenderness of the movement.

Darien gave her a weak smile. "Normal doesn't involve locking your partner in a cage once a month." Placing a hand on either side of her on the couch, he watched her and continued to talk softly. "So, I spend my every waking moment of each day watching over you, helping you, comforting you, and keeping you safe as much as possible."

His eyes stared at her mouth and Remi's breath caught in her throat.

"When all I want to do is hold and claim you." He took a deep breath and got up, moving to stand by the window. "After this morning, it will kill me if you're with another man, Rem and that's not fair to you."

She watched his shoulders rise and fall as he took several deep breaths.

"It's getting harder each day to keep my wolf at bay, to stop every time I'm near you." He made a strangled sound. "Of course, I'm a sucker for punishment and can't stay away." Turning, he placed his hands in his pockets and looked back at her. "Nadine has been making me one of her magic potions for years. The potion barely works now, even with the increasing the strength and using it more frequently..." Heaving a sigh, he moved back toward her with his predatory grace. "I'm not telling you this to make you feel bad or put you on the spot." He shrugged. "I've put it off as long as I can." He gave her a soft smile. "You're only twenty-five," dropping his hands on his hips he shook his head and mumbled, "way too young for me."

Remi waited and he didn't say anything else, he continued to stand there looking at the floor. "So, what now?"

Darien lifted his head slowly and looked at her. He shook his head, an unsure expression on his face. "You're my mate, *Álainn* and there will never be another for me. Ever."

Remi blinked and watched him. Several emotions went through his eyes.

"I refuse to take away your choices." A soft rumbling noise came from his chest. "There's a lot more than the mindless killing that I don't agree with from my clan." He lifted his hands in a move of frustration. "If I don't claim you, I'll have to watch you grow old and eventually die. If I do claim you, then I may lose you anyway. Wolves are very possessive and dominating. Two things I know you won't tolerate."

"I don't know what to say, Darien." It took a lot to shock her, with some of the things she'd seen before she'd always managed her way through, but this had her completely at a loss.

Shaking his head, he lifted his eyes and studied her for several long moments. "I don't know either." He shrugged. "I've been in knots over it for years now. The staff, our friends, have all been running interference for me." Sighing, he rubbed the back of his neck. "Everyone agreed with Doyle at first, that you were too young." Dropping his hand down to slap on his leg, he gave her a lopsided grin that didn't reach his eyes. "That's the big secret you've been sensing."

"It's a pretty *big*, life-changing secret." She sat back, hugging the cushion off the couch into her chest.

"I know and for what it's worth, I'm sorry."

Eyes wide she stared at him. "It's not like you can prevent it from happening, it's part of who you are…"

"You mean *what* I am."

She shrugged. "Whatever. I don't have a problem with what or who you are, Darien, so you shouldn't hold it against you either."

He smirked and then sobered. "This morning…"

Remi held up a hand. "Don't go distracting me with sex talk, there's a lot more going on here than just sex."

"I know." He continued to stand there looking down at her, the expression in his eyes not telling her anything.

"You're very important to me, Dare." She waved a hand around, "Before the sex, before this mate stuff, you have always been my rock and a very important part of my world."

"You're my weakness," he whispered, "and my greatest

strength, *Álainn*."

Nodding, she swallowed the lump in her throat. She wanted to scream, to cry to yell. This was so unfair. Fate could get stuffed for tossing this at her. Her whole world included Darien, but she didn't know if she wanted to be mated happily ever after right now, or ever. It was so much more than a piece of paper and a ring that normals believed were binding. Mating in any of the para cultures was more permanent than stone.

Blinking, she dragged her mind from her thoughts and looked back at the man standing, predator still, in front of her. He hadn't moved, she doubted he had so much as taken a breath while she sat there trying to digest everything he'd just told her. "I'm sorry," she said quietly, "this is huge and is going to take me a little time to process."

He nodded. "It doesn't have to change anything between us right now…"

Remi laughed and shook her head. "It changes *everything*, Darien." She tossed the cushion on the couch and stood up, suddenly feeling restless. "You can't just tell me that then expect me to shrug and go back down to do the dishes."

He gave her an exasperated look. "I didn't mean it like that."

There was a soft growl in his voice making her stop and study him. "This explains the growling lately."

Darien shrugged and lifted his arms in a move of acceptance. "I curb it as much as I can."

If it had been anyone but him that had dumped all of this on her, she would have shooed them away so she could think, but seeing him standing there, pain and anxiety on his face, made her heart ache. He'd always been there for her, for whatever she needed. If she needed to yell, he gave her the fuel and yelled back. When she needed to cry, he held her and soothed her until the tears stopped. If she needed to laugh, he'd made her sides ache from laughing too hard.

Closing her eyes, she took a deep breath and then opened them and looked at him. He still hadn't moved an inch, just stood there tense and silent. "Well, fuck." Moving over, she stopped in front of him and shook her head. "It couldn't just be good sex with us could it?" Leaning closer, she wrapped her arms around his waist and hugged him, resting her head on his chest. She closed her eyes in relief when his strong arms wrapped around her.

"Just good?" His voice was strained.

Grinning, she leaned back and looked up at him. "Okay, explosive." She blew out a breath and then rested her head against his chest again. "I don't know what to do with all of this, Dare, so please give me a bit of time."

Darien squeezed her tight in his arms. "I wasn't even planning on telling you yet." He kissed the top of her head. "I was hoping for some more explosive sex first."

Lifting her head, she gave him a wide-eyed look.

He smirked. "I'm kidding, sort of." His eyes flicked to her lips and then back to her eyes. "With the killings and threats, I think you have more than enough on your plate to handle for now."

"I had actually forgotten for a few wonderful minutes." Biting her lip, she looked back at him. "It's not good that the council is coming, is it?"

Slowly his eyes moved away from her mouth to her eyes. "No, it's not. They're intrusive. They believe nothing is private, it's all their business…"

"You've dealt with them before?"

"Some of them."

She gave him a look of curiosity.

He shook his head. "It was a long time ago." His hand began caressing her back as if he could sense her stress.

"Are they going to be okay dealing with me?"

A low growl came from deep in his chest. "They don't have a choice. Doyle chose to pass Serenity on to you; they have no say." His arms tightened. "It's not like they can revoke the gift. Serenity *is* you." Giving her a reassuring smile, his arms loosened a bit. "Not to worry, if they mess with you, they'll have to deal with me…" his eyes flashed yellow, "and Pascal, and Attis, Finn, and gods forbid, if we have to we'll sick Iris and Vienna on them."

Remi laughed. "I think I'm more frightened for them with the girls than all of you men."

"Hey," he pouted, "don't be like that." The playful look faded from his eyes. "We're good for now?"

Taking a deep breath, she thought about how she was feeling inside. "I'm still a little freaked out, but I think we'll get through it."

The large body in her arms relaxed. Grasping her chin, he tilted her head, so she was looking in his eyes. "Telling you was the scariest thing I have *ever* done in my life." His eyes held hers with such tenderness she couldn't have looked away, even if she'd wanted to. "I should also tell you that I don't plan on making it easy for you to forget."

Eyebrows furrowed and questioning, she searched his face. "Forget?"

"This." Still holding her chin, he lowered his mouth to hers and tasted her lips slowly, savoring them.

Remi's eyes closed as the feeling moved through her. Hard kiss, soft kiss, passionate kiss it didn't matter; the man could melt a glacier with his lips. When he lifted his head, she opened her eyes slowly to look at his hooded ones. "So, you plan on cheating?" She asked slightly out of breath.

Grinning, he dropped a quick kiss on her mouth and then released her. "Damn right, I do." Backing away from her, the smirk still on his mouth he winked. "I'm going down to rustle us up some food." He wiggled his eyebrows. "It's the second night of the full moon."

Shoulders drooping, Remi sighed. "I can't believe I forgot that, too."

"Tsk tsk, where is your mind at, Ms. Foster?"

Baring her teeth at him, she watched him smile wider. "Go away, wolfman, I'm going to soak in the tub and prepare my weary body for pandemonium, the sequel."

With a chuckle, he turned and walked out of the room.

Grasping her head between both hands she sighed loudly.

"A killer, a council, *and* a mate." She groaned. "It's like a bad joke." Dropping her hands, she kicked off her boots. "*This* is my life."

23

Quickly checking the IDs, Darien nodded and let the couple pass. Out of the corner of his eye, he watched Remi drag Berk back into the middle of the dance floor. The young wolf didn't look all that happy to be dancing for what was probably the fifteenth dance. Glancing over at the bar, he waited until Pascal looked over. Lifting his hands, he sent the vampire a 'what gives' look. He'd been making Remi drinks for the last two hours and she'd been slamming them back, one right after the other. Pascal gave him a helpless look, he may be an old vampire, but Remi *was* the boss.

Shaking his head, he turned to watch her again. Watching her dance was a form of torture for him. He wanted to go out on the floor and drag her against his body or pick her up and carry her upstairs. It wasn't right that every move she made jolted awareness straight to his groin. Clenching his jaw, he looked around the bar, he wasn't the only male that noticed how she moved—more than once he had to glare at Finn when he paused to observe her.

Emery walked by with a tray of drinks and gave Darien a worried look. None of them were used to Remi drinking. One drink was usually where she stopped. The only staff that

183

didn't seem concerned were Elise and Vienna, and he didn't know why.

Turning when the door opened, he nodded to the two regulars that were walking in. The song ended and he almost sighed in relief when Berk grabbed her arm and pulled her off the dance floor. The young wolf sent him a quick look that Darien wasn't sure if was pleading mercy and asking for help, or if Darien was going to owe him for trying to keep her out of trouble.

Pascal leaned down and handed her another drink, sending him a quick, apologetic look.

"She needs to blow off some steam, Darien."

He briefly looked at Vienna beside him. "I've never seen her drink this much before." He rubbed his jaw and looked around the bar checking that everyone was behaving.

"A lot has happened in the last week that's never happened before." She rearranged the glasses on her tray. Not waiting for him to reply, she moved through the crowd to deliver an order.

Sighing, he rolled his shoulders and fought to keep his feet planted where they were. He, more than most, understood the need to have a few stiff drinks to blur reality, but he couldn't help feeling it was his fault that she was going overboard. Until he'd told her they were mates, she'd been pretty good at keeping her head up and taking everything on the chin.

Checking to make sure they were still sitting at the bar, he watched her laugh and Berk grin. Berk was damn lucky he was gay, or Darien wouldn't be able to tolerate their closeness. Even with the young wolf's sexual orientation, he still felt twinges of jealousy watching them dance and sit close to each other.

Before he could look away, Remi turned and looked right at him. There was a look on her face he couldn't decipher from where he stood. Finn came over, guiding a customer to the door. With a nod, Darien opened the door and gently nudged them to walk out on their own accord. Closing the door, he turned around to see Remi lean closer to Berk and say something. With a grin on his face, Berk nodded and then toasted in his direction. Frowning, he glanced around again. At least the crowd was calmer tonight, he didn't know how well he'd manage any troublemakers considering the mood he was in.

The group in the corner was suspiciously quiet tonight, which he thought was odd, considering he usually had to issue more than one warning glare each time they were here. He glanced around. For the second night of the moon, it was too quiet. Suspecting the news of the murders and the pending arrival of the council causing his unusually quiet night, he crossed his arms and took his regular stance beside the door.

He's never had this much trouble focusing on his job. Before he could think, he caught himself looking back over in the direction of where she sat. When she jumped up and grabbed Finn's arm, he had to bite back a growl. *Shit.* Finn glanced over his shoulder at him. Turning, he caught Emery's attention and motioned him over. Nodding, he came over. "Watch the door."

With long strides, he went over and leaned on the bar, getting Pascal's attention.

Pascal glided down and lowered his head.

"What is she drinking?" He glanced down at her again.

"Lady's choice." Pascal nodded to a customer to acknowledge them.

"What's that?" Darien watched Finn walk away from her.

"A watered-down version of a python."

Straightening, Darien looked at him. "How many has she had?"

Lifting his arms, Pascal looked down toward her again. "I didn't know I needed to count how many." Leaning closer, he looked right at him. "She needs to let her hair down tonight. It's been a hell of a week for her."

Sighing, Darien shook his head and started to walk in her direction. He needed her to go upstairs so other males couldn't see her, so he could do his job. When he was a few feet away from her, she grinned and then sprung at him, wrapping her arms around his neck. He wanted to pick her up and carry her upstairs, and if he didn't keep his distance, he'd be doing just that. Gripping her waist, he couldn't help but fall into hers.

24

Setting her empty glass on the counter, Remi spun the stool and looked around. Nothing made her happier than seeing a sea of people dancing and having fun. She closed her eyes and listened to the song for a minute and then decided she didn't know it, but it still had a great beat. Turning back around, she leaned over and grinned at Berk. "You," she pointed at him, "should dance with me."

Berk raised his eyebrows and glared at her. "If we dance anymore, we won't be able to move tomorrow." He tipped his glass at her. "Remember we decided we were done dancing for the night."

"Right." Picking up her glass, she looked in it to see it was still empty. Frowning, she waved it in Pascal's direction. He nodded and turned to make her another drink. Sighing, she pushed the empty glass down the counter and turned back to Berk. "Why are you here after dark, Berk?"

Grinning, he leaned closer to her. "Soren agreed to do the early shift tomorrow so I could come out and play for a change."

"Soren is such a sweetie."

"Yes, she is." He laughed. "I will thank her a thousand

times because when I had the idea to come and hang out here, I didn't know I'd be babysitting my drunk boss."

Remi's mouth dropped open. "I am not drunk."

Pascal leaned down on the bar and slid a full glass in front of her. "Your drink, my lady." He winked. "On the house, of course."

Remi laughed. "It better be. It's *my* house."

"So it is." He grinned at Berk and then straightened up and moved in the other direction.

Remi took a sip and closed her eyes. Opening them she looked at Berk. "You should try one of these. It's a new drink Attis and Pascal created."

Berk lifted his glass. "I have been." He lowered the glass. "Although I think you're drinking four to my one."

Taking another drink, she laughed. "Well, you do have to work tomorrow."

He nodded and grinned at her. "So do you." Leaning closer, he rested his chin on his hand. "I can't believe how much you're drinking. I don't think I've ever seen you drink more than a few sips before."

Brushing the hair back from her face, Remi leaned down on the bar mimicking what he was doing. "I needed to burn off some stress." She rolled her eyes. "I'm under house arrest, or confined, whatever, because of some sicko out there making people dead," she huffed out a breath, "and after being attacked, I'm not really complaining about the house arrest thing." Berk nodded and let her continue. "I'm just freaked out a whole lot about the council coming tomorrow, so hey," she laughed, "maybe if I drink myself into a coma tonight, they'll give me a pass and let me miss their visit."

Berk leaned back and looked at her. "Don't hold your breath."

"I'm not." She snorted. "I'd pass out if I tried to hold it right now." Taking another drink, she looked around for a few seconds and then gave him a serious look. "I left out the mate stuff." Sighing, she looked at him with wide eyes. "I can't believe I have a *mate*, one that I've been looking at every day for seven years, and he *just* got around to telling me."

Berk nodded. "It's pretty crazy."

"Craazy doesn't even cover it." She turned and looked around for Darien. "He's kinda sexy though, my mate." She watched him coax someone toward the door. Clearly, they'd done something wrong for Darien to be helping them leave.

"Yes," Berk turned his stool to lean against the bar, "he definitely scores high on my sexy meter." He toasted the glass in Darien's direction and took a sip.

Remi rolled her head to the side and smiled at him. "I think it's pretty awesome that you're gay."

Berk spit his drink back into the glass he had raised to his mouth. "Thanks, I think."

Remi sat forward and grabbed his arm. "You know what we should do?" His eyes widened in question. "We should go find you a mate too."

Pascal leaned down so his head was between theirs. "Need a refill yet, Berk?"

Remi grinned at him. Berk shook his head and looked at one of her vampire bartenders. "No. I'm going to need an energy drink if she doesn't slow down."

Pascal laughed.

"Hey," Remi gave him the sternest look she could manage, "no energy drinks for the wolf. Been there, done that, and it wasn't pretty." She turned and grinned at Pascal. "We were just going to go mate shopping for Berk," she glanced at the dance floor. "Have you seen any pretty gay prospects for him?" Frowning, she looked back at Berk. "Or do you prefer manly? I don't know your preference."

Berk's mouth opened, and then he looked at Pascal with his mouth still open.

Pascal patted her shoulder. "I don't think there's anyone here right now that qualifies, but I'll let you know if any come in."

"Good man." Remi turned back to Berk. "We could always go dance instead."

"Pascal, what the hell is in the drinks you're feeding her?"

Berk spun his stool and glared at him.

Pascal straightened up. "Sorry, trade secret." With that, he turned and walked back down the bar.

Turning around, she watched Finn walk by.

"Finn," Remi jumped up and then grabbed his arm when she swayed a little too far from the momentum. "You should dance with me."

Finn raised one eyebrow and looked from her to Berk and then back to her again. "I would, Remi, but my boss doesn't like it if I fraternize when I should be working."

Remi sighed and leaned her head on his shoulder. "The bitch," she laughed and looked up at him, "Berk's too tired to dance anymore."

Finn chuckled. "Well, I don't think he signed up to have the energizer bunny for a partner." He looked over his shoulder and then back at her. "Here comes Darien. Maybe you can persuade him." He winked at her and moved away slowly like he was afraid she was going to tip over.

Remi turned to see Darien leaning over the bar and talking to Pascal; both kept glancing at her. Shaking his head, he straightened up and walked toward her. She loved the way he walked, a powerful stride with that grace all the para animals had. His stride definitely said he was in charge. *Swoon*. When he was only a foot away, she grinned and launched herself at him. Wrapping her arms around his neck, she smiled up at him. "You should dance with me, Dare." He gripped her waist in his strong hands and looked down at her.

"If you dance much more tonight, you're not going to be able to walk tomorrow."

"Thank you," Berk said, sitting back down.

Playing with the hair at the back of his neck, she bounced to the beat of the song playing. "Please?"

Darien tightened the grip on her waist, making it hard for her to move with the music. "I can't, sweetheart. I have to work." He looked over the top of her head to Berk. "Try to keep her sitting for a bit longer; then Finn can take over at the door for me."

"You owe me, big man. This isn't an easy task."

Remi looked over her shoulder at Berk and rolled her eyes. "You don't have to babysit me, Berk. Go home."

He opened his mouth and then looked at Darien.

"Hey," Darien used his finger to turn her head back to look at him. "Berk doesn't get to come hang out often. He should stay."

Remi sighed. "Fine, but he's too tired to dance." She glanced over to see Kyran walking through the crowd in their direction. "Oh, here comes Kyran; maybe he'll dance with me."

Darien growled and started backing her toward the kitchen door. "We'll be right back," he said to Berk over his shoulder.

Once in the kitchen, Remi looked over at Baker.

"Take five," Darien told him.

He still held her waist, and she was in no hurry to let go of him either. The world wasn't spinning, but it was starting to float, and she didn't want to go with it.

Baker looked at Remi and grinned. "No problem." He danced toward them. "You've got some nice moves on you, Boss lady."

Remi chuckled. "Thanks. I wore out your brother though."

Baker looked from her to Darien, and then his facial expression sobered. "Well, he did work all morning." Moving past them, he went out to the bar.

"So," Remi tilted her head and looked up at Darien, "sure you don't want to dance with me?"

Shaking his head, he smiled. "I didn't say I didn't want to," He leaned down and rested his forehead against hers "After watching you move on the dance floor, I want to do a whole lot." Lifting his head, he backed her up against the wall. "Why are you drinking so much?"

Remi rolled her eyes. "It's not so much." Sighing, she shrugged. "Just unwinding, I think I'm entitled. I can't change forms and go for a run or howl at the moon or whatever," she grinned, "and I want to go dance some more."

Brushing the hair back from her face, he cupped the back of her head and made her look at him. "See, now I'm all for you dancing, even with every male out there staring at your body." He clenched his jaw for a second and then exhaled, "But dancing with other guys," he placed a finger over her mouth before she could say anything, "other guys that *aren't* gay," he sucked in a breath, "*that* I have a problem with right now." He leaned down and kissed the end of her nose. "You know I'm trying to fight all the instincts that go with mates, Remi, but other guys near you," he shrugged, "can't get past it."

A song she really liked came on, and she started moving with the beat, despite being between the wall and his body. She bumped her hips into him and did a bounce, then started to sway. "So, what do you suggest, sexy man? Do I have to stay in the kitchen and dance?" She bumped her hips against him in time to the music. "Hmm?"

Darien gave her a lopsided grin. "Keep the bumping up, and you may get more than dancing."

Remi bit her lip and continued to do it, watching him. "Maybe you should take me upstairs or downstairs..."

A low growl came from deep in his chest. "Baby, don't tempt me."

"I think you should kiss me." She stopped moving and ran her finger over his mouth. "If I'm not allowed to dance, I should be compensated."

"If I kiss you right now, stopping might be a problem." He leaned down and breathed against her mouth.

"I don't see the problem."

Chuckling, he lifted his head away. "*Jesus*, I should have got you drunk years ago." Grasping her waist, he leaned back down beside her ear. "If you can go *sit* with Berk for fifteen minutes, I'll take you upstairs." He nuzzled her neck.

Grasping the back of his head, she held him close to her. "Promise?"

"Promise."

Remi released his hair and sighed. "Fine. Fifteen minutes,

not a second longer, or I'm dancing again."

25

Fifteen minutes turned into forty-five, and Remi kept drinking the whole time. When things finally started to wind down, Darien left the door to Finn and went to rescue Berk, who was starting to lean on the bar more and more.

"Have a good night," Pascal said with a wink as he walked by.

Snarling, Darien kept going without comment and strode toward Remi. She turned in the stool, swayed slightly, but managed to stay upright. She had a smile on her face as she watched him head toward her. He knew why she was smiling. What he didn't know was if he was going to be able to do the right thing and walk away.

Berk lifted his head and then blinked. "Can I go home?" He stood up and sidestepped. "Actually, I think I'm going to crash in one of the empty rooms downstairs."

Darien nodded. "Thanks."

Berk wiped his hand over his brow. "I can't even tell you how happy I am that boss lady doesn't do this often." He turned and took a few steps toward the kitchen, swaying with each one.

Looking down at Remi, he couldn't help but grin at the

194

way she was smiling at him. Holding out his hand, she placed hers in it and got up. He expected her to wobble, but she didn't. *Shit.*

Following close behind her as she danced through the doors into the back room, he mentally talked himself through what was going to happen. *Get her upstairs. Get her to bed. Alone. Come back down and close the bar.*

As they rounded the corner to the supply room, she spun and shoved him back against the wall. As his back hit the cold surface, he grabbed her waist, thinking she had fallen into him. When her eyes moved up his body slowly and stopped on his face, it only took one look at the expression on her face for him to realize *I'm in trouble.*

Her hands moved up his chest to rest on his shoulders; leaning her body against his, she licked her lips. "Can I have that kiss now?"

Part of his brain said *you can have anything you want*; the other part wanted to find the nearest door and remove himself from the temptation. His wolf brushed back and forth against his skin. Gripping her waist, he started to push her to put a bit of space between their bodies when she took hold of his neck in a death grip and pulled his head down to hers.

Momentarily shocked, he tried again to move her as she nibbled his bottom lip. *She's drunk*, he argued with his wolf. The beast didn't seem to mind. *When the hell did she get so strong?* He managed to lift his head an inch. "Rem…"

She took advantage of him opening his mouth to speak, and shoved her tongue into his. Wolf or no, as soon as her flavor hit his tongue, he grasped her by the neck and took the kiss. Her body molded to his, and he had to suppress a moan.

"Hey, Dare?"

Lifting his head, he glared over at Emery, leaning against the doorway. The young vampire had a smirk on his face.

He shrugged, "I'm thinking maybe you should take Remi upstairs." Emery's eyes were lit with amusement.

Remi giggled and began nipping at his collarbone with her teeth.

With a lift of his eyebrows, Emery turned and went back towards the kitchen.

"Come on," Darien growled at her. When she didn't move to start walking but continued up his neck with her teeth, he hissed out a breath and picked her up.

An enthusiastic noise came out of her as she wrapped her legs around his waist. "You're going to pay for this tomorrow, *Álainn.*"

She attacked his neck with her mouth again, "Make me pay now."

Clenching his jaw, he started toward the stairs, not even sure how he was going to make it with her rubbing against him. Each step was torture, with her body rocking against his groin. He should have brought her up earlier before she could drink so much.

Finally reaching the top of the stairs, he paused to catch his breath, and she took that as the all-clear and grasped his hair, jerking his head back down to hers. He intended to resist the urge to kiss her until neither of them could breathe, but the message didn't reach his mouth in time, and before he could think, he had her pinned up against the wall drinking in her flavor.

"Oh!"

Gasping, he lifted his mouth from hers and looked over his shoulder to see Cait standing there, gobsmacked.

"Cait! Dare's helping me bed." Remi's words were slurred.

Both eyebrows raised, Cait looked from the inebriated woman in his arms to him. "Has she been down there drinking all night?"

Darien nodded and gasped out a breath again. Hopefully, she'd lend him a hand in getting her to her room. Cait looked helpless, the side of her mouth turning up like she wanted to smile, but she didn't.

"I'll cover for her in the morning."

With that, she turned and went into her room. Darien

blinked and looked at the door again. Being alone spurred Remi back into action, and she grasped his hair again. Reaching around, he pried her hand loose. "Keep that up, and we're not going to make it to the bedroom."

She stopped and smiled up at him, her legs loosening before she slid down his body to stand on the floor.

Inhaling, he tried to ignore the scent of her. Grasping her hand, he gave it a tug and walked quickly to her bedroom. Once inside, he moved to the bed, hoping to get her to it, and then he was getting out. When he was almost to his goal, she pulled on his arm and shoved him. Stumbling back, his knees hit the bed, and he dropped down to sit.

Remi quickly straddled him, jerking his t-shirt out of his jeans before he realized what was going on. *Jesus, she's made me dimwitted.* Trying to balance their weight and slow her down, he almost lost the fight when she squirmed, dragging her tongue along his bare chest.

His beast was panting, more than happy with their mates' acceptance and attention. Grasping her hair, he gently pulled her mouth away. He needed to come up with a better plan, or they'd be naked in the next minute. "Remi," he paused when her lust-heavy eyes looked up his body at him, *fuck,* "baby, slow down." Pushing up, he released her hair and flipped them so she was lying on the bed.

Moving slowly, he crawled up her body, pinning her wandering hands to the mattress. Shaking, he kissed her throat softly, working his way up. If he could just get her to lay still for a few minutes, she'd be out. "That's better," he crooned beside her ear, "there's no rush." Kissing her jaw gently, he squeezed his eyes shut, hoping that if he didn't look at her, this would be easier. *As if* his senses responded, all he could do was smell her scent, and it quickly chipped away at his resolve.

26

Remi opened her eyes slowly, when the light hit, it was like a thousand starbursts exploded inside her retinas. She closed them again. Pascal was a very bad vampire for feeding her his new concoction. She'd have to spike his blood with rat poison. It wouldn't kill him, but it would make him suffer for a few hours.

Carefully she rolled to her side, feeling for the edge of the bed. At some point, she was going to have to look at the clock and see if she was late. Her stomach churned, all she could think was if she threw up it might moisten her tongue enough to free it from where it was stuck in mouth. It felt like she was still moving, or was that the bed? Why was the bed moving? *Please if it's an earthquake let the ceiling fall on me because, under no circumstance, am I going to get out of this bed quickly.*

An arm rested across her shoulder and her heart jumped inside her chest.

"Drink."

It was Darien and he was placing a water bottle to her lips.

"Drink." His deep voice rumbled next to her ear. Even his voice, which usually she could listen to forever, hurt.

The first sip hit her stomach like a stone. She paused to

make sure it was going to stay down. Opening her mouth again she took another sip. Her poor, dry mouth wasn't complaining as that awful taste rinsed away, so her stomach could just get over it and stop churning.

"Think you can manage a few painkillers? I'll get Naddy to make her remedy as soon as she comes in."

If it meant the throbbing behind her eyes would stop, she was willing to try anything. She nodded, at least she hoped she'd managed to move enough that he'd give her the pills.

Remi swallowed, then waited several seconds until she caught her breath. Who knew swallowing was such hard work? "You conned me last night."

Darien's deep chuckle came from beside her head. "I did not."

Taking a few slow breaths, she remembered, for the most part, everything she'd done the night before. "I threw myself at you," she swallowed slowly, "and you put me in bed, alone."

The bed moved and she felt the heat from his body next to her. His hand rested on her hip as his breath brushed over her cheek. "I am more than willing to give you what you were after last night, now," he brushed the hair back from her face, but she still refused to open her eyes, "but not while you're wasted, sweetheart."

She felt the pillow move as he put his head on it. "You stayed with me."

"I wanted to make sure you were all right." He sighed. "I'm pretty sure I'm partially responsible for your overindulgence last night."

Even with her brain exploding, she couldn't push the blame off on him. "You didn't hold me and pour it down my throat."

"I didn't need to."

Remi licked her dry lips. "It's the bad vampire's fault."

Darien chuckled. "I'll be sure to tell him." He sighed. "Actually, he's the one that told me to let you blow off some steam. I wanted to stop you more than once."

Turning slowly, she burrowed her face into his chest trying to hide from the way she was feeling. "Next time, save me from myself." She was happy that his scent didn't make her feel nauseous, because she was pretty sure she'd just used all the energy she had to roll over. "What time is it?"

"You can sleep some more." He pulled her further into his body and draped his arm over her waist.

"Am I late?" Not that she could have gotten up if she tried.

"You can sleep some more."

Curling into his chest, she moaned. "You're not going to answer me, are you?"

"No."

If she could open her eyes, she knew she'd see him smiling. "Fine."

"Remi?" He whispered softly.

"Mmm?"

"I'm sorry for upsetting you and causing last night."

She focused on his breathing, finding it soothing. "It wasn't you, Darien." Even his heartbeat was making her feel better, or as good as she was going to feel right now.

Holding her closer, he rested his head above hers. "Then what?"

Remi listened to his heart for a few beats, trying to reach through the fog in her brain to explain it. "It was everything, Dare." She swallowed and tried to wet her lips. "Everything from having no parents, no birthdate," she didn't know how to tell him, "just everything."

His hand ran slowly down her back, wiping away the tension as he did. "You may not have parents, sweetheart, but you have family and many that care about you."

What was she supposed to say to that? Snuggling closer, she rested her face against his throat and lay there listening to him breathe. Later when she wasn't dying, she would have to think about all of it. To figure out who she was, where she wanted to go. She needed this threat to Serenity to go away. Her life may not have been normal by most people's standards, but she wasn't about to let anything change it.

"Remi?"

Darien's voice was soft and heavy and didn't hurt anymore to listen to. "Mmm?"

"I love you," he whispered, so softly she was sure she was imagining it, "everything is going to work out."

A tear rolled down her cheek. "I love you too, Dare." Squeezing her eyes tighter, she refused to give in to the emotions that tore at her. When normal life resumed, she was going to have to figure out what to do with Darien and being his mate. What she didn't know was if she was going to break both their hearts and change everything, or if she was going to be able to be what he wanted.

27

It was late afternoon by the time Remi made it downstairs. Cait, Nadine and Darien had done everything possible to stall her; from bringing her lunch in bed to almost carrying her to the tub to relax and soak. She wasn't comfortable with everyone's new mission to pamper her.

When she walked out of the backroom, Darien met her at the door. "You could take a whole day off."

Stopping, she looked up at him. "Are you trying to hide me from the council?"

"No," he grinned, "more like trying to save them from you."

Snorting, she shook her head. "I'm sure I won't pose any threat." She didn't know much about the council, but she knew they were the most powerful in the para community.

"Are you sure about that?"

Searching his dark eyes, all she could find was a soft, caring look. Sighing, she gave him a weak smile.

Tucking his hands in his pockets, he exhaled slowly. "I just talked to Betany, Deane, and Ranae, they'd like to take some time off until the threat is gone."

Remi knew it was bound to happen, it pissed her off that it

was happening at all. "Yeah, I was going to talk to everyone and let them know that I understand if they want to bow out for a while. It will be tough being shorthanded, but we'll get by." She swallowed down the lump in her throat. "What did you tell them?"

Tucking the hair behind her ear, he shrugged. "That you wouldn't have a problem with it, and for them to be really careful where they go and what they do."

Nodding, she leaned her forehead against his chest. "I just want all of this to go away."

His warm hand rubbed the back of her head. "I know." Heaving a big sigh, he dropped his hand. "Hopefully the council will resolve it quickly."

Moving around him, she headed to the kitchen. "I'm not sure what I'm feeling about meeting them."

Darien snorted. "I know what I'm feeling, and none of it's good."

That really wasn't what she wanted to hear.

They were almost ready to open Serenity After Dark when she learned exactly how she'd feel about meeting the most powerful paras she'd ever encountered.

If her life were a movie, this would have been one of those slow-motion moments. The door opened, without assistance and the six glided in. All were tall and beautiful, with an aura of lethal power.

"I think they're here," Emery said in a voice filled with awe.

The first two were vampires and Remi didn't need to ask how old they were. The power radiated from them. *That* kind of power only came from centuries of living, or, in this case not living. The man was tall with glossy black hair that hung past his shoulders. His eyes were closer to maroon, making her wonder if they'd been brown when he was human. He studied her blatantly then smiled slowly, revealing the biggest fangs she'd ever seen. Okay, *if* he'd ever been human. Aside from that, he was probably the most gorgeous male she'd ever seen. Almost feminine, if that were possible.

Attis moved out from behind the counter and went toward him. His frame was rigid, but his head slightly lowered to acknowledge the power of the elder. Remi was shocked, and Attis bowed to no one.

The female vampire was tall and slender with all too-perfect long blonde hair and piercing blue eyes. Remi was certain she could see into her soul. The vampire slowly looked over each of them standing there.

When a chill went down her spine, Remi looked away from her to the massive male on her right. He was, without a doubt, the largest man she'd ever seen; considering the size of all the men at Serenity, that was saying a lot. For a moment, she thought she was sensing a wolf shifter, but then she could see his darker side and realized he was a werewolf. Another shock for her, a werewolf on the council. He looked familiar, which was ridiculous; she could never forget a man that large.

His soft brown eyes moved slowly over her, and then he smiled like he'd known her for years. Stepping closer to Darien, she needed to feel him near so she didn't run away screaming. Something she'd never done in her life, but there was always a first time. The way her heart was thrumming, this could be that time.

Remi watched the tall redheaded female wander across the bar. She was a witch; there was no mistaking the waves of magic coming from her.

"This is quite the place, don't you think?" The witch turned and looked at the tall, light-haired man behind her. He just nodded without speaking.

It took Remi a few seconds of studying to know that he was a mage. A blood mage, if she wasn't mistaken. She didn't know all that much about someone with that skill set or what they could do, but the knot in her stomach told her that was probably a good thing.

"We've heard good things about this place." The last male looked right at her as he spoke. He reminded her of a Greek god, which could only mean something that perfect had to be a powerful faerie. There was something mesmerizing about him.

Emery nudged her from behind, reminding her that a response would be good. "I'm glad." She tried for a smile, but with the way she was shaking, it probably didn't come across as relaxed as she wanted.

"You're the human sensor." The faerie murmured a note of surprise in his voice.

Before she could answer, the male vampire turned toward her. "Oh, I wouldn't go as far as calling her human, Alaric. I think if you look deeply, you'll find *much* more."

"True," he added, his pale eyes moving over her once more.

Remi looked up at Darien, not sure what to do. He placed his arm behind her, letting her know he was close. "My name is Remi," she offered another weak smile, "and this is…"

"We know who everyone is, Miss Foster." The witch informed her.

"Indeed, we do," The huge were said, with a grin and nodded at Darien. "Nephew, how are you?"

Giving Darien a wide-eyed look, he glanced down at her, signaling a 'later' look with his eyes.

"Uncle Garrett. I'm doing well."

Nodding, *Uncle* Garrett looked down at her, a warm smile on his face. Remi wanted to pull her shirt up to cover her throat as he gave it a long leisurely look.

"She's lovely," he told Darien with a surprising Irish burr tickling his words.

Darien's arm pulled her closer without making the move obvious. "Yes."

Feeling like she needed to do something to change the vibe passing between the two werewolves, Remi glanced at Pascal. In seven years, she'd never seen the expression on his face she was seeing now. Fear.

"Donnan, it's been a long time." The female vampire purred.

Turning, Remi realized she was coming towards Pascal.

Donnan? She gave him a curious look. He lowered his lashes and gave a slight shake of his head before taking a deep breath that he really didn't require and pasting a frozen smile on his face.

"Elaine."

Looking away from him, she watched the woman's eyes roam over Pascal. Even though she was absolutely gorgeous, there was something inside her that was so dark it sent a shiver down Remi's spine.

"Let's cut through this tension, shall we?"

Remi saw the mage move in their direction and head straight for her. When he stopped directly in front of her and Darien and extended his hand, she had to fight to not step back.

"Ah," he offered her an apologetic look and lowered his hand, "I understand. You have to be careful who you touch." Inclining his head toward her gracefully, he straightened again. "I am Brome."

Relieved she hadn't offended this powerful man by not shaking his hand, she smiled. He motioned with his hand to the witch as she still wandered around looking at everything.

"That is Hope," he turned to nod at the male vampire, "and Leontes."

Before Remi could say anything, the female predator that was moving closer and closer to Pascal paused and looked over her shoulder at Emery.

"And *who* is this?" She sounded like an excited child, only with an eerie edge to her voice.

Clearing her throat, Remi turned without moving away from Darien's comforting closeness. "This is Emery," she smiled at the woman, "*my* son." She didn't know why she had to make her claim clear; there was just something about the ancient vampire that set her on edge.

An amused look crossed her face. "I had heard that you acquire *strays*."

The way she said it made it sound dirty and wrong. Remi straightened her spine and studied the woman for a moment.

"I don't see it that way." She moved away from Darien and looked into the woman's pale eyes. "My daughter, Cait, is from a troll clan. I adopted her when her entire family was *killed.*" She smiled at her, "And when one of *your* kind turned Emery, they abandoned him to figure it out on his own…"

Leontes moved between the two of them so fast that Remi didn't even see him until he was looking down at her. "We weren't informed." He gave her a look of concern and then glanced at Emery.

Attis glided down and stood beside Remi. "Ah, I see our beautiful leader is stepping right into it." His look told her that he had her back, like always.

Leontes turned and looked at him. "Attis, you were aware of this?"

Attis inclined his head. "I was, Leontes." Looking around for a moment, he continued, "You weren't informed because both Pascal and I were here. I believe we're *elder* enough to oversee things."

Remi ignored the strange look Elaine gave Pascal and turned to look back at the vampire watching Attis. "If introductions are finished, we really need to get ready to open for the night."

Leontes brought his focus back to her. "Yes, don't let us delay you. We're anxious to see if the creature that is responsible for the slayings comes here tonight."

Raising her eyebrows, she glanced around at the council members. "Do you think they will?"

Hope stopped her wandering and gave her a big smile. "We should be so lucky."

"Okay." Stepping away, Remi let out a slow breath and nodded at Emery. "Go make sure Finn is up. Elise and Vienna will be here shortly."

Emery looked only too happy to leave the presence of the intimidating beings. He blurred past her and into the kitchen.

Turning, Remi watched Elaine follow Pascal down the bar. "Pascal, check the inventory out here, and Em will get what you need when he comes back."

Pascal looked at her gratefully. Elaine continued to follow him as he moved over to open the liquor doors and fold them back. Twice he had to move to avoid running into her.

"Um, Elaine, is it?" The woman stopped and looked over her shoulder at Remi. "Perhaps it would be easier for him if you moved to the other side of the bar."

All movement in the place stopped, and everyone turned to look at the woman as she smiled, her eyes almost glowing. "Are you *warning* me off? Asking me not to interfere with *your* hired help?"

Remi shook her head. "No. I'm telling you not to bother my *friend* while he's working. Pascal is as every bit important and necessary to the operation of Serenity as I am."

"*Really?*" She began a slow, graceful glide in Remi's direction.

Locking her knees, Remi nodded. "With his help, we're able to offer a safe and discreet place for every para. I may be the beacon that draws them here and keeps their secrets from regular humans, but without him, or any one member of my team, my family, we'd be quite ineffective."

"Elaine," Leontes moved over so he was across the bar from her, "we are in Miss Foster's domain. Here *her* laws supersede our own."

Elaine gave him a hard look.

He continued, "As long as she's not breaking a council or clan laws, we must listen to her."

Garrett stood beside Leontes and nodded his approval. "The fates brought her here, and it's not our place to interfere."

Huffing out a breath in a dramatic way, Elaine looked from one to the other. "Very well." Sighing, she looked back at Pascal. "Can I at least get some O negative?"

Pascal inclined his head and turned to the blood fridge. "Of course," he added stiffly, glancing at Remi out of the corner of his eye; she noticed the amused look on his face

28

Remi turned when Finn came into the kitchen.

"I don't know what I missed, but that lady vamp is seething."

Baker chuckled. "I caught part of it. Remi put her in her place so she wouldn't grope Pascal."

Grabbing a bottle of water, Remi leaned back against the fridge and opened it. "She wasn't trying to grope Pascal; she was getting in his space."

Finn handed Baker an order. "It must have been something to behold; Em is all puffed up with his *that's-my-mom* strut."

Taking a drink, she capped the bottle and went over to the window to see if everyone was tolerating their guests. They had taken a corner booth and, for the most part, looked like regular customers, all except Elaine, who was pouting. It surprised her that Randell and Kyran were sitting with them. "When did Dell get here?"

Finn paused near the door. "About fifteen minutes ago. Apparently, some are going down to the morgue to check the bodies."

A shudder went through her. "Fun times."

209

"Hopefully, they take grumpy with them," Finn mumbled as he went back out.

Moving along the window, Remi checked on her staff. Vie and Elise didn't seem to be put off their grove by the newcomers. Then again, Elise was a water nymph and somewhat revered by all clans and races, so they wouldn't do anything but respect her. Vie actually seemed to be having more fun than normal.

Baker leaned against the window and looked out. "Vie is having a blast playing head games with the mage." He said it a matter of fact.

"Really?" Looking over to the booth, she saw that Brome was following her head waitress with his eyes, a smirk on his face. "Well, hopefully, he survives it."

Baker snorted and turned back to the fryer. "It's kind of cool that we need to fear for the council's safety from fellow employees."

Smirking, Remi realized it was entertaining. "Wait until they meet Iris."

He laughed. "I might have to come in for breakfast to experience *that* in person."

When she turned back, Pascal's face appeared in the window. She yelped in surprise.

"Have I told you how much I adore you?" He smiled at her.

"Because I saved you from the dragon lady?" She leaned on the edge and grinned back at him.

Lifting one eyebrow, he nodded. "That's just a plus." Stepping back, he inclined his head in a regal way. "I would go to battle under your reign any day." With that, he was gone again.

Glancing over her shoulder, she looked at Baker.

He shrugged. "I don't know about going into battle, but I'll get Berk to bitch slap anyone that pisses you off."

"You're my hero, Baker."

He laughed. "I know, right? I'm the *real* deal."

When she looked back, Emery was walking by the bar with

a big grin on his face. It made her feel good that he was proud of her. Looking over at the door, she saw that Darien was looking right at her. How did he always know when she was watching him? Winking at him, she watched the slow smile appear on his sexy face.

His uncle was standing beside him and looked over, then said something to his nephew. Darien's smile was gone and quickly replaced by a scowl as he shook his head.

"I didn't know Darien had an uncle." She said more to herself.

"Who is part giant, I think," Baker quipped over her shoulder. "Thank mother nature for making Darien just large and not freakishly large size."

Remi shrugged. "I like Darien's size just fine."

Scrunching up his face, Baker glared at her. "Wrong brother. I don't want to talk size with you."

"I didn't mean…"

"Attis told me if I wanted a good strong tea, I'd find it in the kitchen."

Jolting, Remi turned around and looked up at Garrett. "Sure, let me put the kettle on." Turning, she went over and pulled the old teapot Darien had insisted be part of any kitchen off the shelf and filled the kettle. Grabbing the box of tea bags, she dropped four into the pot. Darien said that was the *only* way to make tea.

Garrett nodded his approval. "My nephew has taught you to make tea."

She smiled. "Yes, we learned early on that if you put only one tea bag in, that was unacceptable."

He smiled, and she could see the family resemblance then. "It's the Irish in the blood."

"Is that where the rest of your family is?" Crossing her arms, she leaned back against the counter.

"Darien doesn't talk about his kin?" He looked disappointed.

"Not much, no."

A thoughtful look appeared in his eyes. "They didn't part

on the best of terms." He glanced at the kettle as it reached a boil.

Turning, she poured the water into the pot.

"For the most part, the family remains in Ireland, but there are several branches in the States and Canada now."

When she turned, he was standing much closer. She looked at Baker, unsure, and then turned back to stir the tea bags around in the pot.

"You'll have to allow me to be the prying Uncle, *neacht*," he paused and smiled, "Ah, niece, but why are you still unclaimed?" A serious look of concern was in his soft brown eyes.

Biting her lip, she didn't know what to say. "I just found out that I was his mate."

He gave her a shocked look. "Really? He's been able to deny it that long?" There was disappointment in his tone.

Turning back to the tea, she poured a cup and turned and held it out to him. He nodded his thanks and then took a sip.

"Ah, that's nice." Setting the cup on the counter, he leaned down closer to her. "If you like, *neacht*, I could force the issue with my rebellious Darien, and he would have to claim you as his own."

"Uh," Baker leaned around the huge man blocking Remi's view of him, "pretty sure the big guy has *no* problem with claiming her."

Garrett stepped back out of her space and studied her. "You have denied him?"

Remi made a mental note to corner Darien the first chance she had and find out more about the do's and don'ts of mating. She was starting to feel like she was floundering around, trying not to sink. "I…maybe you'd better ask Darien to explain."

Looking at her for a long uncomfortable moment, he abruptly nodded. "Damn right, I will." He growled and walked out of the kitchen.

Wincing, Remi looked at Baker to see his eyes as worried as her own. "I think that went badly."

Baker nodded quickly as they both rushed to the window to see Darien and his uncle face to face. Remi couldn't hear what was being said, but she did see that Darien's eyes were yellow. "Crap." Rushing toward the door, she didn't have a chance to get out of it before Attis came in and blocked her from going out front.

"I think," he reached over and brushed the hair over her shoulder, "you should stay right here for a few moments."

Glaring at him, she rolled her eyes. "Don't give me the little woman thing. Move, Attis."

Sighing in a dramatic way, he inclined his head and stepped aside. By the time she rounded the counter, she could see a small crowd around the two seething werewolves. Glancing to the side, she spotted Pascal leaning back with an amused look on his face. "You *could* help."

He laughed. "I'm old, not senile. I'm not stepping between two growling werewolves."

Hissing out a breath, she jogged to the door and pushed her way through the crowd. Emery grabbed her arm; the look she gave had him hold up his hands like he'd been stung.

Pushing her way between the two, she glared up at Garrett, ignoring the sharp teeth and neon yellow of his eyes, as she smacked her hand against Darien's chest, which she noted was more muscular than normal. "Enough." Yellow eyes looked down at her, surprise lighting them. "Both of you knock it off. *Now.*"

Remi knew she might live, or not, to regret her next move, but Serenity was hers, Darien too, and for his uncle to cause this disruption was intolerable. She shoved a hand against Garrett's chest while holding Darien's look. "Calm down," she said as softly as she could manage, knowing full well that both would be able to hear over all the noise.

"It's over. Everyone…back to your fun," Attis appeared beside them, blocking the view of most of the gawkers. "The next round of drinks is on me." He purred. Just that fast, the group broke up and went toward the bar. Glancing at her, his eyes moved from one man to the other. "You good?"

Remi nodded, still holding Darien's look. "I got this." Sliding her hand up Darien's chest, she tried to stay calm. "You're scaring the shit out of me, Dare," she whispered.

Garrett stepped back, letting her hand fall away. "I doubt that." He said in a gravelly voice and walked out the door.

Darien inhaled deeply, his eyes starting to go back to normal as he did. With more force than he'd normally use, he wrapped his arm around her waist and pulled her tight against him. Resting her head against his shoulder, she let out a slow breath and closed her eyes for a second.

"Amazing."

Opening her eyes, she saw Brome and Leontes beside them. Brome was smiling at her.

Leontes looked at Darien and then back to her. "Calming two weres, that's quite the feat, Miss Foster."

Remi shrugged as much as she could in the tight hold Darien had on her. "No one fights in Serenity."

The old vampire's lashes lowered, and then he inclined his head.

Brome motioned beside him. "The Detective is taking a few of us to check the bodies."

Remi glanced at Randell and Kyran. Kyran was smirking. Randell had a look of disgust on his face, his eyes moving from her to the werewolf holding her.

"Okay," she said like it was a normal conversation.

Darien pulled her back away from the door but continued to hold her close and inhale slowly. "Sorry," he whispered next to her ear.

Rubbing her hand in a circle on her chest, she looked up into his dark eyes. "It's fine. I don't think your uncle understands, that's all."

He snorted. "You're ..." he tensed.

Turning, she watched Brome, Randell, Elaine, and Alaric leave. Randell and Elaine's expressions mirrored each other, bitter and irritable. *Two of a kind*, she thought. Remi lowered her head so she wouldn't smirk in their direction.

"I need..." Darien growled softly and released her.

Grasping her hand, he walked through the crowd, making her almost run to keep up. Shoving into the kitchen, he kept tugging her along as he went into the back room.

"Dare…"

He spun and pushed her against the wall, covering her mouth with his in one fluid motion. Remi's whole body responded as he attacked her mouth, and she struggled to keep up with him. Grasping the back of her head, he growled against her mouth, and her knees weakened as the sound vibrated through her.

Lifting his head, he rested his forehead against hers, keeping her tight against his body. "Sorry," he gasped and panted.

Swallowing, Remi tried to regain her breath. "For kissing me?"

Darien grinned. "No." Brushing a soft kiss against her mouth, he leaned back. "For losing it twice."

Exhaling loudly, she leaned against the wall and rested her hands on his shoulders. "Well, I much prefer the second loss of control over the first."

Shaking his head, he studied her for a moment. "I can't believe you stepped between us."

Eyes wide, she sobered. "Me either."

"Still, I can't believe my beast listened without hesitation." He grinned, "And my uncle," he blew out a breath, "that's something right there."

Remi chewed on her lip and thought about it for a moment. "Well, I think he was trying to bait you on purpose."

Closing his eyes, his jaw tense, he shrugged. "It wouldn't surprise me."

Poking him in the chest, he opened them and looked at her again. "Later, you and I are going to discuss *you* leaving out the fact that your uncle was council."

"I planned to tell you last night," he smirked, "but someone decided to drink a little too much."

"Oh sure, blame me." She laughed and reached up to

brush the hair out of his eyes. "Are you okay now?"

His eyes darkened as he looked at her mouth. "For the most part."

"Good, let's go see if we can get through this night." He stepped back and gave her more space. "I'm really curious what they're going to figure out at the morgue."

She stepped into the kitchen and was swept off her feet in a hug from Emery. Setting her back down quickly, he grinned down at her. "*You* rock."

Laughing, she shoved at his chest. "Remember that when I make you scrub the washrooms next time."

Emery's jaw dropped. "That would just be mean." Throwing his hands up, he shook his head. "There are germs and *stuff.* I could get sick."

Remi laughed. "You're a vampire."

"Hey, it could happen." He turned and exited the kitchen without another word.

Darien chuckled from behind her. "Probably the first germophobic vampire in history."

"Lucky me," she sighed, with a smile on her face.

29

Kyran glanced over at Darien. They both looked at the clock over the bar.

Darien didn't need to see to know that Kyran was glaring at him. "I know. I've tried to get her to go get some rest. She won't go until they get back."

"At least she's drinking water tonight," Kyran smirked at him.

Darien laughed. "There is that." Turning, he checked to make sure his uncle was still on the other side of the bar and nowhere near Remi.

"So," Kyran leaned back against the wall beside the door, "that was scary as fuck earlier." He gave him a hard look. "Don't do it again."

Rubbing the back of his neck, Darien dropped his hand and rolled his shoulders. "I'll try not to."

"If Remi hadn't been there, what would have happened?"

Darien looked over at his uncle, who sat talking to Leontes and Hope. He loved the man, without a doubt. They'd been really close before he'd joined the council. In any other situation, he'd back his uncle in a heartbeat, but not when it involved Remi. "Do you really want to know?" Turning his head slowly, he looked at the detective.

Kyran opened his mouth and then closed and shook his head. "No, I don't think I do."

"Me either." He slapped Kyran on the shoulder. "Watch the door for a few minutes?"

"Sure."

Moving toward Remi, he had to grin as he watched the way she caught his every move. She may not be ready to be mated, but they were mates. They were always aware of the other when they were in need, regardless of the situation.

When he reached her, he teasingly leaned down and looked into her glass.

She swatted him on the shoulder. "It's water."

Resting his hip against the bar, he turned the stool she was on, putting her legs between his own. "You look tired, *Álainn.* Go up to bed."

Giving him an exasperated look, she shook her head. "I want to wait until they're back."

Brushing the hair back from her face, he moved closer. "They could be gone until dawn. You have to work in the morning."

"I'll still work," she shrugged, "I may just growl a little more than usual."

"With my luck, you'll growl better than I do, and I'll be unmanned."

Smiling, she looked up at him, and the look of adoration in her eyes made his heart speed up. "You need to take your sexy ass up to bed, *a ghrá,* so I can focus on my job."

Moving slowly, she stood up. "One of these days, you're going to tell me what those sexy words you're always saying to me mean." She slid her hands up his chest, her eyes shining at him.

"You like those, huh?" Anytime she voluntarily touched him in any way, his heart would jump into his throat, and the rest of the world could get stuffed as far as he was concerned.

"I think I do," she smiled, "and I know they're Irish now."

He chuckled. "See, there's a reason I keep you away from

my family."

"You mean family, as in the man walking toward us right now?" She dropped her hands away.

Darien didn't turn to look at his uncle; he just continued to watch Remi. First, the man berates him for not claiming her, then chooses the moment they're close to interrupt. He'd never understand his relatives and the way they worked, even if he lived forever.

"I'm sorry to barge in, but I need to speak with the both of you."

Releasing Remi, he looked over his shoulder at his uncle. Without a word, he guided her in the direction of the kitchen, knowing Garrett would follow. Stepping through, he looked around; Baker had the kitchen cleaned up for the night. "You can cut out now if you want, Baker."

Baker gave him a surprised look, and then his eyes went to Remi and the large man standing in the door. "Sure thing, I'll just go hang out front until Bode is done so we can head out together."

Darien couldn't believe he'd forgotten his rule of no one leaves alone. "I'm sure if you bug Pascal, he'll spot you a beer."

"Cool." He grinned at Remi. "Night, boss lady."

"Good night, Baker." She gave Darien a look and moved over to lean against the counter, the furthest from his uncle as she could get.

Garrett rubbed the back of his neck and looked at the floor for a moment. "I want to apologize for earlier." Dropping his arms, he crossed them over his chest and sighed, "I didn't understand what there was between you." A bashful look was on his face. "That young waitress, Vienna, uh…" he shook his head, "enlightened me."

Darien looked at Remi, and they both had the same thought, Uncle Garrett was lucky Vie had been nice about it.

"It's just hard, you understand?" He glanced from Remi back to him. "I didn't know there had been so many…" he waved a hand around, frowning like he was trying to find the right words.

Sighing, Darien tucked his hands into his jeans and studied his uncle. Just the fact that he was trying to apologize told him the man he thought he knew had changed over the years. "It hasn't been a smooth ride for Remi since she got here seven years ago, *uncail*, but trying to force my beast," he gave him a hard look, "that was a bit underhanded." He caught the look Remi gave him, the one that said he was in trouble for not explaining what had happened. She, like everyone else, thought it was a difference of opinion. It had started that way, but then he had tried to force Darien's beast to the forefront so he wouldn't be able to control his actions around Remi, so he would mark her.

"It was. I'm sorry." His uncle moved his eyes to Remi and bowed his head slightly. "You'll have to forgive me, *neacht*, for being old and set in my ways."

Just like that, Darien thought his uncle had won her over, or she had him wrapped around his finger. It was one of those, possibly both, as he watched Remi's shoulders slump and that look appear on her face. It was the same look she got when she decided to adopt Cait and Emery, when she took in Finn and Iris and gave all four of the Lewis quadruplets a job.

"There's nothing to forgive, Garrett." She smiled up at him. "You can't walk in and expect to understand everything in five minutes." Glancing at Darien, she looked of amused. "Serenity is *never* straightforward or simple."

Garrett relaxed and perched on the edge of the sink. "Many from our clan never find their mates, so it seems abnormal to me when you know of each other but don't…" He lifted his hand and rubbed the back of his neck. "If I were to find my own," he sighed, "I would leave the council without a backward glance."

Raising his eyebrows, he gave his uncle a shocked look. "Really? I thought you were honored to be on the council."

"I was. I am." He tilted his head and gave him a serious look. "For the peace," he smirked, "for the love of a true mate…" He sighed again and closed his eyes for a moment, "I'd give anything to feel that grounded."

Nodding, he understood what the elder was saying, at least most of it. Glancing over, he saw that Remi was giving him *that* look again. He'd be doing a lot of explaining later.

"Do you still lock yourself up on the night of the moon, Darien?"

"No, I lock him up," Remi said with a smirk.

Garrett laughed. "That's a bit of justice there." Sobering, he looked back at him, and Darien wanted to jump up and find an excuse to leave. "See, that's where I get lost," he motioned to Remi, "if she were marked, especially with her not being clan, you would have an anchor." He shook his head and looked at the floor. "As long as she's tied to your lifeline, she'd be your tether. The moon wouldn't control you completely." He said the last part quietly while looking at the floor.

Darien didn't need to look to know that Remi's eyes were burning a hole through him.

The door swung open, and Pascal glanced at them one at a time. Frowning, he motioned out front. "They're back."

Standing up, Garrett nodded to them abruptly and left.

Darien started to the door, hoping Remi's curiosity would take precedence over tearing a strip off him. When his hand reached the door, she was in front of him, giving him a narrow-eyed look.

"You and me, wolfman, are going to have a chat later."

He debated whether he should just meekly agree or tell her that he thought it was sexy as hell when she was looking at him the way she was. She continued to glare at him. *Meek it is.* "I know."

30

The doors were locked, Serenity After Dark was empty except for the council and some of the staff. Boden and Baker sat at the bar with Emery, all keeping their thoughts to themselves for a change. The mood in the room was heavy and oppressive. Remi was ready to climb right out of her skin.

Attis and Vienna sat at the bar. Neither was offering their opinion, which worried her. They had their focus faces on at least, which told Remi they were thinking the problem through.

Getting up from the table, she paced halfway across the room and looked back at the group sitting at the table. Collectively, there was enough power and experience sitting there to be able to handle anything. Hopefully, she prayed, that would be the case this time.

Nodding to herself, Remi turned to Baker and Boden. "You boys go home. I want you to fill in your brothers and your folks. It's up to them if you come back tomorrow." Both opened their mouths, determined looks on their faces. "No." She stopped them from speaking. "I can't expect any of you to take a chance coming here with this hanging over us." Glancing over her shoulder, she gave Pascal a look. "Can you do your stalker thing and make sure they get home?"

He grinned and got up. "Of course."

"I'll go with him." Elaine started to stand.

Remi turned and looked at Leontes, hoping he would understand what her eyes were trying to convey.

He made eye contact with her briefly, a look of acknowledgment on his face. "I think your input will be beneficial here, Elaine."

Finn stood up. "I can go."

Pascal clasped his hands in front of his body and looked at her, tilting his head slightly, giving her that look that he always did, saying she needed to loosen the apron strings a bit.

Exhaling, she studied him for a moment and then turned to Finn. When he'd come to Serenity, she'd only been here a year. The man he was now was so vastly different than the run-down, skeletal-thin, almost insane vampire that had walked through the doors the first time. It had taken four years to bring him out of his shell and back to life, as much as you could with a vampire. Now, he was as important to her as Emery and Cait. Finn stood there, a hopeful look on his face, and she knew she was going to have to let him go with Pascal. He was, after all, twice her age. Nodding, she pointed from him to Pascal. "*You* listen to him."

Finn saluted her, a smirk on his face. "Yes 'mam."

It almost hurt to see the expressions on Baker and Boden's faces as they walked out. Remi turned from the door and looked at Darien. The guarded look on his face told her he knew she was aching at the thought that the boys wouldn't be back tomorrow.

"Okay," she turned back to the table to see everyone was watching her. All members of the council were sitting there with patient looks on their faces. That annoyed her that they could be so calm. She knew they were used to enormous threats and danger, but they could at least look mildly concerned. Elaine was the only one that didn't look indifferent. She had this sour look on her face. Remi wondered if she realized how unappealing it made her.

Dell and Kyran stood at the end. Neither seemed sure what to think of the most recent turn of events. Kyran's face was filled with emotion. Remi was beginning to understand that he belonged at Serenity as much as the paras that were her family. Dell, on the other hand, she really wished he would transfer to a far-away-foreign country and stop reminding her how stupid she'd been to fall for him.

Attis, Vie, and Emery were leaning against the bar now, expressions mirroring her own thoughts. *Now what?* Taking a deep breath, she tried to focus and stay calm. "So, back up and fill in some blanks for me." She looked straight at Brome as she spoke. She didn't know him any better than the rest of the council, but he had a vibe she was comfortable with, barely. "Too many traces to count…" She held up her hand and shook her head, "No, let's start with the fact that magic was definitely involved, but not from a witch or mage?"

He nodded. "Correct."

"And how many kinds of magic are there?"

"More than you'd like to know," he answered slowly.

"I'm sure you're right about that." Unable to stand still, she paced across the room. "How many traces did you detect?"

"Innumerable." His voice was serious, practically flat.

She lifted her hands. "Which means?" Holding up her hand, she motioned in the air, "In simple layman's terms, please."

Brome glanced at Alaric and then looked back at her. "That it's somewhere between a large coven and an organization involved."

Remi looked at Darien. His thoughts were the same as hers; that answer hadn't told them anything.

"So," she looked down at the floor, trying to stay calm, "the magic, it's being used to control whoever is doing this, but not to actually kill?" She flicked her eyes back to the table.

Elaine smiled. She looked like she was enjoying her

confusion. "The killer," she glanced at Leontes out of the corner of her eye, "or killers, are the pawns. They're not using the magic."

Hope nodded. "They actually think they're smart enough to not be caught, even though eventually the pawns will be, but they will pay the price."

Biting her lip, Remi closed her eyes for a second. "But they'll still be out there." She looked from one to the next, going around the whole table, meeting only guarded sets of eyes. "They could just find new pawns." It didn't have to be said that the threat would never go away unless they found out who was behind it.

"Can I try something?" Vienna came over and stood in front of Remi. "It may not work, but then again, it could help."

Just the fact that Vie had figured something out with her amazing brain that they all feared and loved made Remi feel like there might be a chance. She motioned to the table. "Have at it."

"I'll try to get you answers." Vie held her look for a moment.

"That would be great." Remi knew she was tired, and she was starting to fight snapping at anyone that breathed the wrong way. Crossing her arms, she waited as Vie walked over to stand beside Brome.

"Did you touch them?" She asked him.

"The bodies?"

Vie nodded.

"I had to." He gave her a puzzled look.

Clasping her hands together, she gave him a hesitant look. "I'd like to try something. I may be able to follow the traces you sensed and get a number or," she flipped her hair back over her shoulder, "something."

Brome pushed his chair back and opened his hands in a welcoming gesture. "Be my guest." His expression was amused.

Remi didn't know what the two had been up to half the

night before he'd gone to the morgue, but there was obviously something between them.

"Okay," Vie rubbed her hands together and then held them beside his head, "this might feel a bit weird." She paused. "Just don't fight me. I don't want to hurt you." He raised an eyebrow at her. She grinned. "I promise not to dig into *all* your secrets."

Brome sat there for a moment studying her face. "I'm an open book for you."

Remi glanced at Darien. He smirked and then sobered quickly. Yep, definitely something going on there.

Everyone seemed to hold their breath as Vie placed her hands against the mage's head and closed her eyes. Brome also closed his, discomfort clear on his face.

Remi started counting in her head to not demand if it was working. She knew better than to interrupt Vie when she was in her zone. A body could get hurt. She'd seen that firsthand a few years ago and didn't want to repeat that experience *ever* again. Hope leaned closer and then looked at her with a curious expression on her face. Lifting her finger to her lips, Remi shook her head. The witch nodded and sat back again.

Brome whooshed out a breath as Vienna lowered her hands. "My gods," he whispered breathlessly and looked up at Vie, "that was…" he studied her for a moment. "You have mage blood."

Remi wasn't sure if it was a question or a statement.

Taking a deep breath and exhaling gradually, Vienna nodded. "Parts."

Darien made eye contact with Remi again. That explained so much, yet didn't.

"Did it work?" Hope asked excitedly.

Vienna steadied herself on the back of the chair and glanced at Remi. She couldn't express how she felt that her waitress and friend was looking at her and not the table of power. On a good day, Remi felt like she was a tiny, insignificant human. Since the council had arrived, she was feeling the size of an ant. With her staff and friends still looking at her, it made her feel invincible.

"I don't have names or anything, but..." Scrunching her face in a look of concentration, Vie wandered slowly across the floor.

Remi didn't need to ask what she was doing. She'd seen Vienna in action or knew the signs of when her brain was processing facts.

"There's something familiar about one of the traces..." she spoke quietly, not looking at anyone. Her head popped up, and she zeroed in on her. "I need Pascal."

Remi glanced at the clock. "He should be back in a few minutes."

Nodding, Vie crossed her arms and stared at the floor again. "There are at least," she closed her eyes like she was trying to remember. Opening them, she looked right at Brome, "twenty distinct paths from the magic that was all over the body."

Brome sat forward in the chair. "Twenty." He studied her in a way that made Remi think he had many questions but wasn't going to ask them. "Why do you need Pascal?" He looked around the table at his other council members. "One of us can't help?"

Vie shook her head and focused only on him. "Pascal and I have..." she looked over her shoulder at Attis, a look passing between them, "done this before, so I am comfortable working with him."

Remi's eyes connected with Darien's. They knew what she was really saying was that she trusted Pascal and none of them. No one at Serenity knew of Vienna's past or even what she was, and despite the mystery, were okay with it. They also knew what upsetting Vie could result in. Some things were just safer left alone.

"Were you able to sense who the pawn is?" Alaric stood up and walked over to her, a brilliant smile on his face. "Or perhaps whether the pawn is para or not."

Vienna looked up at him, an amused look on her face. "Trying to use your fey charms on me is a waste of your time, sparkles." She motioned toward Remi, "It's the same result as if you tried it on Remi."

Frowning, Alaric looked over at her. "I'm not sure what she means."

Shrugging, Remi crossed her arms over her chest and gave him an awkward smile. "I'm immune to all forms of magic, spells…" she waved her hand around, "and all that."

"I see."

Brome started laughing and sobered quickly when the large faerie glared at him.

"How is that possible?" Hope inquired softly. "Alaric can even get me if I let my guard down around him.

Brome got up, a large smile on his face as he wandered in Vienna's direction. "I suspect Miss Vienna has a touch of Fey in her."

Vienna gave him a cute grin. She wasn't about to confirm or deny. Heaving a sigh, she walked away from them both and went behind the bar. Grabbing a bottle of juice, she opened it, waving it in their direction. "The pawn is definitely para."

Randell turned and studied her. "You're sure?"

Vie nodded and then took a drink, ending any further possibility of response.

The fact that normals were killed by paras spawned a noisy discussion with the council and two detectives. Remi noted that Kyran seemed to be more on the council's side than his partner's. Tucking that piece of happiness away for her own enjoyment, she went over and sat beside Emery. He had, oddly enough, been quiet throughout all of this. He also, she noticed, had that lonely, sad look about him, one she had lived more than enough on her own. "Did you send Corey away?"

Crossing his arms over his chest, he studied a spot on the floor by his feet. "Yeah, I sent her to her aunt's before we opened." He sighed. "She called me when she got there and agreed to stay until I told her it was safe to come back."

Rubbing her hand up and down his cool arm, she leaned

down so he would make eye contact with her. "You did the right thing."

He looked at her finally. "Does the right thing always hurt?"

Remi snorted and patted his arm. "Yeah, pretty sure it does." He groaned and got up to stand with Darien and his uncle, also standing on the sidelines, waiting for some sort of decision to be made by those scrambling for the lead position on this investigation.

Brome turned and moved in her direction. Apparently, he'd had enough of the group trying to one-up each other as well. He sat on a stool next to her and watched from that viewpoint for a long silent moment. "Does it really matter who stands in front on this?"

Remi smiled and looked at him. "Give them a minute. They'll figure out what's important once the hormones settle."

He nodded and then sighed. "The council doesn't necessarily represent maturity at all times."

"I don't think anyone does."

Vienna leaned forward from behind the bar and looked at Brome. "How's the head?"

He took his time answering. "I can still feel bits and pieces of you in there."

She shrugged. "It will fade."

Brome turned the stool so they were almost face to face. "Tell me, how can you have a touch of mage and fey inside you?" He frowned. "They're quite incompatible."

Vienna took a drink, her eyes studying him the whole time. "I'm guessing that being on the council means you are privy to many lost files."

He nodded without comment.

"Do you recall reading about a group of brainy scientists from several clans experimenting with gene *splicing*?"

Remi looked from one to the other.

His eyes widened. "There was the Gen project..." he shook his head, "but that was never continued after repeated failures."

Her expression didn't give anything away as she looked from Remi back to the inquisitive mage. "Officially, on paper, it was." She smirked. "Unofficially, the eight scientists decided…" she snorted, "for whatever reason, to toss together their own DNA in a big 'ol stock pot and let it stew and mature, hoping the results might lead to more answers."

His eyes searched her face, a look of confusion on his.

Vienna straightened up and opened her arms. "Tada! They got me instead."

Remi felt like she was sitting on the outside looking in. Her brain wrangled with it for seconds longer than Brome's did.

"That's impossible," he whispered.

Leaning forward again, Vie lowered her voice. "And yet, *here* I am."

He blinked several times, opening and closing his mouth like he wasn't sure what to say first. "That would mean you have eight parents…"

Vienna pointed at him, a bingo expression on her face. "All from different clans and one normal." She held his eyes for a moment. "Let me tell you, family gatherings are *never* dull."

Brome inhaled deeply and then exhaled all at once. "I…"

Capping the juice, Vienna set it on the counter and turned it in her hand for a moment. "I would appreciate it if this stayed between us."

He nodded slowly and then looked at Remi.

Vie grinned. "Remi won't tell a soul," she watched him carefully, "aside from Darien, that is."

Brome stood up quickly. "I vow I will not either."

She nodded abruptly. "Good, because someday it's bound to come out, and having allies could come in handy."

31

Before Remi could fully digest Vie's news, Pascal and Finn stumbled in the door. She stood up and looked them both up and down. It was always a strange thing to see a vampire looking flushed, and from experience, it wasn't for good reasons.

Finn stopped abruptly, the grin fading off his face as he looked a Remi. He held up his hands and then pointed to Pascal. "I did what you said and listened to him."

Pascal rolled his eyes and then gave Remi his most charming smile. "We did not break any of your rules," he glanced over at the table of elders, "or yours."

Feeling like she was out of energy and patience, Remi looked from one to the other. "Did you get the boys home all right?"

Finn nodded. "Yep, they're all tucked in."

Brushing the hair out of her face, she blew out a breath. "Then that's all that matters for now." She motioned to Vienna. "Vie's been waiting for Pascal. She was able to pick up…" she didn't even know what to say next, "I'll let her explain."

Pascal smiled and glided over to Vie. "Tell me your

beautiful brain has found a way for me to track our psycho."

Vie rolled her eyes at his enthusiastic compliment. "I'm not sure, but there is something familiar there."

"Intriguing." He sat down on one of the stools so they were the same height. "May I?"

She nodded, then moved back a few inches. "*Just* that part."

Pascal chuckled. "Not to worry, *I* know exactly how many ways you could kill me, and I'm not eager to test any of them."

"Okay." She leaned forward again so their heads were only a few inches apart.

Remi had never felt what it was like having someone else inside her head, but she was paranoid enough that she didn't want to be too close to either of them while they did whatever they were doing.

Brome, on the other hand, apparently held none of her reservations and moved closer, his eyes going from one to the other like a scientist watching an experiment.

A familiar feeling moved over Remi, and she knew without looking that Darien had come up behind her. His arm circled her waist just as his body heat reached her. Rather than tug her back against him, he stepped forward so their bodies were barely touching.

"I can feel your exhaustion, *a ghrá*." He whispered into her ear.

She nodded and leaned back against him. "If some sort of decision would be made, then I might get to bed before dawn."

Darien's arm tightened around her, forcing her to relax more of her weight against him. Remi looked around to see everyone was watching Brome and Vienna, except for Elaine. She was watching her. Remi tensed in his hold. *What is that vampire's issue?*

Chuckling softly against her ear, Darien turned them so Remi couldn't see if she continued to stare at her. "She's jealous," he murmured so only she would hear.

Of what? Remi wanted to scream.

"A demon," Pascal said loudly and got up from the stool.

Remi pulled out of Darien's hold. "A *demon* is the pawn?" Pascal's sight focused on her slowly, like his mind was returning to him. He nodded. Remi knew, well, pretty much nothing about demons. Like magic, there were too many flavors to ever know them all.

"You're sure?" Leontes rose from the table with his vampire grace and glided in their direction.

Pascal nodded and looked at Vienna for a moment. She had her focused face on. If Remi knew anything about her, it was that when she had that look, you didn't get in her way.

"This complicates things," Hope said, following Leontes. "Demons are nasty creatures that follow their own rules.

Vienna picked up her juice and opened it. She glanced at Remi and then at Darien before taking a drink. There was more, was what the look said, and honestly, Remi wasn't sure if she wanted to know anymore.

"And the traces?" Brome finally spoke, "Were you able to distinguish any of those responsible?"

"We were able to find only twelve or so strong enough to grasp," Vienna said between sips.

Pascal sat back down and rubbed a hand along his jaw. "It wasn't easy," he motioned to Vie, "we had to tag team to follow a few of them." He sighed. "We were only able to follow two completely, leaving at least ten others, maybe more."

"The complexities are fascinating," Brome shook his head, "but that is a discussion for another time." He leveled Pascal with a serious look. "Who are the two you followed?"

"I don't know," Pascal said with an astonished note to his voice. "The familiar part was the pawn." He turned the stool and looked at Darien. "The demon *has* been in Serenity before."

Darien rubbed the back of his neck and then looked to Remi. "That could be a big list."

Remi nodded. "Demons are pretty common around here."

"I might recognize the feel of them if we had names or descriptions." Pascal mused quietly.

"Same for me," Vienna added and looked at Brome.

With a serious expression, he inclined his head. "I as well, after feeling the trace and having a body to target."

Remi's phone buzzed in her pocket. Glancing at the clock, she wondered who could possibly be texting her at this time. Pulling it out, she opened it and then sighed with relief. Smiling, she glanced at Darien. "The Lewis boys *will* be coming back tomorrow. All of them."

His grin mimicked her own.

"How soon can you have a list?" Elaine got up from the table, pausing to make sure all noticed her before she walked over.

Remi tried to focus on each time she'd recognized a demon when they entered Serenity. It could take her hours of thought to remember them all.

"In the morning," Darien said abruptly. "Remi needs to get some rest so she can work in the morning." The way he spoke left no room for objections.

Frowning, she turned and looked at him again. "I'm…"

"Going to get some rest." He finished for her.

"I need some downtime too," Vie said quietly. "All this brainwork has made me tired."

Remi studied her for a moment. She did look drained. Vienna never looked tired. "Why don't you take Em's room upstairs?"

In a hurry to leave, Emery sprang to his feet and blurred around to stand beside Vie. "Come on, I'll take you up."

Finn hopped over the counter and went to the blood fridge. Leaning down, he pulled out a few bottles and tipped them in Remi's direction. "I'm going to bed down for the night as well." His eyes widened. "Tomorrow night sounds like it might be one hell of a ride."

Remi cringed. She didn't want that but knew there was going to be no way to resolve this in any kind of peaceful way.

Alaric moved into her line of sight. "I believe we should adjourn for the night. Miss Foster needs her rest." He tilted his head and continued to look at her. "We're going to need her to use her drawing ability to bring on the demons tomorrow."

She knew what he meant, but the way he said it made it sound like a plague or something evil. They only needed one demon. The rest, as far as she knew, were innocent in all of this. She looked at Darien and was about to suggest starting the list now, but the look in his eyes told her that he had already decided she was done for the night. Sighing, she looked around as everyone was getting up. "I guess we'll resume in the morning," she made a point of looking right at Elaine, "or tomorrow night."

Garrett came over and stood beside Darien. "Brome and I would like to stay on the premises tonight."

Darien looked at Remi.

She was going to say no, then realized if Brome and Garrett took the two rooms in the dungeon, dragon lady would have to stay elsewhere. "You can use the two unoccupied rooms downstairs." Remi glanced over to see Elaine's expression turn sour. Her mouth opened, and Remi expected something vile to spew out.

"I have made other arrangements for us, Elaine," Leontes said before Elaine could get a word out.

Elaine looked down for a moment and then back up with a fake smile on her pale face. "Of course, Leontes. How considerate of you." She glanced at Pascal and then waved a hand to the room as she moved to the door. "Until tomorrow evening."

Remi looked over at Leontes and bowed her head in thanks. He chortled and then followed Elaine out the door.

Alaric and Hope were right on their heels.

Pascal turned to Garrett, "I feel I owe you a drink for *that*." He hopped over the bar and motioned to the liquor bottles. "What's your poison?"

Garrett grinned and sat down. The stool looked smaller

than usual, with his large frame on it. "Irish whiskey, if you don't mind."

Brome turned to look at Attis. "Perhaps you could show me to my room?" He rubbed the side of his head. "I fear Vienna's skill has left me with a bit of a headache."

Attis nodded and motioned to the kitchen door. On his way by, Pascal held out two bottles of blood; accepting them with a grin, he followed Brome into the kitchen.

Remi turned and looked at Kyran and Randell. She made eye contact with Kyran only. "See you tomorrow?"

He grinned. "Only place to get coffee." Patting Dell on the shoulder, he went over to the door.

Dell had a sour look on his face, a duplicate of Elaine's. Without a word, he turned and went out the door Kyran was holding open.

"Well," Remi watched Darien lock the doors, "I guess I'm going to go try to get a nap before I have to work."

"I'll have everything set up for you and Berk," Pascal said over his shoulder while he waited for his blood to warm in the microwave.

"Thanks, Pascal." She stopped at the kitchen door. "Feel free to start the demon list too." He nodded in her direction, making her grin. Of course, he would. "Good night, Garrett."

Turning his stool, he toasted her with the glass of whiskey. "Good night, *neacht.*"

Darien slowed to stand beside his uncle and looked over at her. She raised her eyebrows, telling him she hadn't forgotten they had to have a talk. With a sigh, he smacked his uncle on the back and nodded abruptly to Pascal.

32

Taking the stairs as fast as she could force her tired body to go, Remi made it to her bedroom in record time. Kicking off her boots, she sat on the bed and covered her face with her hands. Dropping back onto the comforter, she lay there with her eyes squeezed shut.

She knew she wasn't old by any sense of the word, but still, she had been through some things that were devastating, things that bordered on illogical without reason. This – this was just so far beyond anyone's scope of normalcy; she didn't know what to think.

Aside from people being killed, which was undoubtedly a travesty, unfortunately, a part of everyday life in this whacked-out world.

Someone, no make that more than a dozen were conspiring, for some unfathomable reason, to harm anyone involved with Serenity. It didn't make sense. What possible reason could there be to kill sweet Mrs. Chaise and Mark? They were both warm-hearted people that probably didn't so much as squash a bug in their whole lives.

It was insane. She couldn't comprehend the reasons at all. Why would they kill the inspector and auditor? Seriously, neither had a profession that was well loved or would win a popularity poll, but why kill them? They weren't exactly loved by those here. If anything, killing them was doing Serenity a favor.

The attack on Emery, she didn't see a point. Opening her eyes, she stared up at the ceiling. It was her, not Serenity. Cait. "Oh my god!" She bolted upright just as Darien was walking in the door. "It's me." She scrambled to her feet, her heart racing. "Go check on Cait."

Darien paused for a moment and then spun around and left the room again.

When he came back in, she was sure she hadn't taken a breath.

"She's sleeping," he stopped and looked at her. "What's wrong? What's going on with *you*?"

Heaving a frustrated breath, Remi sat down and started pulling at her braid to take it out. "It's me. They're not after Serenity. They're after me."

Darien sat down beside her. "How do you know that?"

Rolling her eyes to look at him, she gave him a blank look. "They're choosing either people I have argued with, had problems with—probably trying to discredit me, or people I care about…"

He placed his hand on her shoulder. "Remi…"

"No," she turned sideways to look at him, "listen, they chose Mark and Mrs. Chaise and attacked Emery."

He sighed. "They also attacked you…"

"*Before* Emery and *after*, I told them their powers wouldn't work on me."

Darien gripped both her shoulders lightly. "You need to calm down…"

"Calm down?" Jumping up, she paced over to the dresser and stared at it. "This day just keeps getting crazier the longer it goes on." Spinning, she waved her hands around. "There's a group of paras targeting me and Serenity, and I have no idea why." Narrowing her eyes at him, she gave him her best scowl, "and don't think for a second I forgot about the wonderful information your uncle shared."

He didn't comment, just sat back and looked at her, a defeated expression on his face.

"Seriously, Darien, why didn't you tell me he forced your wolf to surface instead of letting me think he just pissed you off?"

"He did piss me off…"

Leaning back against her dresser, she crossed her arms over her chest. "You know what I mean. How did he even do that?"

Sitting up, he examined the palm of his hand. "Elders can do that to younger wolves."

Giving him a bland look, she shook her head. "It's not like you're a kid."

He grinned. "No, I'm not, but there's a reason he was drafted by the council, Remi. Only the most powerful beings are."

"Tell me dragon lady is just there for her blunt snobbery,"

Darien shrugged. "I'm sure that's a bonus, but no, she's there because she's more powerful than other older vampires."

Remi heaved a sigh and went back over to sit on the end of the bed. "Well, I'm going to just pretend she slept her way to the top."

Cringing, his eyes wide. "She probably ate her partners."

"I've never seen Pascal afraid of anything…"

Rubbing the back of his neck, he nodded. "I didn't think it was possible."

Closing her eyes, Remi tried to breathe out the tension that was filling her. Giving up, she opened them and gave him a serious look. "Why didn't you tell me that having a mate would help you control your wolf on the full moon?"

His chocolate eyes moved over her face before moving back to her eyes. "I didn't want you to agree to be my mate just, so I didn't have to be caged one night a month."

"I wouldn't have…"

Titling his head, he glared at her. "Yes, you would have."

Sighing, he fell back onto the bed and rubbed his hands over his face. "There's no guarantee that it would work either."

"Oh." She studied him and realized he was just as tired as she was. "I'm beat, but I doubt I'm going to get a minute's rest tonight." She picked at the comforter beside her leg. "I have no idea what they think I can do. They expect me to draw these demons here. How do I do that?"

Rolling his head to the side, he shrugged one shoulder. "I have no idea. I didn't know it was something you could actually control." He shifted and propped his head up on one arm. "I'm sure one of them will know how to help you."

"I hope so."

"Darien." Emery appeared at her door. "Hope and Alaric are back. They sensed someone testing the boundaries of Nadine's spell and want to go hunting."

Darien bolted up off the bed.

"They want you to go with them, Attis and Pascal too." Emery pranced on the spot.

Remi got up and started for the door. Darien put his hand against her waist to stop her.

"You stay up here," he said softly, with a tone that told her not to argue.

Emery interrupted before she could say anything. "Finn and I are going to be up on the roof to see if we can spot anyone. Brome is coming up here, just in case anyone breaks the boundary spell."

Remi felt her heart beating in her throat. She knew this was the council's plan, but she didn't like it. "Why are you on the roof?"

Emery grinned. "Backup. No one is expecting us to be up there," he shrugged, "and Leontes is staying downstairs. I'd say whoever tries something stupid is in for a wild ride."

With that, he turned and was gone from her sight. Remi stepped in front of Darien. "Do you have to go out?"

Cupping her cheek in one large hand, he leaned down and placed a light kiss on her mouth. "I won't be alone." Straightening, he stared into her eyes. "Stay up here."

Sighing, she hugged her arms around her waist. "It's not like I could do anything but throw my boots at them and scream my werewolf is going to beat them to a pulp when he comes back."

Grinning, Darien shook his head and turned to the door. "I can actually see you doing that."

"Be careful, please." Remi watched him walk out and inhaled a shaky breath. She wanted them to find those responsible, but at the same time didn't want anyone else she cared for to be hurt.

33

"I feel like a useless human."

Brome laughed softly. "You're not hiding up here if that's what you think you're doing."

"Well, it feels like that's exactly what I'm doing."

Glancing out the window, he was quiet for a minute. "Leontes is downstairs, and your two young vampires are on the roof to stop anyone should they try to get to you." He grinned at her over his shoulder, "I am the last defense in your protection should they fail." Turning, he gave her a serious look, "But it is not because you are a helpless human, Remi. It is because nothing can happen to you."

Remi leaned back and shook her head. "I don't understand."

His smile was warm. "I know." He moved in her direction in a slow stroll. "There is quite a lot you don't understand about who you are."

Crossing his hands behind his back, he continued to look at her, a contemplative expression on his face. "Perhaps it's time someone filled in some of the blanks."

Remi gave him a wide-eyed look. "How is it you know more about me than I do?" She snorted. "I don't even know who my parents were."

242

"Who is not important," he gave her a sympathetic look, "I don't say that to seem cold. I understand the yearning to have family and a connection." Brome waved his hand around. "You have both here at Serenity." He quirked an eyebrow at her, "If you'd known your parents, would you have found your way here?" Shrugging, he sat down in the chair across from her. "I don't think you would have, and then what?"

Studying him for a moment, Remi tried to picture what her life would have been like if she hadn't been a part of the foster care system. There would have been no fleeing when she turned eighteen, no Riverside, and no Serenity. Her chest felt tight when she thought of it like that. Taking a deep breath, she exhaled slowly and leaned forward to rest her elbows on her knees. "Okay, fill in the blanks."

Brome nodded once, a pleased look on his face. "You seem to believe what you can do has something to do with Doyle and his passing." A brief, grieved expression crossed his face. "Doyle had nothing to do with it other than helping you find your way here." He paused and looked at her, his eyes searching her face. "I helped Doyle spell the sign he placed in the window looking for you." He shrugged. "It took five years for it to lead you to Serenity's doorstep." Rubbing his jaw, a faraway look filled his eyes, "we were beginning to worry that we'd missed you."

Shaking her head, Remi squinted at him. "I have no idea what you're talking about."

Grinning, he tilted his head to one side, almost as if he were listening to something. "Your soul," he motioned to her, "the piece that makes you so unique is several thousand years old."

Remi opened her mouth and then realized she had no idea what to say, so she closed it and waited for him to continue.

"If you die," he raised one eyebrow at her, "the older you get, the less likely that is to happen. But possible during early life. We were afraid you'd passed on, and we'd have to wait until the next Keeper was grown enough to seek us out."

"So," she frowned, "I'm a Keeper?" It sounded ridiculous

to say, but she learned a long time ago that a lot in the para world was odd.

"If you must label it, I suppose that's close enough." He smiled at her, a warm expression in his eyes. "You, for lack of a better way to say it, are the balance, the one that keeps the scales even."

Sitting back, she opened her arms and gave him a frustrated look. "You're making less sense the more you say."

Brome laughed quietly. "I suppose Hope would be better at explaining it than I, but let me blunder through the rest and see if we can sort it out." Huffing out a breath, he looked around the room for several seconds. "As you know, there are a vast number of para beings in our world, each with their own abilities." He shrugged. "Not always good, I admit, but still true. No matter the ability of a being, it won't work on you…"

"Yeah, I know."

"You are otherwise in every way almost normal. Almost human."

Remi shrugged her shoulders.

"A few thousand years ago, our world wasn't as civilized as it is now." A look of regret was in his eyes. "One para clan would plunder another, bringing it close to extinction in some cases. There was no council to dole out justice, to patrol the communities and prevent chaos." He motioned to her with a smirk, "By whatever means a seemingly normal human came to exist, one that could tell a specie with a glance, immune to their thrall or magic…"

Remi held up her hand to stop him, "Wait. Are you saying that I, or the past versions of whatever I am, were the…" she stopped, her mouth hanging open, not quite sure what to call it, "Some sort of law?"

Brome nodded. "In a sense, yes. The Keepers defended the normal humans from all the paranormal clans and from themselves as well."

Puffing out her cheeks, she blew out a loud breath. "I don't do any of that."

"It's not as needed as it once was." He stood up and walked over to look out the window. "Yet, you open the doors downstairs each day, allowing normal and paras to mingle among one another in a safe, peaceful environment." Turning away from the window, he leveled her with a serious look. "Do you know how many other places like this there are in the world?"

Shaking her head, Remi didn't even bother to make a guess.

"None." Leaning back against the window ledge, he glanced outside again before looking back to her. "Species from all over this planet keep ending up here." He examined his hand for a moment. "The council has records of registered clans, their origin, and present locations." Nodding toward the window, he glanced at her again. "Within a three-hundred-mile radius, throughout the rural space that surrounds Riverside, are more species from all clans than exist anywhere else." He gave her a soft look. "Your power is like a beacon to them, Remi. The peace of your existence calls to them."

"I..." She frowned and looked at the floor, "I didn't know this."

"Perhaps it wasn't necessary for you to know yet."

Clasping her hands, she looked down at them. "I don't feel at all powerful, Brome."

He laughed softly. "Yet you heal the broken, soothe the beasts, and calm the wild."

Remi snorted. "If you say so."

Pushing away from the window he came over and sat on the arm of the chair. "You don't believe me?" He smirked when she shook her head. "You stopped two werewolves from turning, with a touch."

Remi wanted to say that wasn't true, but now that she thought about it, as soon as she touched Garrett and Darien, they had settled down.

Brome continued before she could speak. "Your Finn was very broken, let me assure you," a sad look entered his eyes, "the council had been monitoring him for several years, it was on the table to end him before he endangered our world."

"End him?" She shook her head. "He was just hungry and…"

"And out of control, believe me." He sighed. "The vampire he is now is so completely different than that creature you first saw." Tilting his head, he narrowed his eyes at her. "Did he ever tell you he made his way from Iceland to here?" She shook her head. "It was what confirmed your powers were beginning to flare."

"I didn't know."

He nodded. "You weren't meant to, then." His serious look changed to amusement. "If he isn't a good enough example, I could tell you from experience that your two charming bartenders are completely reformed because of you."

"Pascal and Attis?"

Smirking, he rubbed his jaw. "Yes, they created more havoc across the globe than any other pair the council has on record." Pinching the bridge of his nose, he closed his eyes for a moment. "They always managed to walk a thin line between outright breaking of our laws, at least we were never able to place them at the incidents…" he waved his hand around. "Let's just leave it there. You may not feel all-powerful, Miss Foster, but you are." Getting up again, he paced across the room. "Emery would have been ended, with no sire claiming him. By all rights, he should be out of control and insanely wild, yet he's not."

She felt she needed to defend him. "He didn't know what he was doing when he attacked me."

"My point exactly. He didn't even know he had been turned." A scowl appeared on his face. "If his maker is ever found, they will be punished."

"Emery is fine now." Getting up, suddenly she wasn't able to sit any longer.

Brome nodded. "I know and it's because of you he is." A

pensive look appeared on his face. "I understand, from talking to Attis that he's more than fine."

Hugging her arms around her waist, she tried to settle the tight feelings in her gut. "What do you mean?"

Giving her a soft look, he smiled. "You can relax, nothing is going to happen to your son. What I meant was the fact that he can get up before two elders like Pascal and Attis is because he drank from you." He sighed. "A death sentence under normal circumstances, you understand, to ingest the blood of a Keeper, but at the same time it's been allowed due to the situation."

"Because I claimed him?"

"There's that, but also mere curiosity. We want to see what else happens. He can already do what vampires wait three or four hundred years to do," he smirked, "rise before sunset. What else may develop?"

Remi swallowed the lump in her throat. "I don't know what I'd do without him…"

"I understand, and no one will take him from you." He studied her for a moment. "His bite has connected the two of you. No other has ever been joined with a Keeper in this way." He chuckled. "Although all the previous norms seem to be broken where you're concerned."

Remi was beginning to wish Darien would come back, so she didn't have to hear anymore. "What do you mean?"

Brome walked by the window and looked out it as he moved. "No other Keeper has ever had a mate."

"Is that bad?"

Stopping in front of her, he looked at her arms crossed over her stomach before he looked at her face. "It's not breaking a law, if that's what you're asking. It's just never happened in the history that we know."

"Oh." Her mind tried to process all the information, as she searched for something to say. "I just found out."

A surprised look appeared on his face. "Darien has ironclad control over his beast then, being this close to your mate for so long without claiming them is unheard of."

"So I've been told." Her heartbeat wouldn't settle down. "Darien told me when, if, we are mated then our lifelines join," she swallowed, "What does that do?" Shrugging, she tried to figure out how to ask it. "You said the older I get the harder it is for me to die and werewolves live a long time…"

Brome grinned down at her. "I suspect Darien may end up being the oldest werewolf in history."

Frowning, she exhaled and rubbed her hands up and down her arms. "What do you mean?"

Turning, he walked back toward the window. "Keepers have been known to live two, even three hundred years."

What? The idea of being that old was more than she could digest. She knew Attis and Pascal were old and Darien was the best-looking older man she'd ever seen, but this was her they were talking about, Remi Foster, tall, average looking, not some para.

"I've stunned you," Brome said quietly.

Blinking, Remi looked at him. "It's just information overload lately."

"I can only imagine what it's been like."

"I doubt that." Remi moved over to the other window and looked out it. "Does Darien know all of this?" She didn't know what she was going to do if he'd known all this time.

"I suspect he senses there's a part of you that's extraordinary." Brome continued to look out the window. "Pascal and Attis probably have an inclination as well, as they've been on this earth for the last few Keepers, but no one knew for certain but Doyle." He turned his head and smiled at her. "He was fiercely protective. He made the council promise to only tell you when you wanted to know."

An ache filled her chest. "I'm glad he did," she shook her head, "a few years ago this talk would have gone very differently."

"How so?"

She watched out the window, not seeing any movement. The night was eerily quiet. "Well, after I threw up from laughing too hard, I probably would have started packing."

Brome chuckled. "I envisioned you throwing me out."

Looking back at him, she started at his feet and took in the size of him. "It would have crossed my mind, but no, leaving would have been easier." Exhaling, Remi glanced back outside. "So, what does all this mean?" She shrugged. "I'm not normal, which I already knew, but what am I supposed to do with all of this?"

Brome came toward her and looked out the same window. "When you need to do something, you will. Until then, nothing has to change." Giving her a quick look out of the corner of his eye he sighed. "Once the threat to you has been resolved, we'll leave, and you can continue your silent magic as you've always done. If that's what you want."

Remi nodded, even though she wasn't sure what that meant. "Then the threat is to me and not just Serenity in general."

"They're coming back," he motioned down the street to where Remi could see the outlines of Darien, Garrett, Hope, and Alaric walking, she couldn't see Attis and Pascal, but knew they wouldn't be too far away. "And yes, the threat is to you. Serenity without you is just a café by day and bar by night."

"I was afraid of that." She couldn't take her eyes off Darien as he got closer. The shadows from the streetlights kept his face hidden from her, but somehow, she knew he was watching her through the window the same way she was him. "Why are they targeting me? Does that mean they know what I am?"

"No harm will come to you or those you love, Remi. The council won't allow it." He studied her for a moment. "I don't know how anyone could know, but we're going to find out." Brome turned on his heel and headed in the direction of the back stairs.

Taking a deep breath, Remi debated on following him or staying where she was. Her head was swimming with information, her heart was pounding a nervous, anxious beat, and her body just wanted to curl up in a warm blanket and sleep for hours. Blowing out an annoyed breath, she turned and slowly moved toward the door, only to stop a few feet from it. She didn't want to see everyone right now, that might make her a coward, but she didn't care. After they debated and discussed, someone would fill her in. Right now, she just wanted a few more minutes of silence to think about everything Brome had just told her. *You could have given me a manual, Doyle,* she thought with a defeated moan— *something to explain what the hell I'm supposed to do with all of this.*

34

Nervous energy had Remi bouncing from one thing to the next. She had the entire café ready for breakfast before Berk could get the food prep finished. After Brome had gone, she'd sat on the couch and waited for someone to come and tell her what had happened. The next thing she knew it was morning and she was in her bed with a passed-out Darien beside her. Wanting to wake him had her second-guessing for several minutes, she wanted to know what happened, but she'd left him there to sleep and come downstairs to help Berk get the morning started.

Holding out a cup of coffee, Berk gave her a steady look. "Your nerves have mine buzzing. You need to sit down and take five before I start bouncing off the walls."

Accepting the cup, she sighed. "I'm sorry. You'd think with only a few hours of sleep I'd be dragging my ass, but I could probably run a marathon today."

Turning back to the grill, he began to take the sausage off and place them on the warmer. "I can't believe no one told you what happened." He scowled over his shoulder at her. "You must have been out cold for the big guy to move you and not wake up."

Leaning back against the counter, she sighed. "I think my brain had a meltdown from information overload and my body just followed suit."

"No doubt." He covered the pan. "Mine went into arrest when you explained what they found out from the bodies…" he made a face, "Eww, by the way, I can't believe someone would do that." He made an exaggerated shiver before continuing. "So, basically we're trying to find a demon that's under some kind of spell?"

"Spell, thrall, I didn't ask for details."

Berk shrugged, "But Pascal and Vie say this demon is a customer?" He huffed out a breath. "I hope it's no one we know, like *really* know." Moving over to the fridge, he pulled out the prepped bowl of mushrooms and set them beside the grill. "Mushroom omelets today." Checking the clock, he leaned back against the table. "So, what happens to the pawn demon when they're found?"

Sipping her coffee, Remi watched him over the rim of the cup. "I didn't ask."

"I don't think I want to know," he added quietly. Tilting his head to the side he gave her a wide-eyed look. "On to the important things…" he smiled, "tell me about the men on the council."

"There's a vampire, a mage, Darien's uncle…" she smirked when he let out an exasperated breath.

"You know that's not what I'm asking."

Leave it up to Berk to shrug off the threat and be more interested in what the men looked like. Setting the cup down, she got up and grabbed the menus stacked on the end of the counter. "They're all…"

"Good morning, *neacht*." Garrett filled the doorway. "Darien told me you'd be down here this early. I'm still surprised you're up and about."

Remi sighed. "All part of the business owner deal." She motioned to the coffee pot. "Would you like a coffee?"

Garrett rubbed a hand down over his chest. "I've never acquired the taste for it."

Nodding, she set down the menus and moved over to get the teapot ready. "I'll brew you some tea."

"Appreciate it." Turning the large man stepped over in front of Berk and put out his hand. "Garrett."

With his mouth gaping open, Berk nodded and wiped his hand on his apron before placing his small hand in Garrett's. "Berk."

With an abrupt nod, Garrett smiled. "You must be a brother to Boden and Baker then?"

Berk nodded and then put his head back to look up at him.

Turning, Garrett gave Remi a serious look. "I'm going out to check the boundary. I'll be back in a moment for my tea." He paused at the door. "Brome should be joining us shortly."

Pouring the water into the pot, Remi turned to see Berk, eyes wide, staring at her.

"OMG" He huffed out a dramatic breath, "you didn't tell me there were giant man treats on the council." He glanced at the door Garrett had gone out then back to her. "That's Darien's uncle?" Berk snorted, "I thought Darien was large…"

Shaking her head, Remi picked up the menus and went out into the café. They'd be opening the doors in a few minutes and she was hoping for a busy morning to keep her occupied. The less time she had to sit and think about everything, the better.

"Morning, Remi."

Brome stood at the kitchen door. "Did you manage to get some rest?" He motioned behind the counter, waiting for her to acknowledge him before getting himself a cup of coffee.

"I managed a few hours, although I think it was just plain exhaustion and not just sleep."

Nodding, he added some cream to his cup. "Sometimes the mind just knows when it needs to reboot."

Remi sighed, "I guess I needed that."

Leaning back against the counter, Brome studied her. "You're doing much better than most would be."

Deciding she didn't want to learn anything else, she

motioned to the paper on the end of the counter. "I started the demon list. Hopefully, everyone else can add some names."

Going over to the list, he turned it with a finger and looked at it. "I talked to Alaric and Hope last night, they're going to help you to hone your skills and draw the demons here." He glanced at her. "If you'd like."

Heaving a sigh, she nodded. "I'd like." Turning when the door opened, she watched Garrett come back in. "I have no idea how to actually control it."

Berk came out of the kitchen and held out a cup to Garrett. "It's strong enough to kill any virus on contact." He went over and began to pull up the blinds.

Garrett chuckled and sat down on one of the stools.

Brome slid the list down the counter to him. "Remi's been working on the list."

Checking the coffee pots, Remi gave them both a few moments to sip their preferred wake-up beverage. "I passed out before Darien could tell me if you found anyone or anything last night."

Garrett glanced up from the list. "We lost the scent."

"But there was a scent this time?" She gave him a hopeful look.

Brome gave her a small shrug. "A very faint one according to Attis."

Remi felt some hope for the first time. At least they'd found a scent. "That's good, right? That there was one this time?"

"If it was an error on their part, yes," Garrett nodded, "if it was intentional then they know we're here and are baiting us."

Brome chuckled. "That never works out well," he gave her a serious look, "for them."

A part of her wanted to ask more questions, but logic told her she was probably better off not knowing. Two regular customers came in. Berk went over and started chatting with them. "How far did you manage to follow it?" Remi poured the customers' coffee and set them on the counter for Berk.

"Pascal said it faded near the old bridge on Dunham Road and then was gone before they reached the tracks." Garrett nodded to Brome's explanation.

Both men watched to see if she knew where they were talking about. Remi had lived in Riverside for seven years but exploring had never been on her bucket list. "Maybe they met someone there and got a ride?"

Garrett shrugged. "Could be."

A few more customers came in, giving her a chance to keep busy and not have to discuss it any further. She wanted to know, but at the same time anytime she asked a question her life got more complicated.

Taking the orders, she clipped them to the rack for Berk and turned to see Darien leaning against the kitchen door. He looked rough, to say the least. The last week of long days and never-ending nights were taking their toll on everyone.

He looked around for a moment before stopping on her. There was something different in the way he looked at her this morning. Questioning.

Going down the counter she poured him a coffee and took it to him.

Taking it from her, his eyes searching hers as he took the first sip. "Are you all right?" His voice was deep and gravelly, he must have climbed out of the bed and come down immediately.

Giving him a puzzled look, she nodded. "Yeah."

"Brome filled me in last night…"

The meaning of the different looks dawned on her. "I'm still processing."

He gave her a soft look. "With good reason." Taking another sip, he looked around again. "I'm a little stunned by all of it." He smirked. "I always knew you were one of a kind but didn't realize how."

For some reason, she needed him to be okay. If Darien could accept it, then it would make it easier. "You're okay with it?"

Remi watched Berk set the two orders in the window but needed Darien's answer before she took them.

"Are *you* okay with it?" He shrugged. "I'll take you anyway, Remi, you should know that."

Feeling like a weight was lifted from her she smiled. "I don't know if I'm okay with it, but I don't think I really have a choice, do I?"

"Not really." He moved by her when more customers came in and sat at the counter.

Picking up the orders, she turned to see Garrett watching her, a warm smile on his face. "I still don't understand the two of you."

Heading out to deliver the food, she raised an eyebrow. "Join the club, Garrett."

By the time the café was busy Alaric, Hope, and Kyran were there.

"Need me to do anything?" Kyran asked as she carried a bin of dirty dishes by him.

"Ah," she glanced around, "if you could make more coffee, that would be great."

"No problem." He went behind the counter. "Who is going to help with Deane, Renae, and Betany gone?"

Picking up new placemats, Remi tucked them under her elbow and grabbed the order in the window. "I think Iris and I have most of it covered. Nadine and Soren will be here shortly."

"How long has Iris Cantrell worked here?"

Remi turned to see Alaric watching Iris take an order. "Three years I guess, maybe longer."

Alaric turned to look at her, a blank expression in his eyes. "We lost track of her."

Glancing back at Iris, Remi turned slowly to him. "Okay. Well, she's found. Why were you keeping track of her?" Her first thought was it was too early, she was too tired for word games or para drama. His answer had better be short and sweet.

"Fey, as you may already know, are either light or dark."

Crossing her arms, she gave him her best *duh* expression. "Yes, I know that." Seriously there were some things she knew.

"Iris is neither," he glanced away from her then his mesmerizing eyes flicked back to hers, "or should I say both. It's rare, almost unheard of. Dark and light do not..." he watched Iris walk toward them, "procreate."

Remi looked at her waitress and then smirked at him. "I'd say they do."

"We had several incidents reported involving Miss Cantrell. How has she been since she's come here?"

"Fine." Remi shrugged, "she has a short fuse from time to time..."

"And the result of those times? If she's a threat to your patrons, we can have her removed."

Removed? "I wouldn't say she's a threat..."

He leaned over the counter, his face getting closer to hers. "Have there been any incidents that should have been reported?"

Remi studied his pale eyes for a moment and then turned to see Iris. For all her faults, she'd grown on Remi. Iris was as much a part of her family as Darien and her adopted children. "I wouldn't label anything," she made quotes signs in the air, "an incident." She shrugged, "more like a miscommunication, but it wasn't anything we couldn't handle." *Without Betany's light magic and Nadine's spells.*

With narrow eyes, he looked at her for a moment. "Just be watchful, Miss Foster, she can be very volatile."

"Noted." She saw Iris loading up a dish bin. "I better see if they need any help in the kitchen."

He nodded, barely acknowledging her as he turned to watch Iris once more. Quickly, Remi headed into the kitchen to wait for the volatile faerie.

Shoving through the door, Iris gave her a lopsided smile. "Is the *all-mighty* Alaric spouting off his usual garbage?"

"I don't know what you did, but he really has it in for you."

Remi stepped out of her way so she could put the dishes by the washer.

Iris snorted. "Typical."

"You pissed off a council member?" Berk asked in a cautious way.

Rolling her eyes at him, Iris wiped her hands on a towel. "I outsmarted him five years ago and I guess he never got over it."

Added to her list of I-don't-want-details, Remi gave her a serious look. "Just watch yourself while they're here. I've already got Dragon Lady gunning for me because I stepped in to stop her from harassing Pascal. I don't need to get caught in a Fey battle as well."

Sighing with a sincere look, Iris nodded. "I'll behave. I want them gone as much as you do."

Moving over to the dishwasher, Remi began to load it. "I just want the threat eliminated and things to go back to normal."

"Amen to that." Berk waved the tongs in the air and turned back to the grill.

Soren came in from the back room. "Good morning." She gave Remi a smile and moved over to the coffee pot while glancing over Berk's shoulder at the orders. "Did Nadine do something different to the boundary spell?"

Remi frowned. "Not that I know of."

"Oh," adding cream to her coffee, Soren took a sip and went over to the toaster.

"That's what was different this morning." Berk spun around and looked at Soren. "I thought I was just exhausted after a restless night."

"Iris, need you out here," Darien called through the window.

With an exasperated huff, Iris looked from Berk to Soren and then went back out front.

"What is different?" Remi asked, hoping her heart speeding up was for nothing.

"Normally when we," Soren motioned to Berk, "shifters

walk over it, our animals feel it."

Berk nodded. "It really stirs them up."

Soren's eyes widened. "Since Nadine's coven strengthened the spell, it's been intense when I step over the line. Except today."

Frowning, Remi pulled her phone out of her pocket. "I'm going to text her and see if they did something to it."

"There's no need," Hope stepped into the kitchen, "I did it."

"You changed it?" Remi erased what she'd typed and set her phone on the counter to give the council witch her full attention.

"Yes." Hope inclined her head toward Berk and Soren. "I'm Hope."

"Changed it how?" Crossing her arms over her chest, Remi leaned a hip against the prep table.

"We want the guilty to be able to come to you." She gave her a small smile, "But they wouldn't have been able, so we changed it." Glancing over Berk's shoulder, she looked at the grill. "Your food is going to burn."

Cursing softly, Berk turned back to what he should have been doing.

"The spell will still prevent violence," Hope continued, "but ill intentions are another matter."

Remi had never completely understood how it worked, only that it did. "Just so long as those that come here are safe."

"They are." She gave Remi another polite smile. "Brome, Alaric, and I would like to help you hone your drawing abilities, if now is a good time?"

Remi's nerves started to tingle. "Things are under control for now, so I have a bit of time." A dozen scenarios flashed through her mind. She had no idea what it was going to involve in learning how to intentionally use her ability.

35

The Keeper, not *a* Keeper but *the* one and only. Darien exhaled loudly and stared at the wall of the small office.

The hair on the back of his neck stood up, letting him know he wasn't alone. Turning, he almost sighed to see Emery leaning against the office door. "I just needed a minute."

Crossing his arms over his chest, Emery studied the floor between them. "I get that." With a slow movement, he looked back up at him. "Did you know?"

Running a hand through his hair, Darien sighed again. "I knew there was something, but I never figured she was The Keeper." He gave the young vampire a sober look. "Do you know what that is?"

Emery nodded. "Yeah, Attis gave me the condensed version," he grinned, "or as condensed as I could get him to make it; he kept going on and on, having flashbacks to a Keeper he once knew. He's pumped that our Remi is the all-powerful, revered Keeper." Pride shone from his eyes. "I knew Mom kicked ass but had no idea there was more to it than her pure awesomeness."

"You know you're an abnormal child, right? Aren't teens

supposed to resent their parents?" Darien perched on the edge of the desk.

"They're supposed to eat all their veggies too," Emery flashed red eyes at him, "I guess I am not the usual teen."

Shaking his head, Darien finally smiled. "You're not the usual vampire either."

"Are you saying Finn, Attis, and Pascal are normal?" He tucked his hands in his pockets and slumped back against the door frame, "because I think they'd be offended." Rolling his eyes, he looked around the small space. "I don't think any of us here fit profile of normal."

"That's true, but," Darien motioned to the clock on the wall, "I meant that vampires shouldn't be able to stay awake this late."

Glancing at the clock, Emery shrugged. "So they keep telling me." He straightened to his full height, reminding Darien that he wasn't a child but a full-grown man...vampire. "I stayed up to talk to Corey when she got up," he sighed, "I'm going to go crash."

Darien watched him leave and got off the desk, some of the council were going to help Remi learn to tap into her skills. He hadn't really spoken to her since they'd left last night, and he didn't know why; only he needed time to think it all through. Of course, this hadn't stopped him from putting her in bed and climbing in next to her. She was his mate regardless of what else she was to become. The problem he was having was whether being his mate was a good thing or a bad thing for her.

Stepping out of the office, he watched the three council members go into the back room; following reluctantly behind was Remi.

She paused at the door and looked at him. "I'm about to learn how to flip the switch to turn my beacon on," her voice was high-pitched like she was excited, but her expression told him she really wasn't. "Coming to watch?"

Going over, he pulled her into his arms. "Wouldn't miss it." He used the same fake enthusiasm she had. Remi rolled her eyes at him making him smirk as he hugged her into his body. "You look like you're on the way to a dental appointment."

Sighing, she relaxed into his hold. "This better not be anything remotely close to *that*."

"It will be fine. *You'll* do fine." He said softly as he tipped her chin up so she would look at him. They hadn't gotten to spend much time together lately, and he missed it. If he had his way, he'd stand here holding her all day. As he looked down into her soft brown eyes, his stomach began to tighten. If he stood here too long getting lost in her, there would be no lessons today. Dropping a soft kiss on her lips, he smiled down at her. "Let's go find out how this works."

Darien stood at the back of the room, staying out of the way as much as possible. It was hard to keep quiet while watching the elders try to explain what she needed to do. Presently Alaric was telling her to open her channels to find her ability. Covering his mouth so no one would see the grin, Darien waited for the words that mirrored her expression to be said.

"Does my soul come with a user guide?" Remi glanced around at them, a grin on her face, only to receive looks of disapproval at her humor. "I'm trying to tap into my magic channel or whatever," she mumbled.

Darien snorted and received an annoyed look from Alaric.

"Perhaps I can try?" Brome moved over to stand in front of Remi.

She waved a hand around. "Be my guest."

Wincing, Darien crossed his arms and leaned against the wall. The council members may not realize it, but he knew that tone all too well. Remi was running out of patience. If Brome wasn't able to help her, she was going to go beyond annoyed and into angry. *That* he'd stick around for, there was just something about her when she got mad that appealed to his wolf side. Of course, all parts of her did that to his man side.

Brome was going on about her being a task-oriented person, which was true, so maybe he'd have better luck. That hope was fleeting as the mage began to talk to her about opening her arms and pulling the wolf shifters to her on the invisible lines she held in her mind.

Remi's hands slapped down on her hips. "Invisible line? Really?" She looked from Brome to Alaric. "What like a mime?"

Coughing to hide the laugh that was dying to come out, Darien shrugged at her when she turned and gave him a look that said she thought they were insane.

Sighing in a way that was almost painful, she gave Brome a stern look and raised her arms again. Darien hoped it would work, for the safety of the three watching her like a science experiment. If it didn't, he might have to step in and rescue them when Remi went berserk on them.

He watched her lower her arms. "I don't feel anything," she said in a flat tone. Brome, Alaric, and Hope turned to watch the door.

Darien tilted his head and looked at it for a second, then at Remi. Her eyes were on him, and it was as he thought; her patience was at its end. She glanced at those watching the door and then back to him, rolling her eyes.

Hope finally looked at her, an understanding smile on her face. "I think my colleagues are going about it wrong. Let me try to explain."

Tucking her hands in her back pockets, Remi nodded.

Keeping quiet, Darien listened while Hope began giving Remi a bit of background and explained how the Keeper's abilities worked. He wasn't sure if Remi was interested or not, but he was. She was his mate and he should understand the powers her soul had passed on to her. After the first few minutes, he watched his mate's expression and understood each little thing she did. As Hope began to explain how Remi could tap into her power, in a very new age slash witchcraft lingo sort of way, his mind began to wander back through the years he'd known of his mate's existence.

They had always been in synch. It had always been that way, he realized. Even when they weren't close, he had been able to just look at her and know her mood and what she was thinking. Last night when the council had explained that Remi's soul was that of the ancient Keeper, he had entertained the idea that he shouldn't mess with fate. No Keeper had ever had a mate, but now to watch her, he wasn't sure if he could do that. Right now, at this very moment, he couldn't even consider never seeing her again. There was no walking away. His wolf was preening and feeling so much pride and agreed completely. Remi was his. Gods help man, beast, or entity that tried to tell him otherwise.

He was jolted back to the present when Remi made an annoyed noise and then blew out a breath. "The only part of what you just said that I understood was *let's try it this way…*"

Straightening, he moved in their direction. It was time to save their high and mighty butts and step in.

36

Remi sat on top of the cases and leaned against the wall; she was exhausted. Learning to use an ability that she'd always thought worked on its own was harder than she could have ever imagined.

After three hours of lessons and practice, she'd been sent to have a nap. A nap was something Remi never did. Even if time was available, which it never was, she couldn't fall asleep. It was one thing to go to bed at night when she knew Serenity was being run by several powerful paras, but to shut her brain off during the day and not worry? Impossible.

She'd been surprised when she'd instantly fallen asleep when her head hit the pillow. Learning how to use her *beacon* was apparently a great way to shut down her mind and drop from exhaustion.

The actual training had been a frustrating experience until she understood what she was supposed to do. Alaric had tried to explain to her how she could just reach inside and open the channels. To Remi, channels were something on the TV, so reaching inward or not, she couldn't grasp what he wanted.

After that failed lesson, Brome thought possibly Remi was

more of a task-oriented person and not mental, whatever that meant. He had suggested she just open her arms and think of invisible lines pulling the wolf shifters she was trying to call to her. Despite feeling like a mime, she tried it, and again, nothing happened.

Hope stepped in at that stage and as much as Remi tried to do what she was asking, she couldn't. The way the woman spoke was like opening a new-age magic or witchcraft book and skipping to the advanced-level spells. Nothing she said made sense to Remi.

Darien had been the silent observer up until this point. Thankfully, after seeing what she was going through, he'd suggested bringing Nadine back to help. The council members seemed a bit put off by his suggestion, but they listened, and *finally,* someone was able to phrase it in a way she was able to understand.

Nadine told her to think of it as taking a deep breath and, as she exhaled to blow out the call for all clans or a specific one…like blowing on hot coals to encourage flames, slow and steady. At this point, Remi found her so-called channels and was able to zero in on one at a time.

She felt like an excited kindergartener that had mastered printing her name when her call brought a confused-looking Berk to the backroom. Right on his heels was Bates and even Les interrupted his lunch and had asked Iris if Remi wanted his help with anything.

As far as pivotal moments in her life, this one was right near the top of the list.

Brome and Alaric wanted to make sure she could 'change channels' so they had her up the strength and page any werewolves nearby. This caused Darien to growl in a low menacing way from across the room, which only got louder when Garrett came to her, a smile on his face.

For Remi, it was affirmation that she did have the ability and knew how to use it. The council members still weren't sure if she could amp it up enough to call the many demons on the list.

Darien, with a smirk, suggested she try to call vampires. Remi laughed thinking he was joking. It had been one in the afternoon at that point…there was no way she was going to wake them up. Brome decided it would be perfect. If she could wake the sleeping dead, then she was strong enough to call any target she wanted.

Reluctantly, hoping it didn't work, she tried to call vampires to her. A few minutes later, she received a text from both vampires sleeping downstairs. Attis suggested that unless the building was on fire, she should leave him be. Pascal's message wasn't even in English, but she thought it was along the same lines, and he wanted to be left to rest.

Finn phoned her to ask if she was all right, at least that's what it sounded like he had whispered on the other end of the phone.

Remi was ready to celebrate her success when Emery came into the backroom. His eyes were red, skin translucent, he moved stiffly and never should have been able to come upstairs at that time of day, but he did. After assuring him that everything was fine, he went back down to his room.

The highlight of the whole ordeal was to see the three revered council members standing there with their mouths hanging open. She was the Keeper, now, even they couldn't deny it.

"You okay?"

Opening her eyes, she looked at Finn. "I'm wiped out, and the night isn't even halfway done."

Finn pulled two bottles off the shelves. "There are a lot of demons out there." He grinned, "You're drawing them in like bees to honey."

Remi grimaced at his comparison. "Except one of the bees is actually the pawn in an evil plan to take me out."

He sobered. "Can I get you anything?"

"No. I think I'll just go get some air for a few minutes and then crank up the *beacon* again."

Finn glanced at the bottles in his hand. "Just let me get these to Pascal, and I'll come with you," he gave her a half-hearted smile, "no one goes anywhere alone."

Waving her hand toward the door, Remi slid forward on the case. "I know. Go."

Finn blurred from the room.

Standing up, she stretched, trying to get the blood flowing and find the energy to walk. With Pascal, Vie, and the entire council out front scanning minds, auras, and whatever else they could, surely the demon pawn would be found, and then she could go to bed.

Stepping into the backroom, she swung the door open and looked outside. In all of it, she'd never asked what happened after they found the pawn. Could they locate the ones controlling them? She assumed they must be able to, or finding them wouldn't be as important as it was.

Glancing behind her, she checked for Finn. He must have gotten sidetracked. Going out the door, she inhaled slowly. There was a soft breeze blowing and it felt nice to have some fresh air fill her lungs.

Remi stood there and debated going further for a few moments. She was a foot outside the door, it was open, the light beaming out on her like a spotlight, Finn would be here in a few seconds, minutes at most, so she didn't see a problem stepping a few more feet from the building. The breeze was just strong enough to be refreshing but not cold.

Tucking her hands into her back pockets, she stood there looking around. The moon was barely a quarter, but it still reflected light on the river, making it sparkle without being bright. Once Finn got out here, she'd go sit at the table and let the sound of the water moving soothe her.

Turning, she noticed how many cars were lined along the street. The parking lot was full. Going over, she leaned against the corner of the building. Unfortunately, from here, the garbage bin blocked her view of the river, but to put it anywhere else would mean the staff had to carry the garbage even further. Scowling, she looked at the pile beside it. Someone had dumped their garbage. Why they couldn't just open the dumpster and put it inside, she'd never know.

Heaving out a breath, she went over and flipped the lid back. Would it be rude to put a sign on the container telling people to place the garbage *inside*? With her luck, they'd think she was rude.

Bending down to pick up the bags, she stopped and squinted in the dim lighting. Jumping back, she stared at it. What she'd thought were dark bags was a body.

Stumbling, she turned and sprinted in the door. Before she took two steps, she ran into a hard chest. Not caring whose it was, she clung to them. Strong arms wrapped around her, and she looked up to see it was Kyran. "There's a body…"

A growl sounded from behind him. Stiffening, he turned them enough to see a yellow-eyed Darien standing there. Before either of them could do anything, Pascal appeared between them as he stood face to face with the irritated werewolf, his eyes glowing red.

"Calm down, Darien," he said in a low voice.

Wrapping an arm around Remi, Kyran turned to face them both. "She's found a body outside," he sounded exasperated.

Pascal and Darien both paused and turned to look at her, their eyes going back to normal.

"Where?" Pascal demanded.

Taking a deep breath, she swallowed the bile in her throat. "By the dumpster."

Pascal disappeared.

Kyran gently pushed Remi in the direction of Darien and then pulled out his phone. "Go grab some council members. I'll get Peterson on the phone." He went out the back door.

Darien wrapped his arms around her. "Are you all right?" He leaned back and looked down at her, "Finn said you needed some air."

Resting her face against his warm chest, she nodded. "I thought someone had left garbage beside the dumpster."

Kyran came over and stood beside them, staring at the river for a few moments. "Hope and Brome say it's the pawn."

Darien sucked in a breath. "They killed their pawn and dumped it outside our door."

"That's what it looks like."

Rubbing his hand up and down her back, Darien hissed out a breath. "Why?"

Tucking his hands in his pockets, Kyran turned to watch the group by the dumpster. "I don't know."

Remi looked over at Randell, Brome, and Hope. Where was everyone else? "Where's Pascal?"

"He's gone with Garrett to see if they can pick up a trail." Kyran cleared his throat. "The body has traces of another scent, so they're trying to follow it."

The idea of smelling a corpse made Remi's stomach churn. She studied him for a moment. There was something he wasn't saying. Darien glanced from her to Kyran.

"What is it?"

Remi took a shaky breath and pulled out of his arms so she could see Kyran better. "What aren't you saying?"

Kyran snorted softly. "I was trying to figure out how to tell you." He blew out a breath. "The harm none spell is completely gone."

Remi jolted. She hadn't expected that. "So…"

"They have a mage working with them." Dairen finished for her.

"That's the theory." Kyran turned back toward the river.

Taking a deep breath, she tried not to freak out because that's what she wanted to do right this very second. She wanted to stomp her feet, rant, and have a good cry, all at the same time.

Darien rubbed the back of his neck, his eyes moving over her like he was waiting for her to crumble. There was frustration etched in his features. "I should go check on how they're doing inside."

Stiffening, Remi couldn't believe she'd forgotten they were still open. "I need to stay outside for a few more minutes."

He looked over to where the coroner pulled up.

"I'll stay here with her." Kyran offered. "There are enough

of us out here that the only way anyone could get to her is if they come out of the water."

Darien looked at the river briefly and then nodded. "I'll just be a minute." He gave her a soft look, asking without words if she was okay.

"I'll be right here," she assured him. With fast strides, he went in the direction of the building. "I don't understand any of this…" Remi said more to herself than Kyran.

"It's way above my pay grade," he agreed, "I mean, I transferred from the city, and killing crimes were the daily norm there, but this…" he motioned to Serenity, "this, I don't get."

Remi looked back at the river; she didn't want to watch them put the body in a bag.

"I also," Kyran continued, "don't understand this Keeper beacon stuff. What good does it do anyone to go after you?"

Remi sighed; it wasn't anything she hadn't thought herself.

"What you can do isn't exactly transferrable or anything. Right?"

"Not as far as I know," Remi whispered. If she could, she'd stand here all night and stare at the water. It was peaceful to watch, flowing almost silently downstream. For the most part, the river was reasonably calm. Sure, the water level went up in the spring, and occasionally the extra water coming in from so many drains caused it to rush with more urgency, but it wasn't a roaring noise, ever. It was a genius idea. Whoever had come up with the water tunnels that ran through the town to prevent flooding saved the residents a lot of worry each spring…

Remi looked back at the building and then at the riverbank. Inhaling sharply, she grabbed Kyran's arm. "I think I know why they can't track them." Turning, she ran toward the building.

"Remi…"

She could hear Kyran running after her but didn't stop. Moving around everyone at the back, she ran inside only to be stopped by Darien on his way back out. "Where's Finn? I think I know why Pascal can't track them."

Dairen frowned. "I'll get him." He went back into the storeroom.

Kyran came running up behind her. "What?" He sounded panicked.

Dell was right behind him, his hand on his gun.

Kyran waved a hand at him. "She thinks she knows how they've been slipping by us."

Straightening, Dell dropped his hand. "How?"

Darien came back with Finn.

Excitedly, Remi gripped the front of his shirt. "Finn, the tunnels."

He gave her a bewildered look.

"The drain tunnels. You practically lived in them. Could they be using them so no one can track their scent?"

Finn's eyes widened. "Holy shit," he turned to Darien and then Kyran, "they could. Their scent would be hidden in miles of rank, musty tunnels."

"Son of a bitch," Dell muttered.

"What's going on?" Elaine glided into the room.

Darien wrapped an arm around Remi's waist and pulled her back into his chest. He hugged her lightly. "Remi just figured out why Pascal hasn't been able to pick up their scent."

"Really?" Elaine raised an elegant eyebrow and looked at her, "and how is that?"

Finn answered before anyone else could speak. "There's old water tunnels running under the town, from one end to the other." He pointed at the back door, "They all lead to the river—*right* outside our back door."

"What are we waiting for?" Garrett stood behind Elaine.

Finn grinned. "Uh, I don't think you'll fit." He looked at Remi, "I had to walk almost bent over through most of them."

Garrett nodded and glanced around at everyone as they came back inside. "My wolf can fit. Will Pascal be able to navigate them? He isn't that much smaller than I am."

"Oh, he'll fit."

Everyone spun around and looked at Pascal. He gave her a cheeky grin, "I was beginning to think I'd lost my skills."

Remi took a sharp breath. "Let's hope my theory pans out." She watched Garrett speak quietly to Leontes.

Nodding, Leontes gave her a hopeful look. "We're going to let them think they've gotten away with it, and then we'll *hunt* them."

The way he said hunt sent a shiver up her spine.

Boden came sliding into the room. "Attis asked me to come and see if we're still working." He wiped a hand across his forehead. "We invited a ton of demons here tonight, and he says if someone doesn't come help contain them, he's letting Vie have fun."

"Oh shit." Pascal was gone before anyone could move.

"Maybe," Garrett said quietly, "we should help close Serenity *before* we go hunting."

Leontes nodded and motioned for Elaine to go back in.

She gave him a startled look and then rolled her eyes, "Fine, but I'm not waiting on anyone."

Brome looked at Remi. She couldn't translate the expression on his face. "I'll help," a big grin appeared on his face, "although seeing what Vienna can do might be entertaining."

Darien cleared his throat. "No, trust me, it's not entertaining at all."

Finn gave him a wide-eyed look. "Oh, come on. That time she made that asshole shriek in…"

Remi silenced him with what she liked to call her 'death looks good on you' look, and he closed his mouth. "Why don't you go back to work, Finn," she suggested softly.

He nodded, "I think I'd better go back to work." With an apologetic glance at Darien and then her, he was gone from the room.

37

It was like take two with a few modifications. Remi stood looking out the window, much like she had the night before, only she had Leontes babysitting her this time. Her young vamps were up on the roof again. Elaine was downstairs while Darien and Garrett prowled around outside in Were form. Alaric, Pascal, Attis, Brome, and even Vie were gone to follow the tunnels and try to find where the scent led them. Remi had tried to send Cait to stay with her friends, but she'd refused and now stood at her back window watching for everyone's return.

"I can feel the waves of emotion pouring from you," Leontes spoke from the other window but didn't turn to look at her.

Sighing, Remi leaned against the wall and crossed her arms over her chest. "I feel like I'm always being left behind."

He glanced at her, a brief surprised look on his beautiful face. "You wanted to go with them in the drains?"

Remi snorted. "No, not really. I just…"

"I'm not upset that I have been left to watch over you." He smiled sweetly, "I consider it a great honor to protect the Keeper."

His facial expression changed, and if Remi wasn't mistaken, he looked excited.

"It's a very thrilling time for all of us. We're personally helping the Keeper, and for the first time since times we remember began, the Keeper has a mate."

She wasn't sure if she wanted to know, but she asked anyway. "Why is that thrilling?"

Leontes glanced out the window again and then turned to face her. "Perhaps," he smiled, "let's consider for a moment that it was never intended for a single Keeper to carry the burden alone. For whatever reason, previous mate's paths didn't cross."

Frowning, she looked at him for a moment. "Wait, is this going where I think it is?"

He flashed her a fanged grin, "If you're thinking the results of your procreating, then yes, it is."

Pushing her hair back from her face, she sighed, "I thought the Keeper was actually the soul with many lives."

He nodded slowly, "It is. The soul seers have confirmed that."

She'd ask what a soul seer was another time. "So, you think if I have a child, they will have a soul like mine or the abilities?"

He waved a hand around, "That's what is exciting. We don't know."

Rubbing her hands over her face to have a reason to break eye contact with him, she glanced back out the window. A werewolf prowled the other side of the street; she didn't need to look long to know that it was Darien. He paused long enough to glance at her and then continued. "I just recently found out I have a mate," she watched him out of the corner of her eye, "I don't think I'm ready to take it to the next level just yet."

"Mmm, quite," he turned back to the window, "all right then, we shall change the subject."

Remi was all for that, anything but talking about her.

A sound of pain came from his direction, turning to see

why she was faced with a lonely expression.

"I had a mate once," he averted his eyes and looked at the floor. "It was a *long* time ago."

She didn't know if she should ask what happened, then wasn't given the chance when he began speaking again.

"She was fey," he gave her a sorrowful glance, "which is taboo. A vampire and fey."

Remi frowned. "I know, but don't understand why."

Resting his hands behind his back, he watched out the window again. "We're too powerful on fey blood. Close to unstoppable."

"But she was your mate…"

He nodded. "Yes, and we ran away to escape punishment." His voice had dropped to almost a whisper, "We almost made it." A strange noise passed his lips. "Two hundred years later, I agreed to take a position on the council to possibly change things. Mates," his eyes briefly connected with hers, "regardless of specie or breed, should never be parted."

Remi felt her chest tighten when his words made her think of ever being without Darien permanently. "I'm sorry."

Leontes tilted his head and studied her for a moment. "Thank you. Hundreds of years have passed, yet the pain is still there."

Several minutes of silence passed, and neither spoke. It made her antsy, and the waiting for them to return seemed longer. She looked over at him, having no idea what his blank expression meant. She broke the silence. "So, all vampires have an ability, right?"

"On record thus far, yes."

"Does it happen immediately, or is it something that they develop as they get older?"

"It can happen either way. Each individual is different."

Touching her phone in her pocket, she fought the urge to look at the time again, "Emery doesn't seem to have one yet."

Leontes grinned, "you mean aside from being able to get up in the sunlight when elders can't…"

Her eyes widened. "Is that his? Will it increase as he gets older?"

"Most likely, or it could turn into something else as he ages." He gave her a bright smile. "Maybe he'll be able to walk in the daylight."

Biting her lip, she considered that for a moment. "If he has ended up that way because he bit me, I hope it doesn't develop any further."

A noise that sounded almost like a chuckle came from him. "I can see that being a problem indeed."

Remi swallowed nervously. "Yeah, Remi on tap isn't happening."

He laughed out loud at that. "I dare say your abilities would give you the power to stop that."

Hopefully, he was right. How long had they been gone now? It was starting to feel like hours. "I guess you have some superpower also."

"I do."

A typical male answer, she thought.

A hard look appeared in his eyes, "I have the skill set for interrogation and intimidation."

"So, I guess it was your job once the demon was found, or would have been?"

"Yes. It is unfortunate I wasn't able to question him." He waved a hand at the window, "It would have saved a lot of time."

"Speaking of that, shouldn't they be back by now?"

Cait came rushing into the room. "They just went in through the back." She spun around and raced back out.

She had hoped to walk in and see looks of retribution, ones that told her it was soon going to stop and go back to normal. Remi had never been as shocked as she was when she saw Pascal with red eyes, elongated fangs, and utter hatred on his face. Attis, who normally would be reining him in, didn't look anywhere near his calm self. His expression was a few notches below Pascal's but still just as lethal.

"The damn trail led almost to her doorstep!" Pascal hissed in a voice filled with venom.

Vie nodded, then shook her head, "I can't believe it's her. I knew she was a drama queen…"

"…and chronic liar…" Finn added.

"…not to mention a bitch, but this?" Attis stomped behind the bar and reached into the fridge for blood.

Remi looked from one to the other. Were they trying to drive her insane? "Who?" She said loud enough that everyone paused and looked at her.

"Margo," Darien said with a growl in his voice.

Her heart jumped. "Margo, is the reason people are being slaughtered? The reason Emery was attacked?" She clarified, looking around, hoping someone would tell her no.

"Well, if she's not at the high end, why would the trail lead to her?" Hope asked, looking at Brome.

"You're sure?" Remi was feeling numb. She glanced at Pascal.

He nodded.

"What could she possibly gain from all of this? I mean, we resolved our differences over a year ago. She comes in here…"

"She must have some end game in mind." Garrett offered.

"Did she show up tonight when I called demons here?" It had been such a draining night for her. Remi couldn't remember half the faces she had seen.

Vie shook her head. "I didn't see her."

"Me either." Finn shrugged.

So much for this all wonderful ability. "Why didn't it work on her?"

Brome sighed, "That confirms it. They obviously have a mage of their own. A mage could. I know I could place a protective barrier around someone, so it wouldn't work."

Remi frowned. "And that would work? I thought what I could do worked on all?"

"It does to those within the range of your request." Brome glanced at Hope, who nodded her agreement with his statement.

"So it's *big* magic that prevented her being affected?" Remi wished for a manual or at least a cheat sheet of instructions for all of this.

"It's the only answer."

"Great, just what we need." Turning, she went behind the bar, heading toward the coffee maker, then changed her mind and grabbed a bottle of whiskey. A few shots and maybe things would be clearer.

38

"We're going to need help." Alaric glanced from Brome to Hope. They both nodded.

"Help with what?" Remi set the empty glass down and leaned on the counter.

"The confrontation may be somewhat trickier than we planned," Leontes said quietly.

Attis' head snapped around. "Confrontation?" He glanced at Pascal, who was smiling. "I'm in."

"I wouldn't miss it." Pascal perched on the edge of the bar, "when?"

"Tomorrow night. We can't wait until they have the chance to plot further." Leontes answered, even though he stood there with his arms crossed and looked at the floor.

Vie went over and stood in front of Brome. "What kind of help are you thinking?"

"Several factions." He smiled down at her, "Would you like to take part?"

"Oh yeah," Vie smiled in a way Remi had never seen before.

"I think we should move Remi somewhere safe until this is resolved." Remi jolted and turned to glare at Darien. How

280

could he even suggest she run and hide? "I'm not going anywhere."

"We don't know what we're up against, Remi…"

Ignoring him, she turned to Brome. "I thought magic and stuff didn't work on me?"

Darien wasn't going to let her pass the decision off to anyone else. "You can still be physically hurt."

She scowled at him. "So, can anyone here."

Sighing, Darien glanced around, and when no one showed signs of helping, he stepped over to stand in across from her. "We all heal a little differently."

Looking around at the various paras in the room, she knew it was true, but she didn't care. Pushing away from the bar, she walked around it to stand almost on his toes and look up into his eyes. They still weren't back to his soft, dark brown ones. "I'm not running and hiding." She said it slowly in the calmest voice she could manage. She watched his eyes streak with yellow as he clenched his jaw.

"Remi…"

Placing a hand on his chest, she searched his eyes, "I am not staying here like a good little Keeper or whatever…" She looked around at the others and then back to him. "If all of you are going to risk your well-being for me, I'm going." His teeth clicked together. "So, if you don't want anything to happen to me, be really good with whatever mad skills you have."

Darien growled deep in his chest, but he didn't say a word.

Remi knew him well enough to know the conversation wasn't over. He would wait until she was alone and then try again.

"We're going to have to call Nadine and…"

"Don't say Iris," Alaric whispered.

Vie grinned. "Definitely, Iris. Betany, and the twins too."

"Better make those calls now," Finn waved his hand around, "some of us don't do daytime meetings."

Vie nodded and pulled her phone out.

"I'll call Nadine and Betany," Cait offered and went over to the phone.

Remi crossed her arms over her chest and watched the others stand closer, talking quietly. She knew they were probably discussing strategy, but she needed a moment...or ten. No matter how she looked at it, she couldn't figure out why Margo was involved. Sure, they hadn't been great friends, and she'd fired her, but this was a little overreaction.

Watching the others, she realized Elaine was practically glowing. Come to think of it so were Leontes and her bartenders. What was it about vampires and battles? Turning, she looked for Emery. He sat at the other end of the bar with Finn, Baker, and Boden. They all stared at the council members, clearly not needing to be closer to hear them. Blowing out a breath, she went toward them.

Em's attention was on her. She didn't need to be a mind reader to know what his anxious expression meant. He wanted to go too.

"I don't think it's a good idea," she said as she leaned against the stool beside him.

He smirked. "I feel the same way about you going."

"I was going to ask you to stay here with Cait and watch over Serenity."

Emery's mouth twitched, "I think the Lewis boys can do that."

She glanced at Boden. He nodded with a solemn expression on his face. Giving Emery a hard look for a few seconds, she tilted her head and made sure she kept her nerves in check before she spoke. "You and Finn won't leave my sight the whole time, and if anything goes wrong, you both will high tail it back here and watch out for Cait."

Finn's mouth dropped open as his eyes filled with excitement.

"Deal," Emery said in a serious tone.

"Yes." Finn hissed under his breath.

"Remi."

Turning, she watched Darien move in her direction. Biting her lip, she raised her eyebrows even though she knew what he was going to say.

"We need to talk." His tone was somber.

"So, talk."

He looked over her shoulder at the four watching them like they were on a stage.

Motioning to the corner, she waited for him to go first. "You're not going to talk me out of going, Dare."

Darien leaned back against the wall and looked down at her. She tried not to look right into his eyes because she knew they'd be all soft and pleading, and she didn't want to give in.

"Is it wrong for me to want you safe?" His voice was soft and pleading.

Grinding her teeth, she took a deep breath and ignored that he wasn't fighting fair. "I have to go. All of this is because of me. Mrs. Chaise, Mark, even the damn auditor. They are all dead because of me…"

Grasping her hips, he pulled her body close to his. "None of this is your fault."

Trying not to focus on how good he smelled, which shouldn't be right considering he'd just spent a few hours in his wolf suit, Remi rested her hands on his chest. "Whatever the reasoning behind any of this, none of it would be happening if it wasn't for me."

"Remi…"

Reaching up, she put her hand over his mouth. "There's no way in hell I am going to be anywhere else when the rest of you are putting yourself in danger…for me." His eyes searched hers. "Please, Darien, I need to do this."

The next few seconds felt like an eternity. He stood there; she wasn't even sure he was breathing. With a low growl deep in his chest, he dropped his hands away from her and tilted his head to the side. It was the closest to an agreement she was going to get. Before she could say anything else, he moved to the other end of the bar.

Everyone watched him. Boden leaned forward and looked at her for a moment, then spoke to Emery. "Was that a yes or a no?"

Vie grinned. "That was definitely a yes, and he's not happy about it."

"He can also hear you," Darien added as he poured a drink of scotch.

Cait came out of the kitchen and gave Remi an abrupt nod. "Nadine and Betany will be here shortly." She glanced at Darien, "And yes, they have someone bringing them, so they're not alone."

Remi tucked her hands in her back pockets. "Cait, go print up a sign to hang on the door before we open. We're closed tomorrow night."

Cait stopped. "Am I giving a reason?"

"Just say we're closed for repairs." She glanced at Darien, and he nodded.

Cait opened the kitchen door. "What are we repairing?"

Darien held up a glass of scotch for her. Not her preferred drink, but it would do. "The balance," she told Cait.

"Okay," she shoved the door open, "so, closed for repairs."

Draining the glass, Remi stood there observing. Inside she was in knots. No, that was a lie. She was freaking right out. What did she know about any of this? Nothing. She didn't know a thing about being a Keeper or what she was actually to do. Magic, mages, and spells she knew nothing about, demons and pawns even less. Until the last few days, all of that was something she thought could only be found in a novel.

Attis and Pascal were reliving their last battle with Finn. Remi couldn't even stand to watch re-enactments on the history channel, never mind being in one. What would this be like? Again, she had no idea.

Darien came up to her and took the glass out of her hand, and then tilted her chin up, so she was looking at him. "Don't worry, *A ghrá*. The council doesn't fail."

"It's not them I'm worried about," she confessed in a hushed tone.

Darien frowned, "Emery..."

Remi shook her head, "him either. I'm pretty sure vampires come with a built-in violence survival chip."

His lips twitched. "It's possible." Lowering his face so it was only a breath away from hers, he held her eyes with a soft look. "You'll be fine. I won't allow anything but."

Kissing her lips softly, he straightened and turned toward the kitchen. "I'm going to check out the windows upstairs and make sure nothing's going on outside."

Remi watched him leave. He always knew what she worried about. She shook her head; he always knew where her head was regardless of what it was. He also seemed to make her feel better.

"It must be bothersome to always have a male stand in your way."

Surprised, Remi looked at Elaine. "He's not really in my way," she shrugged, "he may growl about things, but he'll always have my back." Remi realized she'd never thought of it that way, but it was true. Darien would always be there for her.

"I don't believe in mates," Elaine's tone was mocking.

"So, you've never found yours?"

Elaine snorted. "I've never cared to look. Why limit yourself to one forever?"

"I hadn't thought of it that way." Glancing behind the cynical vampire, Remi saw that not only had Nadine, Betany, and Iris arrived, but they with Vie and Cait, all of them glaring at the back of Elaine's head. Poor vampire better tread carefully, or she'd be in a whole mess of *oh oh*. She gave her the best fake smile she could manage. "I guess it would be trying to have the familiarity and comfort of one that has no other motive to be with you than who you are and no ulterior motive than your happiness."

Elaine frowned. Remi ignored it and continued. "One that knows you as well as you know yourself. One that will go to any length to protect you and keep you safe." She thought of Darien for a moment, and that familiar warmth filled her.

"One that only has to look at you to make you shiver, knowing just a slight touch will make you explode...whose kiss always feels like that first passionate kiss."

Now Elaine's lovely face was marred with a venomous scowl.

"You should feel lucky to have escaped such a fate for so long." Remi leaned back against the bar, trying to look nonchalant, when inside, she was thinking, *'Bring it if you can, vampy.'* Elaine's eyes narrowed, and normally Remi might stop, but she didn't. Lately, she wasn't sure what was going on. It was all foreign to her, but Darien? He was the one constant in her world. Sighing, she started walking away from Elaine. "Maybe you should write a book. You could call it how to be empty and miserable for all of eternity." She glanced over her shoulder and shrugged, "Might be a best seller."

Nodding to Nadine's smirk as she passed her, Remi grinned back. "I'm going to check on Darien."

39

Darien stood looking out the back window, watching the tunnel drain. He doubted anyone would be back in what remained of the night, but it gave him an excuse to avoid being downstairs. There was no need for him to be in on the planning. He was a werewolf. They had three possible purposes in a fight, protection, clean up, and slaughter. Given the amount of magical factions involved, he wouldn't be required to fight. Who was he kidding? The moment Remi said she was going, he had one objective, watching out for her. He planned to enlist a few others to help him. Why did she insist on going? Yes, she was the Keeper, and their skills were well-recorded and legendary. Remi didn't know how to use her gifts yet.

For his own peace of mind, he was going to get Brome to talk to her. Pascal as well, because Darien was almost positive he'd experienced the last Keeper. He wouldn't be surprised if Attis did as well. Some day he was going to ask them how it was that a Greek and a Scot ended up together for the last several centuries. He wasn't a history buff, but he recalled them being on opposite sides at one point in time. The tale was bound to be interesting and, if he knew them, bloody.

He felt Remi's presence behind him.

"Nadine and the girls are downstairs."

"Yeah, I let them in the back." He continued to watch out the window.

Remi stood beside him, "shouldn't we be in on the planning?"

Darien shrugged, "I'm sure someone will let us know if we're needed. I doubt we will be though."

"Too much opportunity for them to use magic or violence?"

She always understood. He chuckled, "Something like that." Turning to look at her, he searched her face. He saw the worry and something else he couldn't be sure of. "No one will expect me to be too far from your side."

"Is it wrong if I feel better knowing you'll be close?" Her eyes moved over his face.

"Not to me."

Darien had to bite his tongue, literally, to keep from asking her not to go. There was something strange in her eyes as she looked at him.

"You know we're a science experiment for the council."

Do I even want to know? "How's that?"

"They're curious about what's going to happen."

"With?" It wasn't like her to beat around the bush like this.

"No Keeper has ever found their mate, so they want to see the results."

She had his full attention now. "Of being mated?"

Remi glared at him for a moment. "Of *procreating*."

Darien blinked. "They want to see what happens to our kids?"

A startled look filled her eyes. "They want to see if we'll produce little Keepers."

"Really? I thought there was only one?"

"Me too." She leaned against the window frame. "They don't know for sure. Leontes finds it very exciting."

"I didn't think anything excited him."

She grinned. "Apparently, a little Keeper does."

He wasn't sure how he felt about it, being under the watchful eyes of the council or having a child of theirs a subject of interest.

"Have you thought about it much?"

"About?"

She smirked. "*Our* kids."

It was one of those questions a male wasn't sure how to answer. Any answer he gave could land him in trouble. He decided to try the truth. "Once or twice."

Remi smiled up at him. Obviously, he'd given the right answer.

"You can see me as a Mom? I don't know the first thing about it."

He shrugged, "You didn't know how to call vampires to you yesterday," he smirked at her, "You're a fast learner." Talking about having children wasn't helping him keep his wolf under control. His wolf was all for mating and breeding.

"You'd make a great Dad."

Snorting, he shook his head. "With Caitlin and Emery pushing my buttons all the time, I've had practice."

She smiled at him again and moved closer. "You think of them as yours too."

He could smell her shampoo, and it stirred his insides as it always did. "I do." Turning, he brushed the hair back from her face, "Anything that involves you includes me."

The next smile lit her eyes, and it reeled him in. Before he realized it, he pulled her closer to him and covered her soft mouth with his. Her flavor filled him. He'd missed being near her in the last few days; sleeping beside her without having her was torture. Before he took it too far, he lifted his head and looked down at her. Her face was flushed, her breathing heavier. "We should get out of Cait's room." Wrapping her arm around his waist, she leaned into his shoulder as he led her to the living room.

Darien paused by the window on his way to the couch. Pascal and Finn were walking down the street with Iris. He hoped they were escorting her somewhere. Otherwise, that was a lethal trio.

"I guess the details have been sorted out."

He nodded. "Looks like it."

"I had words with Elaine."

"Shocking." He steered her to the couch and sat down. She stunned and delighted him when she straddled his legs and sat on his lap. He hoped whatever she said after this didn't require a lot of concentration because *her* like this only took his mind to one place. Remi began playing with the hair on the back of his neck, sending quivers of need through him.

"She doesn't believe in mates," she said it in a preoccupied way.

"That's not surprising. I'd feel," he paused when she licked her lips, "sorry for hers if she had one."

"I feel sorry for her."

His wolf was ready to pounce. The feeling of her fingers running through his hair was driving him crazy. He couldn't stop looking at her mouth. He could taste each breath she took. Resting his hands on her hips, he shifted his body, bringing her closer to him. "For her?"

Remi nodded, "Yeah. Having your mate means all the loneliness is gone, right?"

With each breath he took, all he could smell was her. "I suppose it does."

She tilted her head, drawing his attention to her throat; he wanted to kiss it, to lick it...

"It means you're with someone—you're connected, body and soul. Someone that's faithful and true to you."

Dragging his eyes back to hers, a man could drown in those amber pools. "Uh—I've never heard of mates cheating on each other, that's true."

"It's perfect."

She said it breathlessly, sending a shiver through him. "It's not magic, *A ghrá*." *But you are...* "It's still a relationship and takes work."

"Sure," she leaned closer and kissed his mouth lightly, "but you're linked together in a way a normal relationship could never be."

His blood was close to percolating in his veins; he was that hot. Inhaling slowly, he took all the scents that were her into his body. He could smell the soap she used, blending subtly with her scent, the shampoo that drove him crazy, and he could smell she was aroused. Darien licked his lips, trying to find something to say. "That's true." His wolf was dangerously close to surfacing, and that was the best he could do. Reaching behind her, he tightened his hold and slid her forward on his legs so the center of her heat was pressing against him.

Remi shifted, opening her knees further so there was no space between them. Darien's restraint was strained. Inside, he was quivering with anticipation—places he didn't know could.

"What does it involve, Dare?"

Her breath brushed over his jaw. "What?" She needed to stop making him use his brain—it was in the middle of an erotic meltdown.

She rubbed her cheek against his. "Mating. How does it work?"

Darien closed his eyes and fought through the fog in his mind to try and figure out what she was asking. He opened his eyes. "For—" she kissed his jaw with warm lips, "ah, in most clans, the male marks the female." His wolf shoved up against him in a not-so-gentle nudge, wanting what he was telling her.

"With a bite?" She rasped.

The sound of her voice made him even harder if that was possible. Soon there wouldn't be enough blood flowing to his brain to form any words. "With a bite," he had to fight to keep his fangs from emerging. He knew his eyes were already yellow, but he couldn't do anything about that. With a hand he hoped wasn't shaking as much as it felt, he reached up and brushed the hair off her neck. It was a stupid move. He knew it but was still doing it. Slowly he revealed the pale skin where her shoulder and neck met. Lowering his head until his lips touched that soft skin as he ran his tongue, little by little, over it. "Right here," his voice was deep with lust.

When she hissed out a sound of pleasure, he lost the hold on the reins of his control of his wolf. Grasping a handful of her hair at the back of her head, he held her still and crushed her soft mouth beneath his. She returned his kiss with a needy moan, driving him further away from control. A hundred years could go by, and he'd never tire of kissing her.

"So, are we really going to do it?"

His brain tripped, trying to decide what she was asking. "I think you need to define *it* for me. I'm having a little trouble focusing right now."

Remi gasped as he nipped her bottom lip.

"Mate."

Pausing in his tasting her, he smirked. "If that's what you want to call it, then yes." He boosted her higher on his body, fitting them together.

"Darien..."

She rubbed up against him, and he decided the jeans had to go. Now.

Leaning back, she pulled her hair off her throat. She stopped moving, "Do it."

It took a moment for her words to register. Lifting his head, he looked at her; she leaned to the side. Her neck was bare and exposed to him as she looked up at him with heavy lust-filled eyes. The meaning of what she wanted became clear.

"I want to be your mate," she said softly.

"Uh..." he tensed, not sure he heard her right. His wolf went crazy, almost tearing his insides apart. *Isn't this what I've been waiting years for, my mate to accept me?* Why was he pausing? She attacked his mouth, making it near impossible to think. Tearing his mouth from hers, he swallowed and tried to force air into his lungs, "Remi..."

She covered his mouth with her hand. "I've spent years trying to figure out what I was looking for." Her sexy eyes locked with his. "It wasn't a what. It was who..." Moving her hand slowly, she leaned close enough that he could taste her breath. "It was you, Darien." She began to nibble at his lips, soft, coaxing, and he felt his resolve fading. "It's been you all along." She straightened and got off his lap, tugging on his hand until he stood.

When he was on his feet, she moved into him, her soft body fitting with her like they'd been made just for each other.

"I want this, Dare."

He stood there; the only sound was their heavy breathing. It felt like his heart had paused, waiting. Even his wolf stood paralyzed, hoping. "Baby, there's no going back," why was he giving her one more chance to back away? He didn't know. "You'll be mine—forever."

Remi's amber eyes didn't falter, didn't blink. She nodded.

Grasping her waist, he lifted her so slowly that each inch of their upper bodies slid against the other. When she was level with his face, she wrapped her legs around him, her arms circling his neck. His wolf remained still, afraid if they made one wrong move, she'd change her mind. Holding her to him, he navigated to her bedroom, keeping her eyes captive with his.

By the time he reached the bed, his whole body was shaking, her breathing so shallow he couldn't track it. Lowering her, he pulled the hem of her shirt up over her head, tossing it to the floor. Her bra quickly followed. He had to force himself to go slowly; as he carefully took off her shoes, jeans, and underwear, still not breaking eye contact. He wanted to make this something she would never regret, a moment so perfect she would cherish it forever.

Taking her hand, he nudged her to sit on the bed and then leaned over her to lie on her back. He was barely able to undo his own jeans and take off the rest of his clothes. She was spread out on the bed like a miracle offering, and he had never been so nervous in his life. Knowing you have a mate and finding them was one thing. Making them yours forever was the most intense feeling he'd ever felt.

Kneeling on the bed, he watched her as he lowered himself between her legs. He should speak, say something that would be special, but he couldn't find his voice. His mouth was full of fangs, and he knew she'd seen it before but wanted to ease her into feeling them against her. Placing tender kisses down her ribs and over the softness of her stomach, he carefully nipped the sensitive skin with the tips of his incisors and then licked over each spot.

Remi was quivering beneath his touch, gasping with pleasure by the time his mouth touched her inner thigh. She began to squirm in the most erotic way he could have ever imagined when he tentatively tasted her. Closing his eyes, he savored her taste, embedding it in his memory. Nothing had ever tasted so right before.

Every muscle in his body throbbed with need, and he wasn't sure if he was going to be able to hold off much longer. He wanted to sink deep inside her, both fangs and body at the same moment. To claim her, mark her, and forever take her to love and keep.

She moaned and lifted her hips, pushing her heat against his mouth. She was close to the edge. Lifting his head, he looked up her body to see her eyes on him. Her chest was rising rapidly as she gasped each breath.

Feeling like a predator, he moved up her body, keeping an inch of heated air between their flesh, not touching anywhere. "Are you sure?" He had to ask once more. From here, there was no going back.

Remi nodded, reaching up and touching his face as she did. A deep growl escaped his mouth; she looked at it and then traced a finger over his exposed fangs. *Fuck.* He almost came right then.

Without giving her a chance to object, he flipped her onto her stomach and covered her body with his. He'd thought about it, fantasized, and dreamed about it, but nothing had even come close to how amazing it felt to have her body beneath his.

Shifting, he lifted her hips from the mattress and brushed

the hair away from her neck, baring it to him. Placing a soft kiss against her flesh, he whispered, "I love you," and then drove his body into her wet one.

Her muscles clamped around him. He paused for as many seconds as he could manage to give her body time to adjust to his invasion when she moaned and pushed back against him. A low growl came from his throat as he pulled out. Licking over the muscle near her neck, he opened his mouth and felt his own breath on his face as it bounced off her skin.

Plunging into her, he bit down at the same moment. Remi gasped and then bit into his forearm and screamed a sound of release with a mouthful of his flesh between her teeth. Pain, pleasure, and his wolf exploded through him all at once, and reality blurred into pure erotica.

Nothing had ever felt so perfect as his mate.

40

Remi woke up feeling charged. She didn't know if it was the mate connection or pure adrenalin thinking about what was coming after dark, but she could probably run a marathon and still feel amazing. Darien had groaned when she asked if he was getting up, so she took that as a no and went downstairs without him.

She didn't even make it all the way into the kitchen when Berk spun around and stared at her. She saw his eyes go to her neck, and then his mouth dropped open. Feeling self-conscious, she touched her neck. "It's not visible, is it? I don't want to freak out the normals."

He shook his head, his mouth still gaping open.

"Okay, good."

He suddenly gasped. "You agreed," he waved the spatula around, "I mean, of course, you *did,* or the big guy would be doing self-mutilation penance." He squealed. "Oh my god, if everyone weren't going off to face their doom tonight, I would throw *the* most fabulous party," he grinned, "ever."

Going over, she poured a cup of coffee. "Did you have to mention the doom part?"

Berk closed his eyes and mouthed sorry. Turning back to

the stove, he flipped the home fries. "So, what does Wolfman think of finally getting you?"

Just then, Remi could feel, actually *feel* Darien wake up. Along with his waking, she felt his irritation for leaving him there alone. "I think he's on his way down now, so you can ask him." She took a sip, "I had to persuade him to mark me."

Berk frowned. "Why? He's only wanted this forever."

Setting the cup down, she went over and began wrapping the cutlery. "He wanted to wait until after tonight."

"Really?" Berk tapped the spatula on the edge of the grill, "it's a bonus for tonight, and you'd think he'd know that. You can draw on each other for strength."

"He knows that—" Darien stood in the doorway, "doesn't mean I'm taking a chance on anything happening to Remi tonight."

Berk nodded, but Remi interrupted before he could say anything. "I'm going, Darien. Live with it." Before he could say a word, she went out into the café.

She moved down the counter and then stopped when prickles of heat moved over her skin. Turning, she saw Darien leaning against the end by the door. He had a strange smirk on his face. "Did you do that?"

He shrugged, "part of the mate package." He started walking slowly toward her. "We can project emotion to each other."

"Really? That could be handy." The way he watched her made her nerves buzz.

"I can feel what you're feeling."

Remi rubbed her hands together and tried to relax. "Sorry, I don't know how to not feel."

He grinned as he stopped in front of her. "I don't mind. I've spent years trying to get inside your head," he grasped her hip and pulled her closer, "and now I don't have to guess."

"I felt it when you woke up."

Running his finger over her braid, he moved it to hang

down her back. "You mean when I woke up alone, my mate gone without so much as a kiss?" He pushed the neck of her shirt aside so the mark was visible. As he did, she could see her own teeth marks on his arm. A mark he would wear with pride. He'd told her when he put salt on it so it wouldn't heal the next time he shifted.

Remi shivered when he ran his finger over her mark. She leaned into him, wanting to be closer. That was new; she thought as heat and awareness flooded into her—making her want to climb him. Darien's attention came back to her face, and her knees shook from the heated look he gave her. She suddenly didn't care about making coffee or filling sugar containers. She just wanted to stand here and touch him, kiss him…

Someone coughed.

Leaning to the side, she saw they weren't alone. In fact, the entire staff was huddled together, some leaning out of the door, others peeking over shoulders, everyone smiling at her.

Nadine smirked and then shrugged. "We're here for a quick meeting before the vampires have to sleep."

Sure enough, the four tall vampires stood at the back of the group, grinning at her.

"Meeting?"

Darien kissed the top of her head and turned around. "Is the council part of this?"

Iris shook her head, the new shade of bright pink hair not to be missed. "Nope."

Darien started setting up the coffee brewers. "Good."

Remi wasn't sure if she'd ever seen the entire staff together before. "So, what's going on?"

Deane and Ranae pushed their way through the group. Deane's expression was more serious than Remi ever recalled. "We wanted you to know we're all in."

Ranae nodded, "members from each of our clans will be present tonight."

Remi stood there, wide-eyed, not quite sure what to say.

"Elise and I are going to stay here tonight with the wolves

and Cait." Soren motioned to Elise, "Her brother is coming to stay with us. With the river so close to the café, they'll be strongest here."

Betany stepped up to the counter. "I'm going to stay back too," she glanced around before continuing, "If there are injuries, I'll tend them."

Berk leaned out the server window from the kitchen. "Soren and I will have food," he grinned at Pascal, "and blood prepared."

Vie moved over with slow steps and sat on one of the stools. "I'll be going with a few from Betany's clan." She shrugged, "I don't have a clan, so…"

Remi leaned a hip against the counter. "I hear you there." Her heart ached with both pride and worry. "None of you are expected to go."

Iris snorted, "Of course not, but you're ours to protect." She waved a hand, "And not because you're the Keeper. You've gone to bat for each of us at some point.

Finn stood behind her, "and protected us, even from ourselves."

Nadine moved away from the door and came down to the brewers. "You believed in us when no one else would."

Emery moved beside her and started pouring coffee, "or afraid to."

"We don't know what we're dealing with…"

Pascal's smile stopped what she was going to say.

"Actually, we do." He motioned to Vienna, "Vie and I have been tracing those lines, or as many as we can."

Nadine set a cup of coffee on the counter beside her.

Remi nodded her thanks and looked back at Pascal. "And?"

"Well, we already knew they had a mage, but I imagine Brome and Alaric can take him on without too much trouble. We only need him distracted so the rest of us can get close." He paused for a moment, waiting for input she imagined, but none was offered. "There are a few vampires which will *thrill* Elaine and possibly Leontes. He does hate traitors of our kind." He snorted, "There are a few minor shifters, but I believe Iris and her clan are up to that challenge."

Iris made a noise that was either a giggle or a snarl. Remi wasn't sure. "It feels like Christmas," Iris sang softly.

Afraid to ask what that meant, Remi looked back to Pascal.

His expression was more serious. "There are demons of every flavor," then he grinned, fangs showing, "Attis and I will handle as many of those as we're able."

Attis moved down behind the bar to the blood fridge and pulled out four bottles. He set three on the bar. "Nothing tangier than demon juice," he opened the bottle and took a drink, "I look forward to the taste of fear."

Remi's stomach churned, but she kept that to herself and glanced from Finn to Emery.

Finn smirked and picked up one of the bottles. "Not to worry, we've been assigned the task of sticking to you like glue." He offered a bottle to Emery.

Taking the bottle, Emery nodded, "Like a second and third skin." He took a small sip and motioned to Darien, "Just like I'm sure your *mate* plans to." He grinned at Darien's confirming nod. "Congratulations by the way, and I think everyone will agree when I say it's about damn time."

She felt her cheeks flush and scrambled for a way to keep the subject off mating, despite the warm feeling Darien was sharing with her. "Does anyone have any thoughts on what I can do to help?" Remi looked at Darien, who was opening his mouth to speak, "Staying here isn't one of them." He closed his mouth and crossed his arms over his chest.

"You have more power over the clans than any of us." Attis played with his empty bottle on the bar top.

"I doubt calling them to me will be of help."

He smirked, "No, that's true, but the Keeper—*you*, have more skills than that."

"Really? Like?" She picked up the coffee and held the cup in both hands while hoping these supposed skills were something she could do.

Attis shrugged, "You can paralyze them…"

Pascal chuckled, "it's more like freezing them for a few moments."

Attis rolled his eyes at his companion. "You'll have to wait until we have them all occupied, especially the mage and witches…"

"Witches?" Nadine turned a scowl on her face.

Vie held out an empty cup to her. "Yeah, at least two," she glanced at Pascal, "we're not sure how strong they are though."

Nadine took the cup and turned back to fill it. "Leave the witches to me. I'm bringing two others from my coven, and between the three of us, we could peel the skin from any traitor a mile away."

Eyes wide, Remi looked back to Vienna. She was smiling.

"Anyway," Pascal gave Nadine a surprised look, "there's most likely too many for you to hit them all at once, so we'll distract and cut down the numbers a bit for you."

"What about the normals?" Vie asked, looking over her shoulder at Pascal. "Who's going to deal with them?"

Shocked, Remi set the cup down again. "There are people involved?"

Boden put up his hand, "Are you saying we're not people?"

Leave it up to him to crack a joke at that moment. She glared at him. "You know what I mean." Blowing out a breath, Remi leaned on the counter and looked down at it. "Not that I understand why me, why Serenity, but what stake would normals have in any of this?"

"That's what I want to know." Kyran came out of the kitchen and then stopped abruptly and looked around. "A little early for a party, isn't it? Why wasn't I invited?"

Berk chuckled in a dramatic way, "No one was able to get near you without a council member attached to your elbow."

"Ah," Kyran walked behind the counter and headed straight for the coffee. "Understandable, they're a very serious bunch." He fixed his coffee and turned to lean back against the back counter. "So, I'm guessing I missed the battle plan." He didn't wait for comment. "I'll be the normal people's justice—oh wait; I am the plain old no-special-skills cop."

"You'll need to stay clear," Deane said quietly, "there's going to be a lot of power surging."

Kyran nodded almost nonchalantly. "No problem there." He shrugged, "the way I see it is the normals involved are going to be paralyzed with fear or freak out and run when all this goes down. I just need to be on the sidelines and then grab them as they stumble by."

Darien chuckled at that. It lasted about three seconds before his face turned to stone again. "Pascal, do you know how Remi can do that freeze thing?"

Kyran lowered his cup and mouthed *freeze thing* at Remi.

She shook her head, not wanting to try and explain what she didn't understand. Remi looked at Pascal.

"No, I've witnessed it but have no idea how. Brome would know." He smirked, "I think he's memorized every move ever made by the past Keepers."

Remi groaned. She wasn't up for another lesson from the council.

Nadine gave her an easy smile. "It's inside you, Rem, just like the calling was. You'll find it." She glanced around and then gave Remi a wide-eyed look and played with the collar of her shirt.

It took a second before she understood. Trying to seem casual about it, Remi pulled her braid back to cover the bite on her neck.

"I'd be running around shouting it from the rooftops if I was newly mated," Elise said with a big grin.

Kyran hissed out a breath. "Mated?" He looked at Remi, her neck, and then back again. "How the hell long did I sleep? I missed the strategy meeting and a mating announcement…"

"Mated?" Garrett's deep voice boomed from the kitchen door. He inhaled slowly and then smiled. "Well, thank the Gods, it's about bloody time…" he stopped as he noticed everyone. Shaking his head, he came down to the counter, grinning at Remi. "Welcome, *neacht*." Then he glared at his nephew. "What the hell are you doing down here?"

Darien stepped closer to her back and rested a hand on her hip. "Opening the café."

Garrett snorted. "Is nothing like it was? Any newly mated pair I've ever seen all but vanishes for a honeymoon month."

"A month?" Remi stuttered and then felt her cheeks heat when she realized why the couples would need to do that.

Glancing around for a moment, Garrett pointed to Berk. "Get your grill going and make me a brew while you're in there."

Berk opened his mouth and then saluted the big were before going into the kitchen.

Remi turned to the kitchen, but Garrett stepped in front of her.

"Not you. You get today off."

"I…"

Wrapping an arm around her waist, Darien pulled Remi back from the counter. "He's right. You have to figure out what this ability is before tonight."

"I don't need all day…"

"We'll stay," Ranae said and started to take the chairs off the tables. Deane went into the kitchen with a brief smile and nod.

Garrett grinned at her and then at Darien. "Off you go. We'll see you at dinner."

Attis went over and put his arm over Finn's shoulder. "Dawn is a few minutes away. Time for vampires to retire."

Nodding, Finn glanced at Emery. "I'm ready to drop, and he doesn't even look tired."

Lowering the bottle, Emery gave him a bloody smile. "I'm tired, just not ruled by the impending light."

"Lucky bastard," Finn mumbled as he walked down the bar.

Remi watched a few more minutes as everyone either went to work or wandered out the back door.

"Go," Nadine said softly as she refilled the brewers. "I'll

text you when Brome is up, and you can pick his brain."
Remi sighed.
"Go," she repeated, "spend some time with your mate."

41

Remi moved through the room, agitation churning inside her. In twenty minutes, they'd be leaving, and as she studied each being there, she realized she was the only one not prepared.

Brome's instruction had basically amounted to telling her when she wanted it—her ability would be there. She just had to want it bad enough…in summary—absolutely no help at all, in *any* way.

The energy inside Serenity was charged with so much tension her skin felt like it was charged—or was that her own power? She had no idea.

By the kitchen were those staying at Serenity. Keeping the home fires burning, as Boden had put it, she hoped those were hypothetical fires, but with the Lewis boys, you could never be sure.

Remi was thankful Cait would have so many to watch out for her, and the building that was her home. The Lewis brothers had the most serious looks she'd ever seen on any of their four faces. Betany, Soren, and Caitlyn just looked worried as they talked quietly. In a way, she was glad Cait's clan didn't come into their power, whatever it turned out to be until they were in their twenties. Otherwise, she'd be freaking out with Cait wanting to go too.

Elise stood in the corner with her brother, Cedric. He was a very pretty man, with all fair hair and a tanned complexion, all nymph males were fair and appealing. Nice on the eyes or not, the expression on his face said he didn't have a sweet disposition. Cedric had never been one to come inside Serenity, much to the female patrons' disappointment.

Remi suddenly felt Darien's disapproval. Looking over to where he stood, she met his eyes. His expression said he wasn't happy her thoughts were on another male, but then a feeling of warmth and love flowed through her, telling her she was forgiven for looking. Letting her eyes move over him for a moment, she quickly looked away. Hadn't they just spent most of the afternoon wrapped around each other in bed? Studying him like something she wanted to taste wasn't where her head needed to be right now.

Kyran and Dell stood by the entrance. Both looked almost bored, then again, they were used to impending violence in their jobs. Kyran said something to Dell, who turned and looked at her for a moment before he glanced at Darien. When he looked back at her again, she didn't need to be a mind reader to know he wasn't happy she was mated to the *were*. If anything, he looked disgusted by it. With an abrupt nod to Kyran, he went outside. Kyran grinned at her then shrugged and went over to talk to Iris.

Iris, her deep red hair replacing the bright pink it had been earlier in the day, was standing with four fey, Betany's clan members if she had the introductions right. Even though the other four were also fey, they didn't have the warm vibes Betany always seemed to have. Compared to Iris, however, who was radiating vengeance, they could have been choir girls.

Was it strange that so many women were going? Another difference between the two worlds Remi was part of, the paras had no problem letting women fight—or if they did, they were smart enough to keep it to themselves.

Ranae and Deane had four family members with them, and there was no mistaking they were related in some way. They all had similar features, only different shades of hair. Even the two males looked the same. A family with strong twin genes, Remi mused as she let her eyes move to the four council members standing away from everyone else in the room.

They didn't talk to each other, just observed. Elaine still looked positively radiant; Leontes seemed to have a glow on. Hopefully, her blood supply was holding up with this many vampires in the house; at least she hoped they'd been drinking bottled blood. Tomorrow—if she had a tomorrow, she'd have to order more.

Alaric leaned against the wall, his eyes not leaving Iris. He either hated her like no other or was seriously crushing on her because even Iris wasn't *that* interesting.

Hope, well, Remi wasn't sure if Hope was even completely present. Her eyes were glazed and other than her lips moving every few seconds, there was no indication she was aware of anything happening around her. Remi would never get witches. Her best friend may be one, but that gave her no insight into how they worked.

Remi looked to where Nadine stood with her two coven mates Darien and Garrett. She barely recognized Naddy, for a moment she thought it was because her long pale hair was down, and then realized it was the way her eyes looked. They were basically glowing, she didn't know what a group of witches did to get ramped up, but her friend had done it in spades. The two from her coven with her were just plain scary. She was glad they were on the same side.

Garrett, *Uncle* Garrett looked jovial for someone going into a metaphysical war, then again Remi was pretty sure once he changed it wouldn't be *meta* with the big man, but *all* physical—and violent.

Darien, she glanced at briefly, to find his eyes on her. It was typical really, for him to observe her while she watched everyone else. When he winked at her, warmth spread through her and she looked away. Right now, he was a distraction from the silent mental meltdown she was busy tackling.

Attis and Pascal sat at a booth with the two younger vampires. To see them, you would think it was a normal night from their relaxed demeanor. She remembered their ages, or estimated ages, and figured they'd probably seen more wars, revolts, and battles, tonight wouldn't even register on their mayhem scale.

Finn's body language said he was laid back and cool, but he had a wild look in his eyes. The same one he'd had when he first came to be at Serenity. She hoped tonight wasn't going to set him back to his old ways. He turned and looked right at her, and the look faded slightly. She didn't know how, but for some reason, she seemed to be his anchor. His mouth quirked in a small smile, which she returned with a nervous one of her own before exhaling slowly.

Emery, *her* Em, was sitting there watching everyone in the room. Every few seconds, he'd nod or shrug to whatever the older vampires were saying, but she knew he was observing and sizing everyone up, just as she was. Their eyes met and she could see he was resolved and going for her and no other reason. No one, in his mind, could threaten her and get away with it. Remi didn't know what had occurred when he'd drank from her that night years before, but she felt deep in her soul that it would never fade. She tried to relax her posture a bit while he studied her, hoping to give him a sense that she was just dandy with the events to come, but when he tilted his head and smirked, she knew she'd failed.

Finally dragging her eyes away from him, with a silent wish for him to be okay through tonight, she looked at Vienna and Brome. They were standing close together and seemed to be oblivious to the others around them. It was odd, though pleasing, to see Vie talking with a male, it was something Remi couldn't ever remember happening. If it were any of her other staff cozying up to a council member, especially an all-powerful mage, she'd be concerned but Vie, she knew, could more than take care of herself. If anything, Brome should be worried.

Kyran came over toward her, his usual easy walk was stiffer, less smooth, the only indication he was hyped up in any way. Stopping on the other side of the bar, he tucked his hands in his pockets. "You were given the run down?"

Remi nodded, "Yeah," she exhaled and rolled her shoulders, "we meet at the tunnel exit near Margo's house." She was glad most of the thirty here had decided driving was better than going through the creepy tunnel. "Leontes and Elaine are going to the front and hopefully drive them all out the back." Remi glanced over at the two vampires, yeah seeing them on your doorstep would cause you to flee. "The rest of us will be waiting in the trees by the field behind her place."

Kyran nodded. "And the rest, they say, will be history."

"We hope."

He shrugged. "I'm not under the impression it's going to be easy, but the rest of the para team are going to be nearby."

"So that's the department you're part of?"

He nodded again. "Yep."

She had to wonder more about his history. "Been on the para-force for long?"

He flashed her a smile. "Did five years in the big bad city." He shuddered, "that wasn't a fun time."

Crossing her arms over her chest, she tried not to visibly shake. "I can imagine."

"No, you can't." Kyran turned when Garrett moved up beside him.

Garrett grinned like it was a party. "We're leaving." He looked at Remi, his eyes softening, "I'm shifting and going through the tunnel with the vamps. Darien's going to ride over with you and the cops."

Remi nodded and dropped her arms. "Okay." She moved quickly to the end of the bar and went around it, avoiding making eye contact with Cait and those at the end. She needed to get her head in the game, considering she had no idea of the rules or how to play, she couldn't be having any anxious feelings for those staying behind. They'd be fine. They had to be.

It felt as if Remi was standing in the middle of a scene in a horror movie. The treed area was down in a small hollow, with trees of various types around the edges, complete with a big open space in the middle. The moon was a bright quarter with a few clouds hanging from it, the fog on the ground seemed to be an extension of the clouds. Yep, if she was a character in a movie and walked into a place like this, she would high-tail it in the other direction.

Hidden through the barely visible trees surrounding this little grove were her friends. To her right she could make out only Vie and Brome. The only reason she could; he was doing what looked like a slow-motion tai-chi, waving his arms around aiming them all around the space they stood.

"He's casting a cloaking spell," Darien said softly from beside her.

Nodding, Remi pretended this was a normal event in her life.

Vie stood with Brome, her lips moving but she kept her arms down at her side, her eyes focused on the opening facing Margo's property.

Taking a deep breath, Remi exhaled it slowly and looked to the left. Nadine, her coven mates, and Hope were there. The fog circled their ankles making it look like they were floating on air. None of them were watching the opening, all had their heads tilted back looking at the sky, arms open. She could hear a chant but couldn't make out what was being said.

"Not sure what they're up to," Darien whispered, "pretty sure we don't want to know." He made a low growling sound, "All this power is playing havoc with my wolf."

A deep growl came from behind them, Remi turned to see a huge—scary, up to her waist, huge werewolf prowling on all fours behind them. It stopped and looked right at her and how she wasn't sure, but she recognized it to be Garrett.

"I'm going to have to change shortly—"

Looking up at Darien, she searched his face, his eyes were already yellow, but there was something hesitant in his expression. "I've seen you change before, Dare."

He shrugged, "Don't be afraid of me…"

Remi grinned, "It's a little late for that isn't it?" She rubbed a hand over his chest. "Do what you have to do, just…" she stretched up and kissed his mouth softly, "don't get hurt."

Darien smirked and shook his head.

The two young vampires standing on her other side chuckled. Glaring at them, she turned back to Darien. "Go, do what you have to, we're fine."

A movement above her made her look up. Attis and Pascal went over their heads and landed gracefully a few feet away. "Elaine and Leontes are almost on their doorstep." Was it shocking they looked like two excited children?

Darien kissed her hard on the mouth and then walked over behind a tree. She'd thank him for that later. Knowing he changed, seeing him as a werewolf was okay; watching it happen, well yeah, she'd have to work on that.

Pascal came over and stood where Darien had been. "Take some deep breaths and start finding that ability." He placed a hand on her shoulder and made sure she was looking at his blood-red eyes, "Attis and I are going to play right and left wing," he nodded to Finn and Emery, "They're your defensemen."

Remi blinked, realizing he'd just put the game plan into hockey lingo. "I guess that makes me goalie?"

He grinned, "when you're ready to come out of the net, we'll cover you."

She blew out a breath, "Okay." As far as playing *hockey* went, Remi was pretty sure she should be on the other side of the plexiglass, behind the goal, or on the bench.

Attis glided on her right side, he nodded abruptly to her and then looked over at the two fledglings, "Think of all those times someone pissed you off and you wanted to take a bite…" Finn's eyes went red, his face lost the handsome smooth lines and his fangs came out. Stepping out of the way, he motioned for Finn to take his place beside her. "No one gets remotely close to our Keeper." Finn nodded and turned to watch the opening.

"You're up," Pascal said stepping out of the way and motioning for Emery to stand on her left.

Emery looked at her, took a deep breath, and in a blink of an eye became that feral vampire that had bitten her.

It was a momentary pause for Remi, remembering that the boys she worked with every day, that she thought *she* was protecting were lethal beings.

"Go," Emery said in a deep almost unrecognizable voice to the elder vampires.

As soon as they glided forward the two werewolves moved up to stand in front of her, she felt like some fairytale queen. Darien paused long enough to look over his shoulder, his yellow eyes connecting with her briefly and then he turned his long snout to watch the opening in the trees.

Movement near the opening had her turn her attention, the others were there now, and it wasn't surprising at all to see who was going to be at the front line of this battle. Iris was there with the other fey, Alaric included. He stood right beside her and both, for reasons she'd never understand, looked like they'd done this before. An aura, a bright powerful one emanated from Alaric, and then blended with the darker, more foreboding one Iris was giving off. Remi decided they were each other's exact opposite and that suddenly explained their resentment. They'd probably make an amazing couple if they could get past that polar opposites thing.

Ranae and Deane, along with their relatives practically blended with the tree line. The only thing Remi noticed was their usual beautiful appearance was now somewhat scarier. She didn't understand precisely what elves did, but she had a feeling she was about to find out.

She sensed more than saw that all movement stopped, and

all eyes were on the opening. Someone near her said "Showtime", but she didn't look to see who.

Iris and Alaric faded to nothing, and before Remi could think beyond that, three people she didn't recognize came running through the opening. Her ability to see what they were flared, and she said "human," more to herself than anyone. They veered to the left and out of the trees Kyran and Dell appeared, tackling them before dragging them out of the way. Later, when her heart wasn't lodged in her throat, she'd ask how they knew as quickly as she did what they were.

A man came through next, only he didn't look like he was real, more like a mirage. He had to be the mage.

"Gris!" Brome bellowed and moved toward the center of the clearing. His hands were moving in strange patterns, an energy coming from him that made Remi's breathing falter. Before he reached the center, the other mage seemed to solidify; now he looked real. He had a vicious smile on his face.

"We meet again, *cousin.*" He hissed.

Remi was glad at that moment she had no blood family, it seemed to her that it was a horrible complication, she swallowed the lump in her throat when Brome's cousin began to raise his hands.

Brome made a guttural noise and stepped back a few feet. "Not this time, dear Gris." He stepped forward and threw his hands out in front of him making the other mage step back this time. "It ends tonight. You will find justice is your new bedmate."

Holding her breath, Remi watched as each time they moved their hands it seemed to hurt the other. Finn hissed and stepped a few feet in front of her. Remi knew he wanted to do something, but what could a fledgling vamp do against a powerful mage? "No, Finn." She said softly.

Looking quickly back to Brome, her heart stuttered to see him hunched over. That Gris jerk had a big smile on his face. Remi felt a heat moving through her, this was bad. She started to take a step forward when Vie stepped into sight.

She had her hands raised out from her sides her mouth was moving but Remi couldn't hear what she said.

Remi watched as Vie raised her hands and Gris stumbled back several feet, his head snapping around to look at her, the shocked expression on his face made Remi want to shout, 'Go Vie,' but she kept silent.

Gris grabbed his head and winced. "How…"

Brome had recovered by this point, "Cousin, may I introduce the lovely Vienna." He started walking toward the other mage, "She's like no one you've ever met before, or ever will again." Gris fell to his knees, moaning as Brome stepped up in front of him. Reaching into an invisible— Remi didn't know what, his arm disappeared up to his elbow and then he pulled it out and held up a glowing blue pair of handcuffs.

"I've got him, Vienna." He moved behind his cousin and put the cuffs on. Immediately, Gris didn't seem big and scary. Now he just looked like a normal man, about to face a hefty sentence. Remi guessed the cuffs suppressed whatever abilities or magic he had.

Vie stumbled a step and then leaned down over her knees. "That's all I have in me."

Brome yanked Gris to his feet and dragged him in her direction. "That's all we were meant to do in this." Reaching her, he put his arm around her and headed back to the trees they'd hidden behind.

Darien's growl brought her attention back to look across the field. In the time she'd been caught up watching a mage battle, all hell had broken loose. Nadine and the witches were scattered around the field, each taking on one or more, witches. Hope looked like she was bored with the whole thing as two young girls chanted loudly while facing her. With a flick of her hand, they stopped talking and clawed at their own mouths. That would be a handy skill. Hope laughed, "If your strength lies in saying words aloud, you'll never be skilled enough to last." She stomped toward them, a pair of blue cuffs in each hand.

Shaking her head, Remi turned to see how Nadine fared. Her two coven mates were backing in her direction, five others walking toward them. Naddy had a scowl on her face, the look one of complete concentration. Those pressing toward her paused, but it didn't last long. Remi started to head toward her, not sure what the hell she was going to do, but Emery stepped in front of her.

"Focus," he said around a mouthful of fang.

Nodding, she stopped and took a deep breath; reaching…she still didn't feel anything. So much for this happening when she needed it.

Pascal appeared a few feet away from Nadine and with a grin on his face glided in the direction of the witches Nadine and her mates were trying to stop. Remi saw the look of determination appear on her friend's face as the vampire distracted the younger witches long enough that she could toss a spell, or whatever, their way.

Satisfied they would prevail, Remi turned her attention to the twins, Ranae and Deane were flanked by the not-so-pretty relatives now. What sounded like hisses and cursing came from them and the horde they faced. Deane laughed as one of the male elves opposing her fell to his knees and clutched at his throat. Scary.

Deane yelped and then spat out blood. No one was even standing near her, so Remi had no idea who was responsible. In an instant Leontes was there, hauling a woman up in the air, so her feet were dangling off the ground. Deane grinned, evilly, but still a grin, and moved closer. With a tilt of her head, the woman gasped and kicked her feet. Satisfied the elf had it under control, Leontes blurred out of sight.

A shrill laugh, one she knew was Iris' brought her attention to the right of where Remi stood. Iris and Alaric, both looking like this was some kind of party were advancing on half a dozen fey. The fey didn't even seem slightly concerned as the large elder fey and crazy red-haired one moved toward them.

She was so far out of her league here, Remi decided as she

took deep, deep breaths and tried to stir this supposed skill that was hidden inside her.

Iris made what Remi could only call a rebel yell and launched herself at a tall fey.

Garrett emitted a low, menacing growl and moved in the direction of the fey action. Darien now stood right in front of her like a giant guardian. The sound of pain made her look back, all she caught was Iris flying through the air and landing on her back with a loud moan.

Fury filled Remi, so strong it took her breath away. Without thinking, she ran toward Iris, Emery, and Finn right on either hip. As she reached her the fey man that had hurt her faerie friend stood over her. Pushing right past logical thought, Remi stopped and glared at him. He stopped, his eyes moving to her with shock on his face.

Finn flew through the air and tackled him to the ground, then paused and looked over his shoulder at Remi. "You did it, he's paralyzed."

Stunned for a second, Remi nodded. "Stay with him. I don't know how long it works."

Finn stood up and placed a foot on his chest. "Got it."

Alaric shouted to Iris, as she sat up slowly. He tossed something to her, blue cuffs landed beside her. Remi recognized the look of vengeance on the little fey's face and stopped moving in her direction.

Iris got up, cursing under her breath, and went over to the faerie Finn all but stood on now. "Flip him over on his face."

"With pleasure." Finn leaned down and rolled the large fey over like he was a small child.

"Are we winning?" Iris asked as she snapped the cuffs on the man.

"It's a tie so far, I'd say." He told her.

Getting up, she brushed off her pants and ran a hand through her messy hair. "Then let's get back to work."

The fog suddenly thickened and Remi turned trying to see, only to find white all around her. It had to be magic.

Fifty fifty, Remi thought as she looked around. There was so much commotion she wasn't sure where to look. Bodies moved in and out of the fog, sounds of pain and victory echoing in the darkness. "Darien," Remi whispered and in an instant, he was at her side. "Go help. Emery will stay with me." She watched the hesitant look in his yellow eyes. She shook her head. "Go help our people." Growling softly, he glanced at Emery and then turned and disappeared into the fog.

"Attis," she said quietly knowing he was lurking somewhere nearby. He appeared out of nowhere. "Find Naddy or Hope, get them to clear this damn fog somehow." He studied her. She shrugged, "I did it once, but if I can't see anyone, I can't do much." Nodding abruptly, he sent Emery a look and then blurred into the darkness.

Looking over at Emery, she took a quick sharp breath and exhaled. "Let's go find someone to help." He didn't bother to give her a tentative look, just held out his arm and motioned for her to pick a direction.

Stepping through the fog, Remi kept her hands loose at her side, she had no idea who she would see first, but she needed to be ready.

Emery stopped so suddenly Remi came close to walking into him. Damn, this fog. He hunched down, his stance widening telling her that they were close to someone, and unless his vamp senses weren't working, she was pretty sure it was someone they didn't want to be near.

Before Remi could decide what to do, Emery was knocked back, sliding across the dirt with another vampire on top of him. A growl unlike any sound she'd ever heard came from him as Em jumped to his feet, the other vampire dropping away like he'd been nothing more than dust on his shirt. Emery stood straight and glared at him, his eyes glowing red. A haunting fanged smile appeared on his face as he stepped closer to this other vamp.

Remi's heart surged, a tingling heat bursting through her. Raising her hand toward the stranger, she felt a chill go down her arm.

Emery stopped and then his shoulders slumped slightly. "Killjoy," he said glancing at her and she realized that the vampire was stopped where he stood, a look of hatred on his face.

"So sue me," Remi uttered and then looked around but couldn't see anything in the fog. "Cuffs!" she called out.

Elaine appeared out of the fog. She stopped and looked at Emery and then to the other vampire. "I see you've figured it out, Keeper."

"Let's hope," Remi told her as she turned to go back into the fog. "How are the witches making out lifting this fog?"

Elaine shook her head, "Brome has gone to lend a hand." She snapped the cuffs on the vampire, "It's taking all the fun out of it when you can't see the mayhem."

Emery gave Remi a wide-eyed look and then motioned to the left.

"Just think of it as hide and seek." Remi offered as she followed him into the void hoping all of it was over soon. Elaine's eerie laugh echoed around her.

42

Leaning back against the tree, Remi sipped the water Emery had given her. Where he got it from, she had no idea. As soon as it was over, her legs felt like jello, so she found the nearest tree willing to hold her upright.

Emery squatted down beside her. "That was something else," he grinned, "when you paralyzed six of them at once."

She still wasn't sure how she had done that. "What about you *herc-u-vamp?* Tossing off elders six times your age," she smiled, "pretty impressive."

He shrugged, "I'm told that's your fault," he snorted, "or your blood's."

Emery still avoided her eyes whenever that was brought up.

"Hey, if it gives you an advantage and you stay in one piece, I'd say it's a win." She leaned her head back against the tree, "Speaking of…how is everyone doing?"

Em glanced over his shoulder, "Mostly everyone just looks wrinkled and tired. A few minor scrapes and bumps, but fine otherwise."

"Good." She patted his shoulder, "Go lend a hand loading them up. I'll be right here."

Leaning forward, he kissed her forehead. "I'm on it." He stood up.

"Hey," he looked back down at her, "don't forget to call Corey and tell her she can come home."

He chuckled. "She's already on the road." Pausing, he glanced around before looking at her again. "How taboo is it to turn a normal to be your mate?"

Remi's heart bounced against her ribs. "I…"

Emery cracked a grin. "Just kidding."

Glaring at him, she pointed toward Kyran. "Go help." She could hear him laughing still halfway across the field.

Warmth filled her just as Darien came out from behind the tree that was stopping her from lying flat on the damp grass. He sat down facing her, his hip against hers. "How are you holding up?"

"By bark right now," she said with a smirk to see his eyes light up as she did. "I'm beat." Reaching up, she brushed the hair back from his eyes. "You, however, don't look tired at all."

He tilted his head. "There wasn't much for me to do, other than run around like an excited puppy occasionally sounding fierce."

Remi choked on a laugh, "Yeah, that's it." She took a sip of water, "I guess I have you to thank for that sudden boost of energy at the end."

"I had it to spare. You were busy kicking ass." He grinned, his eyes almost back to the chocolate shade she loved.

"Well, metaphysically, anyway." She motioned to Emery. "Did you catch my boy in action?"

Darien looked over at him, "I did. I guess he got some of Mom's power."

"Does that mean you might too? You bit me."

He laughed, "I don't think it works that way."

"I know." She studied his profile as he watched the others walking those in cuffs to stand together. The nerve in his jaw ticked visibly. "What aren't you telling me, Dare?"

Turning his head slowly, he met her eyes again. "I was just

talking to Brome and Randell before I came to check on you."

"And?" She quickly glanced at where they stood, hovering near the lineup of the losing team.

"According to some of the lesser members Margo was at the root of this plot." His eyes searched her face.

Remi frowned. "Why?"

Reaching, he pushed the hair back from her face with a gentle touch. "She had an idea that the power was passed to the holder of the deed for Serenity."

"So, she thought if Doyle gave it to her, she'd become more?"

He nodded.

"That's ridiculous," she stuttered for words, "we-I…didn't even know a thing about this Keeper bit until lately…"

"Apparently, she overheard a conversation before you came along. She knew that the sign Doyle put up—the one you saw, was looking for someone to be the *Keeper* at Serenity."

Remi leaned forward and looked over at Margo and then back to him. "She thought the power was in the building, not a body?"

"Something like that."

Realizing her mouth was hanging open, she closed it and sat there for a moment. Innocent people had been killed for nothing. "None of the followers knew, not even that mage—Gris?"

Darien frowned when she used his name.

She waved a hand around, "He's Brome's cousin."

"Okay." Sighing, he got up. "None of the followers knew, and if *Gris* did, he kept it to himself." He held his hand out for her.

Taking his hand, she let him pull her to her feet. Her head was a bit light, but at least her legs cooperated and kept her upright. "They killed innocent…"

"I know," he wrapped an arm around her and started walking.

Leaning into the warmth of his body, she looked over at the lineup. "What will happen to all of them?"

"The normals will be prosecuted by Kyran and Randell's system. The paras have to face the council's justice." He kissed the top of her head. "I don't know what that is, and I don't want to."

A shudder went through her. "Me either." As they walked, she searched for each one of her staff and family that had come with them. As far as she could see, none of them were seriously injured. Emery's description covered it. They were wrinkled and tired. A few had some scrapes and dirt on them, but everyone was on their feet and looking happy. Remi was proud of each one of them. Finn and Iris were doing some sort of victory dance. Remi laughed, "There's going to be a celebration at Serenity tonight."

"It can't be avoided." Stopping, he pulled her in for a hug. "My heart is almost bursting with pride right now."

It was one of the most emotional statements she'd ever heard from Darien. Hugging him, she leaned her cheek against his heart. "Mine too."

He stiffened slightly, and then his arms loosened. Turning, she saw that Leontes and Alaric were coming toward them. Darien didn't step away, just pulled her into his side. She could feel his emotions, and they felt like jealousy to her.

"Relax, wolfman. They are *so* not my type."

Darien kissed the top of her head. "I know." He grinned down at her, a heated look in his eyes.

Leontes bowed his head when they stopped in front of them. "A successful evening."

Remi shrugged. "Sure."

Alaric smiled down at her, "You did well tonight for no training."

"I didn't really have time for the full program."

He laughed, "No, you did not."

"We're going to go secure the prisoners and then we were going to come back to Serenity, if that's agreeable." Leontes gave her a hopeful look.

"Absolutely." Remi looked over to see Brome and Vie laughing. "I don't think anyone would mind."

"Hey, pretty boy!" Iris bellowed as she came toward them.

Alaric spun around and glared at her.

Iris jogged over and didn't stop until she was almost standing on his feet. "Nice tricks tonight." She grinned, "But I still pulled off a nice ten, so you owe me that drink."

"I recall you picking yourself up off the ground a few times…"

"Diversion tactic that worked." Iris shrugged and gave him a look, daring him to call it anything else.

Alaric made a hissing noise. "Fine. I owe you a drink."

"And?" She rocked back and forth on his toes.

The tall fey grinned, "And we'll discuss the rest."

"Deal." With a smile, she made a dramatic bow in Remi's direction. "Keeper, wolfman, I'm heading back to Serenity with Ranae and Dee."

"We'll see you there," Remi said, trying not to smile at her theatrics.

Alaric watched her walk away and then cleared his throat when he glanced at Leontes' questioning look. "We should get moving too."

Leontes motioned for him to lead the way. "We'll see you shortly."

Darien stood there with her and silently watched them leave.

"That was…"

"Yeah," he finished for her and pulled her sideways so they could go to the other side of the field where they had parked the cars. "Let's go home, mate."

"I'm not too thrilled with being called in if needed by the council…"

"You are the Keeper." Darien pushed her gently so she had to walk backwards into the bedroom.

"I know, but I don't like being at their beck and call." He gripped her hips and guided her down the small hall and around the corner against the wall.

"It's more like they're at your bidding." He dipped his head down and kissed the side of her neck.

"I'm sensing you don't want to talk about this right now."

His mouth moved sensually up her throat and across her jaw. "Are you picking that up through our mate connection?"

Remi grinned and nipped his bottom lip, "No. It's a by this…" She rocked her hips into him. His arousal was more than obvious.

"You're so observant," he licked her lip, "can we talk about this later?" Grasping her hips, he boosted her up so she could wrap her legs around his waist. Resting her shoulders back against the wall, he pushed her shirt up and leaned down to kiss the exposed skin. "Our in-house vampires are kicking everyone out in an hour." His lips traveled up over her ribs, "Betany is going to make sure they all get home safely," lifting his head he kissed her softly on the lips, "The threat is gone…" His mouth crushed her in a long breath-taking kiss.

Through the link between them, she could feel his desire; mixed with her own; she was on fire on the inside. He lifted his head and looked at her, "So you're saying I'm all yours for the night."

"I'm saying your all mine for the night," he kissed her again, "every night…"

"Whoa—that's—sorry."

Remi pulled her shirt down and looked over Darien's shoulder to see Emery standing there looking flustered.

A soft growl of frustration came from Darien as he lowered her to the floor.

"So much for vampire grace," Cait called from the hallway.

Emery scowled and looked down the hall, "You knew what I was walking in on, didn't you?"

Remi heard Cait laugh, "I was just going to close their door when you ran through it."

Emery blew out a frustrated breath and then grinned at Darien. "So, does this mean I have to start calling you Dad?"

Darien growled. "Why *are* you walking in?"

"Oh, right." Emery smiled, "Corey just got here." He looked at the floor and then avoided Darien and looked at her. "She's going to stay downstairs with me tonight—ah," he looked around the room, "can you see her off in the morning, Rem?"

The tension in Darien's shoulders eased slightly.

"Sure, Em." Remy straightened her shirt. "Be careful—okay?"

Nodding, Emery gave her a serious look. "I will." He spun back toward the door. "Night, Mom—Dad." Then he was gone.

Sighing, Darien rested his forehead on hers. "He tries to get on my nerves, doesn't he?"

Remy wrapped her arms around his neck. "Maybe, but you're a good *dad*."

He smirked, "If you say so." He ran his hands up the back of her shirt and pulled her against him.

"I want a little one of our own."

He lifted his head and looked at her. "You want a little vampire of our own?"

Shaking her head, Remi grinned. "No. I want a little baby of our own."

"Ah—" he swallowed, "not yet, right? I mean, someday—yeah, but I'd like to have you to myself for a little while at least..."

Reaching up, she put her hand over his mouth. "I didn't mean right now." She rolled her eyes, "I still don't know if we should try for a Keeper-werewolf crossbreed, but someday, probably."

"You'd be great with a little one," he smirked, "look at how you herd the lot downstairs."

"I don't..." she bit her lip, "Okay, maybe a bit."

Darien laughed and swung her up into his arms. "No more words tonight." He dropped her gently onto the bed and then crawled toward her. "No battles, no worries, no interruptions..."

"Very demanding, aren't you?"

"I've been more patient than a thousand saints…" He hovered over her on his hands and knees.

"That many, huh?" Remi was trying not to laugh at the serious look on his face.

"I broke every rule regarding mates." He undid her jeans and began working them down her legs. "Seven years, Remi, *seven* years I kept my hands to myself and beat back every basic instinct I had…"

"Darien?" he stopped and looked up at her, "No more words tonight."

Grinning, he crawled back up and leaned down. "No more words." Lowering his head, he kissed her.

KEEP READING FOR AN EXCERPT OF

HEART

Animal Senses Book 1

Jacqueline Paige

Chapter One

Blinking, Rayne glanced around. She was in the underground parking space in her apartment building and didn't even remember the drive. Her chest hurt, hands were vibrating and reality felt far away. Three times, she tried to extract the keys from the ignition, finally after fumbling she managed. *Come on, Rayne, get it together. Think!*

Her mind didn't want to accept the words that had come from Aiden's mouth, her fiancé. In all the years she'd known him, never had he used that tone. Scared her enough to send chills through her spine. She believed he meant every word. *I am not an idiot, I've always known he was a hard man, but the words turned my blood to ice and a part of me knows I'll never feel the same for him again.*

Taking a shaky breath, she groped around for her purse, feeling like she was moving through mud. Somehow, she managed to move and get out of the car. Her legs still felt like rubber, but she couldn't stay in the parking garage all day. Turning, she forced herself to move to the door.

What am I going to do? I can't marry a man like that. I'm not even sure if I can look at him now.

Stopping, she looked at the elevator door. Just the thought of stepping inside left her feeling suffocated and trapped.

Hugging the purse again, she turned toward the stairwell. *Keep moving*—she had to.

Trapped, I am, aren't I? Trapped in a relationship. Just that one word showed her the next move. She had to get out of this relationship. Aiden was not her dream man, if such a thing existed, but he had been comfortable. Admitting that, she now accepted that the relationship was too comfortable to be real.

When she reached her third-floor apartment, she wasn't out of breath. But, as numb as she felt, she wasn't sure if she *was* breathing. Maybe this was just a dream and she'd wake up any second now. Giving herself a small reprieve, she let that thought marinate for a few seconds before reality came crashing back.

It took her two tries to get the key into the lock. *What had his associate said just before my world darkened? "We haven't found a body or any sign of him, Aiden."* Him, who? A body? A body!

As Rayne stepped inside her apartment the dreamlike veil lifted away, revealing reality. *A reality I'm not sure how I can live with.* She quickly locked the door, all three locks. Not it would protect her, Aiden had keys. Leaning back against the door she tried to calm down and think.

Aiden was some sort of mob, mafia...*whatever*? Standing there she waited to feel her doubts were unsubstantiated, but it didn't happen. Her fear *was* the truth. This explained the dangerous looking misfits he had in his employ. They had never quite *fit* she thought. Aiden wasn't a boy scout—she knew that. He was a powerful man, as his father had been, but what kind of power was now very clear to her. Closing her eyes, Rayne held a trembling hand over her heart, it was still beating too heavily. *I can't look at him again. Ever.* This only meant one thing...

She looked around the pretty apartment for a moment, taking two steps towards the kitchen before stopping. She had to leave, now. Everything was *his*. *He* paid for everything in this apartment, she worked in *his* gallery. Her whole world was controlled by *him*…

Moving in a slow circle, Rayne studied everything in sight.

Every. Single. Thing.

Bought by him, in one way or another. Taking a deep breath, she tried to exhale slowly. Failing, her breath huffed out in one loud whoosh. There was no alternative, she had to get out of here.

Today.

Right now.

Kicking off her shoes, she bent down, scooped them up, and headed towards the bedroom.

Faster than she ever changed before, the skirt was stripped off and tossed on the bed. Barely having both legs in her jeans, Rayne began pulling open drawers and cabinets, dumping the contests all over the bed. All she really owned were clothes, her beloved camera, laptop and a few mementos to remind her of her parents. All of it was going in her car. A thought made her freeze as she held the empty drawer over the bed— her car was in *his* name. Dropping the drawer on the pile, Rayne sat on the bed, defeated. In the mirror, a frightened woman stared back. Seeing herself was enough to jolt her back into action. Giving the frail looking reflection a determined nod, she made a solid decision. To hell with him. She was taking the car. He hated it, called it girlie, and complained it wasn't comfortable. *The car is now mine.*

Forty-five minutes later Rayne surveyed the bedroom. There was nothing left that she wanted. Leaning down and picking up the last bag, she went to set it with the rest. "This is pathetic, Rayne Andrews. Your entire life fits in six cases and a couple of purses."

She walked through the apartment for the last time, working out how to get all of the cases downstairs to the car without causing suspicion, when the ring of her cell phone pierced the silence. She looked over at her purse, the ringtone was Aiden's. A few seconds after it stopped, the phone on the table began to ring. *Can I do this?* Taking a deep breath, "Buy some time," she whispered aloud just before answering it.

"Hello?"

"There you are. You didn't answer your cell."

He may be using that soft tone, but she now *knew* what he was. "Oh, I was taking the garbage to the garbage room." Her hand shook as she held the phone and prayed that her voice didn't give anything away.

"Where the hell is that girl I pay to do that?"

Just the way he said it made her tremble. "I-it's Wednesday, Aiden. She doesn't come in today."

"Right. Listen baby, I may be here awhile. Could be most of the night..."

"That's—fine. I was heading to the spa shortly." Closing her eyes, she waited to see if he questioned that.

"Do you want me to come by in the morning to pick you up?"

For what? "Pick me up?"

He chuckled. "We have a brunch with Donny and his wife."

Letting out the silent breath she'd been holding. "Oh, yes please." *Please let me sound normal.*

"Okay baby. You go get all beautiful for me and I'll see you in the morning. Ten o'clock."

"Okay, Aiden."

"Love ya, baby."

"Me too." She hung up quickly. Suddenly gasping for air, Rayne tried to settle her nerves again. *Ten o'clock.* Looking over at the clock and doing the math, she had seventeen hours to disappear.

It took almost as long to get all the bags down as it had for her to pack them. Of course, if you're planning to pack your whole life up and vanishing, it would probably be easier if you didn't drive a *Cabriolet*. Fitting everything into the microsized car had taken more than one attempt. In the time it took to finish, she was much calmer about her decision to leave. Not that she had a choice, but she could always have a mini breakdown and cry her heart out, later. Right now, she needed a plan to figure out the next step.

The first stop was the gas station. Getting out of the car, she looked around, checking for Aiden or one of his men. *Great, paranoia already.* After she assured herself that he couldn't possibly know yet, Rayne walked over to the pump. As she lifted the card up to the slot, she realized that he could track her cards. As if the machine was going to grab it, she jerked her hand back and turned to get her purse. She'd need all the cash she had available. Looking over her shoulder again, she walked to the cash machine. This location was close enough to the apartment to not point in any direction—when she finally decided on which direction. Her hands weren't the steadiest as she punched in the numbers and requested the limit the machine would allow, the shaking increased when she grabbed the cash and stuffed it in her wallet.

Glancing around, she walked back to the pump, inserting a card to pay for the gas. It only took her a few minutes to decide she would hit a few more cash machines in the area to bypass withdrawal limits. Aiden might not drive by, but now she suspected he had people everywhere that would recognize her.

After the gas was pumped, she thought that a map would be a good thing, unless she planned to drive around Chicago endlessly—because that's the only place she'd ever driven. Reaching down, Rayne pulled out the nearest one, only to put it right back, it was a map of the one place she knew. Bending down, she studied the title of each map before spotting an oversized atlas with Canada in it. She grabbed that one. Before she could second guess the decision, she set it on the counter and waited for the clerk to ring it in.

With the receipt and atlas clutched in her vibrating hand, she went back to the car, hoping she could get through the next few moments without questioning what she was going to do next.

An hour later, she sat in an empty parking lot, trying to force a bagel down her throat. The atlas she'd purchased was propped against the steering wheel, endless lines of varying colors stared back at her. So many places and no idea where to go. She looked over at the glove box where she'd put her money—in a make-up bag no less. It had taken five different bank machines to empty her accounts of every cent she had. Her cards were now at their limits, accounts were empty and on a whim, Rayne had taken out a cash advance on the card Aiden had given her for emergencies. If this wasn't considered an emergency, she didn't know what was.

Focus, Rayne. Looking back at the map, she tried to wash down a bite with the lukewarm coffee. She knew making maps took a lot of work and was complicated in a way she didn't really care to understand, but they really weren't telling her anything. She needed her laptop and the internet to make a decision that the squiggly color co-ordinated lines weren't telling her. Sighing, she glanced around the parking lot. A hotel was at the far end. She reached down to pull the laptop case off the floor. Setting it on the passenger's seat, she opened it and hit the power button, praying for it to pick up a signal as she flipped through another few pages. There was a signal, not a strong one, but it would do. Bringing up a mapping site, she entered Chicago as the starting point. *Now what?* A starting point generally meant you needed a destination and that she didn't have. Flipping a few more pages, Rayne picked the first name that jumped off the page. Destination? Timmins, Ontario, Canada. Her heart was pounding as she hit enter.

Strangely, she felt relieved knowing she had decided on a location. Her resolve only faltered for a few seconds when she discovered there was a fourteen-hour drive to get there. Biting her lip, she looked out the windshield, not really focusing on anything. Was she ready for a fourteen-hour drive that would take her far away from Aiden? If she had translated the map correctly, where she was heading was right in the middle of nowhere. That meant there was less chance of her being found. Yes, she was ready. Picking up the notebook that was waiting for the details of *the* game plan, she started to jot down the directions, deciding after a few lines that she'd only write down the first five hours and then reassess her route from that point. She had no idea what it was going to be like driving this far.

Closing the laptop, she put it back on the floor and just sat there. Was she crazy for doing this? Yes, but she couldn't stay here and that left few options. She was alone, just like when her parents died. This time all the decisions to be made were going to be her own.

~

Her eyes felt completely dried out. Was such a thing even possible? She didn't know, but at the first drug store, she was getting some eye drops. Glancing at the time— again, Rayne squinted back at the road. *How long have I been driving now?* Four hours? No, closer to five, she needed to stop soon. A few hours ago, she had foolishly thought she would be across the border before planning a stop, but that wasn't going to happen. Driving at this speed meant she still had at least an hour and a half to go before reaching Mackinaw City and then another hour to the border. Considering the longest she'd ever driven passed an hour back, Rayne knew she wasn't going to make it. She had a newfound respect for people that drove for a living. The quick bathroom stop a few hours before hadn't been long enough. If she didn't stop soon, she was going to make mistakes and end up lost, or worse. Stopping would be for the best.

Blinking quickly, she tried to make her eyes not feel as dry and then focused on the sign she was coming to. A motel was thirty miles from here. Looking at the speedometer, Rayne attempted to do the math and calculate how long that would take, less than a minute later she gave up and decided it wasn't important. As long as she arrived at the motel before falling asleep. A few hours of rest, something to eat and a shower became the new goal.

After what felt like ten hours she could see the hotel's sign not too far ahead. Elation and a bit of pride filled her as she realized she'd made it to here without help. She was slowing down when she noticed two police cars sitting at the motel. All the hair on the back of her neck stood up. Aiden couldn't know she was gone already, could he? Would he involve police? Biting down on her lip, she thought he probably wouldn't, but she wasn't going to take any chances. Gripping the steering wheel tighter, her heart was crashing against her ribs at the thought that Aiden might find her. There would be more motels further away, and another chance to take a break.

It took several seconds for the sign she'd just passed to register. *I've done it!* She was almost to Mackinaw, at least that's what the sign had said. Taking a deep breath and fighting the grogginess that had been closing in for hours, she forced herself to keep going. Maybe a little air would help, not that it had a half hour ago, but it couldn't hurt. She rolled the window down, hoping it would help. Seven hours of driving, minus two very brief bathroom breaks and a stop for gas, and she'd managed to keep going. If she wasn't ready to pass out, she would be pretty impressed with what she'd managed.
After a few minutes of taking deep breaths she groaned, the open window wasn't working. Reaching for the radio, she fumbled with the buttons and flicked through the few stations that were clear, anything to sing to or even pretending to sing might work. She scowled at the radio. Turning it off, she stared at the road once again. "Okay," she tried to ignore how slurred her voice sounded. "Use your brain, get the blood pumping and drive." Wiggling a bit, she tried to sit straighter. "Great, my brain is already sleeping,"

she yawned while trying to see the sign that was getting closer. "Oh. Interstate one twenty-seven. I've been looking at that for what seems like forever," she mumbled to the eyes in the mirror. "And before that it was I31." She bobbed her head and tried to recall the roads before that. "One ninety…something, not that it matters really—It's not like I'm going to be going on the return trip," Rayne snorted and then laughed, not sure if it was delirium or exhaustion that had her talking to herself. "And what are you going to do when you reach your middle of nowhere in Canada, Ms. Andrews?" She glanced at the speedometer, even though she had no idea what it had said on the Mackinaw sign she'd just driven past. Clearing her throat, she looked at the reflection again. "I have no idea what I'm going to do. I didn't sit down and plot out a course of action before fleeing," she giggled quietly this time and then squealed as she drove by another sign. "What–ah, miles…" biting her lip a couple of times, she looked at the time. "Oh! A half hour!" Gripping the steering wheel with the very last of her energy, she focused on the road. "You did it. And the reward?" She attempted to smile, but yawned and erased what would have been the smile. "The reward is sleep."

Rayne stood, clutching the room key in her hand and looking at the car, deciding. With the way she'd stuffed the cases into the car, there was no easy way to get to the one that had the clothes she wanted, without taking everything out of the car. Did she care if she slept in something fresh? At this point, no, she would come back out later and sort out what to change into. As she started to head for the room, her brain flashed a warning. She wasn't feeling very trusting now. Turning back, she unlocked the car and reached in to grab her purse, money, camera and laptop. If anyone decided to pick up the tiny car and carry it away, she could get by with just this.

Stumbling into the dark room, she kicked the door closed.

Her shoes were off in two steps, it felt glorious. Her leg smacked into the bed. Setting the precious items down on it, she shoved them to the other side and flopped down, face first. Had she asked for a wakeup call? The chances of a yes were high, but there was no way she could summon the energy to find out.

KEEP READING FOR AN EXCERPT OF

The Huntress

Alterealm Series

Book 1

By J. Risk

Chapter One

I didn't even get both eyes opened and focused before I knew something was wrong. Where was the color? I was only seeing sepia? Everything was brown. Blinking rapidly, I tried to readjust my eyes to see if there was any other hue. It didn't change a thing and for the life of me I couldn't figure out why.

Sitting there, I tried to decipher what was going on and why I was sitting on the ground. Looking down I ran my hand over the dried dusty surface. Why was I on the ground? Craning my neck as far as I could in all directions, I looked around. Okay, where was the pavement and cement? The buildings and streets I called my natural turf?

The why's flying around in my brain suddenly decided the top question, was what the *hell* was going on?

Squeezing my eyes shut, I struggled to recall the last thing I remembered doing. I was hunting down a bounty—a nice one with a large dollar sign attached to her. I had tracked her ass down and...

I confronted her? Yes, I was minutes away from calling Frank and telling him to get out his shiny pen and sign my check.

So what happened between then and now? Not to sound repetitive, which is something that drives me nuts, but *what* the hell was going on?

Startled, I started to check for bullet holes or the deep crevices that knives leave behind in flesh. That had to be it, I'd taken a beating and this was that in between place you sit when your near death's door, but not quite ready to see what lies on the other side.

Finding no critical injury, I slumped forward and rubbed my head. There was some rational explanation for this, there had to be. Had I been drugged? It could be some crazy hallucination. Any minute now I was going to either wake up in my bed at home or some hospital with a cheery nurse leaning over me, reassuring me we are going to be *just* fine. I only had to wait it out a little longer and all would be normal.

To kill time until I woke up, I looked around some more. Wherever this was it looked like a burnt-out world. Not the charred kind of burn, but depleted and completely used up sort.

Vacant.

Sitting still wasn't really a strong trait of mine, so I figured I'd get up and take a look around, there had to be something to see around here. If my body was actually somewhere else for safekeeping, what harm could come to me, right?

I staggered like I'd never stood before, struggling to get my balance. Whatever was going on with me, my equilibrium was totally shot. Standing there swaying like grass in the breeze, I turned carefully trying to see if there was anything around me except rust tinted dirt and nothingness.

My heart stumbled around in my chest when I spotted someone coming in my direction. Yes! I wasn't the only one in this soulless place.

The closer it got to me made me the more I questioned my original conclusion. I didn't know, exactly, but it was not some*one* it was a some*thing*. No one label could describe it. Standing over six feet, it had the shape of a man dressed in jeans and a large, very out of fashion gingham snap up shirt.

When I reached the face, I can only describe it as part wrinkle puppy dog with floppy skin crossed with Freddy and Jason after the slash scenes.

It stopped in front of me and instinct had me reach around behind me under my jean jacket for my raptor claw knife, which I put on as regular as underwear when dressing; and that would be everyday, by the way. Relief washed over me when I felt the small circular handle. At least while waiting to survive I got to bring my toys with me.

Big brown eyes assessed me slowly and I wanted to make the call that it was harmless, but yeah, having tracked down anything from a sicko killer to a card shark in the last three years, I knew better than to fall for sappy looks.

"Are you a magishian? You juisht appeared."

A male voice, even though he spoke with a heavy lisp that randomly inserted *ish* into his words. Then again if I had saggy lips like he did, I'd be happy to talk at all. I sized him up for a few more seconds, trying to gauge whether he was really in front of me, or if I was having some sort of psychotic episode. Was a magician good or bad? I decided the play dumb, being blonde did have *some* advantages. "A magician?"

Those brown eyes developed a nervous quiver. Magician equaled bad. "No…"

He looked relieved. "Oh good. I didn't want to have to bash you over the head."

I grasped my raptor tightly and shrugged. "Yeah, me either."

The sky brightened and began to glow a rust orange color. When I asked for some color, I'd hoped for something out of the orange family.

"We better go, they'll be coming soon."

"They?" I glanced around quickly, not wanting to take my eyes off him for long.

He nodded and pranced on the spot, the nervous movement had me on high alert. "The daywalkers." He whispered.

Daywalkers? Did I even want to know? I didn't think so, but this bizarre nightmare wasn't going to be complete if I didn't ask.

Looking me over a few times, his eyes widened under the pressure of his drooping forehead; *that* was quite the expression. "You're not one of them, are you?"

I walked in the day, night and even at dusk, but I wasn't going to tell him that. I decided honesty might work, if not violence was always a good backup. Judging by his expression daywalker ranked on the bad list with magician. "I—I don't know what you'd call me."

Those sappy eyes looked me up and down a few times trying to figure me out. "You better come with me. It's not safe to leave you wandering around." He looked behind him and then motioned behind me and started walking.

I knew in my gut it was a mistake, but as I had no other real options… I didn't know where I was or what was going on and so far he knew more than I did. "Where are we going?"

Pausing he glanced over his shoulder and then lumbered along again. "I'll take you to Troy, he'll know what to do."

My eyes were starting to strain as the sky brightened. "This Troy, he's in charge?"

He stopped so suddenly I almost ploughed right into his back. When he turned and looked at me, his eyes weren't a sad brown any more but were leaning more towards red. It had to be from the strange color of the sunrise. "You're not from Alterealm are you?"

"Is that where we are?"

He nodded.

"Nope."

That nervous jitter of his seemed to return all at one. "How did you get here?"

A reasonable question that I had nothing to offer that resembled an answer. "I don't know that either."

His red eyes darted to the sky. "We have to go."

Turning, he began jogging toward, well, nothing that I could see. Not wanting to find out what he was afraid of, I ran along behind him. All I could think was this Troy person, if he was a person, better have some answers.

He stopped again and dropped down onto his knees. Was he hurt? Surely that short jaunt hadn't winded him that much. He began tapping his hand on the ground. What was he doing? Looking all around us, I kept watch for anything really, not wanting to meet these daywalkers in the slightest. Just when I'd had about enough of his short break, he grasped something in the sand and pulled a door in the ground open.

"We're going to have to use the shortcut. We don't have time to get to the main gates."

Looking down into a hole with a ladder, I glanced around again and despite every muscle in my body telling me to run and get the hell out of here, I started down the metal rungs into a deep hole that would take me, hopefully back to friggin' reality.

About Jacqueline

Jacqueline is a multi-published author of 'all things paranormal'. Her book list proves this is her niche with stories of witches, ghosts, psychics, shifters, and more now on the shelves. Her current genres are paranormal romance, paranormal fantasy, and paranormal romantic suspense.

Her books are available in many formats around the globe, including book/reading apps. Since adding them during the pandemic, her books have had over a million reads and her 'to be written' list is growing longer each day. She can't write fast enough.

Jacqueline began her writing career in 2006 (as a joke) and her first book was published in 2009. She hasn't stopped since then. She is an avid reader and will read 'anything with words', whether it's a novel, article, or even every sign she passes.

Jacqueline lives in Ontario, Canada in a small town that's part of the popular Georgian Triangle area. Even though she can see the mountains, she does not ski.

When she's not in one of her writing worlds, she spends time with her grand-monsters. She has nine of them (so far) and looks forward to corrupting them in the years to come.

Jacqueline also writes under the pseudonym of J. Risk

Jacqueline loves to hear from her readers, you can find her at

http://jacquelinepaige.com/